The Forsaken Rose

Meagan Walker

The Forsaken
Rose

A NOVEL

———

MEAGAN WALKER

For Katelyn.
I have been and always shall be
your friend.

And for Mom and Dad.
For keeping me motivated.

The Forsaken Rose

"So, so you think you can tell
Heaven from hell
Blue skies from pain
Can you tell a green field
From a cold steel rain?
A smile from a veil?
Do you think you can tell?"

-Pink Floyd

Prologue

Buckeye, Arizona

To say that the sun was hot would be an understatement as it bore down on the parched dirt with monumental force. The only foliage able to force its way through the dry earth was scraggly and coarse. Heat reverberated from the surface and rose in thick, hazy waves to bring drenching sweat on any patch of human skin it could find. But she ignored the heat. And the way the fabric of his oversized t-shirt clung to her sticky skin. The sleeves had been cut off ages ago so that the exposed skin could catch any hint of a breeze. Nevertheless the white cotton had yellowed and darkened within a month after she had been forced to make her stay in Arizona permanent.

She lifted the mug to her lips and blew a steady stream of air across the surface of its contents. Steam rose and fled lazily. She took a sip of tea and licked the drops from her upper lip before setting the cup back on the saucer. The heat from the strong black tea warmed her insides to match that of her skin, which was beginning to take on the texture of leather.

Seven years ago, she wouldn't have thought twice about switching to an iced coffee when the temperature rose above sixty-five degrees. But now ice took forever to freeze in its tray and they couldn't afford a coffee maker. Not with her job and his holey pockets. Besides, she had always preferred tea. This sorry excuse for tea, however, was something she would have blanched at not a year prior. Not to mention the only method of brewing she had at her disposal. Seth Williams would turn over in his grave if he caught sight of her heating her cup of water in the microwave.

But these were different times and she took what she

could get. She lit a Pall Mall and took a long drag, holding the smoke hostage in her lungs before slowly releasing it.

The screen door opened behind her, pulling her from her limited supply of cheerful memories, the few she allowed herself to dwell on. The door creaked and slammed shut. She didn't look up from the distant mountains as he lumbered groggily and collapsed into the faded lawn chair next to her.

"You're up early," she said, blowing ripples across her tea, miniature waves climbing at the white ceramic.

"Am I?" he grunted. He always sounded more southern when he was tired, a trait that had made her smile once upon a time.

"The sun's up, isn't it?" *How could it not be? It's so bloody hot.*

"Is that what the sun looks like?" He quipped, laughing at his own joke. When she showed no signs of amusement, he cleared his throat and tried to think of something to say.

"You workin' today?" he asked stupidly. He already knew the answer.

"I work every day." The ice in her tone did nothing to cool the surrounding temperature.

"Right," he drew back. "Do we have any aspirin?" he asked. His head was splitting. It was no wonder why he never saw the sun. The sun made everything worse.

"Nope," she answered. "Ran out last week. If you need aspirin, you buy it. That was the deal."

He leaned forward with his elbows on his knees and massaged his temples. He thought she'd been bluffing when she'd made that rule. He mustered up the energy and rose to go back inside.

"Get some water and a rag to cover your eyes," she said when he got to the door. "But come back out here. Our air conditioning unit's broken again. You'll at least get a breeze." She sighed to herself when she heard the fans cut on in the living room. That man was so stubborn. She considered making him pay the electricity bill, but dismissed the thought. He wouldn't pay it, the electricity would get cut, and then how would she heat her tea?

A smile teased the corners of her lips as she downed the last few sips. Wiping sweat from her brow, she got up, grabbed the backpack at her feet, and climbed on the bicycle that was leaned carefully against the house.

The afternoon sun burned against her skin as she pedaled eight miles to Serge's Bar, a ramshackle pub that had long passed its prime. She leaned the bike behind the old building and went in through the back entrance. She slid into the bathroom to change out of her gym shorts and into a sleek pair of old jeans and a gray tank and leather vest. Elizabeth would have a heart attack at her style choice and the old hiking boots caked in a layer of dust. But Elizabeth wasn't here, and she'd given up on style a long time ago. Throwing her head under the sink, she turned on the faucet and let the almost cool water soak into her scalp and rinse the sweat away. She wringed the excess water from her hair. Too short now to curl, it dried in awkward waves. She tossed her backpack across the handlebars of her bike outside before heading to the front of the building. It seemed quiet for a bar in Buckeye, but then again it was only three in the afternoon.

"Afternoon, Sergeant," she called colorlessly at her boss. He had a name of course, but everyone called him Sergeant. She never understood why. He wasn't a military man. She also never cared to ask the nickname's origin. Or his real name for that matter.

"You've got a thing in the mail," he gestured to a small parcel on the table. Serge was never a man for too many words. Their customers saw him as a grump, but she didn't mind. The less conversation, the better.

A frown creased her face as she approached the package. She racked her brain for any possible explanation. None of her old friends knew where she was going when she left all those years ago, and those that knew her whereabouts didn't bother to care about her wellbeing. They sent her royalty checks for her handful of songs when the obligation arose, but other than an added *Hope you're doing good* in Mike's slanted handwriting, they seemed to have forgotten her.

She picked up the package and felt her heart turn to stone in her chest when she saw the return address. Her brain stalled in stunned silence before catapulting forward with a hundred questions, each a variation of *How?*

With trembling fingers, she tore open the package. Inside were a letter and a smaller envelope. She hastily read the letter and felt her still heart jolt back to life, pumping what felt like acid through her veins. Her legs failed her and she collapsed onto the barstool, staring blankly at the letter.

Dead? How could he be dead? The questions filled her mind, but no answers came.

"Customer!" Serge called from the back room. She blinked away her tears and looked up with a feeble smile. Work passed in a blur of refilling glasses with every variation of alcohol and wiping crumbs and spillage from the counter. She didn't notice when men hit on her or that her inattention earned her a rough night of meager tips.

Finally at two o'clock in the morning, she let her bike fall in the dust in front of the shabby house. She was alone for the night. Again. She collapsed at the handmade kitchen table. A ghost of a breeze flitted through the open windows as she lay with her head on the wood for over an hour.

She woke just before the sun was to rise over the mountains with a stiff neck and back and a sore forehead. She leaned back in her seat for a moment before packing her few articles of clothing and the cigarette pack full of folded, damaged photographs in her backpack.

She considered leaving without a note. It would be a few days, she judged, before he even noticed her absence. But when she thought of how he would fare without her, how he would end up homeless and hungry, begging on the streets to fund his alcoholic escapades, she scratched a note on the pad on the counter, grabbed the envelope of plane tickets, and rummaged under her bed for her box of cash.

Leaving him enough money to cover the next two months of rent, she climbed onto her bike without so much as a backwards glance.

Part One.

"For she had nowhere to turn! Do you
  understand, sir, do you understand
  what it means when you have
  absolutely nowhere to turn?"
                        -Fyodor Doestevsky
                        Crime and Punishment

Chapter One

Plaistow, East London

Audrey groaned as she rolled over and pounded her fist on her alarm clock, silencing the incessant beeping. She pulled the covers over her head to guard herself from her dog's wet tongue, but after a few short minutes, the angry growl in her stomach had her rolling out of her warm bed. Her toes met the hard floor with an unpleasant chill as she stumbled the few feet from her bed to the kitchen to make coffee. Throwing two pieces of white bread in the toaster, she opened the back door to let her dog out into the garden. She dumped too much kibble into Hermione's bowl, spilling it into the floor. Dismissing the mishap with a wave of her hand, Audrey dropped into the chair at her little table, fighting the urge to put her head down on the plastic surface and drift off to sleep.

The smell of fresh coffee soon filled the room and lured Audrey out of her chair. She buttered her toast heavily and layered it with cinnamon. She wolfed it down in seconds, ignoring the unremitting voices intent on torturing her with remnants of the past. But that's why she ate it every morning was it not? To remember while trying to forget?

Shaking the thoughts from her head, Audrey wiped the crumbs from her hands on her comic book boxer shorts. She poured black coffee into the only mug she owned. It was cheap and had a large Union flag sticker wrapped around it with LONDON written in bold letters. Etched in red on the inside rim was the English cliché Keep Calm and Carry On. She'd bought it at the airport more than four years ago.

Sipping on her coffee, she went to fetch Hermione. The greyhound walked immediately to her overflowing bowl and gorged herself loudly on the round pellets while Audrey pulled on an old pair of sweat pants and a hoodie, fastening a leash to a very excited Hermione for their morning walk.

The airy chill of the early October dawn soothed Audrey's characteristically crowded mind. The slight breeze rustled the yellow leaves in the trees above them. The black, starless sky was beginning to glow in a dull grey over the heads of neighboring buildings, hinting at the imminent rise of the sun. Hermione walked happily by her side, stopping every now and again to investigate a foreign smell. They walked down their street and the street parallel, passing identical rows of connected houses with lines of parked cars out front and enjoyed the quiet of the East London morning. Audrey tried to harness the serenity of the dark streets and weightless atmosphere to last her through the day ahead.

By the time they made the loop back to her flat, the entire sky had brightened in a wash of pale blue and yellow with clouds stained slightly pink and grey. Audrey unhooked the leash from Hermione, who lapped at her water dish and groggily jumped on the small black sofa across from the kitchen. A dim 7:00 shone in the green light of her alarm clock on the floor by her bed as she walked to her bathroom. She took a long shower, letting the near-scalding streams relax her tense muscles.

"Audrey Wyatt! Get out of the shower NOW! Before I drag you out by the hair!"

Audrey slammed the water off and stood naked and trembling. She leaned against the shower wall with her hands clasped on top of her head, counting to ten and burying the memory back down where it belonged. It had gotten easy to push the escaped voices down, but they seeped through her protective walls much more frequently as time went on.

Pushing back the shower curtain, Audrey dried off and squeezed her dripping hair in a towel. She walked across her flat to the clothing rack against the wall behind her mattress to dress. She was pulling on a pair of old, black oxfords when her laptop started ringing. A small smile twitched across her cheek when she saw her best friend's Skype picture on her screen. Audrey had barely hit the answer button when a thick mess of dark hair and bright green eyes popped up excitedly on her screen and shrieked.

"Audrey!"

"Hold on a second," Audrey laughed, "I'm trying to get ready." She went to fetch her makeup bag.

"Where have you been?" Her friend demanded. "I've tried to call you eight times already!"

"Sorry," Audrey sat down at her table, running her fingers through her tangled, wet hair, "I haven't turned my phone on yet."

"I have some amazing news!" she gushed. When Snow smiled, she smiled with her entire face, wrinkling her nose, widening her eyes, raising her brows, but something about the zealous animation in it put Audrey on edge.

"Why are you even awake?" Audrey stalled her. "What's it, 11:30 over there? You're usually asleep by now or waist deep in lesson plans."

"I couldn't go to sleep before I called my best friend with the news!" she half squealed. Audrey felt Snow's enthusiasm like a brick in her stomach. She had a sense of where the conversation was heading.

"Well," she started, pulling her damp hair around her shoulder to braid it, "are you going to tell me or not?"

"Look!" she yelled eagerly. Audrey looked up from tying off the braid to see a sparkling diamond ring on her finger.

"So Ganesh finally popped the question, did he?" she asked. Audrey knew she should be excited for her friend. She should be ecstatic that she had found her own happiness. But she wasn't. She knew what Snow's engagement entailed. It was clear what would happen next. She wasn't ready. She didn't think she would ever be ready for this.

The next few minutes were filled with one girl burbling over the details of her new fiancé's proposal while the other applied more makeup than she normally wore as an excuse to avert her eyes.

"Hey Snow," Audrey cut her off in the middle of an exhaustive description of how her handsome lover had gotten down on his knee at their favorite rooftop restaurant with glistening eyes and a gorgeous smile. "I have to be at work in twenty minutes. I need to go," she lied, hoping to end the conversation before she received a proposal of her own.

"Wait, I have something to ask you." Snow yelled from the now half closed laptop. Audrey's breath caught somewhere between her lungs and her nose, unable to escape. She reluctantly opened the laptop back up and looked down, picking at the chipped orange nail polish. Snow continued. "Remember when we were kids and we promised to be each other's maids of honor?"

Audrey sat in silence, unable to respond, unable to look at her best friend. Maybe if she didn't answer now, she'd never have to. She heard Snow sigh.

"Audrey, I know how much has changed since then and what this would mean for you, but I wouldn't want any one else as my maid of honor. We even thought about having a London wedding, what with his parents there and all, but my family simply wouldn't be able to afford the trip." Audrey lifted her eyes to the ceiling, trying to steady her breath and fight against the stinging tears. Snow offered a smile, but Audrey kept her head turned away.

"Just think it over, okay?"

"I'm going to be late," Audrey lied again, standing up abruptly. "Congratulations on your engagement," she mumbled as she slammed her laptop shut. She let out the breath that burned in her lungs and stared at the ceiling again, blinking ferociously and biting the tip of her tongue. She couldn't go back. She'd finally been able to somewhat enjoy herself after so long. She couldn't just up and move across the world, back to the country she'd fled four years ago. She couldn't abandon the security she'd finally been able to establish. She just couldn't.

Hermione, sensing the change in atmosphere, jumped off the sofa and sat at her feet, looking up at her and whining. Audrey slumped to the ground and leaned against her kitchen cabinet. Hermione walked between her bent legs and stared at her owner, nose to nose, and Audrey ran her hand down her dog's back. A sad smile spread across Audrey's face at the large brown orbs that implored her.

"What are we going to do, Hermione?" she patted her on the head and hoisted herself up. Audrey grabbed her bulky leather jacket and leashed Hermione before walking out the door.

The sun had risen and some of the neighbors were awake and getting into their cars to begin their days. A young blonde boy in a primary school uniform sat on the front steps of his house, pulling at the strings of his backpack, presumably waiting for his mother to walk him to the bus stop. Hermione wagged her tail happily at him, and he raced across the garden to the concrete wall that was painted a rudimentary white and stood at the edge of the lot.

"Hey, Hermione!" he exclaimed, reaching across the barrier to pet her. Audrey fixed her eyes ahead, tugging her dog along before the boy could touch her.

"Good morning, Miss Wyatt!" he called, and she gritted her teeth at his voice.

She walked out onto the bright and busy street, passing shops opening for a day of slow business, university students racing to the tube station, and tennis players on bicycles on their way to the nearby courts. A double-decker bus whizzed past with a groan and a plume of exhaust, but Audrey saw none of this. Her thoughts warred with contemplation of the decision she had to make and the memories that caused her mind to want to shut down completely.

She made the half-mile trek to the Plaistow train station by sheer muscle memory and a bit of guidance from Hermione with no real thought to where she was going. Hermione pulled her off the train for their transfer at Whitechapel station and again when they arrived at Shoreditch High Street. It wasn't until she gained sight of the Book Worm's Hole that she regained total consciousness. The little second hand bookshop that sat at the base of the metal arched bridge looked ancient with three stories of aged white brick apartments stacked on top of its black paned windows and green and gold sign.

"Morning, Wyatt," Mr. Williams called. "Leave the door propped open, will ya? It feels lovely out there." She did as she was told as Hermione bound expectantly to the old man, who gave her some sort of treat that Audrey would probably disapprove of and patted her on the head. Audrey gave a genuine smile for the first time that day when Mr. Williams promptly delivered a cup of tea. She sipped at the reddish, steaming liquid and eyed his robust attire with another grin.

Mr. Williams was the closest relationship Audrey had made since moving to London. She'd left her home on a whim a few days after her twentieth birthday with nothing but a bag of clothes and her dog. Having had an unsuccessful day of flat hunting, she'd decided to unwind a bit with a book, to ward off her own emotions with someone else's. An escape that could only be found through the fictional diction of some faceless author. The Dostoevsky in her pack, however, had been one she refused to look at, afraid she'd do more unraveling than unwinding. She'd walked down several streets before stumbling across an oddly named bookstore with an oddly dressed old man at the counter. He'd worn a blue pinstriped button down with a dark green vest, a grey tweed coat, and a yellow and brown striped bow tie, topped with a dark green fedora, a thick gray mustache, and an old pipe in his mouth. Before saying hello, he informed her that he'd stopped smoking thirty years before when he and his wife moved to the city from their home in Warrenpoint, Ireland, but he still enjoyed the feel of a pipe between his teeth. He'd opened the store when his wife passed away, leaving behind countless books. Some of them were borrowed, while others were bought, and through the years hundreds of readers had enjoyed her tattered, yellow pages. He also accepted book donations, so his inventory fluctuated often, creating a diverse melting pot of old and new stories and giving Audrey an endless supply of reading material. He kept three or four of his wife's absolute favorites on a shelf behind the counter with a framed photograph from their wedding in 1951. Audrey went to the bookstore every day the week of her arrival to see Mr. Williams and to borrow a book. When she'd found a flat available with only a thirty-minute train ride from Book Worm's Hole, he'd offered her a job. He'd given her liberal hours and a generous paycheck. The way she saw it, he'd quite literally put a roof over her head, and she loved him for it.

Seth Williams had known from the beginning that Audrey was a broken young woman. It wasn't just the fresh scar that told of the agonizing journey of something sharp and heavy traveling from the corner of her eyebrow into her hairline, but the vacancy in her silent eyes screamed of recent horrors and of ghosts that followed her from America. She was withdrawn and quiet, shying away from his friendly gestures the first two days she'd visited, but she'd kept coming back. He never pushed to know the story behind her misery, but he wanted to do everything he could for her, having lost two children to miscarriages and his daughter, who died at the age of four, something he never shared with Audrey. After their daughter passed, his wife had turned to books and he to work. Book Worm's Hole was his fourth business and seemed to be the one that would last.

Audrey went about her morning duties, taking inventory, straightening up the sofas and lounge chairs, making coffee, and boiling water for tea. She was again in a sort of haze, trying to forget the occurrences of the morning, promising to return to the matter later.

"She's getting to be an old fart, isn't she?" Mr. Williams gestured to Hermione's snoring form on the sofa. She was curled into her usual ball of bony legs.

"I wouldn't go as far as saying she's a fart," Audrey laughed. "She's only ten."

"Well then," he chortled, "she's almost as old I am!" Audrey shot him a questioning look. "In dog years that is."

"Well I guess considering you're an old fart, then it makes her one, too." He stuck his tongue out at her, a glistening daub of pink beneath his grey bar mustache, and they laughed for a moment. Audrey's smile soon turned to one of sad contemplation. She watched Hermione's stomach rise and fall steadily as she breathed. She had, what, three years left? Five years at best. Then what? Hermione was all she had. She was her sole companion and her only living, breathing reminder of...

Hermione rolled over on her back in her sleep, kicking her legs up in the air and contorting her body to where the side of her head almost touched her ribcage. Audrey and Mr. Williams burst into laughter again, and questioned for the hundredth time how she found comfort in such distortion.

Customers trickled in and out throughout the day, keeping Audrey busy making tea and giving advice on which novel to choose, but the spaces between customers were brutal. They left Audrey alone with her thoughts. Alone with the possibility of uprooting and moving back to America. The possibility of losing Hermione. The possibility of never seeing Mr. Williams again. The list grew longer with every passing hour of the things in her stable life that could easily be turned upside down with the ominous decision ahead of her. She was once again in a haze that didn't subside when customers came in.

Seth watched with concern at Audrey's state. He knew something was wrong, but he couldn't place it. Around four o'clock that afternoon, he saw her dump a scoop of tea leaves into the coffee maker. After correcting her mistake, he told her to go home early.

"No, I'm okay," she protested. "Just a bit tired is all."

"Audrey, you gave a Stephen King novel to someone

requesting romance," he said gently. "Go home, make some tea – preferably with a kettle not a coffee maker," he joked, "maybe watch a movie, but just get some rest." Audrey started to object when he put his hands on her shoulders. "This wormhole will still be here tomorrow."

"Okay," she yielded, nodding in defeat.

"Now go before I fire ya," he winked. She tossed him a small smile before walking out the door, but she didn't feel like going back to her flat.

She walked Hermione down a few streets, admiring everything about the great city she'd come to love. The road was lined with shops and businesses, cafés and bars, expensive apartments, and old brick walls cluttered with graffiti. She stopped to marvel at the self-expression of decades of troubled and passionate souls. London was a city where modern advancements and contemporary architecture shared the same sidewalk as buildings that bled history, archaic remnants of lives lived centuries before her time. It was a place that held onto its past while moving forward in a race to some unknown finish line.

Audrey reached out a hand to run a finger over a painting of an eye budding like a rose on the crumbling bricks when she heard the soft grunt at her feet. Hermione lay panting on the sidewalk still wet from the previous day's rain. She sighed with a heavy heart and made her way to the nearest tube station that would take them back to Plaistow.

The trip took a little over half an hour, but in that time, Audrey had reached a decision. She knew then that there was never really any decision to make. She knew all along what she would do. Now was just the hard part. Making that decision a reality.

They walked the last half-mile to their flat at an exceedingly slow pace. Audrey unlocked the door and stepped inside. Hermione trudged slowly over to the sofa, but upon examining the small height she'd have to jump, she opted for the mattress on the ground.

"Guess we aren't going for our afternoon walk tonight, huh?" Audrey hung her jacket on the hook by the door and looked around her flat.

She didn't have much to her name, and the decoration showed it. Her clothes were old and all hanging on one rack. She didn't have a bed, just a mattress on the ground with grey sheets and a grey duvet. An old black leather sofa sat in front of the kitchenette. The bay windows were bare with no blinds or curtains on the rod that crowned the top of the panes like some newly dubbed king, too poor to fill his crown with jewels. Her walls were white. Her cabinets were white. Her small kitchen table and chair were white. The only bit of color that broke the monotonous cycle came from the bright Union flag bunting that was strung across the wall above her sofa and mattress. Snow had sent it to her when Audrey finally made contact with her a year or so after she moved in.

Audrey crossed the small room and lay down next to Hermione, who rested her head on Audrey's stomach. She stared at the ceiling for a while, collecting her nerves and reassuring herself that she was making the right decision. She looked over at her alarm clock on the floor. 5:48. Without having to calculate it in her head, she knew it would be nearing ten in the morning for Snow, and she would be at work. Not wanting to give herself time to change her mind, Audrey typed out an email to Snow and hit send. She squeezed her eyes shut, her stomach sinking into the mattress beneath her.

I'll do it. was all it said. It was all that needed saying.

Chapter Two

Plaistow, East London

The alarm clock beeped its normal hateful tune. Audrey reached over to turn it off and stared at the ceiling above her. Four o'clock was too early to be getting up for such circumstances. Too early, even, for Hermione. She rolled over on her side to look at the dog curled up next to her. She slept on her side with her whitening head just below the pillow. Audrey pet her gently a few times, careful not to wake her up before rising off the mattress, taking the duvet cover with her.

She wrapped it around herself like a cocoon as she made toast and coffee and sat at her table, flipping open her laptop and logging on to Skype. Seeing that Snow was online, she clicked video call and went to pour her coffee.

"Audrey?" Snow answered before she sat back down.

"Yeah, hold on," Audrey called, sprinkling cinnamon on her toast and waking Hermione. She sat down in front of Snow whose hair and makeup were still done from her day. She thought again how unfair it was. She could only imagine how much she looked like Frankenstein's monster.

"Good morning," Snow smiled.

"Shut up," Audrey grouched, making Snow laugh. She took a bite of her toast.

"Do you still eat that every morning?" her friend asked, the smile slowly fading as Audrey took a hefty gulp of coffee, willing the caffeine into her system.

"Yep," she answered through a mouthful. Snow opened her mouth to comment, but Audrey broke her off with a question of her own. "So you have a rough itinerary for me?" It had been a month since her decision to move, and the plan was to leave when her flat let was up in December.

"Er, yeah," Snow looked down, rustling some papers. She had some sort of indie band playing in the background, probably Iron & Wine if Audrey could guess. "There's a flight available through Icelandair. It's the cheapest by a pretty big margin. You should leave London on December twenty-seventh and arrive here at one thirty our time. So that'll be a bit over twelve hours travel time."

"Oh, dear god," Audrey whispered. She didn't mind the flying. It was Hermione that she worried about.

"That includes an hour and twenty five minute layover in Iceland, though," Snow added, looking at her papers.

"Iceland?" Audrey's interest peaked. Snow looked up and nodded. "Where in Iceland?"

"Reykjavik."

"Is there a way I could get a longer layover?" she asked. "Possibly overnight? I've always wanted to go to Iceland."

"You've always wanted to go everywhere," Snow teased. "Let me check what else is available," Audrey waited as Snow down screened their chat to look up different flight times. The prospect of spending the day in Iceland lifted some of the trepidation from her shoulders. "Looks like there's a flight on the twenty-sixth with a layover in Reykjavik a little more than seventeen hours, but you'd have to be cool with red-eye flights."

"Sounds perfect," Audrey answered.

"Great," Snow smiled broadly. It was the first positive remark Audrey had made. She'd kept her comments neutral so as not to betray her dread and anxiety. "Looks like you'll still land at SEATAC at one thirty on the twenty-seventh, and I'll be there to pick you up!" She went over the rest of the details on what Audrey would have to do before making the trip regarding things such as packing and preparing for international flight with an animal. Audrey yawned several times, hoping to no avail that Snow would cut it short.

"Do you know what you're doing with your furniture?" she asked, clearly checking things off a list.

"Yeah," Audrey answered, rubbing her forehead, "leave it." Snow looked confused. "It's a furnished flat let. None of this is actually mine but the clothes rack, which was only six pounds so there's no real point in bringing it." Snow nodded in understanding and returned to her checklist. After a few minutes Snow's attention was diverted when her fiancé returned from his shift at the hospital. His dark, thin figure wrapped in unflattering scrubs soon came into view with his head and shoulders cut out by the top of her screen. Audrey groaned and dropped her head to the counter when he bent down to kiss his fiancé hello.

"Could you at least move out of the bloody frame before you do that?" she grunted with her head still on the table. She heard his throaty laugh.

"That word sounds bloody ridiculous coming from an American mouth," he teased. She lifted her hand up to flick him off. "Good morning to you too, Audrey," he laughed. She raised her head, her matted curls falling in her face, and gave him a sarcastic smile, eyes half closed from her almost nap on the table. She hated to think that she would soon find comfort in the familiarity of his English accent.

"Ganesh," was all she said. He rolled his eyes, having given up on reminding her of his first name. He squeezed Snow's shoulder before walking out of the frame. Snow stared after him for a while, her smile lingering.

"I have maybe five minutes left to chat, and you have the rest of your life to stare at that butt," Audrey reminded her. Snow snapped back to her laptop, a blush shining brightly on her ivory skin. They talked for a few minutes before making plans to call again the coming weekend and saying their temporary goodbyes with Snow heading to bed and Audrey to her morning walk with Hermione.

Exchanging the duvet cover with her usual sweats, she clipped the leash to Hermione and set out. It was a cold morning, colder than any they'd had that season, sending Audrey back inside for her bulky leather jacket. They'd begun to cut their walks in half to save Hermione's shrinking supply of energy.

Back inside, Audrey showered and dressed in her usual beat up oxfords. Her hair dried in its customary curls and fell past her shoulders. She made a mental note to cut it before she moved so Snow wouldn't attack it as soon as she landed.

"Morning, Wyatt," came the daily call when she walked through the door of Book Worm's Hole.

"Good morning, Mr. Williams," she smiled, and Hermione ran to get her treat. They chatted about the late November weather, which led to stories of the Irish winters of his childhood. Audrey took her wonted place on the sofa next to Hermione, pulling a pillow into her lap. She smiled as he told his stories, listening with a childlike fascination

"I do remember it snowed one Christmas when I was a lad," he stared past her, his eyes unfocused as he watched the memory unfold before him. "Granddad came on Christmas Eve, a day earlier than he planned so he could dress up as San Nioclás for us. Oh how I bawled and blubbered when he gave me a sack of coal. It was meant as a joke, of course, but I never took to practical jokes well. He had to pull off his hat and glasses to show me it wasn't real," Mr. Williams chuckled to himself. "Of course, I feel awful now. The old man worked for months to grow his beard long enough to have a good disguise." Audrey smiled as his laughter grew. "Christmas was always my favorite. It was the only time Granddad would make the trip up from Dublin. He ran a pub there, you see. He always planned on Dad taking it over so he could retire, but after fighting in the Great War, Dad moved out to Warrenpoint with my mam." Mr. Williams paused. The smile faded, smoothing the laugh lines. Audrey tilted her head to study his weathered face. There was a somber look in the old man's eyes as he stared off into a time long past. He snapped suddenly back and smiled at Audrey. "Guess it made the old man mad, dinnit?"

"Guess so," Audrey offered a small smile. Mr. Williams turned his attention to the papers on the counter.

"Any holiday plans for this year?" he asked after a while, glancing up from the bills.

"Ah, you know me," she answered, putting the pillow aside and walking over to the tea pot, "I don't do Christmas." She plugged in the kettle and turned to face him.

"Well," he looked up at her, pushing his maroon fedora back out of his face, "I still live in the flat upstairs if you want to come keep an old man company." He smiled, pointing at the ceiling. She nodded, promising to come by as long as he didn't make a big deal about the holiday. He promised and turned back to the bills. Audrey poured steaming water into the teapot and dropped in the strainer. She looked out the window above her, waiting as the tea steeped.

"I'm taking a trip the day after Christmas," she said.

"Oh, that sounds lovely," she could hear his smile. "Where

to?"

"Iceland."

"Odd time of year for Iceland, isn't it? What's the sun up for? Five hours?"

"Four."

"Hmm. Taking Hermione?"

"Yeah," she nodded and looked down at her tea.

"Just the two of you?" he asked.

"Don't worry. The crime rate in Iceland is virtually nonexistent," she laughed softly, knowing her safety wasn't the motive for the question.

"Right then," he grinned sweetly. "I hope you two have fun. When do you come back?"

Audrey shifted uncomfortably. "I'm not." She glanced up to weigh Mr. Williams' reaction. He looked at her questioningly. "I'm moving."

"To Iceland?"

"No," she smiled softly and shook her head. The smile faded as she struggled with the words. "To America."

"Ah. Back to your family, then," he guessed, meeting her eyes. She shook her head again, swallowing down the lump forming in her throat.

"No," she whispered. "Snow's getting married and wants me as her maid of honor. I have to help her plan her wedding."

"You?" he laughed. "Planning a wedding? Oh I need to see this wedding. Should be disastrous."

"Hey!" she snapped. "Thanks for the faith in me!" They laughed softly for a while before falling into silence. A customer came in, interrupting the quiet. Audrey directed him to the mystery novels. She handed him an Agatha Christie when he said he'd never read a detective story before. She promised Christie was an excellent introduction to the genre and that this one in particular would prove to be nail-biter. They exchanged smiles and currency, and he walked out the door. Audrey continued to avoid eye contact with Mr. Williams. After what felt like hours, he broke the silence.

"So Seattle, then?" he asked. She nodded. He pulled his lips into a tight line, a smile of sorts to hide the way they tugged into an involuntary frown under his mustache.

"It's not for another month, though," she reassured him, and he nodded in her direction before staring blankly down at his bills. They spent the rest of the day helping customers and reverting to such small talk as weather and restaurants and rising cab prices. When it came time to close at eight o'clock that night, they said their goodbyes, and Mr. Williams climbed the short staircase to his flat. Audrey collapsed onto the sofa next to Hermione, who looked up at her with sleepy eyes before resting her head on her thigh. Audrey absentmindedly caressed her dog's back.

She felt hollow. She asked herself for the hundredth time if it would be worth it, leaving everything that held her together. She leaned foreword, resting her elbows on her knees, and dropped her head in her hands, taking a few deep breaths. Hermione whined and pawed at her leg.

"Come on," she said. "Let's get out of here."

Their trip back was slow, but took no time at all. Audrey had pushed all thought from her mind and sat in the tube in a blank, vacant stupor. Before she knew it she was at her flat, pulling her keys from her jacket pocket. She took the carton of ice cream from the freezer, grabbed a spoon, and set her laptop up on the kitchen counter.

"What should we watch, Hermione?' Audrey asked over her shoulder, flipping through the small DVD case. "We've got Die Hard," she suggested. "Oh, Phone Booth! That's a good one. What about I am Legend? Nice and creepy, that one." She flipped to the next one, and her heart stopped. She stared down at the disk, the voices swarming.

"Well," she raised an eyebrow, "since we're going to hell." She pulled the disk out and raised it to show her dog, who looked up from her bowl, chewing loudly. "May as well get used to it." Audrey loaded the DVD into the side of her bulky laptop and turned to plop down on the old sofa, popping the lid from her ice cream. Hermione jumped up and lay next to her, staring at her with pleading eyes.

"No, ma'am," Audrey shook her head, "you're watching your diet." She licked her spoon tantalizingly, making Hermione whine softly.

The movie started. The white silhouette of a boy fishing off the side of a crescent moon signaled its beginning. Soon a zebra was rope swinging and frolicking through a group of singing penguins who took flight before he could run through a beautiful terrain, unaware of the lion in the bushes stalking his prey. Audrey watched the movie intently, eating her ice cream, barely registering the freezer burned taste. She was distracted when Hermione's gruff, begging whine turned into a sharp, wheezing bark.

"Oh, piss off!" Audrey snapped. Hermione laid her head down, sinking in dejection. Tinged with guilt, Audrey rubbed her playfully on the side. It had been years since she'd watched Madagascar, but she still found herself quoting certain parts. Mainly Alex the Lion's lines. He was always her favorite. Audrey smiled and even laughed at several points. She could hear theirs too. Both of them. She could pick out the difference, a loud cackling, head thrown back, belly laugh and the giggle through closed teeth and smiling lips. She heard them as if they were sitting on either side of her, but she didn't push them out this time. She let the laughter seep into her bones like an aching blanket. She grit her teeth against the unpleasant feeling that came with the happy memory. She endured it.

Towards the end, Alex caged himself in a cave guarded with spears that kept him inside, kept him from hurting his friends. Audrey felt a small tear escape from her eye and roll down her cheek, drying before it reached her chin. She shot up, bolted the short distance to her laptop, and slammed it shut. She threw her hands in her hair, scraping nails against scalp, wrapping fingers in the roots, squeezing until her eyes burned with the pain, and crumpled to the floor. Tears burst from her eyes in rivulets, months of held back, pushed down emotion came boiling to the surface. She curled in on herself and buried her face in her knees, covering her head with her arms as if her ceiling was collapsing on top of her. She wished it would. She wished her house would cave in and crush her. The pain coursed through her, like a stabbing knife and a dull ache simultaneously. A vast, vacant black hole at the core of her being, sucking the life from every limb, every extremity of her body.

After a few minutes, Audrey felt Hermione's cold, wet nose on her trembling arms. She lifted her head and blinked the tears from her eyes to focus on Hermione's whitening face and large, brown eyes. She wiped her cheeks on her sleeve and wrapped her arms around Hermione. She cried onto her dog's shoulder like she had done countless times in the past decade. She cried like a child with her dog sitting stoically, waiting for it to pass.

Audrey lay flat on her back on the floor with Hermione next to her, her body stretched against the length of Audrey's side with her head on Audrey's shoulder, eyes gazing intently at her master's chapped cheeks and glassy eyes. Audrey ran her hand up her spine and stared at the white ceiling. Her eyes felt heavy, but she knew sleep wasn't an option. She lay there in the silence for a while, feeling the Earth's gravity pull her against the floor.

"I forgot how good that movie was, Hermione," Audrey said after a while, her voice cracked and raw. "No wonder they loved it so much," she looked at her dog and sighed. "I wonder how he liked the second one."

Audrey turned back to the ceiling and resolved to give herself the rest of the night. She'd let herself miss them. She'd feel the rest that was left to feel. The guilt. The regret. The overwhelming urges to pick up the phone. She'd feel it all. But tomorrow would be just like every day. She'd bury it all back down.

Groaning with the effort, Audrey sat up. She walked across her flat to find her wallet and pulled out the old folded photograph. She kept it with her at all times as a reminder but always left it folded. She needed a reminder, not torture. She carried the photograph to the sofa and sat down. Hermione stretched out at her feet, too tired to jump onto the couch next to her. Audrey felt a fresh wave of tears sting her sore eyes as she unfolded the photo.

It had already started to fade with age and wear, the fold lines whitening, damaging the color, but the image came alive to her as if they were standing right in front of her, arms draped around each other's shoulders, Dan's gloved hand pressed against the side of his big brother's face. His mischievous smile, eyeing his brother. Ethan with his eyes closed and his mouth open, laughing. Their blonde hair flying out at sweaty angles from their baseball caps. Their jerseys had an excessive amount of dirt caked into the fabric due to unnecessary sliding into home plate.

Audrey felt the punch in the gut. The regret of what she left behind so long ago. But she'd made a choice. And Audrey Wyatt never went back on a decision. No matter the consequences.

She pulled her legs up onto the short sofa and laid her head on the armrest. Tears fell silently across the bridge of her nose and puddled around her cheek.

It was what it was. She couldn't change it. No matter how badly she wanted to. She'd never hear their laughter again. Never hold them in her arms. Never attempt to tame Dan's hair or drag Ethan out of bed. Never make their breakfast and get them ready for school. Never have endless Madagascar marathons with popcorn and Twizzlers for Audrey, Reese's cups for Ethan, and Sour Patch kids for Daniel. They'd been unstoppable, inseparable. Now none of them were even in the same country. An irreparable cavern lay between them, dividing them forever.

Audrey closed her eyes as another tear fell.

Chapter Three

Boaz, Alabama
November 2000

The family SUV cut through the chilly autumn evening, the blue paint melting in with the pinks and oranges of the Alabama sunset. Driven by a man still hoping to make a good impression, apologies shot behind him at the three kids in the back after every unavoidable pothole. The two boys in the middle row laughed exuberantly with every jolt, while the teenage girl lounging across the back seat rolled her eyes and attempted to readjust her book.

"Whatcha reading, Audrey?" Mark asked, leaning up to look at her in the rearview mirror.

"*Crime and Punishment*," Audrey mumbled.

"What'd she say?" he asked the woman next to him, who shrugged indifferently. He raised his voice so Audrey could hear him, "What'd you say?"

"*Crime. And. Punishment*!" Audrey shouted, enunciating every word sharply and blinking in his direction. A miffed expression crossed Mark's baby face for a split second before he turned back to the road.

"Bit of an advanced book for a girl your age, isn't it?" he asked, eyebrows raised.

"I'm fourteen, I'm not stupid!" she wondered whether it would help to mention her birthday was in a month and a half, but the following silence went on too long for the added comment to still carry any weight.

"She's on some kind of weird book kick," Audrey could see Sheryl wave her hand in the air to dismiss whatever her daughter had said. Just like she always did. "She read the *Iliad* for fun over the summer," she scoffed.

"Actually it was *Ulysses*, which is one of the most difficult books to read," Audrey corrected. "I haven't read the *Iliad* yet, although I plan to, but I'm proud of you and your extensive knowledge of classic literature," Audrey sang, dripping with sarcasm.

Sheryl didn't turn around but held her hand out to flick her daughter off in full view of the little boys in the middle row, who let out unsurprised "ooohs" while the older of the two yelled "Mommy that's a bad finger!" Mark's eyes flicked around for something interesting to look at. Or maybe he was searching for a soft patch of ground that wouldn't kill him if he jumped out of the speeding SUV, but all that passed were cotton fields and rows of corn. Audrey rolled her eyes again and turned back to her book, leaning the side of her head against the fabric of the seats, wishing she had something to throw at Sheryl.

After a few minutes of awkward silence, Mark tried to salvage the shred of their discarded conversation.

"Do you want to be an English college professor or something?" he asked tentatively.

"I'm not talking about my future with you," Audrey said before he could get the question fully out of his mouth. His teeth clacked shut almost audibly.

Audrey had a justifiable cause for distrusting any man her mother brought home, but Mark, as of yet, had only annoyed her by his blatant, obsequious bootlicking. In addition to taking Sheryl out on luxurious dates she didn't deserve for the past several months, he had begun to inject himself into her family. He'd taken them all out for dinner every other Friday since the early summer. Audrey had objected the first few times of course, but there were only so many excuses she could come up with. Now he was dragging them out to the middle of nowhere with the intention of buying their love with a bunch of puppies of a high-class breed from a white trash trailer park. But who was she to judge? If anything, the rows and rows of mobile homes would remind her of the one she grew up in.

Audrey looked out of the dirt caked back window. The only visibility was through the thin Wash Me written with the point of a finger. Daniel hadn't been able to reach, of course. Audrey had held him up so he could temporarily vandalize Sheryl's truck, instructing him on how to spell it correctly. Although a fresh coat of dust from the dirt road had begun to fill in the words, the corn and cotton fields were still visible, streaking past as the sky darkened.

They reached their destination a few minutes later. The dilapidated trailer stood a few yards from the main road with an old GMC in the driveway. Mark opened their doors, and the boys filed out excitedly while Audrey went through the door on the other side, leaving Mark standing awkwardly before following after them.

"Puppies!" Danny squealed the moment he walked through the door and rushed at the jumble of paws and wet noses stationed at the corner of the room. Over half of them scattered at the sight of a young boy lumbering towards them. The other three ran to meet the excited newcomer. He collapsed on the floor and was soon giggling, covered in rambunctious puppies. Ethan wasn't far behind.

Audrey trailed at the back, ignoring Mark as he held the screen door open for her. The odor of wet dog and urine rolled over her, and she felt a wave of nausea. A tired-looking greyhound, undoubtedly the mother, lay across the dirty sofa while seven puppies bound elatedly across the living room. Audrey wondered if this was even legal and if the breeder had a license. Mark's face mirrored her surprise and skepticism as he leaned out of the door to check that the house number was the same as the one in the paper.

"Be careful! They're babies!" Sheryl cautioned, worried the boys would unintentionally snap the puppies' fragile bones. The four in the corner soon overcame their fear and approached the throng of ungainly limbs. Audrey stood back and watched, suppressing the urge to join them. She wouldn't give Mark the satisfaction of seeing her smile.

"They have giant eyeballs!" yelled Ethan, scratching a black and white pup behind the ears. A lone pup wandered over to sniff out the other strangers in her house. Audrey couldn't contain herself any longer. She bent to pick up the small gray and white pup. She held her against her as the puppy put her paws on her chest and sniffed her face, leaving a trail of moisture from her chin to her nose. Audrey smiled to herself and ran a hand down the dog's skinny back.

"Looks like you've found the one, huh?" Mark nudged

Audrey with his elbow. Her smile vanished.

"She's pretty cool," she shrugged.

"I'm getting all three of you one if you want her," he said.

"I'll take this one," she said to the breeder, not breaking eye contact with her mother's boyfriend. She reached into the pocket of her bulky leather jacket and produced enough cash to cover the price of the puppy. She followed him to the kitchen and signed the papers handed to her. Then she walked out on the porch with her new dog, zipping up her jacket against the cold. She sat on the steps and played with her little bundle, fighting back the moisture that gathered in her eyes and gave a tangible proof of her weakness.

The crisp wind blew her straightened hair into her face, and she fought to keep it tucked behind her ears. Crickets chirped from seemingly all directions, and a lone cow bellowed somewhere in the distance. After a few minutes she heard the screen door slam behind her.

"Audrey Joanna Wyatt!" Sheryl yelled in that shrill, nagging tone that warned Audrey to brace herself for another lecture. Audrey mouthed along with her mother as she said, "You can't keep doin' this!"

"Oh but I thought you'd be proud of my level of responsibility in paying for my own dog," she retorted sardonically.

"Mark's just tryin' to do somethin' nice for you." Audrey ignored her and scratched her puppy on the head. They'd had this same conversation countless times before and would countless times again, but it never changed anything. She hoped her mother would eventually just give up.

"Can't you at least pretend to appreciate what he's tryin' to do?"

Audrey made a face at the puppy, shoving her hand in its little face and shaking her fingers as the dog tried to catch each appendage in her mouth.

"Audrey!" When she got no other response, Sheryl sat down with a huff beside her and started lighting a cigarette. Audrey eyed her and bit her lip, planning her attack. She watched her raise her long, thin fingers to her mouth, and without warning, Audrey snatched the cigarette from her and tossed it into the front yard. Sheryl let out a cursing roar at her daughter.

"Don't smoke around my dog, Sheryl," Audrey interrupted

matter-of-factly.

"Do not speak to me like that, young lady," she fumed. "I am your mother!"

"Oh and don't you like to remind me?" Audrey shrieked. They both sat trying to contain their outbursts for a while. Sheryl sighed and shook her head.

"What's it gonna take to get you to soften up to Mark? Hmm?" she asked. "Seriously." She waited for an answer, but Audrey remained quiet, chewing on the inside of her cheek. After a minute, Sheryl huffed and was about to stand up when she heard Audrey's whispered voice.

"I never met my real dad," Audrey said to her puppy, whose giant eyes were in her face once again. "I don't even know his name. You tried to get me to accept Richard as my own father, and I tried. I really did. For Ethan and Daniel's sake even though I could see him for what he was. A monster." She turned to look Sheryl full in the face, her anger rising again. "I wanted him to be my dad because he's theirs, but he was a freaking monster! And you let him half raise those boys. You keep bringing home men I don't want, somehow thinking they'll replace the dad I don't know, when all I need is answers!" her voice was getting shriller as her words tumbled out. Lowering her head and turning it away from her mother, Audrey bit her lip and blinked rapidly, trying to block away the tears. Sheryl sat there, stunned.

"Audrey," she placed an awkward hand on her shoulder.

"I bet you don't even love Mark," Audrey exploded, jerking her shoulder away from her mother's grasp. "You just love to spend his money." Audrey shot up and stalked off to the car.

"Audrey Wyatt!" she shouted after her. She got up to charge after her when the boys burst out of the trailer with Mark and began running around in the dead grass with their new puppies. Audrey sulked in the back of the SUV, watching Mark with his big, stupid grin on his long, little boy face yell to Ethan to put his coat on. He went over to Sheryl, who shook her head with her hands thrown in the air and started herding her sons toward the car.

Once on the road, the boys continued an emphatic argument over the name Flash in the row in front of her. Ethan played the older brother card while Dan said he deserved it since Ethan knocked his tooth out during the baseball game several months ago.

"Ethan, you do realize that your puppy is a girl, right?" Audrey blurted out after a few minutes of loud, incessant fighting that Sheryl refused to quiet. The boys sat for a second in utter silence before a hissing snicker leaked through Daniel's teeth like fizz through the cap of a shaken soda bottle as he declared that Flash was all his. Ethan's face fell, which put it in range of his puppy's tongue. He jolted back in disgust when she lapped at his mouth. Audrey felt a moment of guilt at her outburst towards her little brother.

"What about Dazzle?" he nearly shouted, turning around in his seat to implore his sister with round eyes, his excitement returning with a new avidity.

"Dazzle's great, Ethan," Mark answered before she could open her mouth. She clacked it shut, fuming her annoyance through the cab of the SUV, shooting flaming arrows of frustration in his direction. Ethan sat back in his seat repeating Dazzle's new name in an attempt to have her memorize it before they got back to the house.

"Flash and Dazzle!" Daniel announced in a funny voice. Ethan repeated him, disguising his own voice into a throaty squeak. They said it back and forth in different tones, with new inflections, experimenting with not only the names but with how many different intonations they could distort their own voices into.

"Flash and Dazzle!"

"Flash and Dazzle!"

"Flash and Dazzle!"

"Dash and Flazzle!" Ethan mixed up the names in their rush from his mouth, a wide-eyed surprise flickering across his face.

"Dash and Flazzle?" Daniel repeated, his voice climbing an octave with each syllable in preparation for a laugh which came out in a long spew and tapered off into a closed-mouth, shoulder-shaking giggle.

Audrey dropped her head back on the headrest with a sigh. Mark was doing everything in his power to inject himself into their lives like a vaccine against a disease that he suspected would cripple their family. But to Audrey, he was just a saline injection, easing her brother's minds as the placebo took its effect. But he couldn't fool her.

She turned her attention to her own nameless, trembling puppy and ran her hand from her head to her tail a few times to comfort her. Ethan was holding Dazzle up by the paws and making her dance. The pup turned her head to bite his fingers, and he dropped her back down onto his lap with a howl of surprise. Daniel's face contorted and reddened as he laughed and pushed his long blonde hair out of his teary eyes.

At eleven years old, Audrey had promised them as she held them both close to her in the closet floor, whispering comfort to them despite her own terror at the shouts outside the door, that she would always take care of her baby brothers.

She looked down at her now sleeping puppy and continued to pet her.

"Hermione," she whispered. She smiled, thinking it fitting and turned her gaze to the window to watch the night fly past her.

Chapter Four

Plaistow, East London

Christmas, she thought, staring up through the ceiling. She'd made it to another one, and on each one she'd wish it was her last. The days leading to the holiday were always rough, to say the least, but Christmas day, a day where families around the world were gathering for their holiday feast and giving each other gifts and wrapping everyone in loving embraces, meant something entirely different to Audrey. She hated leaving her flat and seeing the cheerful neighbors with wreaths on their doors and lights in their lawns, but she couldn't be alone. She didn't trust herself. On her first Christmas alone she'd tried to end it all with a bottle of pills, but she'd just slept for two days and woken up with a migraine.

Hermione grunted in her sleep and shifted, contorting her body at a severe angle with her head lodged between her front legs, her nose touching her back thigh. Audrey turned her gaze to her dog.

"We forgot to get presents for the doggies!" She could hear his desperate cries vividly. Mark had come to save the day, loading the three of them in his truck with their puppies and hurrying off to get chew bones and squeaky toys early Christmas morning.

Audrey stared at the ceiling, feeling her body sink into the old mattress, imagining it turning to quick sand, slowly swallowing her, ceasing her existence. She allowed herself to remember, careful not to envision faces in too much detail or let the voices match so clearly to the bodies they belonged to, but she needed to remember. If she didn't remember, she'd forget. If she forgot, she'd have nothing. She lay in her hazy, muffled memories until the weak morning sunlight stretched in a lazy pillar across the floor in front of her.

Hermione raised her head and looked at Audrey with sleepy eyes for a minute before standing up, stretching, and stepping off the mattress. She turned to face Audrey expectantly. Audrey watched her for a moment. Oh, how she envied her. Today was just another day for a dog. They didn't really care if they didn't get chew bones or squeaky toys or if they got a special piece of meat for their holiday meal. They had no use for calendars. They simply lived and loved until it was time to die with no real care at all.

Audrey sighed and pulled herself out of bed. She went about her morning with the usual hollow cavity in her chest, the edges of which were slowly freezing and spreading outward. She skipped the toast and coffee, made a cup of tea, and walked to her kitchen table, gazing down at the tattered book that always lay there. Day in. And day out. Her eyes stung, but no tears came. She didn't have the energy to cry.

She took her tea and the old copy of Fyodor Dostoevsky's *Crime and Punishment* to her sofa and wrapped herself in her duvet. She pulled back the front cover and wrote December 2010, running her finger along the list of dates, going back almost a full decade. Some of the corners had torn off from being folded as a place marker through the years. She read for a few hours, not really paying attention. She knew the story by heart. Concentrating wasn't really necessary.

She tipped her tea back, draining the few remaining cool drops and carried her mug to the sink. Sighing heavily, she opened a kitchen cabinet, reaching for a small box in the back. She pulled it out and dusted off the top.

"Merry Christmas Audrey!" they exclaimed in practiced unison.

"Oh, it's beautiful!" she smiled, pulling their present from the box.

"Mark picked it out," Daniel blurted out, earning a punch in the arm from his brother. Mark smiled softly and shook his head while Sheryl yelled at the boys not to fight on Christmas.

Audrey opened the box and pulled out the bracelet. It was supposed to be a charm bracelet they'd build onto every year, but it only contained a small heart that had come with the chain. She fastened it around her wrist and stared at the charm as it dangled, suspended in the air by a single, thin link of chain. Lowering her arm, she looked at the small box. She ran her finger across the velvet fabric of the drawstring bag at the bottom.

"Sorry, we didn't get a chance to wrap it before..."

Audrey put the lid back on the box and retied the ribbon back around it, placing it carefully in the back corner of the cabinet, blocking out Mark's cracked whisper.

Grabbing her coat and a scarf, she walked to the station with Hermione. It was packed, even for Plaistow, crowded with excited families carrying bags full of presents and children wearing Christmas hats. Hermione sat at Audrey's feet, nervously eyeing the strangers around her. They climbed into the train car packed with nervous excitement and impatience. Audrey felt small, like a gray dot in a sea of bubbling reds and greens and golds. She felt as if she were being compressed and continuing to shrink. Smaller. Smaller. Until her very existence was less significant than the dirt caked into corners of the train.

It felt like hours before they came to their stop. The doors almost closed on them by the time they finally made it out. Audrey carried Hermione up the stairs, and they walked the remaining few yards to Book Worm's Hole. She rang the bell, and he buzzed them in. Mr. Williams met them at the bottom of the stairs to take her coat and walk her up to his flat above the shop.

"Nollaig Shona Dhuit, Wyatt," he smiled. Audrey gave a confused look.

"I don't know what that means."

"Happy Christmas," his smile broadened and he nodded, looking exceedingly pleased with himself.

"Ah, snuck that one in on me," she offered a weak smile in return. "Nice bow tie."

"Bow ties are cool," he grinned, giving the tie a slight tug. Audrey rolled her eyes, wondering who had lied to him. With the gold bow tie adorned with Christmas trees, he wore a white, sparkling button down with a vest made of dark green velvet and a bright red blazer. A red ribbon was wrapped around his burgundy fedora, matching his burgundy pants. Though they looked expensive, his clothing was old and worn.

"You have outdone yourself, my good sir," Audrey laughed.

"I couldn't help myself," he smiled broadly, flashing his

oddly white teeth at her. "Is the tie a bit much though? I can take it off if it's too Christmassy for ya."

"Are you kidding? I wouldn't recognize you without those ugly things," she offered an encouraging smile, patting his shoulder and walking past him into the flat. He hung her coat and scarf in a closet in the hall and went to the kitchen to put the kettle on. Audrey looked around the small living room. With only a few lamps casting a dim light around the room she could see the old maroon armchair across from a bunny eared television sitting on the floor. A newspaper lay on the coffee table along with a thin, hardcover copy of James Joyce's "The Dead" that looked like it had seen better days. A record was spinning on the turntable, playing some Celtic classical holiday music. Audrey eyed the burned out candle in the window and smiled to herself. Every year he snuck in more and more "Christmassy" things, hoping she wouldn't notice. She did. But they weren't her traditions, so it didn't really bother her.

"How was church?" she asked.

"Fine, I guess," he grinned awkwardly. "Fell asleep by twelve thirty."

"Wow, you really are an old fart aren't you? Can't even hang through midnight mass!"

He spit his tongue out at her. "You should come with me next time so the old granny that sits next to me doesn't punch me when I snore."

"Yeah, let me fly in from Seattle next year just to keep you awake during church," she shook her head sarcastically. He smiled at her, but she could tell he'd forgotten she'd be gone by next year.

"The ham should be ready in fifteen minutes," he said, turning his head to hide the way his face fell as he fiddled with the potatoes. Audrey sat sideways in the living room chair and swung her legs over the armrest. Hermione jumped up with her and curled up in her lap. Audrey scoffed at her dog, who never seemed to grasp that she wasn't a puppy anymore. She grunted with the weight as she reached for the book on the table, flipping it open to read.

"Granddad used to read that to us every Christmas," Mr. Williams called from the kitchen. "I could probably recite it by memory." Audrey tried to read it, but the voices were too pungent.

"Audreeeeey!" Ethan whined with a stamp of his foot. "We read that every year!"

"That's why it's called a tradition, Ethan," she snapped, cringing at the way he elongated her name.

"Can't you read something else?"

"No. I've read A Christmas Carol to you guys since you were babies."

"Pleeeeease?" he begged, his brother joining in to sing in unison.

"Okay, how about this," she suggested. "I read it, and you guys can act it out. Dan can be the Ghost of Christmas Past, you can be Christmas Present, and Mark can be Christmas Future."

"But who will be Scrooge?" Ethan asked after a moment of contemplation.

"Sheryl," she grinned mischievously. "Obviously."

Audrey pushed out the hearty laugh and the quiet giggle that accompanied the memory. Shoving Hermione from her lap, she got up to help Mr. Williams set the kitchen table.

"What kind of relish is this?" Audrey asked when they sat down to eat, pointing to the glazed ham with her fork.

"Mango," he answered, covering his mouth as he chewed.

"Well it's delicious."

"I can send a box of the leftovers home with you. I won't be able to eat all of this by myself."

"Thanks," Audrey looked down at her plate, "but I'm leaving for the airport first thing in the morning."

"Midnight snack then," Mr. Williams offered with a smile. Audrey smiled back. After dinner they took dishes of mince pies and tangerine tartlets to the living room. Seth sat slowly down into his chair, sinking into the permanent indention that conformed around his body. Audrey sat in the floor opposite him with one leg bent and leaned against the wall, fending off Hermione's begs and pleads for a taste of the pies.

"These are delicious!" Audrey exclaimed through a mouthful of tart. "How'd you make them?"

"The old granny made them," he admitted sheepishly.

"She definitely has a thing for you," Audrey laughed. It occurred to her that she'd never seen Mr. Williams with anyone. He never spoke of anyone but his wife on rare occasions, usually in reference to the books in the shop. Did he have anyone? Or would he be completely alone when she and Hermione left?

They spent the rest of the evening talking. Audrey subtly

encouraged him to ask "the old granny" out, but it didn't seem to appeal to him. Mostly Mr. Williams reminisced on life before London. Audrey wondered where he went in the minutes his milky blue eyes stared vacantly at the wall, his sentences trailing off to silence. She didn't disturb him. She let him remember, knowing all too well how it felt to be jerked from the reverie of happy memories back into the empty reality. She stared at her shoes, memorizing the placement and depth of the scuffs on the surface.

"Audrey," Mr. Williams started in a soft voice, "can I ask you something? You don't have to answer if you don't want to." Audrey nodded, her voice trapped in her throat. She knew before she came that Mr. Williams was bound to ask the questions that had been boiling in his mind for the past four years.

"Will you ever go back to your family?"

Audrey felt the blood leave her face. She set the empty dish aside and looked down at her hands as Hermione lunged forward to lick away the crumbs. "I don't have a family," she answered numbly.

"Oh, I think you do." She looked up to see Mr. Williams flatten his thin lips and bunch his cheeks in a soft smile of sorts. "And you love them fiercely. Otherwise you wouldn't still be so broken."

"You're wrong," Audrey whispered, her voice too thick with emotion to gain much volume. He didn't know. He didn't understand. But she saw their faces clearly in her mind as her vision of the dark apartment blurred. Mark's soft, boyish features he never seemed to grow out of. Ethan's near constant red face and carefully brushed golden hair. Daniel's missing teeth and chapped lips from sucking on them when he was in trouble. He was always in trouble. She saw them as if they were standing right in front of her. She thought that if she reached out, stretched far enough, she could touch them. They disappeared, however, as quickly as they had come, falling away with the tears that leaked from her eyes, but not before Sheryl's angry scowl tainted her memories.

Suddenly aware of where she was, Audrey wiped her face and blinked away the tears, hoping Mr. Williams didn't notice. He got up from his chair and went to the kitchen, giving Audrey a moment alone to compose herself. He returned several minutes later with two mugs of hot chocolate.

"I didn't think you could make cocoa," she sniffed.

"Nestlè," he winked. They sat back at the kitchen table sipping their cocoa. Audrey stared down at the swirling brown liquid steaming in her mug.

"It's all different now," she whispered. "Even if I went back, it wouldn't be the same. I don't really even know where they are. We all fell apart," she swallowed the lump in her throat. "And it's all my fault."

"Oh, I'm sure it isn't – "

"It is," she snapped. She looked in his face, aware that he was trying to read her. She realized how much she'd said and buried it all back down, carefully wrapping up her emotions and storing them where she could easily get to them later, never too far out of reach. She smiled at him. "But I'm okay. I'm not broken as you say. And I'm going back to Snow. She's all the family I really need."

Seth gave her a sympathetic smile. He figured he had gotten as much out of her as he could. He reached across the table and squeezed her forearm with his cold, waxy hands. They sat in silence for a while before going back to small talk. When Audrey announced that it was time for her to go, he went to fetch her coat and scarf. He walked her downstairs and to the door. Audrey looked out at the city and up at the cloudy sky.

"I wouldn't have made it," she said. "Not without you."

He smiled and gave a small nod. "I'm going to miss you, Wyatt."

"I'll miss you, too, you old fart," she tried to laugh, but the forming tears smothered it in her throat. "Can I write to you?"

"I'd be quite cross with you if you didn't."

Audrey gave him a teary grin and walked away. She fought the urge to turn and run back, asking for her job back because she wasn't leaving, but her feet kept moving forward against her will. When she crossed the street, she turned to look back at the old man that had saved her life. He was still standing in the doorway underneath the green and gold sign of the little shop beneath the bridge. He pulled his pipe from his pocket and put it in his mouth. Audrey couldn't help but smile. He offered up a wave, which she returned before lumbering to the station.

Audrey stood on the street and stared at her door. The

cheap gold numbers 220 stood out against the black paint. The tan bricks needed some work, and the white boarder around the bay window had started yellowing long before she'd moved in, making the bleached white doorframe appear to glow, pulling all attention to the curves and swirls of the molding caked with dirt in its alcoves. She stood there with her hand resting on the short concrete wall that separated her tiny front garden from the sidewalk, staring until Hermione's wheezing whine drew her attention. They walked through the little black iron gate that she almost never closed and went inside.

This flat had been her refuge. The place she'd go to every day after work to curl up in her solitude and find a kind of happiness she'd allow herself to feel. Audrey hung her coat and scarf on the rack and looked down at the empty suitcase on her unmade bed. It was a little after nine o'clock. She had to leave for the airport in thirteen hours, and she hadn't even begun to pack. It didn't worry her. She'd packed in eight minutes the first time.

Putting the kettle on, Audrey changed out of her day clothes, folding them and placing them in the suitcase, leaving the oxfords out for the next day, and pulled on her comic book boxers and a black sweater. She poured the tea in her Union flag mug and lifted it to her face. She let the warmth seep through the ceramic and heat her numb fingers. She took a sip and eyed the words on the rim.

Keep Calm and Carry On

She could do this. She sucked in a lungful of air and held it, channeling as much British vigor as she could and carried on. She took all of her clothes from the rack and rolled them military style the way Snow's dad had shown her when they packed for their trip to New York. She left two outfits out and packed them in the duffle bag she'd used to shoplift with Snow in junior high. She stuffed what little toiletries she had in the bag and zipped it. Cramming her teakettle in her suitcase, she had to sit on it to zip it.

Taking a trash bag, she filled it with the remainder of her belongings that wouldn't be taking the cross-planet trip with her. She cringed as she dropped the coffee maker in on top of her shower curtain. It was faulty anyway, she told herself. She set the bag aside for in the morning when she'd throw her sheets and duvet in it too.

She crouched down and opened the kitchen cabinet to

retrieve the small bracelet box. Opening it, she saw the small velvet bag at the bottom. Five years. It had sat at the bottom of that box, unopened for five years now. Maybe what they say about time was true. Maybe it does heal all wounds. Maybe she was numb from the amount of emotions spent in the past few days and decided it couldn't really get worse. Maybe curiosity simply killed the cat. Whatever the reason, Audrey decided to finally see what charm Mark and the boys had gotten her those painfully long five years ago.

She pulled the small blue velvet bag out of the box and sank to a seat on the cold floor. She closed her eyes and pushed her fingers through the opening of the bag, pulling it apart and dumping the contents into the palm of her hand. She sat there for a moment, not sure if she was ready to see it. Audrey breathed and audibly counted to three before opening her eyes.

It was a small silver guitar.

At fist she didn't know what to feel. She scrounged around her memories, trying to figure out if she'd forgotten some sort of inside joke that would compel Mark to think a guitar held any relevance to her at all. But of course she wouldn't have forgotten. The last days with her family were still sharp in her mind. She remembered every detail. Maybe the boys had planned on explaining to her why they'd gotten her a guitar charm when she'd opened it, but there was no way of knowing that now. The only thing she was certain of was the confused anger swelling within her. All those years fingering the fabric of the bag at Christmas time, careful not to press hard enough to feel the outline, toying with the idea of finally opening it. Anticlimactic was the only word that came to mind.

Audrey sighed, hooking the charm onto the chain, and looked around. Even with her stuff gone, the flat looked virtually the same. She grabbed *Crime and Punishment* from the kitchen table and collapsed oblong onto the sofa to read. After a few minutes her phone chimed. Audrey furrowed her brow, having forgotten what device made that noise. She crossed the room and pulled her phone out of her coat pocket, flipping it open to find a text message.

GET ON SKYPE! AND GET READY FOR A SNOWPOCALYPSE!

Audrey groaned and went through the painstaking process

of opening her suitcase. She dug her laptop from the middle of the case and set it on the table, deciding to leave the suitcase open until the absolute last minute. She pulled up Skype and called the only person on her contact list.

"Merry Christmas!" Snow's exuberant voice split through the quiet. Audrey closed her eyes and raised her eyebrows, forcing a smile to spread its way across her face. "It's still Christmas for you, right? I'm so excited for tomorrow!" She had half a glass of white wine in her hand, held pristinely between her fingers like a member of the royal family.

"Yeah, you know I'm not actually seeing you tomorrow," Audrey clarified. "I'll be in Iceland."

"But the thought of you being that much closer to me!" She smiled and raised her green eyes to the ceiling.

"Isn't it smashing?" Audrey smiled broadly, brimming with sarcasm. Snow called her a name that wasn't very princess-like, and Audrey burst into laughter. She always liked Snow better when she was a little buzzed.

"So, are you packed?" Snow's eyebrows disappeared behind her new bangs and she sucked her lips into her mouth.

"Yeah, just finished." Audrey gestured with her thumb to the suitcase on her mattress.

"Righteous," Snow said with half closed eyes. A high school chortle burst through Audrey's mouth.

"Are you drunk on Christmas?" she laughed. "It's still early for you."

"No," Snow shook her head and waved an unsteady her finger at her. "Not drunk. Yet. And we had lunch with my family. We just got back. My prince is in the shower." Audrey tried not to gag. "Speaking of which, I have to go!" Snow winked and repeatedly raised her eyebrows in a provocative fashion.

"Get out," Audrey stated blandly. Snow laughed hysterically and fell out of her seat.

"Merry Christmas!" she yelled from the ground. Audrey watched as she struggled to her feet and staggered out of view, leaving the Skype call running. She heard a few words not intended for her ears and slammed her laptop shut. Despite her own discomfort, Audrey made a mental note to mention the encounter to Snow on Monday. She chuckled to herself, imagining the way her green eyes would widen and her red lips would scrunch in a ball.

Humiliation always looked frame-worthy on Snow's ivory skin.

Audrey pulled herself from her seat and made her way out into the garden. An icy blast chilled her bare legs and had her running back inside for her sweat pants and leather jacket. She came back outside and climbed the fence into her neighbor's garden, grabbing their ladder and setting it up to the roof against the fence. She climbed up, walking carefully over the peak to sit down on the gray shingles of her own roof.

She looked down at the street of identical houses and old cars, but the view beyond was what held her attention. She could just make out the lights of Central London shining like a beacon off on the horizon. The night sky shone as bight as day over the heart of it, reminding Audrey of a lighthouse, beckoning the lost souls to the safety of its harbor. The center of life was still going strong while her sleeping street remained in a quiet calm.

She remembered the dream boards she and Snow had made in junior high. Snow filled hers with pictures of celebrities she wanted to meet. It was really just a board of John Travolta with a few Kevin Costners thrown in. Audrey had pasted clippings from a travel magazine on hers with destinations such as New York, Paris, Venice, Hong Kong, Madrid, Cairo, and of course, London. They'd put the boards up on their walls with a strange sense of pride. Snow eventually took hers down when in 2000 her crush evolved from John Travolta to Brad Pitt. Audrey left her board unchanged on her bedroom wall until the day she left.

When Mark saw it, he took the girls to New York the summer before their junior year of high school. They spent their first day staring with awestruck eyes to the tops of the towering buildings. They had thrived in New York, declaring they'd found where they belonged. When they ran into Courtney Cox on the street, they'd frozen where they stood, making Mark be the venturous one to get her attention. They'd taken a picture with her with Snow's disposable camera. Audrey was sure the photo was in a frame somewhere in Snow's apartment.

From that point on, Audrey and Snow had dreamed of sharing a brownstone apartment in Manhattan, but Audrey had enough of a hold on reality to know it would never happen. She would never give a voice to the truth, however, wanting simply to enjoy the blissful prospect of an enchanting future and watch her friend dream with a hopeful gleam in her eye, feeling herself privileged to witness Snow's blissful euphoria. She certainly never pictured herself living in London. Much less leaving it behind.

Though she had countless regrets stored away in a locked chest somewhere inside of her, London was never one of them. London with its old buildings and palaces, rich and thriving culture, teeming with diversity at every corner.

Audrey pulled the sleeves of her sweater past her hands and drew her legs to her body against the bitter wind, wrapping her arms around them and resting her chin on her knees. She stared out at the light of the distant city until the sun came up at dawn, content to remember the good times while the ever-present ache reminded her that the good times were over.

Chapter Five

Madison, Alabama
February 2002

"Audrey, come here for a second!" Mark called from down stairs.

"No, thanks," she yelled, "I'm good!"

Sheryl had married Mark on New Years Eve and moved them all into his double-decker, four-bedroom house. The boys had been so excited that they no longer had to share a room with each other or their gross older sister. Audrey, however, had not been so thrilled. He'd moved her to a different school district, away from her friends, and she found a way to get him back for it. She'd stopped at a hardware store on the way back from school and used the emergency credit card her new step dad had given her to buy several cans of black paint. She'd hidden them in her closet until he took her mother out of town for the weekend. She then coated her walls in thick black paint. Her mother had become enraged and screamed profanities at her daughter until her husband came to investigate. Mark, however, saw it as Audrey's form of "personal expression" and complimented her on her artistic touch. His encouragement had infuriated her. She considered painting them white again, but she'd grown quite attached to it.

"Audrey," he called again, "I'm taking you to breakfast, let's go!" Audrey rolled her eyes and slammed her book shut, throwing it aside. She slung her legs over the edge of her bed, stomping to the top of the stairs with Hermione hopping at her heels. She ignored his presence in the foyer as she sauntered off to his truck, pausing only to block Hermione's escape through the door with her. They drove through the already crowded streets in silence.

Audrey ignored all attempts Mark made at conversation.

They parked in front of the Waffle House down the road from their neighborhood and pulled on their jackets to walk inside, where they were directed to a table by a window, and Mark ordered a pot of coffee.

"So," he started, making Audrey roll her eyes, "how's school going?" He leaned forward a bit with his hands clasped in his lap, an eager grin decorating his plushy cheeks. Out of his normal work suit, he looked strange in a Captain America t-shirt and a gray zipper hoodie.

"Yeah, you don't have to do that," she snapped. Mark looked at her in confusion. "I know why you took me out here. You just want to lecture me on how I should and shouldn't treat my mother. I don't doubt that she put you up to it, but you weren't there when – " she stopped when a waiter brought the coffee. They avoided eye contact until he walked away. "Look," she started, regaining her composure, "I know you're trying, but you weren't there when she spiraled and took everything out on me. I'm glad she found you, really. She just kind of ignores me now, which is definitely an improvement, but you're not my dad." She grazed her eyes over his face for a moment, scrutinizing his youthful complexion. "You're not even old enough to be my dad. So just leave it alone."

"I'm the same age as your mom," he looked confused.

"Yeah well she's not old enough to be my mother, either, is she?" Audrey added. Mark offered a small smile to alleviate the tension.

"Well, you're right," he said, "I'm not your dad." He took a drink of his coffee, sucking in his breath when it burned his mouth. "Your dad had much redder hair." It was a few moments before his comment registered, and Audrey's head shot up.

"You knew my father?" she asked, bewildered.

"Yeah, I knew him," he fought a smile at her wide eyes. He stalled, pouring syrup over his waffle.

"Well?" she asked, her frustration and impatience building. He shoved a large wad of waffle in his mouth, causing a yelp of protest from Audrey.

"You can't just do that!" her voice climbed an octave. He moaned dramatically, exaggerating how delicious the bite of waffle was. "Mark!"

"Okay, okay!" he laughed and wiped his mouth. "What do you want to know?"

Audrey's mind went blank. She'd pictured her dad so many times in so many different ways and had come up with a list of questions she'd ask him if she ever met him, but now she couldn't think of anything to say.

"What was he like?"

"We weren't very close, to be honest," Mark admitted. "We liked the same girl, so I only knew him as a rival," he looked up and met Audrey's engaged, expectant eyes. The corner of his mouth tugged back in a sideways smile, and he leaned back in his seat. "You remind me of him, and it isn't just your hair. You've got his stubbornness. He knew what he wanted, and he went after it no matter what or who – " he gestured to himself " – stood in his way. And he was reckless. He was always getting into trouble. Got arrested a few times actually. We were all surprised when he actually made it to graduation. Of course, he was almost old enough to legally buy his own alcohol, so I figure the school just wanted to get rid of him."

She was smiling by the time he finished his story, reveling in the first account she'd ever received of her father. Audrey noticed the almost smug look on Mark's face and cursed herself for letting her feelings show so blatantly. The more she got to know him, the more she liked him, and it annoyed her. She worked so hard to hate him, but he was a genuinely kind man. How could someone like Mark marry someone like Sheryl? The thought repulsed Audrey enough for her to regain control of her expression and suppress her smile. Then she remembered something.

"Wait, were you the one Sheryl cheated on in high school?" she asked. Mark pursed his lips and furrowed his brow, two thin wrinkles creasing the otherwise smooth skin between his eyebrows.

"She told you about that?"

"She was drunk," Audrey explained, averting her eyes. "She doesn't know she told me that. She told me I was the product of an affair that lost her the love of her life." Mark looked shocked at the statement and the offhand manner in which it was delivered.

"She said that to you?"

"I've heard worse," she waved it off with her hand and tipped her glass of orange juice back to avoid eye contact. "Was it you, though?"

"Yeah, well," he started casually, adjusting his hoodie, "she was fifteen. You can't expect a fifteen year old to make responsible decisions."

Great, Audrey thought. She was the apparent result of her father's recklessness and her mother's irresponsibility. Sounded promising. She stared off in the corner, burying away the new and unwelcome feelings.

"Which is why," Mark leaned over into her view, "parents have to take on the extra responsibility that ya'll lack. But I'm not technically your parent, and you're much too old to be my daughter," he said, standing up from the table and scrunching up his face at her as if the idea disgusted him. "I'd rather be your friend than your father if it's all the same to you. Don't tell your mother I said that. It isn't something most people in my position would say, but I didn't bring you here to lecture you on her like you guessed. I brought you here to stall you from my own irresponsible decision."

Audrey followed him out of the restaurant and back into the truck in a puzzled daze. She questioned him the whole drive back until they pulled onto their road. Mark stopped the truck about half a mile from their driveway and turned to face Audrey.

"Tie this around your eyes?" he pulled out a bandana from the center console and held it out to her.

"Fat chance!" she snorted, crossing her arms across her chest.

"Well just close your eyes then," he continued down the road and pulled into the driveway. Audrey's jaw dropped at what lay before her.

"1993," Mark informed her. "I know she's a bit old, but-"

"He," Audrey corrected. "He's perfect." Mark's face stretched in a smile of smug satisfaction as he got out of the truck. Audrey followed and took a few tentative steps toward the white convertible mustang GT. The top was down revealing newly installed gray leather seats. She ran her hand along the side, still not believing he was hers.

"Happy sweet sixteen," Mark said smiling, his hands clasped behind his back.

"My birthday was last month," she corrected.

"Well, you weren't here on your actual birthday. Besides, I

had to ship it here from Kentucky. They were delivering it while we were at breakfast," he beamed. "Only downfall is no CD player."

"Oh," she tried not to sound disappointed.

"But I took the liberty of digging around the attic for my old cassettes." He produced a cardboard box full of miscellaneous cassette tapes from his truck and handed it to her. "Some are actual albums, but others are mix tapes. Snow says you like classic rock." If he smiled any longer, it would permanently engrave itself in his face. "Classic rock," he repeated, shaking his head at the concrete. "Is it really considered classic rock already?"

"Thanks," she said to the cassettes, not entirely ready to look him in the eye. She knew that with the job she'd had at the farm for the past few years, she might have been able to afford a puppy, but never a car. "Really," she looked up at him, "thank you." Mark smiled back at her, opening his mouth to say something when he was interrupted by the devil, herself.

"What in god's name is this?" Sheryl screeched, slamming the door to her beat up SUV. Her fried blonde bangs flew straight up in the wind.

"Just thought she needed a car to go with the license," Mark answered calmly. Sheryl ensued with a rant on how she didn't trust Audrey with a sports car and how Mark should have told her his plans ahead of time. Her voice shook with poorly controlled anger. She carried on for a few minutes before Mark, seeing Audrey's raised eyebrows and open mouth ready to fight back, intercepted before she had time to interrupt. He suggested they take the argument inside, leading Sheryl into the house. He turned and tossed the keys to Audrey. They landed in the box of cassette tapes, and she looked up to see him wink at her.

"He's not so bad," she said to herself as she threw the box in the passenger seat floor. Hermione bounded from the open garage door to Audrey. She'd undoubtedly escaped when Mark opened the door leading into the house.

Putting the convertible top back up to guard from the cold, Audrey grabbed the keys and climbed into her new car, turning the key in the ignition. The engine erupted to life, sending chills down her arms. She pushed a tape in the player and smiled as Nirvana blasted through the speakers. She threw the car in drive and sped down the driveway. She raced down the back roads, the adrenaline running wildly through her veins with a limitless liberation. She flew out of the urbanized Madison, Alabama, until she hit the dirt roads of the aptly named town of Hazel Green, making her way to Snow's and arriving in record time.

Audrey screeched to a stop in front of the light blue house and honked. She didn't get a response so she honked two more times before a large, balding man in a Nascar t-shirt swung the door open. Audrey opened her door and got out of the car.

"Hi, Mr. Bailey!" Audrey yelled, and waved emphatically. "Is Snow home?"

"Audrey?" Mr. Bailey held his hand up to shield his eyes from the weak but bright sun. "Is that your car?"

"Yes sir!"

"Nice!" he gave her a thumbs up before turning back to the house to fetch his daughter. Snow appeared in the doorway. Her face lit up, and she threw her arms in the air, pulling her tight pink sweater up above a pair of low-rise jeans.

"You got a car!"

"I got a car!" Audrey yelled, throwing her own arms in the air, mimicking her best friend. Snow bolted across the small front yard to hop in the passenger seat. The girls sped off, driving to nowhere in particular. Hermione sat in the back seat, leaning forward to lick Snow's face in welcome.

They drove to a local dive nearby and sat, sipping on milkshakes and testing out the various cassettes, the NO pile growing in the back seat while the YESes Snow organized alphabetically in the center console. The finished assortment mainly compiled of eighties rock and nineties grunge with a bit of pop thrown in on the mix tapes. They put the first cassette in and danced in their seats and played air guitar along with Alice Cooper's "House of Fire".

"You're saying Mark just bought it for you?" Snow asked dubiously, raising her voice to drown out the blaring guitar. "Just like that?"

"Just like that," Audrey beamed.

"He's not such a bad guy," Snow ran her hand affectionately across the dashboard.

"No, he's pretty great," said Audrey, still smiling broadly.

"What happened to 'He can't buy my love'?" Snow inquired, lowering her voice in attempt to mimic Audrey.

"It's a GT, Snow. Convertible. But seriously, though, think

about it for a second. Tell me one negative thing you've noticed about him, and I'll take back what I said."

Snow thought for a moment, sucking on her strawberry shake. "Well he married Sheryl for one."

"Oh, yeah. Forget what I said. He's a dunce."

They had gone through a few cassette tapes and numerous orders of chili fries when the sun started to set. Audrey put her mustang in reverse and pulled out of the parking lot.

"Toretto," Audrey yelled over the music.

"What?" asked Snow, pulling the straw from her mouth, the pink milkshake half melted and sloshing in her cup.

"I named my car Toretto."

"When?"

"Just now."

"Hm," Snow contemplated, chewing on her straw. "I don't get it."

"You know," Audrey coaxed, "Dominic Toretto?" she looked over at Snow's still clueless expression. "Fast and Furious?"

"Oh," Snow nodded in understanding, making Audrey sigh with relief, "yeah, I haven't seen that." Audrey stared at her with round eyes before shaking her head and turning back to the road.

"How are we friends?" she muttered. "You're staying at my house tonight. We can't continue this friendship until you see it."

Snow sighed. Audrey was always dragging her to her house to watch some macho action packed movie with over the top stunt sequences and guns that never missed a shot, usually about spies or conmen, she never really knew. She never really paid attention.

"Oh, hey," Snow piped up, remembering a conversation from earlier in the week. She turned down the volume to give Audrey the news. "Nicole told me that she overheard Scott talking to Andrew, and he said he was going to ask you out!" she half squealed with excitement.

"But I don't even go to that school anymore," Audrey said.

"Oh, but distance makes the heart grow fonder," Snow replied dramatically with her hands clasped on her heart. Audrey smiled but felt a mix of nervous excitement. She'd been crushing on Scott for months, but the idea of actually going on a date with him, having a one on one conversation with him, terrified her.

"He won't like me when he gets to know me," she said.

"Oh, shut up," Snow groaned. "Can you ever just enjoy the moment?"

"I just have a lot of baggage he won't want to deal with," Audrey mumbled, staring blankly at the darkening road before her.

"You don't have baggage. You have one bad experience," Snow corrected, sucking what was left of her milkshake. "Everyone has a story like that these days anyway."

They drove in silence for a while. Hermione's face appeared in between them, tongue lolling out the side of her mouth. Snow laughed as they both pet Hermione behind each of her ears.

"Mark knew my father."

"What?" Snow's shrill gasp jolted Audrey, almost causing her to run off the road.

"Yeah," Audrey sighed, "from what I gather, Mark was Sheryl's boyfriend in high school, and she cheated on him with my dad. He sounds exceptional, doesn't he?" She stared past the road and told Snow of her breakfast with Mark and of their informative conversation.

"Are they sure?" Snow asked. "Mark could actually be your bio-dad."

"No," she shook her head defiantly. "No way. I don't even look like him. And where would I have gotten my hair? Or my eyes for that matter."

"Genetics is weird."

"No," she asserted sternly.

"Okay fine," her friend conceded with her arms raised in mock surrender. "Do you know his name?"

"Yeah. Jesse. Mark wouldn't tell me his last name. Guess he thought I'd try to find him."

"You're disappointed," Snow judged, turning with her straw in her mouth to assess her best friend's pale face in the passing street lamps.

"Yeah."

"Audrey, you put him on such a pedestal. I told you the higher you held him, the harder you'd fall when he let you down." Snow shook her head.

"I just enjoyed the idea of someone out there, waiting for the right moment to come and save me. To get me out of that house."

"He's not a super hero," Snow reached over and put her hand on Audrey's shoulder.

"Of course, he isn't," Audrey shrugged out of Snow's reach and tried to sound lighthearted, as if the lifted veil of her mysterious father hadn't been sinking in her heart all day. "There are no superheroes. It's just a childhood fantasy to give kids false hope in how great their life will be."

"I was going to say something about being your own superhero," Snow huffed, unsurprised by her friend's morbid comment, "but you just had to be depressing, didn't you?"

Audrey grinned and turned up the volume of Queen's "Somebody to Love", drowning out Snow's voice. They finished the drive in silence, Snow going over in her head everything Audrey had said while Audrey buried everything down. By the time they pulled into Audrey's driveway, they were ready to start their Fast and Furious marathon, laughing at each other and declaring their love for Paul Walker.

Chapter Six

Reykjavik, Iceland

"Miss," Audrey woke up to a tap on her shoulder. She picked her head off the plastic wall and looked up, squinting at the woman in front of her. Her soft smile barely wrinkled her olive skin, but her hazel eyes looked tired. "Miss, we've landed."

"Right," Audrey grunted. She yanked her ear buds from her ears and switched off her bulky iPod. She walked out of the plane, cursing herself for sleeping through the descent. An aerial view of Iceland would have been absolutely beautiful.

Hermione was drowsy from the flight when Audrey picked her up. She slept soundly as Audrey pulled her to a kiosk to buy a bus ticket, thankful for the wheeled dog kennel. She walked outside and pulled her coat tightly around her, digging around her duffle bag for a toboggan. Sitting on her suitcase, she stuck her fingers through the bars of the cage to pet Hermione. The vast expanse of the concrete in front of her faded noiselessly into the pale grey of the brightening sky as the bus pulled up, and the driver got out to help her with her luggage.

"Beautiful dog," he said as he tossed her into the bus, making Audrey's stomach drop at his rough handling of her precious cargo. She smiled and took a seat at the front of the nearly empty bus. Audrey stared in wander out the window as they drove. The dark, grassy terrain zipped by while the far off mountains remained still like lounging giants reaching every now and again into the grey sky. Soon the rich-colored rooftops of Reykjavik came into view, sending waves of euphoria through her stomach and down her arms as she squeezed her hands into fists and smiled.

Stepping out of the bus onto the wet road, she asked the driver for directions to the bed and breakfast Snow had suggested.

Still brimming with elation, she barely felt her feet touch the concrete as she and Hermione walked down a few streets to the peeling cream-colored house. The bunched buildings were just as she'd always pictured. Some were white with red roofs while others were yellow with blue roofs, red with black roofs, black with green roofs, or cream with tin paneled roofs. Everywhere she looked, the buildings decorated the earthy landscape with muted color.

They reached the bed and breakfast within a few minutes and booked a small room upstairs.

"Where are you from?" a thickly accented voice asked from behind her. A stunning woman with a strong face set aside a magazine and rose from her perch on the sofa to meet Audrey at the counter. "I'm Simone. My husband and I are traveling from Germany."

"Audrey," she said, holding out a hand to Simone. "I'm just passing through. London to Seattle."

"London is a very beautiful city," Simone gushed. "We went a few years back. Seattle is in America, yes?"

Audrey nodded. "Washington State."

"How long are you visiting there?"

"A year tops. I'm not sure what's after that."

"It's as I always say: no plan is the best plan." she smiled brilliantly and wished Audrey a pleasant stay.

Audrey was shown upstairs to a little room the size of a closet with wooden flooring and a pastel accent green wall. A large square window overlooked the street and the colorful buildings across it. Audrey tossed her suitcase on the white sheets of the twin-size bed and grabbed *Crime and Punishment* before setting back out in the city.

They walked through the streets in the direction of the Old Harbour, passing by ticket shacks advertizing for whale watching, puffin tours, and sail boating. They stopped to buy some fish and chips, and Audrey sat at the edge of the water to eat her lunch, watching the boats bob up and down with the wakes. Hermione sat next to her, eyes jerking suspiciously at the unfamiliar world around her. Audrey lay back on the damp rock wall on the edge of the shore and pulled her book out to read, dangling a leg above the water until the sun sank so low on the horizon that the words blended in with the page.

They walked back into the town, trudging through the wet streets. Hermione stopped to smell every pile of melting, dirty snow that they passed. They walked until the sun had completely vanished and the streetlights turned on. When they came to the famous Hallgrímskirkja Church, Audrey stopped, her jaw dropping in astonishment. She'd seen pictures in magazines and online, but nothing compared to gazing up as it towered above her with spotlights illuminating its base. The clock at its peak seemed to glow, suspended in the air, an omnipotent eye to watch over the city during the long winter nights. She stood in front of the statue of Leif Eriksson in awe, and a smile found its way to her face.

Making a note to visit it again in the daylight hours before she left for the airport, Audrey turned to continue walking. They only made it a short distance, however when they saw a café that caused Audrey to grin childishly.

"What about that, Hermione?" she bubbled, and Hermione wagged her tail. The sign read Icelandic café Loki, reminding her instantly of Mark's comic books she'd found in the attic and studied religiously on late Friday nights. She tied Hermione to a table outside and walked through the doors.

It was a small restaurant with wooden tables and chairs, white walls, and hanging light fixtures. A group of teenagers sat in the corner laughing to each other. Abstract art pieces hung on the walls and a small counter sat directly across from the door. A large mural covered the length of one wall depicting what she guessed was the life events of Loki Laufeyjarson, the Norse god of mischief, trickery, and lies. It was quite different from the stories she knew from the comic books.

Audrey ordered a Loki Tea and a pancake and sat at a table by the window where she had a view of Hermione lounging under a chair outside. The pancakes were much different than what she expected. They were thin and rolled into spirals with brown sugar and icing stuffed inside. Audrey took a bite and rolled her eyes back in her head. She finished off her plate and leaned back in her chair, rubbing her bloated stomach, and sipped on her tea as she looked out at the view of the church, barely visible through the thick night outside the window.

A man wrapped in a large coat stopped outside and bent to pet Hermione, who wagged her tail in excitement. Audrey smiled and put her own coat on. She walked outside where the man was speaking to her in a language she couldn't understand. He stood up to walk away before Audrey made it over to say hello.

"Making friends everywhere you go, huh?" she untied Hermione and walked in what she hoped was the direction to the bed and breakfast. They made it back at around five thirty and walked up to their room. Audrey took a shower and pulled on an old gray t-shirt and her usual boxer shorts, opening the curtains to look out at the town.

She should go to bed. She had a long and trying day ahead of her. She should just read and rest, take a small nap to help ease the jet lag she'd suffer the next few days, but the thought of staying in bed on her only night in Iceland, alone with the voices... It didn't appeal to her.

On impulse, Audrey grabbed her makeup from her duffle bag and hastily painted on a new face. Applying mascara for the first time in half a decade, she dropped the wand and cursed as the creamy black substance streaked down her hair. But a smirk graced the face that stared back at her in the mirror at the idea that sprinted through her brain.

Pulling the rarely used brush from her suitcase, she ran downstairs to ask the innkeeper for a newspaper and a pair of scissors. Layering the floor with the paper, she wet her hair and stood in front of the mirror, hitting play on the CD player that sat on the tiny dresser. "Krókurinn" by Sálin hans Jóns míns filled the room, and she threw her arms in the air, dancing along to the guitar and horns and an Icelandic voice that slightly reminded her at times of Steven Tyler.

Audrey winced as she tugged the brush through her tangled mane. She hadn't brushed her hair in months, never needed to. When she was finished, her thick hair fell in wavy rivulets down her shoulders and stopped a few inches above her elbows. Taking the shears, she grabbed a small section of her hair on the side and held it out in front of her. Trapping the section between two fingers, she took the shears and snipped at it, sending her heart to her throat. She looked down at the floor at the nearly ten-inch strand of red hair lying on the newspaper. She looked back in the mirror. The shears were in her hand, half open with her left hand clasped over her mouth. The strand next to her face stopped just above her shoulder.

Audrey took a deep breath, realizing she'd gone down a road she couldn't turn back from. Shrugging away the slight tinge of regret, she continued cutting her hair in small sections to her shoulders. She cut and snipped and swayed to the beat as a red circle formed around her feet like a stain, a puddle steadily spreading outward. She held the last strand in her fingers and took a deep breath before closing the shears on it. She looked down at the floor and smiled. Turning back at the mirror, she ran her fingers through the short, wet hair that looked so foreign on her own head. Her fingers itched with a need to keep going. She pulled strands straight in the air and started cutting meticulously, giving herself shaggy layers. After a while, she thought it was best to stop before she went bald. She rewet her hair before cleaning up her mess.

Walking back to the suitcase and squeezing what was left of her hair in a towel, she searched for the right outfit to wear. She settled on a black t-shirt with a grey blazer and jeans.

Audrey turned to the mirror to check her makeup and stopped dead. Her new hair had dried in curls that lifted the length from her shoulders and now rested just at her jaw line. The layers created more of an Afro than any coherent shape Snow would have given her. With the weight gone, the mass of big curls around her head made her wonder if the mirror had turned into a window into another world and the woman looking back at her was a complete stranger. Audrey fluffed her new short do and smiled. She imagined Ethan and Daniel pointing and laughing and declaring that she looked like a boy.

Saying goodbye to Hermione, she had to fight against her to keep her in the room when she left. She went downstairs to the dining room where the innkeeper was serving dinner to the Simone and the man Audrey guessed to be her husband.

"Oh, Audrey," Simone's hands shot to her mouth, "your hair!" The innkeeper turned around, eyes widening when she saw Audrey, who smiled nervously, gauging their reactions.

"It looks beautiful!" Simone smiled. "Doesn't it Hendrik?" Hendrik grunted and raised his beer bottle to her.

"Thanks," she fidgeted with the hem of her shirt.

"Want dinner?" the innkeeper asked. "There's some more baked fish in the kitchen."

"No thanks," Audrey smiled and grabbed her coat and scarf

from the coat rack. "I was actually wondering where a good place for live music at this hour would be."

"Oh," Simone piped up. "Hendrik and I went to this pub on Friday. I'll give you directions. There's a band there playing every night this week. They're supposed to be 'the next big thing'." She bent her fingers as quotations around the phrase.

Audrey walked the few blocks to the pub Simone had directed her to. She stood in front of what looked more like a coffee shop than any pub she'd ever seen. She contemplated going back to her book and her dog and her bed. She decided to turn around, but her legs carried her through the brown, faded door.

It was much larger on the inside than she expected. Through the dimly lit, hazy room, people filled the tables, pulling extra seats to accommodate their large groups. Several others stood lining the white, peeling walls. A few smoked cigarettes, but beer bottles were everywhere. No one was dancing or obnoxiously drunk. They just sat around talking. A stage sat in the corner with a few microphone stands and chords.

Audrey took a seat at a small empty table in the back corner and ordered a tea. She looked around at the smiling faces talking to each other quietly as if this was some sort of Sunday afternoon gathering and not a bar. They were mostly her age and younger, but Audrey felt extremely out of place. She was about to gather up her things and leave when a man stood in front of her, speaking in Icelandic. He was a bulky guy with a round face, soft blue eyes, and a thin beard that was only slightly darker than his sandy blonde hair, and his pleasant smile revealed dazzling white teeth as he spoke.

"I'm sorry," she smiled apologetically after a moment, "I don't know what that means."

"Oh, American," he smiled again. "I was just asking if I could sit here."

"Be my guest," she gestured to the chair in front of her. He sat down and peeled off his coat.

"So what brings you to Reykjavik?"

"I'm on a layover. London to Seattle."

"On a holiday?"

"Relocation."

"Yeah? That's a big move."

"You're not kidding."

They smiled, and Audrey sipped at her tea.

"Can I buy you a beer?" he asked.

"No, I don't really drink."

"Come on, you can't come to Iceland and not have a beer."

"Okay," she smiled and nodded. He flagged down the waitress and placed an order she didn't understand.

"I'm Björgvin, by the way."

"Audrey," she smiled, hoping she wouldn't have to use his name, knowing she would never be able to pronounce it properly. They talked for a few minutes, drinking their beers. Audrey tried not to wince at the bland taste of it.

The band finally appeared on stage and started tuning their acoustic instruments. There were six of them. Five men and a woman dressed casually in jeans and sweaters. A few wore toboggans and two had beards. The girl pulled her guitar strap over her head and approached the mic stand.

"Hello, everyone – "

The small crowd erupted with claps and whistles, interrupting her. A smile broadened across her face as she turned to the rest of the band.

"English," Audrey observed.

"Lucky you," Björgvin nodded with a grin. The woman on stage started softly playing her guitar, silencing the crowd. She sang in a soft voice as the band entered in intervals. The sound grew into one harmonious melody that brought a smile to Audrey's face.

"So, what's their story?" Audrey asked, raising her voice over the music as she leaned over the table to Björgvin.

"I think she's the one that got them all together. They won Músíktilraunir earlier this year," he paused, taking in Audrey's confused expression. "It's an annual music competition here in Reykjavik." Audrey nodded and drank her beer tentatively.

"We're going to slow it down a bit," the man at the front of the stage announced. He started singing, strumming his guitar slowly, his words sinking into Audrey's bones, a familiar sting threatening her eyes.

We set fire to our homes,

Walking barefoot in the snow...

Baby lion lost his teeth,
Now they're swimming in the sea.

Troubled spirits on my chest
Where they laid to rest.
The birds all left, my tall friend,
As your body hit the sand...

So hold on.
Hold on to what we are,
Hold on to your heart.

They started in on a stretch of *la la la*'s, and Audrey felt her heart constrict in her chest. As soon as the song was over, she grabbed her coat, thanking Björgvin for the beer, and bolted for the door. Outside, Audrey gasped in the cold air and blinked away burning tears as a wave of anger built inside of her. Iceland had succeeded in being a place of respite, a place where the voices couldn't touch her. The beauty and tranquility of its atmosphere calmed even her crowded mind, seeming to heal her chafing wounds. But a few words in a song sent the images flooding back. Images of pain, of blood, and of her own betrayal. Images of each set of eyes as they stared into her, waiting for a reaction, an explanation, or some phrase to falsely portray a sense of security, of a denial to the reality she'd forced them all into.

The music inside grew louder as the door creak open and closed behind her. Björgvin walked over and stood next to her.

"Are you okay?"

"Yeah," Audrey worked to regain her composure.

"I got you this," he held out a cardboard square. "Thought you seemed to like their music."

"I did, thank you." She took the CD from his hand. Of Monsters and Men was written across the surface.

"When does your plane leave?" he asked after a short silence.

"Early tomorrow, morning," she lied.

"That's a pity," he sighed. "It was nice meeting you,

Audrey." They smiled, and he stood there awkwardly, not knowing if he should hug her or shake her hand.

"You too," Audrey blurted out when he stepped in her direction. He smiled and went back inside the pub. And with that, the closest thing she'd come to a friend in years was gone. Audrey sighed, watching her breath billow out in a cloud above her head. She took her time walking back to the bed and breakfast, kicking at loose stones and hoping against all hope that she would be able to silence the voices and get some rest that night.

Audrey woke the next morning and took a moment in the darkness to figure out where she was. Hermione lay stretched out at the foot of the bed and raised her head at Audrey's movement. In the mirror across from the bed, she caught sight of her hair, sticking out in every direction. The corner of her mouth curled into a smirk at the image.

Today was the day. Audrey's smile vanished. Groaning, she pulled herself out of bed to beat the Germans to the shower. She nicked the Garg CD she'd listened to the day before, packing it with her things and went on her way, leaving her luggage with the innkeeper. They spent the morning in cafés and sightseeing. Audrey bought a lopapeysa sweater and pulled it on over her black dress. After spending the few daylight hours reading on the rocky shore, Audrey and Hermione made their way back to the bed and breakfast to get their luggage before going to the bus stop. She watched with a deepening sadness at the back of the bus as the town grew smaller behind her and the mountains faded away. Despite the events of the night before, Iceland had served as a needed rejuvenation before her own silent and introspective world clashed with Snow's boundless energy and jubilant smiles.

At the airport, Audrey sat on the floor alone at the gate with her iPod. As they rose into the air, she pulled out *Crime and Punishment*. Less than nine hours were left to go before she found herself in the exuberant arms of her best friend on American soil.

Chapter Seven

Madison, Alabama
February 2003

"Come on Ethan, it's time for school," she said softly, walking to his window to draw back the thick, blue curtains. Ethan groaned and pulled the covers over his head. "Come on, big guy," she sat on the bed next to him and pulled down his blankets.

"Go away," he mumbled. Audrey leaned down to kiss his golden hair before popping him on the butt.

"You better be up and dressed when I come back in here," she half-heartedly threatened before walking to the next room. The door creaked open noisily despite her best efforts. A quick movement caught the corner of her eye as stifled laughter leaked out from under the covers pulled tight over the bed. Daniel's tangled hair jutted out from underneath the blankets. His dog was already standing, staring at Audrey and wagging his tail.

"Morning, Flash!" Audrey whispered. "Have you seen Danny?" Giggles erupted from underneath the Power Ranger bed cover. "Well, I'm tired, and this looks like a very comfortable bed." Audrey walked over and lay on top of the squirming comforter. "Oh well this isn't comfortable at all, Flash!" she rolled away from Daniel's little form and poked at him. "It's all lumpy!" Daniel giggled and jerked the covers off his head. His white blonde hair formed an orb of static electricity around him.

"There he is!" Audrey feigned surprise.

"I'm too old for this game," Daniel said, flashing his crooked teeth at her.

"Oh, you are huh?" He nodded dramatically. "Then why were you hiding from me?" He seemed to think about it for a second before shrugging his shoulders.

"Happy birthday, buddy," she smiled.

"Since it's my birthday, can I have cinnamon toast?"

"Cinnamon toast? You know you can only have a sugary breakfast on the weekend."

"Aw, but Audrey!" he whined in protest, sticking his bottom lip out.

"Oh, come on, you're too old for that."

"Please, Audrey!"

"Okay fine," she conceded. His crooked-toothed grin made her smile. "Get dressed. I'll go make it." He lunged out of bed, flinging his comforter in his sister's face and ran to his dresser. Audrey went back to Ethan's room to drag him out of bed, let the three excited dogs out into the large, fenced yard and walked to the kitchen. Ethan lumbered in wrapped in his bedspread and dropped in his seat at the bar.

"Is that what you're wearing to school?" Audrey asked, handing him a glass of orange juice. He nodded and rubbed his eyes. Daniel bounded in wearing a holey pair of jeans and a green baseball t-shirt. His new Nikes lit up as he walked, blinking like sirens on emergency response vehicles.

"Hey, Ethan, guess what!" he said as he climbed into the chair next to his brother. "You aren't older than me any more!"

"Oh, shut up, Daniel," Ethan groaned, leaning his head on his hand. His cheek squished up, wrinkling his eye closed. "You say that every year." The boys were only ten months apart, so for a little less than two months, they were the same age, giving Daniel a false sense of entitlement. Audrey smiled as she placed plates of scrambled eggs in front of the boys. Daniel looked down in disbelief.

"But you said – "

"You'll get the cinnamon toast if you eat all of your eggs."

"But Audrey – "

"No buts. Just eat it."

Daniel complied and began eating his eggs in silence.

"Good morning," Mark called as he walked into the kitchen. "Happy Birthday, little man!" he playfully ruffled Danny's hair, the long strands covering his eyes.

"Coffee's ready," Audrey nodded at the coffee pot on the counter and took a bite of her orange.

"You are a godsend!" he said as he poured coffee in his mug and ladled in sugar and cream.

"Hey Mark," Daniel piped in through a mouthful of egg, "since it's my birthday, can I have coffee, too?"

"No, stupid," Ethan interjected. "We can't have coffee until we're double digits."

"I'm not stupid, stupid," Danny spit his tongue out at his brother.

"Hey, if you two don't straighten up, I will eat your toast in front of you," Audrey threatened.

"Burn!" Mark bellowed, bringing a laugh even from the early morning grouch that was Ethan Mills. "You guys can have some coffee this weekend if you don't give your sister any more sass this week," Mark offered.

"We don't sass, Mark," said Ethan.

"Yeah, Mark, we're not girls," Danny backed his brother, smiling broadly. Mark spit his tongue out at both of them behind Audrey's back, making them snigger and return the gesture when she looked down at her food. Audrey rolled her eyes and gave the boys their toast.

"What're y'all still doing here?" Audrey looked up to see Sheryl coming down the hall in her sweats. Her bleached tangled hair had been hastily pulled back, leaving her thick bangs stuck to one side of her face. "They'll be late for school! Morning, babe," she kissed her husband good morning and turned her attention back to Audrey.

"I wanted to make them a special breakfast today," she explained to her coffee.

"Well you should have gotten up earlier then. They're late," Sheryl glared at her before hugging her boys and wishing Daniel a happy birthday. Audrey seethed, staring at her mother as she plopped down on the sofa and flipped on the TV. Daniel ran after her and hurtled into her lap. They laughed while Audrey squeezed too tightly to her coffee mug.

"Go get dressed, Ethan. We need to go." Audrey instructed coolly under her breath as she finished her morning duties, which consisted of cleaning up their breakfast mess, packing their backpacks with the lunches Mark had probably stuffed with Little Debbie snack cakes, and herding them to the garage.

"By the way that outfit went out of style years ago," Sheryl called over the click of her cigarette lighter. Audrey stopped in the doorway and turned to face her mother.

"Just like those bangs, Sheryl?" Audrey shut the door before the boys noticed her mother's responding shouts and walked to her car.

"Shotgun!" Daniel yelled and hopped in the front seat of Audrey's mustang.

"No, you're still too young, buddy," Audrey watched them cram together in the small back seat and headed off the elementary school. Once out of the car pool line, she raced the four miles to the high school. She whipped into her parking spot, grabbed her backpack, and ran in through the side door.

"You're late again, Miss Wyatt," the assistant principal stopped her as her foot hit the red and blue checkered floor.

"I know," she sighed and trudged to the attendance office to sign a tardy form.

Audrey pulled up to the elementary school after a long, arduous day of dull classes with teachers who lectured her on things she already knew. Soon her brothers came into view, lost in a horde of children running from the school.

"How was your day?" she greeted them with a smile as they climbed into the car.

"Awesome!" Daniel yelled before Ethan could answer.

"Oh, yeah?" Audrey asked. "What made it so awesome?"

"Ms. Bletchley brought cupcakes for my birthday!" he said. Audrey noticed the bits of chocolate frosting still on his mouth when she eyed him in the rearview mirror. "She said it was for all the February birthdays, but I know she just likes me. She didn't do it last month."

"What if there weren't any January birthdays?" Ethan challenged.

"Yeah well I'm still her favorite."

"I'm sure you are," his sister reassured him.

"Oh, and she gave me this note to give to Momma," he added. Audrey looked questioningly at Ethan in the rearview mirror, who just shrugged and tore open a Swiss Cake Roll he'd saved from lunch.

"Uh, no sir!" Audrey reached her hand behind the seat and

took the snack cake, placing it in the cup holder. "You know there's no eating in Toretto."

"Sorry," Ethan muttered.

"I'm not the one you need to apologize to," Audrey suppressed a smile as Ethan apologized to her car. "Anyway, Daniel, let me see that note."

She unfolded the yellow piece of paper when they stopped at an intersection and hastily read the letter scrawled on it.

"What did it say?" Daniel asked, eyeing his sister nervously when she leaned over to shove the note in her back pocket before the light changed.

"You, young man, are in deep trouble," Audrey lowered her voice dramatically. Ethan's eyebrows traveled halfway across his forehead, and a broad grin stretched his face as he turned to gawk at his brother, who was shrinking in his seat.

"But," Daniel started with a shaky voice, "but I didn't do anything."

"Are you sure about that?" Audrey asked, receiving a ferocious nod in response. "Okay," Audrey said, losing the accusatory tone. "I just wanted to see if you had anything to admit up to. You're just blind. Ms. Bletchley says you can't see the board and you need glasses."

"That's not nice!" Daniel shouted after an audible sigh of relief. Ethan threw his head back and laughed loudly. Audrey grinned, turning her car into their long driveway, and parked in front of the open garage.

"Alright, hurry up and change into your practice uniform so we can go," she called as the boys ran to the house. Flash and Dazzle jumped elatedly at the return of their masters, placing their front paws on the boys' shoulders and licking their faces excitedly, and Hermione ran out to meet Audrey in the garage. Audrey had repeat herself several times before the boys finally ran to their rooms to change. Sheryl was visible through the large windows in the living room, smoking a cigarette and reading a romance novel on the back porch. Audrey sighed and threw her bag down, making Hermione jump. She ran to fold a bit of laundry before rounding up the boys, making sure they had their gloves and bats.

Putting on an encouraging smile when they reached the ballpark, Audrey waved goodbye as the boys bounded off to their coach. As soon as they were out of sight, she threw her mustang in drive and sped out of the parking lot.

She parked in front of the little, blue house and sighed at the truck in the driveway, not in the mood to deal with Snow's latest in a string of ephemeral boyfriends.

"Hey, Carrot Top," Tyler called from the couch in the living room when Audrey let herself in. She rolled her eyes and set an armful of grocery bags on the kitchen table.

"Hey!" Snow trotted into the kitchen with a blinding grin.

"Well, now that you women are where you should be," Tyler grunted, reaching for the remote to flip to ESPN. Audrey raised her middle finger in the air so he could get a good view of it. Snow jabbed her in the ribs.

"You said you'd stop doing that," she hissed.

"Did I?" Audrey pretended to have forgotten. "You should have known it was a lost cause."

"You have way too many ingredients for one cake," she observed, ignoring the comment.

"Boss man only let me off of work on the condition that I bake him a cake too," Audrey explained.

"Okay, you make Daniel's cake, I'll make Royce's?"

"No," Audrey slapped Snow's hand away from the box of cake mix. Snow drew back, mouth wide with dejection. "You can do many things, Snow Bailey, but baking is not one of them."

"Fine," Snow pouted. She bounced to Audrey's backpack and pulled out a notebook and pencil. "I'll draw you a purty picture!"

"What'll it be this time?" Audrey asked absentmindedly, counting eggs to crack.

"Hm," she thought for a second. "Oh! Let's make your dad!"

Audrey smacked the egg against the edge of the bowl with too much force. The shell shattered, sending yolk splattering across the counter. Swearing loudly and getting an equally loud reprimand from Snow, Audrey reached for some napkins. Her stomach clenched.

"Oh please, let's not do this again," she managed to utter.

"Come on," Snow begged. "It'll be good practice for my portfolio!" Audrey met her friend's pleading eyes for a second before conceding. Snow smiled broadly in triumph and leaned over the counter to get a good look at Audrey, who was purposefully avoiding eye contact. Audrey's pencil danced across the paper with

Snow's steady hand.

"We know he'll look like you, obviously. You don't really look like that wench." Snow said, mainly to herself. "Except for a few things of course."

"I have her chin," Audrey pointed out, grazing her finger in the dent of her pointed, cleft chin. She realized too late that it was a bad idea and looked around for another rag to wipe the yellow cake batter from her chin.

"You have her nose too," Snow mused. Audrey jerked up to face Snow for the first time since her observation began. "What? You do! It's all short and pointy, kind of poked up a bit. Like hers. Your face is very angular, and – if you haven't noticed – so is hers."

"I look nothing like her, huh?"

"I didn't say nothing like her," Snow corrected. "Anyway you're safe as long as you don't grow the wart on her nose."

"My mother does not have a wart on her nose."

"Yet," Snow enunciated with a tap of the pencil on Audrey's shoulder. "I'm waiting for it to grow."

Audrey chuckled softly and poured the batter in a greased pan while Snow continued to awkwardly analyze her face, her vivid green eyes taking in every detail. After a few minutes of silence, Snow had all she needed of Audrey's face and sat on the counter, leaning against the side of the refrigerator and pulling her knees up close to her face. The notebook sat inches from her nose as she scratched away at the paper. The only noises that eased the painful silence were Audrey's deliberate movements and the racecar engines roaring on the television in the living room. Audrey slammed the cake pan in the oven and twisted the dial on the timer. She sighed and pulled her badly straightened hair into a ponytail before preparing to make the second cake when Snow's emphatic exclamation made her jump and drop the plastic bag of mix into the bowl she was pouring it in.

"It's done!" Snow leapt from the counter and ran across the small kitchen, shoving the paper in Audrey's face. Throwing Snow an exasperated look, Audrey grabbed the notebook and pulled it away from her face to let her eyes focus on the drawing.

"I probably should have used my sketchpad," Snow mused. "Would have turned out better that way." Audrey's breath caught in her throat. Snow's artistic skills had definitely improved in the year that had elapsed since her last feeble attempt at creating

Audrey's father out of thin paper and a cheap mechanical pencil with a bad eraser.

Piercing gray eyes shot up at Audrey from the paper beneath a pair of thick eyebrows and a lined forehead. His hair curled as much as its short length would allow, giving him an unruly, rebellious look. He had a strong jaw, a squared off chin, and a slightly pear shaped nose complete with a stylish mustache and soul patch combo. Audrey was just about to comment when a large hand reached out and snatched the picture from her grasp.

"This is really good, Liz," said Tyler, "but doesn't he have darker hair?"

"Who?" Snow looked confused.

"Is this not supposed to be Sean Penn?" he barely got the words out before Snow grabbed the notebook. She took a short look at it before slamming it against her thigh.

"Dang it!"

Tyler jumped back at Snow's reaction and looked to Audrey with a pleading expression, wondering what he had said wrong.

"I drew Sean Penn!" Snow tossed the notebook at Audrey who scrambled to catch it, slinging cake batter across the kitchen from the spoon in her hand.

"Shocker," Audrey muttered. "You have so many posters of him in your room, his face has probably seeped into your subconscious at this point."

Snow cursed under her breath and slumped down in a wooden chair at the kitchen table. Audrey's eyes widened with disbelief. She'd never heard Snow say anything worse than "crap" and "dang it" in her life. Audrey put her spoon down and sat down across from her friend.

"It's not that big of a deal, Sn – "

"Yes it is!" Snow cut her off. "I can't be an FBI sketch artist if all I draw are celebrities. I'll have half of Hollywood arrested!"

"Well they'll probably deserve it," Audrey quipped. Snow let out a small giggle and took the notebook back from Audrey to examine it.

"And you never know," Audrey added, "Sean Penn may be my dad."

"Oh that would be awkward!" Snow barked with laughter. "When he marries me, I'd be your step mom!"

"I've already got one step parent that isn't really a parent. What's one more?" Audrey laughed, ignoring Tyler's yelp of disapproval at his girlfriend's blatant crush on another man. "Besides you'll probably be in love with some other old man before you even move out."

"Nope, Sean's the one," Snow said dreamily.

"You said that about Travolta," Audrey reminded her. She got up from the table to resume her baking, calling over her shoulder. "And Brad Pitt. And Mel Gibson. And who was it before that?"

"Adam Sandler," Snow answered sheepishly. Audrey made a scene of gagging into the mixing bowl while Tyler threw his hands up in the air and stormed back to the sofa, grumbling about his presence going completely unnoticed. "Hey," Snow chuckled in her own defense, "to each her own, Audrey. To each her own. Adam Sandler is one good-looking hunk of man."

With her back turned and Snow running off to laughingly console her dejected boyfriend, Audrey let her face fall. The picture had unnerved her. Despite it's slight resemblance to Sean Penn, the drawing of her father was a more tangible reflection of the face she had begun to imagine, the face that had shaped and developed in her head at night though the years. He had her own almond shaped eyes with barely visible eyelashes and curling hair. His mouth had curved with the same arc across the bottom with a thin upper lip that didn't really match the fullness of its partner.

An hour later the cakes were finished and frosted, Snow's parents were home and obviously displeased with the state of the kitchen, and Audrey had boxed the cakes and loaded them in Toretto.

"Are you sure you don't want to stay for dinner?" Mrs. Bailey asked. "I'm making enchiladas."

"That sounds delicious Mrs. B, but I have to go make dinner for the birthday boy," she smiled politely before telling everyone goodbye, and walked out to Toretto.

"A Power Ranger cake?" Dan almost squealed with excitement at the nine candles that burned in the shape of a lightning bolt on top of the heavily layered green frosting. He jumped from his chair and rushed to Audrey's side, wrapping his arms around her waist in an excited grip that choked the air from her lungs.

"Go blow out your candles, bud," Audrey laughed, watching the melted wax meander slowly toward the mound of frosting at the candle's base.

"You missed a spot," Ethan called, gesturing to a section of the cake where his finger had wiped away a chunk of icing.

"My bad," she answered with a shrug, running her own finger along the bottom of the cake and wiping it down the bridge of his nose, smearing his face with bright green frosting. "Looks like you need a tissue there, big guy," she gibed. Ethan blanched in horror and turned to her with his blue eyes blazing.

"You're an idiot!" he yelled.

"Oh yeah?" Audrey got down in his face, daring him to fight her.

"Yeah!" Ethan tried to get closer, to show his own bravery, but he over adjusted for the distance and collided his nose with Audrey's, passing on a glob of green to her pale skin. Tears flooded both of their eyes at the pain before bursting into giggles.

"Hey guys! Birthday boy over here!" Daniel regained everyone's attention, and they all sang happy birthday before digging into the cake. It was half eaten in a matter of minutes and presents were soon strewn across the table, ranging from baseball gloves to plastic nunchucks and a remote control car. They spent a few minutes testing out the new toys while the grown ups cleaned the kitchen and Audrey went to her room to work on her English paper.

Like clockwork, the boys were bathed and in bed with their teeth brushed at nine o'clock sharp. Audrey listened to Sheryl hug and kiss them both good night and then to Daniel's bare feet as they scampered across the carpet to Ethan's room where they waited for their step dad to come in with their favorite book. She heard heavy footsteps coming down the hall, waited for the slight creak of Ethan's door to signal that the coast was clear. She slid out of her room, locking Hermione inside, and crawled the short distance to the wall beside Ethan's door where she sat, leaning against it, listening eagerly.

There was a rustle of pages and movement as the two boys settled into Ethan's bed and prepared for the next chapter. Chapter Twelve, if Audrey remembered correctly. Mark cleared his throat to begin and Audrey turned her head to hear him more clearly. He launched into the story without a moment's hesitation, his voice carrying the weight of each word with a resonating fluency that captivated his nine year old audience as well as the regular visitor, of which he was left unaware.

Audrey smiled as Mark read and leaned her head against the wall, listening as he read the whole chapter of a book she'd read and reread numerous times on her own. She strained her ears to hear the quiet gasps and reactions of her brothers and the different voices Mark used for each character, every one of them armed with a dreadful English accent.

For a short time, Audrey wasn't playing the role of mother to boys only half her age. She wasn't running around like mad looking after them and attempting to keep her own life under control. She wasn't reading college flyers or preparing for scholarship applications or studying for exams. For the time being, she wasn't even a seventeen-year-old hiding outside her little brother's room, eavesdropping on their bedtime story. She was a little girl sitting in her own bed, clutching an old teddy bear and listening to her own father read her a story.

She closed her eyes and let herself imagine it all. She yearned for her imagination to be more than just a dream, but a memory. Her father would sit in a chair across from her bed like Mark did, or better yet, lie down next to her and let her curl up against him. No one would have been able to guess where his red curls ended and hers began. She would have tried to fight her own exhaustion to make sure to catch every detail of what was going on in the story. Her father's voice would transport her from her little bed in her little room into the vast and magical snowy realm of Narnia to find Aslan and defeat the White Witch, bringing back summer for all who lived there. He would have looked down at the end of the chapter to find her sleeping, kiss her forehead, and gently slide his shoulder out from beneath her head, careful not to wake her.

Audrey was roused from her reverie by Mark's sudden change of tone as he told the boys good night and coaxed the half-sleeping Daniel to go back to his own room. She jolted upright and sprinted to her room, quietly closing her door and jumping on her bed to get back to her writing. Hermione raised her head lazily when the bed jerked underneath her with Audrey's leap. A few seconds later there was a knock on her door, and Mark stuck his head in.

"Still working on that essay?" he asked.

"It's a poem, actually," Audrey said sheepishly.

"You write poems?"

Audrey nodded.

"What's it about?" he seemed intrigued.

"Nothing," she said, closing her notebook.

"Ah well, in that case, I'm going to bed. Good night, Audrey. Don't stay up too late, okay?"

"Hey Mark," she called as he turned to leave.

"Yeah?" he asked, swinging the door back open. Audrey's voice caught in her throat, unable to form the question she'd been longing to ask for over a year. Mark stared back at her expectantly. His loose brown hair looked tousled and greasy from a long Monday of running his fingers through it in frustration.

"I," Audrey stammered, looking down at the pencil in her hand. She cleared her throat before meeting his pale blue eyes and continuing. "What was his name?"

Mark's posture softened with his sigh, and a sympathetic look crossed his face, sending fire across Audrey's skin. "I told you," he started gently, "his name's Jesse."

"But his last name?" she swallowed the lump that was forming in her throat.

"I'll tell you someday, but I can't risk you going after him," he offered her a smile that barely reached his eyes. Audrey looked back down at her white bedspread and picked at the seams of the raised, sheer fabric rose design.

"Can you tell me what he looked like?" she mumbled.

"Audrey, I haven't seen Jesse in seventeen years," he said, his voice slightly tinged with agitation. "And it's not like I studied him for an art project or something."

Audrey nodded but didn't look up. Her fingers moved more frantically as she tugged at the fabric. Tears pooled in her eyes and she tried to blink them away, holding her breath to keep it from quickening audibly. She could hear Mark take his hand from the doorknob and sigh at his austerity. She waited for him to mutter a good night and close the door, but he stayed where he was. When her lungs began to burn with lack of oxygen, Audrey sucked in a shaky breath and turned to Mark standing awkwardly in her doorway.

"Why did he leave me?" she choked out before her flooding eyes overflowed. With only a moment's hesitation, Mark crossed her oddly decorated room and sat on the edge of her bed. Audrey wiped at her cheeks furiously and tried to avert her eyes, looking in every direction but his. Hermione shifted to rest her head on Audrey's thigh and stared at them with her round, knowing eyes.

"Hey," Mark whispered, feeling ill equipped to comfort her. "He didn't leave you, Audrey."

"Well then where is he? If he didn't leave me, then where is he?" her voice rose in pitch with the emotions that spewed from her like a bottled soda that had been dropped to the concrete. She turned away again, but Mark put his hand on her forearm to pull her back.

"I don't think he even knew about you." She shot her eyes back to him and searched his face for an explanation. He tried to smile comfortingly at her. "Well, I'm sure he knew you existed. Sheryl blew up like a balloon, but she had already ended things with him. Everyone just assumed you were mine. Most people hated me after that actually. They thought I left her when I found out she was pregnant." His eyes clouded with the memory as he stared through Hermione. "Well I did actually. But how could I watch my girlfriend have someone else's baby, especially when we were just kids ourselves?"

Audrey sniffed and stared down at her empty hands.

"So I guess if anyone left you," he said after a few minutes of silence, "it was me." His voice was thick with what seemed to Audrey as pent up regret.

"Don't be stupid," Audrey scoffed, wiping at her cheeks.

"Audrey, you grew up without a father," he said, bringing a fresh wave of tears to her eyes. "I could have been that for you. If I had stayed with Sheryl then, you would have had a dad." He cleared his throat and tried to smile before continuing. "So if you want to blame someone, Jesse shouldn't be any higher than third in that list, after Sheryl and me." He attempted a laugh.

Audrey opened her mouth to assure him that she could never have expected a boy of sixteen to willingly raise someone else's child, but her words morphed quickly into sobs. Mark moved next to her, wrapping his arm around her shoulder as she leaned into him.

Anger mixed with the frigid emptiness in her, writhing through her veins, making words impossible. It had been easy to both blame and long for a man who should have been her world but who instead had willingly abandoned her. Now she only had Sheryl, who had not only allowed her to grow up without a dad but also a mother. Audrey had always had to take care of her own emotional and sometimes even physical needs while her mom drowned herself in self-pity. Her anger quickly boiled to hatred as she yearned for the elusive man who should have been the one to raise her.

Despite his confession of the guilt that he carried, there was nothing fatherly in the way Mark held her. They had come to terms over soggy waffles that he would never truly be her father or even a true stepfather. The small age gap between them alongside Audrey's forced early maturity had crushed any bud of a parental relationship they could have had, but they were comfortable with being friends. She could never see him as her dad, and he could never view her as a daughter. He was protective like an older brother, and maybe that was okay. Maybe after playing house on a daily basis with her little brothers, all that she really needed was someone to be there when she fell and scraped her knees on the concrete.

And if she couldn't have a dad, she'd have a friend. An older brother.

With that thought, Audrey allowed herself to let out what was left of her bottled up soda onto Mark's gray t-shirt.

Chapter Eight

Seattle, Washington

The plane made its descent over Seattle, and Audrey couldn't help the smile that teased at her face. The tall buildings at the heart of the city rose into the sky from the otherwise flat land and water but still looked like nothing more than Lego structures from her position in the clouds. Ferryboats and barges crossed the Puget Sound as the plane flew lower still and made its way to the airport. The mountains in the distance stood majestically, willing all that laid eyes upon them to become enraptured by their serenity.

Audrey pulled her suitcase from the overhead compartment and followed the slow line of people off the plane. Cruising through the crowded airport proved more difficult than she'd originally anticipated. She got lost twice and had to ask for directions from the bored looking staff members. Finally with Hermione's cage wheeling behind her, Audrey walked in the direction she hoped was the exit, searching every face for a wash of dark hair and lively green eyes.

Then she saw her. Still wrapped in her rain-splattered overcoat and a thick purple scarf, Snow stood scanning the crowd, fiddling with a pendant on a long chain around her neck. Ganesh stood at her side in a brown blazer, checking his watch and saying something to his fiancé that got lost in the jumbled ambience of airport conversation. Snow smiled and replied with raised eyebrows. Audrey watched them for a moment. They seemed happy together. Sickeningly so. Like an image in a picture frame, the generic, posed images with overly joyful models propped up on display shelves in stores to show the various possibilities one could use the frame for. And Ganesh was much better looking than he was on her computer screen.

Snow caught sight of her, and her face lit up as she ran to her and threw her arms around her. Audrey laughed and patted her friend on the back, and Ganesh smiled, taking a back seat to Snow's enthusiasm.

"I can't believe you're actually here!" she squealed through the squeezing hug. "In real life person!"

Audrey eyed Snow's fiancé over her shoulder and reached out a hand in his direction. "Nice to finally meet you Ganesh," she managed to grunt as Snow's hold began to choke her.

"Officially," he added with a dazzling white smile and shook her hand.

"And, omigod, your hair!" Snow pulled back and grabbed handfuls of Audrey's curls, ignoring her duties of introduction. "I love it! Do it yourself?" Audrey nodded. "It needs touching up but I can do that easily. Why hello there, Hermoninny!" she bent down to stick her fingers through the bars and greeted the greyhound, who squeaked and wheezed with excitement.

"Come on!" Snow beamed. "You're in Seattle, baby! Let's get a coffee!"

Audrey couldn't help the feeling of whiplash as she followed her old friend to the parking lot, pulling Hermione behind her. Ganesh stashed her luggage in the trunk of his car as the four piled inside and weaved through the crowded streets until they pulled up in front of a beautiful brick building on 4th Avenue with slanted canvas awnings and large windows. Although it was eleven stories high, it was dwarfed by the neighboring towers.

Snow pulled her along, chattering about all she had planned for them as they took the elevator to the third floor. The walls of their vast apartment were painted a light cream color that contrasted beautifully with the dark hardwood floors. The living room arced with the wide curve of the building, decorated with heavily draped windows that let in the gray, winter sunlight and overlooked the rising city of brick, glass, and concrete. The sofa was pastel blue with dark accent pillows, and several framed photographs sat atop a burlap place mat that covered the center of the coffee table. A thick sliding door separated the living room from the apartment's only bedroom.

"Cute," Audrey said, dumbfounded at how adult it all seemed as she remembered Snow's high school bedroom, plastered with magazine cutouts of celebrities.

"Thanks," she huffed, kissing her fiancé's cheek.

"I'll see you in the morning," he said. "I've got the late shift."

"Well it's nice to finally meet you," Audrey repeated herself awkwardly as Snow grabbed her wrist and tugged her back to the door.

"I'll give you the tour later," she said. They ran back out to the street and walked the short distance to a nearby café. Audrey tied Hermione to an abandoned table outside while Snow went in and walked straight to the counter.

"Two hazelnut mochas please," she ordered. "You're gonna love it!" she exclaimed dramatically as they walked to a table by the large window with a view of Hermione. "So tell me about Iceland! Was it everything you'd dreamed it would be?"

"For the most part, yeah," Audrey smiled. She gave Snow a short description of her time in Iceland, knowing the laidback pace of her vacation would bore her energetic best friend.

"We have to listen to that CD when we get back to my apartment. They sound awesome!" Snow interrupted.

"They were."

"Of Monsters and Men, you say?"

"Yeah."

"Clever."

Audrey nodded and sipped at her hot hazelnut mocha, trying not to blanch at the sweetened flavor. "So, how's the job, Miss Bailey?"

"I love it!" Snow beamed. She launched into several accounts of a room full of rambunctious second graders and her attempt to teach them math and read *Willy Wonka and the Chocolate Factory*.

"You know," Audrey laughed, "I'm still amazed that you moved across the country to go to an expensive school and get a degree readily available in any state and then move to the complete opposite coast to teach kids, which, may I remind you, there's plenty of children in New York. You could have just as easily been a rocket scientist with your grades."

"Well I don't know about that," Snow smiled humbly. The afternoon passed with Snow spewing tips on city life as if Audrey hadn't spent the last few years in London.

"I need to find a job and a place to live soon," she said. "Do you know of anything cheap close by?"

"About that," Snow tried to hide her grin as she dug through her small purse. Audrey stared in disbelief as she proudly produced a key dangling from the metal ring on her finger. "Follow me."

Snow got up from her chair and pulled Audrey out of the cafe. She never loosened her grip on her arm as she tugged her down the street and around a corner faster than Audrey could read the road sign, and within a few brief minutes, they stopped in front of a short, brick building. To Audrey's horror, they walked right past the front desk and straight to the staircase. A metal bar hung on the wall to guide their steps, and paint peeled off the baseboards and doorframes. Audrey lost count after four flights of stairs. Finally Snow led her out into a hallway, stopped in front of a door marked 901C, and held out the key, exhilaration uncontrollably seeping through her grinning face.

"Did we just walk up nine flights of stairs?" Audrey huffed. Hermione plopped down, panting heavily at her feet. Snow rolled her eyes and grabbed Audrey's hand, raising it and slapping the key in her hand.

"I was too excited to use the elevator."

Audrey looked down at the aging key in her hand and stared at her friend in disbelief. "You didn't."

"We felt bad for dragging you across the world, so we took out a lease on an apartment we thought you'd like. Don't worry, the rent bill starts going to you in February once you get settled in," she added at Audrey's look of protest. "Well come on then! Go in!"

Audrey closed her hand around the key and fought a smile at Snow's enthusiasm. She turned the key in the lock and opened the door. It creaked loudly as it swung on its rusted hinges. The studio stretched out into a long rectangle before her, double the size of her London flat. The wall on the left was exposed brick while the kitchen area across from it had recently been painted white. Small, black-framed windows cut into the wall ahead and looked out onto the brick of the neighboring building. A long AC pipe ran along the length of the ceiling, and a spiral, black metal staircase suspended to the ceiling in a cutout corner on the far side of the kitchen, leading up to a small loft.

Hermione wandered through the door ahead of them to

explore while Audrey took a few tentative steps forward. Snow smiled her scrunched proud smile and studied her friend's face to gauge her reaction.

"It's gorgeous!"

"I know," Snow beamed with pride.

"There is no way I could ever afford this," Audrey added, bitter disappointment sinking in.

"Yeah you will," Snow said confidently. Audrey turned to look incredulously at her friend. "I said it's old, didn't I? The heater doesn't work properly, and there's a mouse problem in the winter. I figured it wouldn't be a problem since you have Hermione." Snow beamed with pride.

"Oh she could definitely catch the mice," Audrey started, shaking her head, "if she was a bloody terrier! Greyhounds aren't exactly known for killing pests."

Snow rolled her eyes. "The next apartment at this price is well out of the city. We can get you a lease there if you want, but there's no guarantee it'll be rat-free." Snow huffed. "Oh and since Al's working the night shift at the hospital, you're staying at my place until we can get you a bed tomorrow." She rambled on about how Audrey should decorate her new apartment as they walked around the small space. Audrey felt a strange sense of sadness when they finally turned to leave the apartment. The empty space had softened her anxiety. They took the elevator down to the lobby and walked out into the dark streets.

"So, what's for dinner?" Snow asked.

"Call in a pizza?" Audrey suggested. "And what's the latest overdone action film? Big explosions, impossible stunts. I haven't seen a new one in half a decade."

"Yeah, they don't really make movies like that anymore," Snow admitted, eyeing her apologetically.

"Seriously?"

"Seriously. Sure, there's big explosions and impossible stunts, but not in the way you like it. They try to make it more realistic now, more believable."

"Well that's rubbish," Audrey complained. "Okay fine, we should have a Netflix night then."

"Netflix?" Snow looked confused.

"Yeah, isn't that a thing here?"

"Yeah, but I don't have Netflix."

"Well you're getting it tonight," Audrey smiled as she tried to wave down a taxi.

"Oh, no I'm walking distance." Snow looped her arm through Audrey's and led her down the street.

"Should have known," Audrey slid her hands in her coat pocket and smiled to herself as they walked. A sense of nostalgia washed over her at the so familiar way her friend breached her derelict sense of emotional security and ignored the way her muscles tensed when they linked arms. Being with Snow took the edge off of the ever-present pain and regret. She couldn't help but wonder how different her life could be if she'd gone with Snow to New York like they'd planned all those years ago instead of squeezing too tightly to her brothers.

Pushing the vision of the boys, grown and grinning as they visited her in New York, she focused her energy on memorizing the route to Snow's apartment. They ambled several blocks down, passing markets full of people clutching their coats against their necks, and made a left at Pike Street. She marveled at the passing buildings while Hermione stopped to sniff each passing tree that was rooted into the concrete. They passed parking garages, coffee shops, hostels, restaurants, and a construction site before making a right turn onto 4th Avenue. Snow pulled Audrey along as she watched the city breathe around her until they reached The Cobb apartment building.

Inside, Audrey collapsed onto the sofa and scanned the photographs on the coffee table. She smiled at the one of Snow's graduation. Only Audrey noted the terror in her own eyes as they gazed at Snow, wondering if she would never see her best friend again.

They spent the rest of their night binge-watching Heroes, a show Snow assured Audrey she couldn't continue being her maid of honor if she hadn't watched it all the way through at least twice.

Audrey found herself laughing, really laughing, for the first time in years at Snow's commentary to the TV drama. She then remembered how she'd gotten through all those years of Sheryl's pre-Mark, alcohol infused, berating insults and the heavy silence that often went on for days once Mark came and put an end to her abuse.

After devouring the entire box of pizza, two bags of popcorn, and the first seven episodes of Heroes, Snow hobbled to the kitchen to presumably make coffee.

"Snow," Audrey groaned dramatically, throwing herself across the couch, "can't I just go to sleep? You've been pumping my veins with caffeine all day, but my jet lag is about to be the death of me." She laid her head on the curled up Hermione as she spoke and already felt herself slipping into a deep, intoxicating sleep.

"Nope," Snow walked in from the kitchen carrying two pints of Ben & Jerry's ice cream and spoons. "You just have to eat this and watch the next episode. Then you're free to sleep for three days if you want to."

"Cookie dough?" Audrey grinned sluggishly and pulled herself upright.

"Nothing but the best," Snow handed her a carton and sat down on the sofa, pulling her legs underneath her and hit play to begin to next episode. They both took turns shrugging off the begging whines and pleading eyes of the persistent greyhound. A little while later both women were asleep, and Hermione had free range to the ice cream.

Chapter Nine

Madison, Alabama
April 2003

Spring had always been a time noted for rebirth, especially in Alabama. Dead trees blossomed with pink and white buds while dogs barked greetings at the joggers coming down their roads, and families laid blankets across the lawn for picnic meals of sandwiches and chips with French onion dip. Weekends found people filling motorboats and pontoons that would crowd the rivers, fishing poles jutting out from all sides, and Tim McGraw's voice and sliding guitar reverberating off the surface of the water. The breeze would come alive with the scent of honeysuckles for the few days before the neighborhood children would pick them all from their stems and drain the succulent juices from the base of the flower. Yellow pollen covered every surface, and birds sang their own independent choruses well before the rising of the sun until the pinks and oranges of the sunset blackened to a pitch and stars littered the sky. Crickets chirped in a monotonous symphony, and whippoorwills whistled their lullaby while children asked for ten more minutes of sword fighting in the front yard before their bath.

At least that was spring for most Alabama residents.

For Audrey, it was something else entirely. Spring smelled like freshly cut grass and dirt and sweat. Not the grown man musk that some women found arousing, but the smell of a hormonal boy entering puberty that hadn't yet discovered the importance of deodorant. It seeped into every article of clothing and deep into the upholstery of her eleven-year-old mustang. Dried mud caked in her floorboards no matter how many times she attempted to scrub it away. She thanked Mark every day for trading the original cloth for leather seats that she could wipe clean every afternoon. She never joined her friends at the creek on Saturdays or climbed on the back of a guy's motorcycle on Sunday evenings. She spent every weekend perched at the bottom of a beat up set of bleachers, cheering on her brothers as they ran laps around a baseball diamond.

Audrey woke at dawn on the season's opening day and went downstairs to fill plastic bottles with Gatorade and to make sure her brothers' bats and practice balls were packed in their bags. She stuffed the side pockets with cheese and cracker snacks that would go forgotten once the boys caught sight of the concession stand. Going through her mental checklist, Audrey threw several pieces of bread in the toaster and flipped the television on to NBC. She climbed the stairs to where the boys had spent the night together in Ethan's room.

"Come on, Red Sox!" she cheered as she opened the thick curtains. "It's game-day!" Daniel sat up slowly and squinted against the bright morning sunlight. Suddenly his eyes shot open and he turned to shake his brother awake.

"Ethan! Wake up!" he yelled. "It's our first game!" Only after ensuring he had beaten awake the sleeping bear next to him did he bolt to his room and slam the door. Audrey turned to see Mark standing in the doorway.

"Mornin'," he yawned.

"Good morning," Audrey smiled. "Don't worry. They're both awake, and breakfast is made."

"Oh," his brow furrowed.

"Bags are packed, cartoons are on, and I'm pretty sure Dan is putting his uniform on over his pajamas," she pointed toward his door. "I should probably check on that."

"Audrey," Mark interrupted her, his voice still thick with sleep. "You do too much. I could have done all of that."

"Nonsense, you're up too late," she waved him off and turned to knock on Daniel's door. "Buddy, that's your practice uniform. Your game day uniform is in the laundry room. Ethan! Toast!" She caught Mark shaking his head in her peripherals just before Ethan came lumbering out of his bedroom wrapped in his comforter. She herded the boys to the breakfast bar and set two mounds of buttered toast in front of them.

"Tell me when," she instructed, shaking the premade sugar

and cinnamon concoction over Ethan's toast. He watched meticulously as she poured the brown and white powder over his toast, stopping her precisely when a thin layer covered it evenly.

"And for the little demon," Audrey turned to the other boy, who sat wide-eyed with anticipation. Dumping it on heavily, she hid the surface of the toast from view, watching the cinnamon blacken as the butter soaked it up. Daniel let out a maniacal laugh and carefully carried his treasure to the living room for his morning segments of Kenny the Shark and Tutenstein.

Ethan turned to follow when Audrey cleared her throat to get his attention. He looked at her suspiciously. She nodded her head in the direction of the coffee pot. A broad grin stretched across his face and he burst into a sprint towards the coffee. He filled his cup with more cream and sugar than actual coffee, turning the black liquid a creamy tan. Audrey wrinkled her nose at him and took a glass of milk to Daniel before heading upstairs to hastily get ready.

Her hair had already begun to curl, breaking free from the board straight form she'd worked hard on the night before. Sighing, she wrapped it in a long, thick braid, and threw on her Red Sox hat. Clad in holed jeans and her Mills Sister t-shirt, she ran downstairs to find the boys sitting on the barstools, fully dressed with Mark standing behind them, arms crossed and leaning on the bar. Pride beamed across his face like a beacon in a lighthouse, demanding the attention of all who stood near.

"Very nice," Audrey nodded in affirmation, "except Ethan's number eight and Daniel's ninety-nine." Mark's eyes widened, the smug look vanishing.

"You lying little dirt bags!" he exclaimed.

"That they are," Audrey pulled her drawstring backpack up to her shoulders. "Go change," she ordered. Ethan held out his fist for his little brother to bump, and they jumped down from the barstools. Daniel's uniform sagged while Ethan's clutched tightly to his body.

"Seriously?" Audrey laughed. "That's as much on you as it is on them." Mark's head fell in his hands on the counter as he laughed and let out a loud groan. Audrey smiled and patted him on the back in mock comfort.

"Where are the boys?" Sheryl demanded, abruptly announcing her arrival. "We're gonna be late."

"They pulled a joke," Mark explained. "They're changing." Sheryl nodded and went for her purse. Her bleached hair puffed out at the bottoms with the dead, fried ends, and her dark eyes were lined heavily in black. The words I TAUGHT THEM TO HIT AND STEAL was emblazoned across the front of her sequined t-shirt in bright orange lettering above a skull and crossbones logo made of a baseball helmet and bats. Audrey scoffed at her mother. The only thing she'd ever taught those boys was how to shout every word they said and use their lollipop sticks as fake cigarettes.

The boys came back downstairs correctly clothed, and they all filed out into the garage. Mark tossed their baseball bags into the bed of his new fire engine red Dodge pick up and loaded up with his family. Audrey called for Hermione before climbing into her mustang. The morning sun warmed her bare arms and brought a smile to her lips as she put the convertible top back.

She tailed Mark's truck the short distance to the Recreation Center's baseball field and helped them unload and find the coach. Hermione tugged at her leash at every child that passed yelling "Puppy!" and trying to pet her. Mark settled the boys in the dugout while Audrey and Sheryl found a seat on the bottom row of the sun-baked, metal bleachers. Sheryl turned to the other moms to boast about how wonderful her children were.

"Hey Audrey!" Snow appeared out of nowhere and plopped down next to her. "Hi, Mrs. Fields," she waved at Sheryl.

"Hey darlin'!" Sheryl smiled broadly, flashing teeth that bore hints of nicotine stains. "How're you?"

"I'm good," Snow replied cheerfully. "Just ready to graduate!"

"I bet! Have you decided what college you're going to?" Sheryl only smiled this much when under the public eye.

"No," Snow shook her head, "still looking for the best scholarship. I'm hoping for NYU though. Audrey and I have wanted to go for years." She smiled and nudged her best friend. Sheryl let out a short squawk-like guffaw, wiping the smile from Snow's face.

"Audrey? At NYU?" she chortled. "I wouldn't count on that one."

"Thanks, Sheryl," Audrey shook her head.

"Oh, by the way, Audrey," Snow attempted to change the subject, "you and Scott are in our prom group."

"Did you run this by Scott?" Audrey asked, holding back a cynical laugh.

"Well, no, but I assumed he'd go wherever you are."

"Ha!" Audrey snorted. "I wouldn't put money on it. We broke up last Sunday."

"What?" Snow gasped. "You just started going out! Finally – if I can show my impatience for a second. Y'all were so cute! What happened?"

"He went to Nick's party last Friday and came back with a hicky." Audrey was startled by another sharp laugh.

"Nice pickings there," Sheryl chuckled, lighting up a cigarette.

"Piss off, Sheryl," Audrey spat as her mother continued to laugh and turned back to Snow, but just then, the umpire blew his whistle and the game started.

Mark rushed over and sat next to Sheryl, smiling down at her and wrapping his arm around her waist, leaning down for a kiss. Audrey made a face and gagged loudly. Mark crossed his eyes at her and turned towards the game.

The field filled with awkwardly skinny boys in high socks and cleats and caps. The bustling crowd cheered as the first boy from the Patriots went up to bat. On the second pitch from his coach, the ball hit the bat with a loud ping, sending the ball through the air to land in the dirt just in front of the short stop. He picked it up and shot it towards first base, but the baseman caught the ball too late to get the runner out. The crowd on the opposite side of the field erupted with cheers at the little accomplishment.

Everyone came to the opening games. Parents, grandparents, aunts, uncles, cousins, second cousins, brothers and sisters, their boyfriends and girlfriends, third cousins, and the step grandparents once removed. The stands were packed with families, crying babies, and a dog or two. Hermione pulled tightly against her leash, nose to nose with a beagle of probable foul intentions. Adults munched on sunflower seeds while kids sucked their sodas through Sour Straws and made dirt and rock castles next to the fence.

The first inning ended quickly with the Red Sox trailing by a point. Audrey cheered loudly as Daniel came up to the plate, his knobby elbows peeking out from beneath his rolled sleeves. He grinned and waved a gloved hand at his obnoxious family before slamming the tip of his bat on the ground like he saw the professionals do on television. The coach pitched the ball at him with just enough force for it to slowly pass over the plate. Daniel swung three times, never making contact with the ball.

"Out!" the umpire shouted, sending Dan back to the dugout, shoulders slouched, bat dragging, leaving a dented trail in the dirt. His family shouted encouragements at him, which he ignored. Three more innings passed without a score on either side. The crowd didn't lose stamina, however, desperate to keep the players heartened and excited about the game.

"Next up, Ethan Mills!" the decrepit commentator announced. Audrey's family erupted with cheers again, and Ethan shot them a shy smile. The first ball flew past him and slammed into the catcher's mitt.

"That's okay," Audrey yelled. "That's alright! Eye on the ball!" The next pitch connected with the bat with a loud ping and sailed deep into outfield. Audrey jumped up screaming, cheering her brother on. Ethan didn't look to see how far the ball went. He kept his eye on first base and charged. The first base coach swung his arms, yelling for him to keep going. The crowd screamed louder as he rounded second base and raced towards the beckoning third base coach.

"Go! Go! Go!" Audrey and Snow screamed at the top of their lungs. Ethan's scrunched face was red between the earpieces of his bobbing helmet. He ran with an agility that seemed to age his features with every powerful step as he sprang further with each stride. As he neared home plate, he dropped to his butt and slid across the plate, sending up a cloud of dirt and knocking the catcher out of the way. The ball was still making its way across the field. Audrey laughed at the unnecessary slide as the crowd cheered and the commentator announced a score for the Red Sox. Audrey ran to the side of the dugout and shoved her hand through the diamond-shaped wiring of the fence.

"Way to go, big guy!" she smiled at her brother's panting, beaming form. He slapped a high five at her extended hand and pulled off his helmet.

"I didn't know what the coaches were trying to get me to do," he heaved, the ends of his short, spiky hair dripping with sweat. "I didn't think I hit the ball that hard!"

"It went all the way to the fence!" Daniel yelled, throwing

his arms in the air. "It was awesome!" He smiled admiringly at his big brother, his own shortcomings going completely forgotten as he celebrated Ethan's victory. Audrey stayed and talked to the team for a minute, most of them sticking their skinny arms through the fence to pet Hermione, before heading back to the bleachers.

They added a sixth inning as overtime. The Patriots scored again, winning the game, but it was nothing to deflate the swelling ego of the newly dubbed Mills Powerhouse, who was still floating on cloud nine from his triumphant home run. They all stood for a while at the bleachers, talking with Mark's parents before heading back to the cars. Snow climbed into her Camry with an invitation to dinner extended to Audrey and drove away.

"Can we ride in Toretto?" Ethan asked.

"Yeah and go get milkshakes?" Daniel piped in.

"Sure," Mark answered. "Just be home before dinner!" He smiled and walked hand in hand with Sheryl to the truck.

"Shotgun!" Daniel yelled and hurtled towards Toretto with Ethan hot on his heels.

"Cleats in the trunk!" Audrey called after them. They tugged off their shoes and tossed them in the trunk, racing around to the passenger side door.

"You're still too young to ride shotgun, bud," Audrey said. Daniel spit his tongue out and rolled his eyes at Ethan's smug grin.

"Fine," he pouted and climbed in the backseat as Audrey lowered the top, "but I get to choose the music!" He leaned forward to rummage through the center console, pulling out a David Bowie tape. Soon they were racing down the highway on the sunny afternoon, singing and dancing along to Bowie's "Let's Dance." The wind ripped strands of hair from Audrey's braid and threw Daniel's shoulder-length mane in his eyes. They pulled into the crowded Sonic Drive-In and searched for an empty spot. Audrey put Toretto in park and ordered the boys out of her car. She leaned back in the driver's seat with her arm resting on the side of the door, watching her brothers chug their milkshakes on the curb. Ethan screamed with a brain freeze, and Daniel bobbed his head up and down with a smile that wrinkled his eyes into slits, the only physical evidence of his laughter. They drank their shakes and ate burgers, fending off Hermione's jealous and intruding advances, and then ordered a sundae to split, promising not to tell their mother, promises that they would most likely break.

"I know what I want to do when I grow up!" Ethan announced triumphantly.

"What's that?" Audrey asked. She scooped the hot fudge from the bottom of the sundae, thankful the boys hadn't figured her trick out yet.

"I want to be a professional baseball player," he answered.

"Well, you have the talent for it, for sure," Audrey smiled.

"Oh, me too! I want to be a baseball player too!" Daniel chimed in. Audrey offered him a smile, hoping he'd change his mind and avoid the disappointment life would surely send him if he continued down the sports road. "We can play on the real New York Red Sox team, Ethan! Together!" Ethan burst into fits of laughter much to Daniel's astonishment.

"The Red Sox are in Chicago, stupid," Ethan corrected when he'd caught his breath.

"Nope," Audrey interjected. "That's the White Sox." They shot her identically dumbfounded expressions, making her snort. She let them argue for a minute over the true location of the Red Sox before loading them back in the car to head home.

"Shotgun!" Daniel shouted, adding a "Please?" and a protruding bottom lip. He climbed in the passenger seat before Audrey could protest.

"Ethan gets to DJ, then," she sighed in defeat. Ethan grinned and jumped up to search through the tapes. Danny screamed "NO" as if he had just found out Darth Vader was his father when the first notes of the Eagles' "Peaceful Easy Feeling" came through the speakers. Audrey drove aimlessly for half an hour, listening to Ethan sing and Daniel scream. She pulled into the long driveway and sent them inside with instructions to remind Sheryl of where she was going, hoping to avoid the griping lecture that ensued whenever she didn't tell Sheryl where she was going. Hermione jumped in the front seat and let her tongue loll out of her mouth as they raced out of the municipal area of Madison and into the country. Forty minutes later they pulled into Snow's driveway. Audrey let herself in and walked in the direction of Snow's room.

"Well hello there, Hermione!" Mrs. Bailey hollered in surprise as the greyhound jumped up on the sofa next to her. "Hi, Audrey. You doing okay?" she smiled up at Audrey.

"Yes ma'am," she answered. "You?"

"We're fine, thanks for asking. Lizzie's in her room," Mrs.

Bailey pointed Audrey in the direction of Snow's room as if she didn't already know where it was and turned her attention back to the television program. Mr. Bailey nodded in acknowledgement of the newcomer but never turned his head. Audrey walked down the short hall to Snow's room and stuck her head in. Snow looked up and smiled, pulling the ear buds from her ears.

"Omigod, guess what!" she practically jumped off her bed in her excitement. "I got that scholarship from NYU! I'm moving to New York in the fall!" she exclaimed, shoving an already well-read sheet of official looking paper in Audrey's hands.

Audrey shifted to autopilot. Her face smiled and congratulated her best friend on her accomplishments while her heart faltered and her mind became a feeding frenzy. Snow was leaving. Moving across the country. Leaving her alone with her mother and her ridiculous responsibilities. Snow had swept into her life in junior high, helped her through her mother's nasty divorce, coaxed her into accepting Mark, and above all kept her grounded when her crazy life made her want to fly off the rails. And now she was leaving. They could lose touch. She could never see her again. Audrey wasn't even sure she knew how to talk to new people or how to socialize and make new friends.

"You're panicking," Snow observed, breaking Audrey from her reverie.

"What?" Audrey asked, disoriented.

"I can see it in your eyes. You're panicking." Audrey was almost offended by how matter-of-fact Snow was about it all. "Don't worry," Snow smiled and put her hand on Audrey's arm, "we'll keep in touch. And then I'll be back for Thanksgiving, Christmas, and then summer. You can even come visit me in New York, and then you'll be there with me the next year. And we can room together. In New York! Can you believe it's actually happening?" Hope flooded Snow's eyes and flowed from her mouth, but Audrey's hardened skin kept that hope and positivity from penetrating and seeping into her own heart.

"I can't," she whispered. Snow looked taken aback, momentarily confused.

"I don't understand," her brow furrowed with perplexity. "It's what we've been planning for years, ever since the girls trip. You've worked your tail off to keep that 4.0!"

"I can't leave my brothers," Audrey worked to keep her

anxiety at bay and hidden away.

"But that's what Mark's there for," Snow offered.

"Yeah well, we know how Sheryl is with men. I have no doubt that he somehow loves her, but she'll tire of him and that'll be that. Besides," Audrey offered a smile, "my brothers are my life."

"But they're not your children, Audrey," Snow protested. "They aren't your burden. You shouldn't mold your own life to accommodate them."

"I know that."

"And Sheryl may have sucked at raising you, but she's a good mother to them when it counts." Audrey didn't recoil at the truth in Snow's gentle words. She'd already known it. Her brothers didn't really need her. She needed them.

"I'm not making any promises," Audrey feigned an sly smile, "but I have plenty of time to think about it. Besides this is your moment, not mine."

Snow smiled and gushed with excitement, going into her dreams for the big city.

"Ugh," she groaned, looking at her hand still perched on Audrey's arm. "I can't wait for that summer sun to come back. I'm so pasty!"

"Like it will do you any good," Audrey quipped. "You'll just burn."

"I know, but any color is better than this! I'm paler than you are!"

"And I'm a ginger," Audrey added, trying to rub salt in her wound.

"Yeah, but you're some sort of mutant ginger. You tan better than any redhead I know!"

"Mark says it's probably just that I freckle so much, all the freckles join together to make a fake tan," Audrey laughed. They sat on her bed for a few hours talking about the baseball game, Ethan's budding talent, Daniel's exuberant personality and dire need of a haircut, Snow's small town girl in a big city plans, and Scott's infidelity.

"Speaking of," Snow started, "how are you? Really."

"I'm fine," Audrey shrugged. "It's not a big deal."

"Well dang it!"

"What kind of friend are you?" Audrey asked, shocked by Snow's reaction.

"A friend who was prepared! Wait here," Snow climbed off the bed and left her room, returning moments later with two pints of cookie dough ice cream and spoons. Hermione followed at her heels, suddenly interested in Snow and the food in her arms. "I expected you to be a normal human being and at least show some strange kind of emotion when your boyfriend of almost two months cheats on you, so I bought these and rented that Tom Cruise movie that came out last year."

"Minority Report?"

"How the heck should I know? He does spy movies like you like, doesn't he?

"Well, yeah but that's not a spy movie."

"Oh well!" she exclaimed, exasperated. "Just shut up and watch it so I can look at Tom Cruise!" Audrey laughed and snatched the pint of ice cream out of her friend's hands, popping the disk into the DVD player and lounging back on the bed.

"Oh, and I ordered a pizza," Snow announced with a mouth full of ice cream.

Chapter Ten

Seattle, Washington

"Rise and shine sleeping beauty!"

Audrey pulled her pillow around her ears to drown out Snow's unwelcome wakeup call.

"Hey that should be your name! Sleeping Beauty," she mused. "I'm still looking for your princess parallel by the way. It's harder than you'd think." She plopped down on the couch armrest.

"Obviously," Audrey mumbled through her pillow. "I'm not a princess."

"True," Snow seemed to contemplate that for a minute before shaking Audrey vigorously and walking to the kitchen across from her. "Wake up!" she called.

"No!" Audrey's muffled shout brought a grin to Snow's face. Audrey could hear Snow rummaging around in her refrigerator, but it wasn't until several minutes later when she smelled coffee brewing in the pot that she emerged from beneath her pillow and tumbled off the sofa.

"How and why are you here?" Audrey asked dryly, slumping down onto the metal barstool with a pale yellow seat that Snow had bought for her the week prior.

"The landlord gave me two keys when we signed the lease. I just kept one of them," Snow's exuberant smile was too much for Audrey to witness so early in the morning. She dropped her head onto the counter and covered it with her arms, only to jolt back up moments later at the sound of a mug clinking against the bar.

"And we're going furniture shopping," Snow informed her. Audrey was still eyeing her coffee suspiciously.

"But we just went last week," she complained, standing up and taking her mug to the sink. She poured out the hot contents and rinsed the remainders from the bottom. Snow lowered herself onto the second barstool and watched as Audrey refilled her mug, turned, and leaned against the counter. She sipped her coffee and stared at Snow, waiting for her response.

"I'm sorry, I don't understand," said Snow, at a loss.

"You put sugar in it."

"You could tell that just by looking at it?"

"Yes," Audrey said matter-of-factly. "I don't drink anything in my coffee."

"But you had that latte when I picked you up from the airport." Confusion plastered itself onto Snow's pale complexion.

"You paid for it."

"But you were there when I ordered. You could have said something!"

"You didn't ask," Audrey sipped on her coffee again. Hoping to change the subject before Snow turned a conversation about hot beverage preferences into an in depth psychological discussion, she asked, "So why do I need more furniture?

"Because you spent all of your furniture money on a couch," Snow said with a hint of irritation. "You at least need a mattress."

Audrey looked past Snow's scowl to the sofa in the living room. Under several haphazardly hung charcoal drawings Snow had sent her through the years was a camelback sofa printed with a Union flag. Although the colors were navies and maroons instead of bright reds and blues, it grabbed one's attention, vibrantly standing out against the browns of the brick wall and the industrial grey floor. Snow's fiancé had given them enough money to kick start Audrey on furniture. At the fourth secondhand shop of the day, Snow had left to get coffee and take a breather. Audrey had been stubborn and hadn't agreed to buy anything, but when Snow came back, men were loading the gaudy sofa onto a truck with Audrey grinning proudly up at it.

"But it's a bloody awesome couch," Audrey whispered, a ghost smile curving the corner of her mouth.

"It is, but you can't sleep like that every night," Snow argued, her teacher voice making an appearance. "You should have seen Hermione earlier. Lying on her back between your legs with her paws up in the air. One shift from you, and you'd have kicked her in the face!"

"Fine, I'll get a dog bed."

"No, you'll get a human bed."

"Snow, I have to save what I have for rent until I can find a job!" Audrey insisted.

"I know," Snow's eye narrowed in a mischievous way that made Audrey nervous.

"It's your birthday, and I'm buying you a bed and a dresser, and you're going to cooperate." Snow flashed a credit card in her face. Audrey noticed a foreign name written out on it before Snow put it away.

"Did you steal that?" she asked nervously. "I'm not going to prison over a mattress I don't need!"

"No, silly, this is Al's." Snow stashed her wallet in her purse and walked to Audrey's clothing rack.

"Tell me why you're still teaching brats how to add and subtract when you're marrying a freaking surgeon," Audrey voiced the question that had been growing since she moved to Seattle.

"Being a teacher is more rewarding than just a paycheck, you know," Snow sang, flipping through Audrey's clothes.

"I should hope so," Audrey said under her breath. Teachers were known to be well underpaid. "But you know I haven't celebrated my birthday since I was nineteen right? We aren't doing this now."

"It's really rather sad that you don't celebrate your birthday. I had been planning your twenty-first birthday party for years."

"With what? Virgin piña coladas and Mean Girls?" Audrey teased.

"Piña coladas in January? Gross," she resumed her search for an outfit, flipping through Audrey's clothes like advertisement pages in a magazine. "I do drink wine, you know."

"Oh that's really living it up. I regret leaving now," Audrey rolled her eyes.

"Audrey, come back! Please don't do this!" the shrill scream was almost lost in the wind as Audrey pulled her jacket close around her and raced down the road, Hermione's long legs pulling her swiftly ahead.

"You don't even drink," Snow scoffed as Audrey swallowed back the memory with a hot gulp of bold coffee. She spluttered and coughed as it burned her mouth. "You okay?" her friend turned to look at her. She was holding a grey sweater and a plaid button down in her hands.

"Yeah, fine," Audrey gave a thumbs-up, sucking in air through her teeth.

"Stop! You can't just leave now! Please..." her best friend screamed again, the sound fading as she put distance between them.

"Shut up!" Audrey seethed, squeezing her eyes closed against the scream in her head. Snow stared at her with sad understanding and held up the two shirts.

"Which one?"

Staring at the steady rainfall hitting her window until her trembling subsided, Audrey set down her coffee, walked past Snow, and grabbed her lopapeysa sweater from the hanger. Snow groaned. "Or neither. That works too."

Six and a half agonizing hours later, Audrey and Snow were collapsed on Audrey's new bed with Hermione stretched between them. They'd shopped at mostly secondhand shops and thrift stores to get everything on Snow's "Operation Domesticate Audrey Wyatt" list that seemed to Audrey to grow longer in every car ride. Audrey's apartment had a more relaxed and intimate feel to it now, something that put her on edge. It looked like someone's home.

The mattress that they were now fighting a doze on was situated beneath the loft and behind the staircase. It sat on an iron Victorian era bed frame and was wrapped in cream-colored sheets, a dark grey comforter, maroon pillows, and a cream blanket that looked like it had been made from an old sweater. A dark stained dresser was placed against the wall a couple yards from the sofa and a few used copies of classic novels sat on top of it.

Jerking awake from a half-sleeping state, Audrey slung her hand at the body next to her, slapping Snow in the stomach.

"Wake up," she groaned. "I want food."

They ordered a pizza and sat at the bar in silence, waiting for the delivery guy. They both drooled like dogs when the box was finally on the bar in front of them. Two pieces in, Audrey asked the question that she wanted to avoid but thought necessary.

"So, have you and Ganesh set a date yet?"

"Yeah," Snow said, wiping the grease and crumbs from her

mouth. "May twenty-sixth." She took a rather large bite of pizza and began to look around the apartment. Audrey noticed a level of uneasiness rolling off of her friend in waves.

"Well that's not far off! We should probably start plan– "

"Next year," Snow blurted out, shoving her straw in her mouth and venturing a glance at the dumbfounded Audrey.

"Next year," Audrey repeated. "As in sixteen months from now, next year? As in there was absolutely no rush in my leaving London, next year?"

"Please, Audrey," Snow turned her entire body to face her with eyes, huge and pleading. "I wanted you here! There's so much more that goes into planning a wedding than you – "

"Oh, and I have to be physically present for every second of it, do I?" Audrey gaped at Snow in disbelief.

"It's my wedding," Snow's voice was shrill. "I only plan on having one of those, and I wanted you here for all of it."

"You gave me almost no time to prepare," Audrey's voice was low and cold, "all so you could have the perfect wedding. Do you know how long it took me to actually feel somewhat settled in London? I had my life set up there. One that didn't quite – " Audrey stood up, made the short trek to the door, and swung it open. "I need you to leave before I get too pissed off and say something I'll regret."

Snow sat with a defeated expression for a moment before collecting her things. She stopped just outside the door and turned back to Audrey. Her face was firm, her voice unwavering.

"I did it because it wasn't healthy for you to live there alone and wallow in self hatred like you were. Not for as long as you did. It was time for you to come home."

The silence that followed weighed down on Audrey's shoulders. She was already regretting her reaction, but she couldn't retrace her steps. Snow left, and after a few seconds of standing in the open doorway, Audrey stepped back out.

"Snow, wait," she called, but stopped short when she made eye contact with a blushing man walking in her direction. He raised his hands in surrender and muttered an apology, staring at his feet with drooping eyes as he walked past her. Audrey turned her head to look after him, puzzled. He stopped halfway down the hall to unlock the door to his apartment.

"Your girlfriend caught us making out," came a voice from

behind her. Audrey's short hair whipped her in the face as she slung her head toward the voice. A tall, bony woman about her age with shoulder-length braids tied halfway back was leaning against the doorframe of the neighboring apartment. Her voice hinted at a long unused accent that Audrey couldn't place. Somewhere in Africa maybe? "Madison's easily embarrassed."

Audrey nodded politely and turned to go back to her apartment.

"My name's Margaret," she called after her. Audrey looked back to see Margaret walking her way. Groaning at the inconvenience of the introduction, Audrey tried to paint on a convincing smile as the woman continued, "My friend's call me Ruby."

"Nice to meet you Margaret," said Audrey, ignoring the nickname. "Do you make a habit of sleeping with the neighbors or is it just Madison?" She couldn't keep the malice out of her tone.

"Yeah, actually," Margaret said brightly. "But I'm only into guys though. So don't get any ideas."

"Right," Audrey stared at her incredulously.

"You're Audrey, right?" her neighbor smiled. "I saw your name on the buzzer downstairs."

She nodded.

"I baked you some brownies when you moved in, but then I ate them. Then my dealer got arrested so I couldn't get more ingredients for a while, but expect some brownies some time soon. It was nice to meet you neighbor!" Margaret gave a hearty smile and turned back to her apartment. Once inside her own, Audrey sighed heavily.

Well, she thought, if I've scared off Snow, I'll at least have Ruby for company. And some weed brownies too.

She rolled her eyes and collapsed on the couch next to Hermione who laid her head on her thigh and resumed her dozing. Audrey stroked her dog absentmindedly and thought about Mr. Williams and the letter she had written him earlier in the morning. In her four years in London, she had only once seen him with someone other than herself. "An old mate from school" he'd called him. She'd gone with him to his funeral. Mr. Williams was alone in a big metropolitan area. Even with Snow, Audrey felt just as alone, but she had Hermione. She got up and walked over to the windows. Looking out at a brick wall that was part of a city with a completely new culture, she couldn't help but miss London.

When she left Alabama and arrived in London, she had felt as though she had gone into hiding. That she would stay there until she died of loneliness and grief, which at the time hadn't seemed like very far away. Now, standing in her Seattle apartment, she felt as though she was just passing through. She was only here for Snow's wedding, and when that was over, she wouldn't stay. Being with Snow was great, but it brought back too many unwelcome memories. Since her arrival, the voices in her head had become more frequent, more intense.

As soon as Snow was married, Audrey would be on the first plane out of Washington. To where? She had no idea. But Snow was wrong. Alone wasn't unhealthy. Being alone was all she had known for the past four years. It was the only sort of comfort zone that she was allowed. She planned on returning to it.

Chapter Eleven

Madison, Alabama
June 2004

The rising sun stretched in a long beam across the kitchen, and birds twittered their early morning song. Audrey sat at the breakfast bar and stared ahead vacantly, the spoon in her hand resting on top of her soggy cereal.

Mornings were usually Audrey's favorite time of the day. It was why she continued to set her alarm for six o'clock during the summer months. The boys were still in a deep slumber, recharging their batteries for another rambunctious day in the pool and tracking puddles of water all through the house. Mark would be down any minute for coffee before work, and Audrey would have at least four more hours before Sheryl woke up and made her daily feeble attempt at conversation.

She'd been doing that lately. Her attitude toward her daughter was the root of the problems she'd been having in her marriage. She and Mark had tried to hide their arguments from the rest of them, but when one leads as unstable a life as Audrey Wyatt one learns to be perceptive.

Mark explained to Sheryl during one of their late night conversations at the dinner table – a conversation Audrey had casually kept her door open for – that he had officially had enough with Sheryl's blatant aversions towards Audrey and urged her to start performing more household and motherly duties so that Audrey could "be a kid." Sheryl predictably didn't take kindly to what she believed to be an accusation, but as time went on, she held back her snide remarks and began taking unconvincing measures to establish a relationship that seemed as though forced through gritted teeth.

Audrey humored her mother's advances for Mark's sake, but as far as she was concerned there would never be a bond between them. Too many drunken condemnations sat between them, forging an insurmountable wall that neither could cross.

All of that mixed with the sparse appearances of her best friend, who kept herself shut in her room tending to her online summer courses, made things a little more hectic than usual. Audrey sat in the silence, sipping her coffee while Hermione resumed her hibernation on the couch behind her.

The ominous atmosphere of this morning, however, put Audrey in a foul mood. The birds annoyed her, and the sun was most likely already too hot.

It was Richard's weekend with the boys, and with Mark at work and Sheryl on vacation with her friends in Savannah, the responsibility fell to Audrey to transport her precious brothers to the McDonald's parking lot and hand them over to her mother's pig of an ex husband. Audrey hadn't seen him in seven years and the prospect of having him in her line of vision again was not one that she found appealing.

Bare feet slapped against the boards of the stairs shortly followed by the swift scratching of clawed paws. Audrey turned to see Ethan slogging down the stairs, wrapped in his comforter with Dazzle at his waist. Hermione jumped down from the couch to greet her sister.

"Hey, you," Audrey grinned at Ethan's droopy eyes.

"Hi," his voice cracked with sleep. He walked over to the back door to let the dogs out into the backyard before slumping onto the stool next to Audrey and dropping his forehead to the bar with a loud thud.

"Dazzle wake you up again?" Audrey asked, suppressing her giggle. Ethan nodded against the granite counter and rose with a dramatic sigh.

"Can I have some coffee?" he requested, leaning heavily on his hand.

"Yeah, big guy," Audrey whispered and kissed the side of his head before walking over to pour coffee into the mug she'd gotten him for his birthday. She made a large plate of cinnamon toast and placed it before him. He looked up at her quizzically.

"But I can only have a sugary breakfast on weekends."

"Oh, can it, Goody Two Shoes," she said, shoving a large bite of toast in her mouth. "Dan told me about the garbage your dad tries to pass off as cinnamon toast. I'm doing you a favor. Say thank you and eat it." Ethan grinned and made a sandwich out of two pieces of toast. They sat in silence, eating their breakfast and sipping their coffee for a while before Mark trudged in. They exchanged their good mornings, and Mark stopped dead in his tracks in front of the coffee maker.

"Who drank all the coffee?" he asked incredulously, picking up the pot as if checking for the escaped liquid underneath it. Ethan let out a breathy, suppressed giggle and grabbed at his mug to hide in his lap. He looked at Audrey with wide eyes and a gaping, grinning mouth.

"I don't know," Audrey winked sideways at her brother.

"You're slacking, Audrey," Mark added theatrically. "I expect my coffee to be ready for me every morning when I wake up. Understood?" He eyed her suspiciously while he filled the back of the coffee maker with water to brew another pot.

"Yes, sir," Audrey saluted him. Ethan bit his lip to hold back his intensely building laughter. Mark filled his mug before stomping back to his bathroom to get ready for work.

"Oh, and Ethan," he called from the stairs, "get your mug out of your lap before you spill it." The floodgates were thrust open, and Ethan erupted into fits of laughter.

"Go get dressed," Audrey said when their hysterics dissipated. "And wake your brother, we've got to leave in an hour." Ethan jumped from his seat and dashed up the stairs, the caffeine beginning to course through his system. Audrey let the dogs inside and followed him up to the second floor. She pulled her tangled curls into a loose ponytail, traded her sweatpants for a pair of faded jeans and converse, and went to round up the boys.

"Thanks for doing this," Mark stopped her in the hallway, hurriedly pulling the knot of his tie up to his throat.

"It's not a problem," Audrey waved it off. He gave her the raised eyebrow look that told her he didn't believe her light-hearted façade and left for work.

Audrey's mustang seemed to shrink in size once the backpacks were in the trunk and the back seat was loaded with a boy and two greyhounds. Ethan folded his legs in the passenger seat – with instructions to take his shoes off – so that the third dog could have room in the floorboard. Before making it out of the driveway Audrey threw the car in park and hastily put the top back to allow for a bit more airflow.

The already stifling, thick Southern heat whipped in their faces and made it hard to breathe as they made the half-hour drive to the meeting spot. The boys rattled on in raised voices about all they were going to do at their dad's house that weekend while Audrey steeled herself over for the confrontation that awaited her. She shouted ferociously behind her every few minutes when she would glance in the rearview mirror to find Flash getting brave and hanging his front paws over the side of the car, leaning out into the full blast of the wind.

"Do you see him?" Audrey asked as they pulled into the McDonald's parking lot, suddenly aware that she had no idea what Richard was driving these days.

"No, I don't see him," Ethan said after a glance up from his Nintendo. They waited for what felt like ages. Ethan and Daniel argued over which cassette they wanted to listen to, and after the fourth tape was harshly ejected from the stereo, Audrey banned music altogether.

"There he is!" Daniel shouted excitedly when an old Chevrolet pickup pulled into the parking lot. Ethan threw his door open and jumped out, releasing Dazzle with him. Audrey busied herself by rounding up the wild dog and leashing Flash and Hermione, still unwilling to look at Richard while the boys greeted their father with exuberance. His deep, Southern accent brought back the memories with more vivid intensity. Audrey pushed them out before they could punch a hole in the strength she had been building up since Mark apologetically broke the news to her two days before.

"Here I'll take that." A large, sun darkened hand reached out for the backpacks Audrey was pulling from her trunk.

"I've got it," she snapped, jerking the bags from his grasp, looking him in the eye. At over six feet tall, he towered above her. His skin was heavily tanned like she remembered but leathery from all the years of excessive hours in the sun. His hair was the same shaggy, dirty blonde but showed no sign of the horns Audrey expected to have grown over the past seven years, and his eyes were still watery blue. Premature wrinkles creased his skin, cigarettes and sunlight aging him far past his thirty-nine years. His old cowboy boots were caked in dried mud.

The stale hatred burned anew in her stomach as she flung the backpacks into the bed of his truck. She handed Ethan and Daniel the leashes, mixing up which dog belonged to which boy, and hugged and kissed them goodbye with a plastered smile. Closing the door, she turned to make a break for her car, but Richard was standing in her way.

"Hey, Audrey Jo," he tried to smile, but his eyes were full of regret when he looked at her.

"Hi," she spat.

"How've you been?"

"We really don't have to do this. I'm just here to deliver the boys. Not to chat." She tried to get around him, but he moved to block her.

"Audrey, don't do that," he pleaded. She looked again at the remorse in his eyes and leaned back against the side of her car with her arms raised in surrender. Richard cleared his throat. "You graduated this year, right?"

Audrey nodded.

"Bet that's exciting."

"Yep."

"Do you have any plans?"

"I have a job," she kept her answers short. The sooner he got bored with conversation, the sooner she could leave.

"Oh, that's great," he smiled at her with his dazzling white teeth. "Where at?"

Her wall broke. Suddenly the six years of living in his trailer flooded back to her, played like a film in her head. She kicked off her car and moved closer to him, blind with rage. The loathing seared from her stomach and spewed out of her mouth.

"Okay, listen here, you filthy bastard, and listen well because I'm only going to say this once," she fumed. He backed away, shocked by her outburst. "Folks at AA may have hope in this 'changed man' routine you've got going on, and you may even have Sheryl fooled enough to give you joint custody, but if you so much as think about laying one of your dirty, calloused fingers on my little brothers, I swear to god I will hunt you down and cut off each finger a knuckle at a time, and I am not exaggerating."

Richard stood dumbstruck for a moment before a smirk stretched the corner of his lips.

"You aren't eleven anymore," he muttered, "are you, Audrey Jo?" Audrey's fingers clenched into fists. Her nails bit into her palms.

"I would slap you right now," she spat through gritted teeth, "right in front of your sons. But I know what that's like to witness."

The muscles in Richard's jaw tightened as he tried to swallow down his own rising anger.

"I would never hurt them, Audrey," he said, firmly enunciating every word. "They're my sons." Audrey stepped back and fought the tears that threatened to spring to her eyes as her fury dissipated, leaving her raw and vulnerable.

"Yeah well I gave up on parental love a long time ago," she continued to glare at him for a moment before stomping to her car, leaving Richard standing there, still looking slightly shell-shocked and angry. She jumped in the driver's seat with a happily panting Hermione and turned back to him.

"Mark will be here Sunday at four to pick them up. Don't give me a reason to see you again," she threatened. Through the corner of her eye, Daniel's face was plastered to the window with Ethan craning his neck behind him, but she wouldn't look at them, afraid their wide, innocent eyes would cause her to lose stamina.

Throwing Toretto in drive, she peeled out of the parking lot, flinging Hermione against the cushion of the passenger seat, and refused a glance in her rearview mirror. She throttled forward, not turning back towards town but trekked deeper into the country, screeching to a stop in front of the little blue house. Audrey slammed her door shut and tramped through the green lawn to the door, ignoring the possible scratched paint when Hermione jumped over the side of the car to join her. She marched through the empty house and barged into Snow's room.

Snow started, looking up at first in fear and then in relief, a broad smile stretching across her face. Adorned in yet another new NYU t-shirt, she had several open textbooks and notepads splayed out in front of her.

"Hi," her beautiful best friend beamed up at her.

What was left of Audrey's fury at once evaporated. Her chest fell with the weight of the memories that crashed into her. The same image played before her on repeat. It was like watching through the slit of the closet door all over again as Richard loomed over Sheryl, shouting hoarsely, and clocked her across the face. Audrey remembered all too clearly how desperately she had pulled her baby brothers' heads to her chest, clapping her hands over their exposed ears, entreating them to shut their eyes while her own flowed with tears. And she had just handed over those same babies to his solitary supervision, to those same hands that had bloodied her mother, for three full days.

Audrey woke with a start, jolting Hermione awake with her. Her phone was ringing blaringly on the coffee table in front of her. Sitting up slowly with a pounding headache, she opened the phone and brought it to her ear.

"Hello?" she croaked.

"Audrey?" Mark's voice came through the speaker. He sounded worried. "Where are you?"

"I stayed the night at Snow's," she answered, getting up from the couch and walking to the kitchen to check the time on the microwave. It was still early.

"Oh," Mark sighed. "Well do you still want to get breakfast?"

"Yeah, of course, I'll be back to the house in about half an hour to drop off Hermione, and then we can go," she tried to sound chipper as she flipped her phone shut and grabbed Hermione's leash.

They drove with the top back and nothing on the radio. The green fields whizzed past them, illuminated by the golden morning light, and slowly the scenery shifted to businesses and fancy restaurants.

Audrey's chest was sore, and she was sure her eyes had swollen. She dug in the center console for a pair of sunglasses as she neared the house. Rushing inside and grabbing an aspirin for her head before Mark discovered her arrival, Audrey ran upstairs to shower. Her hair was still damp and curling wildly when she galloped downstairs and climbed in the truck with Mark. They talked and laughed on the drive to the Waffle House and took their usual booth in the corner. Within minutes they were presented with the coffee and waffles that had already been prepared for their arrival.

Being with Mark and enjoying their routine helped to

soothe her throbbing nerves. She wondered if he took her to the same Waffle House every other weekend for the past few years as a way of distracting her from her brothers' whereabouts or if he simply enjoyed her company as much as she enjoyed his. She didn't really care which. She was just grateful that he never brought it up, never talked about Richard or Ethan or Daniel or Sheryl. Their conversations were made mostly of memorable moments with Snow or the wild parties Mark had gone to as a teenager and sometimes venturing to literary topics.

Audrey was aware that Mark knew nothing of Shakespeare, J.G. Ballard, or Oscar Wilde, guessing he had researched his ready information on Wikipedia, but she appreciated the gesture nonetheless.

They never breached the subtly structured barriers into important topics. Well, not until that morning anyway.

"So, I've got to ask," Mark said through a mouthful of waffle, "what exactly are your plans now?"

"You know I just got that new assistant management job at Chili's," Audrey answered with a sense of unease. She knew this conversation would come eventually, but she hoped they could have skipped over it given their situation. "And I've still got that position at the farm. It doesn't pay as much now that Royce left, but – "

"I know, but I thought I'd offer to pay for your college," he suggested. "Higher education is getting more and more important these days."

"Mark, I've missed all of the scholarship deadlines, and I'm sure I wouldn't be accepted – "

"Oh, please you're a freaking over achiever!" he looked astounded at her protest. "Besides I still have some contacts at Alabama. I can probably pull some strings and get you a scholarship."

"No, thanks," Audrey interrupted before he could continue. "I'm not really a U of A kind of girl if you haven't noticed. Besides I wouldn't even know what to major in."

"No one does," he encouraged. "I went in freshman year and declared an art major!"

Audrey looked at him incredulously and laughed. "You can't even draw a stick figure!"

"I know!" he laughed. "Point is, I think you're brilliant. I think you should give college a try, be it at Alabama or NYU or –" he choked on his words "– Auburn, or even some of the local schools. We have more than is really necessary around here. You know that, right? And you'd still be here with the boys."

"Look, I don't want to go to college yet," Audrey argued, her irritation rising. "I'm not ready. I just want to work for a year or two and save. Maybe pay my own way through it." Mark nodded, yielding for the time being. Audrey sighed and looked out the window at the busy street.

"This waffle is amazing!" Mark exclaimed, breaking the tense silence.

"You say that every time," Audrey chuckled.

"It's amazing every time!" he smiled at her, and they continued on with their breakfast as if they had never had the conversation.

In truth, she would have loved nothing more than to join Snow in New York and get some degree she would never really use, but the thought of giving up her routine and possibly leaving her brothers alone with Sheryl and Richard frightened her more than anything else.

College had changed Snow. Not in a bad way necessarily. She just seemed much more grown up now. She was constantly dividing her time between studying and working, but it was the stories of her new life that made Audrey nervous. Snow had a new city, a new boyfriend, a new style, and new friends. Her taste in music had changed, and she no longer had the same one length, board straight hair. It was layered and slightly curled at the ends, making her look older. She had already changed her dream of becoming a forensic sketch artist for the FBI, crossing over the spectrum to ballet.

Audrey wasn't ready for that kind of change.

Chapter Twelve

Seattle, Washington

Audrey was curled up on her Union flag sofa, scratching pen against paper with Hermione stretched out with her head resting on her master's feet. The words in her head had spilled out onto the paper with no rhyme or reason, and she worked at editing it, changing words and shortening phrases until it had a poetic flow that satisfied her. As she lifted the paper up to reread her poem for the eighteenth time, her phone rang. Snow's smiling face lit up on her screen. It was an old picture Snow had emailed to her when she was in London. Ganesh's black hair and dark jaw was barely visible from where Audrey had cropped him out.

"Hello?" she sighed into the phone.

"Audrey, I'm so sorry!" came Snow's desperate voice. "Well I'm not sorry I got you out of London, but I'm sorry for how I told you. I know I'm right in what I did. I just hate it when you're mad at me."

"That's funny," Audrey said dryly, biting her lip against the laugh building in her stomach. Snow always got so worked up over their arguments and stayed in that state long after Audrey had moved past it.

"I really am sorry," she apologized again.

"You'll just have to make it up to me," Audrey said, reading back over her poem.

"I'll do anything!"

"I get to choose the color the bridesmaid's wear."

There was a silence at the other end. Audrey covered her mouth to stifle the oncoming snort. If there was anything that gave tangible evidence of the differences in the two, it was their color choices.

"Technically the maid of honor doesn't have to wear the same color as the bridesmaids," Snow struggled for a loophole. "They just have to coordinate."

"Okay, fine," Audrey sighed dramatically. "I get to choose the color of my own dress."

"I have to approve of it of course," Snow interjected.

"I feel like I'm being gypped, Hermione," Audrey said to her dog, who looked up at the sound of her name. Audrey smiled as she scratched her grey head, listening to Snow's strained voice search for reasons why Audrey was still in control of her dress decision.

"Snow, Snow, it's fine!" Audrey interrupted, giggling audibly.

"Oh, okay good," she sighed. "So I was thinking. We should meet up at our café and start planning."

Audrey sprinted down 1st Avenue and onto Pike Street, pulling her coat tightly around her as she shielded her hair from the rain as best as her thin fingers would allow. Hermione shook the drops from her short fur and sat in her usual place once they were under the blue and white striped awnings that shaded the small tables underneath from the pouring rain. Through the glass, people could be seen lounging in sofa chairs and sitting at tables with laptops and papers strewn in front of them. A bell pinged when she walked inside the café. Without glancing at the menu, Audrey walked to the counter.

"Hi, can I get an earl grey tea, splash of milk please?" she asked politely, pulling a few crumpled bills from her back pocket.

"I'm sorry, we don't carry any earl grey," the barista apologized.

"What?" Audrey glanced up, taken aback. She recovered quickly. "Fine. Black tea then. No milk."

"Sorry, we only carry flavored and chai teas," he repeated. He smiled and pointed to the stand full of boxes of flavored tea bags. Audrey's jaw dropped. She opened her mouth to say something when she was interrupted.

"Just get her a cup of hot water," Snow reigned in beside her. She grinned and held up a Twining's Earl Grey tea bag between her fingers. Audrey snatched it, keeping her distasteful expression.

"And a milk on the side," she yelled back to the barista. "I don't trust you petty Americans to do it properly."

"You do realize you are in fact an American, right?" Snow couldn't contain her giggling.

"Oh piss off," Audrey scoffed before breaking and laughing herself. When the barista returned, her affronted expression snapped back into place. "Buffoon," Audrey spat at him, "you wouldn't know a good tea if you were drowning in it!"

"Audrey!" Snow tried to chastise her, but she was laughing too violently. The barista grinned uncomfortably and handed her the cups of steaming water and milk. Audrey took them with a sardonic smile and brought them to a table in the far corner of the shop. Snow joined her moments later. She tore open three packets of sugar at once, pouring them into her already tan-colored coffee. Audrey eyed her with disgust but decided not to mention it.

"Do you just carry bags of tea with you wherever you go?" she asked.

"When I'm with you," Snow shrugged. Audrey passed her an incredulous look. "What? It came in handy didn't it?" She rummaged through a purse the size of a small country and pulled out numerous wedding magazines and catalogues with various color-coded sticky notes protruding from every side at all angles. Audrey took a deep breath and felt every muscle in her body tense up despite the soothing jazz music pouring through the speakers implanted in the ceiling tiles. She picked up her tea, and took a large gulp of it, spluttering wildly when it burned her mouth.

"Good job," Snow giggled without looking up from her magazines. "I marked the pages with dresses you can choose from with the pink stickies, the flowers with green, the cake with..."

"Wait, have you lost your mind?" Audrey interrupted her. Snow looked up in confusion. "Pink? I thought we agreed that I was choosing the color."

Snow rolled her eyes. "Black or gray right?" She turned the magazine around so that it faced her maid of honor and opened the page to the first dress she had selected for her. The dress was simple. Made of a dark gray material, it would coordinate well with her other bridesmaids' lavender.

"I approve," Audrey stated with a nod, taking a more tentative sip of tea. Snow's answering smile stretched her face to new lengths and even pulled at her the corners of her eyes. She jumped up and yanked Audrey out of her chair. Taken aback, Audrey flailed awkwardly to keep her balance and figure out the situation enveloping her with arms like tentacles with an unbreakable hold. She eyed Hermione through the window, pleading for help as Snow wrapped her in a great bear hug that somehow engulfed Audrey's thin frame. After a moment, her enthusiastic friend pulled back to look her full in the face.

"Thank you for agreeing to this," she said. Audrey softened just enough to carry on with the wedding planning.

After two and a half grueling hours of floral arrangements, table settings, and questions like "Do I want a live band or a DJ?" "Strawberry cake?" "Chocolate cake?" "Chocolate covered strawberries?" and Audrey's one million "Why are we friends, again?", they finally came to a close for the day.

Outside, Audrey put a cigarette in her mouth and fiddled with the lighter. Snow mouth gaped in horror. "Since when do you smoke?"

"Do you even know the ordeal you just put me through?" Audrey huffed, watching the smoke rush from her mouth. "I deserve this one."

"Well in that case," Snow averted her eyes, "you may as well light another one." Audrey raised an eyebrow at her friend's unsteady voice. "I need to run something by you, and I need you to stay calm, okay?" Audrey felt her chest tighten with more than just the smoke.

"Sure, what's up?" she tried to sound lighthearted.

"Well," Snow began, "I was talking to Mom last night about the guest list, and obviously I want to invite my family."

"Right," Audrey coaxed when Snow paused.

"Do you remember my cousin, Cecilia? She was ten when you left."

"I think so, why?" Audrey saw no reason to be alarmed, but her heartbeat rose anyway as if it sensed the imminent threat that her brain hadn't yet noticed.

"She wants to bring her boyfriend." Snow's tone became more and more reserved.

"As she should. What does this have to do with me?"

Snow looked down at the wet concrete, and everything became clear to Audrey. She suddenly felt lightheaded. The buildings began to whirl around her.

"No," she whispered. "She can't bring him. She can't. I can't – " the words fell from Audrey's mouth with no coherent thought behind them. Giving up on the attempt at speech, she pulled hard on her cigarette. When her hands began to tremble, she felt Hermione's wet nose as she nuzzled her owner's clear distress.

"That's what I told Cecilia, but she wants you to think it through." Snow's voice was almost pleading.

"Oh does she now?" Audrey began to feel defensive. "Because she knows exactly how it will feel to see him again after so long. After everything that – " Her throat tightened as her anxiety mounted and her breathing quickened. She groaned and gripped the small iron fence to keep the world from spinning. "He's the reason I left, Snow," she whispered, squeezing her eyes shut against the voice that clanged like a gong in her head.

His voice.

"Audrey! Come look! There's a giant rocket in there, and you can touch it and get inside of it! Hurry up!"

"I wish you would try," Snow said in a soft voice, placing a hand on Audrey's arm. "It would do you good to see him again, to see how well he's doing."

"No, I called shotgun first! You can't do that! I'm telling Audrey!"

"It would do him good, too," Snow added.

"Please don't make me do this," Audrey whimpered.

"I won't make you do anything," Snow sighed, taking a step out in the rain to give her friend some space. Audrey stood upright to catch her breath, searching Hermione's dark eyes for an answer.

"But I do want you to consider it. He's been asking about you ever since you contacted me in London. He really wants to see you."

Audrey scoffed and turned back to Snow. "Don't you dare lie to me." Her face was menacing, but her eyes were desperate. "He doesn't want to see me."

"Where are we going?"

"Of course, he wants to see – "

"Stop lying to me!" Audrey slammed her fist on a nearby table, picked it up and slammed it back down, freeing Hermione's leash and drawing the eyes of concerned passersby. Snow smiled reassuringly to them and ran to Audrey's side.

"You can't do stuff like that!" she hissed in her ear. "You

need to calm down!"

Audrey's head whirled as tears flooded her eyes. "I killed his brother, Elizabeth." She pulled herself from Snow's grasp and took Hermione's leash. "He doesn't want to see me."

Without waiting for a response, Audrey ran down the block in the direction of her apartment building. Snow watched her leave and shook her head.

"Audrey, Where are we going? Slow down! Please! You're scaring me!"

Chapter Thirteen

Hazel Green, Alabama
December 2005

"For crying out loud, sit still, demon!" Snow trapped Daniel's head between her hands and turned it back to its original position. He giggled mischievously, flashing his shining new braces. Snow fought her own smile as she pulled a comb through his damp hair and threw an uncertain glance at Audrey before clipping an inch of white blonde hair from the ends. Danny would only come willingly to get a hair cut if he believed he was only getting a trim, but since he rarely brushed his shoulder length hair, Audrey had to take measures in her own hands.

Ethan, who sat at the head of Snow's bed, looked at his sister with wide eyes when he saw the shears clamp down on Danny's hair higher than the agreed upon length. Audrey put her finger to her lips and winked, pulling Ethan's Nintendo from her backpack and tossing it across the bed at him. He sucked his smiling lips into his mouth to keep from laughing and settled down with his Teen Titans game.

"Hey, Snow, guess what!" Daniel piped up. "I made the travel team!"

"Did you?" Snow asked, trying to keep the tone of surprise out of her voice. Danny nodded emphatically.

"I'm so proud of you, demon!" Snow grunted, grabbing the sides of Danny's head again. She kept a smile as she turned to Audrey again and raised her eyebrows questioningly. Audrey looked up from her book and mouthed that she'd explain later.

Sure, Daniel had gotten better at baseball when he had dawned a pair of glasses and started practicing with his brother and step-dad in the front yard, but he was nowhere near the skill level to be on the travel team. Ethan, however, had far exceeded the talent of a regular baseball player, and playing on the local team was no longer a challenge for him. Both boys tried out for the travel team, and Ethan, predictably, made it through while Daniel was cut. Mark mustered up all of his charm and subtle threats to inform the coaches that they couldn't have Ethan if they didn't take his brother too. After a few minutes' deliberation, they conceded, unwilling to miss out on Ethan's talent.

"Are you kidding me, Audrey?"

Audrey looked up from her book again at Snow's face in the mirror.

"I'm flying back in the morning and you're reading?" Snow asked incredulously. Audrey opened her mouth defensively, but Daniel cut her off.

"She says she prefers Raskolof's company to real humans," he said.

"I did not!" Audrey objected. Daniel eyed her in the mirror and crossed his arms. "His name is Raskolnikov," she corrected.

"Oh, big difference!" Ethan shouted, his gaze still fixed on his game.

"Wait, is that *Crime and Punishment*?" Snow turned around fully to get a good view of the book that Audrey was now trying to hide under the multiple blankets on Snow's unmade bed.

"No," she lied sheepishly.

"I swear," Snow sighed. "Do you not have that book memorized by now?"

"She does!" Dan nodded, earning another grab at his head.

"She quotes it in the car," Ethan added, still staring at the screen.

Snow shook her head. "What are we going to do with her?"

"Hey, I can't help it I'm surrounded by a bunch of uncultured losers!" Audrey teased. Ethan shot her a look from under his eyebrows. Daniel twisted in his chair, causing Snow to throw her arms up and stare at the ceiling in exasperation.

"I'm eleven!" he shouted.

"So?" Audrey argued. "You can read, can't you?"

"You!" Snow dawned her authoritative tone and pointed sternly at Audrey. "Go back to your book and shut up!" The boys burst into laughter at Audrey's affronted expression before Snow turned on each of them. "Demon! If you don't sit still, I'm shaving your head! Ethan, turn down that game. I can't hear Green Day." The Mills boys gave each other wide-eyed, bitten-back grins in the mirror.

"You should be a teacher," Audrey broke the short silence that followed Snow's outburst. Snow fought in vain at the laugh building in her throat, bursting through her nose with a loud snort. They all laughed at that. Ethan threw his head back with such force it collided with Snow's wooden headboard with a loud thud. The room erupted with even louder laughter that woke Hermione who had been spread out, filling the space between Ethan and the foot of the bed where Audrey lounged. She jumped up, thinking something dramatic had happened and began racing around Snow's small bedroom, throwing up a trail of blonde hair clippings and the ends of the newspapers that littered her floor.

"Calm down, Hermoninny!" Snow coaxed in a baby voice. Hermione ran to sit at Snow's feet, looking up at her with her tail wagging enthusiastically. Snow scratched her on the head before turning back to Daniel.

The afternoon passed into evening and found all four of them spread out across Snow's room, none of them willing to leave. Snow was flying to Pennsylvania the next morning to spend Christmas with her boyfriend's family. Colin had come to Alabama for Thanksgiving, and the deal they had struck was to alternate holidays. For this reason alone, Audrey strongly disliked him. Otherwise Colin was a great guy.

Audrey flipped open her phone and sighed. "It's almost six, guys, and we have a long drive ahead of us." Audrey sat up and looked down at her best friend who sprawled across the side of the bed next to Daniel, tears welling in her eyes at the collective, whining *awwww* that came from both boys. Daniel wrapped his arms around Snow who hugged him back fiercely.

"Hey, Snow," Audrey started and cleared her throat against the lump that formed there, "why don't you come over? We're having a Wednesday night movie night."

"Yeah Snow! Please come!" Daniel pleaded, looking up at her. Snow ran a hand through his hair that now flipped out in unruly layers an inch above his shoulders.

"Wednesday night movie night?" Snow repeated. "Is this any different from your Thursday night movie nights? Or Friday or

Saturday?"

"No," Daniel laughed.

"It's just like the Friday one, only on Wednesday," Ethan added.

"We're watching The Grinch," said Audrey.

"No!" Daniel shouted, making Snow jump.

"I thought we were watching Madagascar!" Ethan protested.

"It's, what, four days until Christmas?" Audrey pointed out. "I want to watch The Grinch!" she stamped her foot like a child throwing a tantrum. Daniel giggled and Ethan stared up at her with his mouth gaping.

"You're an idiot," he said, shaking his head. Audrey pointed her finger at him warningly, and he pursed his lips against his grin.

"I don't think I can," Snow answered. Three hearts sank almost audibly at her words. "I have an early flight, and I still have to pack."

Nodding and forcing a smile, Audrey rounded up her brothers and led them to her car. Snow kissed their foreheads as they climbed in. Turning to Audrey with eyes full of unshed tears, she lunged at her. It took Audrey a second to realize what had happened before awkwardly returning the embrace.

"I miss you so much," she whispered in her ear.

"I'll be up there next fall, remember?" Audrey tried to comfort her, attempting to ignore her own discomfort at the lingering hug. "Once the boys are both in middle school. That was the deal with Mark. Remember?"

"Yeah," Snow sniffed, releasing her.

"You do this every time," said Audrey. Snow let out a breathy laugh and looked at the ground.

"Sure I can't cut your hair?" she asked, trying to sound light hearted. "You've seriously fried it." Snow tried to laugh as she grabbed a strand of Audrey's straightened hair, holding up the frayed end so they both could see it. Audrey shook her head and dislodged her hair from Snow's grasp, letting it fall back well below her shoulders.

"You've got a plane to catch," Audrey winked and climbed in Toretto. Snow stood in the driveway and watched them drive off.

"Will she come back here when she's done with school?" Daniel asked from the back seat as they drove through the dark, country roads, surrounded by barren fields.

"I don't know, buddy," Audrey answered. "She may stay in New York, or get married and move to wherever her husband lives."

"Well she's marrying me," he said confidently. "So she'll be back here."

"No, you can't do that!" Ethan shouted, not looking up from his game. "I called dibs a long time ago!" They argued back and forth over who was going to marry Snow.

"You know it's supposed to actually snow, tomorrow?" Audrey suggested, desperate to calm the argument going on in her tightly compacted car. They immediately began planning what they would build and play in the mountains of snow that would pile in their back yard the next day. Audrey hoped against all odds that these impossible mountains of snow would delay the plane that would take her Snow away again.

When they reached the house, the boys bolted through the door and were ambushed by their expectant dogs. Dazzle put her front paws on Ethan's chest and licked his face while her brother rolled over on his back, begging for Daniel to rub his belly.

"It's been five years, and I still can't get over how big those dogs are," Mark said from the kitchen. Audrey walked over to him, tossing her keys on the counter, her own dog following her closely.

"They're average sized greyhounds," Audrey said, a perplexed expression wrinkling her brow.

"Yeah, well, I was thinking of the Italian ones when I saw the ad."

"Idiot," Audrey jeered.

"Jerk," Mark retorted.

"Dweeb."

"Goober."

"Yeasty maggot-pie."

"Piss licker."

"Dear god," Audrey laughed. "Can you be any more disgusting?"

Mark smiled proudly, wrinkling the corners of his eyes. "Yeasty maggot-pie, though? Really?"

"Nothing beats Shakespearean insults," Audrey shrugged with a roguish grin and went to the kitchen for popcorn.

"Okay!" he shouted, clapping once over the noise. "Who's

up for Madagascar?" The boys roared and ran for the couches.

"But," Audrey protested, "it's almost Christmas! What about The Grinch?"

"We'll watch The Grinch tomorrow. I freaking love this movie," Mark gushed excitedly.

"You're such a child," Audrey muttered under her breath about the time Mark sprinted to the couch and lunged onto it, sending it flying backwards. Ethan, almost falling from the couch, yelled out a word that sounded strange and too vulgar for his young mouth. Daniel's eyes widened as he looked from Mark to Audrey, his lips a small O before covering them with his hands and shaking with silent giggles.

"Say that word again, and you're home schooled," Mark warned menacingly though Audrey could see the laughter behind his eyes.

"Yes sir," Ethan said.

"Uh, no Mark," Audrey called. "He wants to be home schooled!"

"Say that word again, and you're staying in school," he retraced his steps, using the exact tone as before. Audrey received an ugly look from her oldest brother while the other continued to giggle.

"Did I hear someone say Madagascar?" Sheryl walked in with a broad smile stretched across her face. Audrey's own smile dropped and was replaced with a wrinkled nose as though a putrid smell followed her mother into the room.

What had once been Audrey and her brothers piled on the sofa with popcorn and candy watching some animated film had now turned into a huge family fiasco. Daniel would curl up next to Sheryl and Ethan would steal Mark's recliner while Mark sat in between his wife and Audrey. He'd pop too much popcorn that would inevitably be thrown piece by piece at the pack of begging dogs.

When the movie was over, Sheryl and Mark herded the boys upstairs to bed, and Audrey began the arduous task of cleaning the living room. She had just picked up the last of the plastic cups when Sheryl walked in.

"I'll get the rest of it, sweetheart," Audrey couldn't help but notice the way her mother grunted the last word. "You can go on to bed if you want." Audrey stayed where she was, watching her mother pick up the candy wrappers scattered across the living room.

"The boys in bed?" she asked, trying to start up some kind of a conversation.

"Yeah," Sheryl answered without looking up at her. "Mark's readin' to them."

"*Half-Blood Prince*?" Audrey grinned to herself. Those kids would be in for a shock soon.

"How should I know?" snapped Sheryl. "It's some wizard book, so probably."

Audrey didn't recoil. It was the most civil Sheryl had been to her without Mark's supervision in a long time.

"Actually, can you get the rest?" Sheryl changed her mind, peering at her watch over the wads of candy wrappers in her hands. "I'm meetin' Jennifer and Becca for a late dinner." She tossed the wrappers on the counter and bolted through the door before Audrey could answer, running back in for her forgotten keys.

Audrey sighed and finished cleaning the living room before climbing the stairs to her room, listening in passing to Mark's booming voice. She grabbed *Crime and Punishment* from her bag and flung herself on her bed, dropping the bag on the ground by Ethan's old shoebox that was barely stuffed underneath.

Three hours and eight chapters later, Audrey's phone buzzed on the top of her bookshelf. She groaned and bent the corner of the weathered page to mark her place before lumbering off the bed and reaching up to grab her phone.

"Hello?"

"Can you do me a favor?" Sheryl's words were whispered and slurred.

"What is it?" Audrey sighed and pinched the bridge of her nose.

"Can you get Mark? He isn't answerin' his phone and I need a ride back home."

"No, he's asleep. I'll get you. Where are you?"

Within minutes Audrey and Hermione were in Toretto, driving across town to pick up her inebriated mother who sat in the bed of a truck with two other equally wasted women smoking cigarettes. Audrey got out of the car.

"Come on Sheryl," she said. "Time to go." Sheryl jumped down from the bed of the truck, rolling her eyes and losing her balance. Audrey lunged to catch her. "Come on," she grunted against her weight, turning to lead her to the passenger side of the car. She noticed over a dozen cans of beer and cigarette butts tossed haphazardly in the truck bed behind the cackling women. Shaking her head, she dropped her mother in the car and shut the door, running around to the driver's side.

"I love this car. Have I ever told you that?" Sheryl cooed, hitting play on the stereo and turning up the volume. Deafening classic rock blared through the speakers, and still Sheryl screeched over it, singing along. Hermione put her head between her paws in the back seat and whimpered. Audrey turned the volume down to a reasonable level, receiving curses from Sheryl.

"I was listenin' to that!" she shouted.

"Well I'd kind of like a dog that can hear, thank you," Audrey snapped.

Sheryl muttered "fun sucker" repetitively under her breath. Suddenly and without warning, she doubled over, vomiting onto the floorboards. Audrey yelped in surprise and disgust, rolling her windows down. She planned to yell at her tomorrow, knowing she'd get nowhere with her when she was this drunk. She'd wait until the massive hangover that was sure to follow to scream at her.

Audrey parked her car in front of the open, empty garage. Mark sat in a lawn chair where her car should be.

"Waiting up for me?" Audrey teased halfheartedly when she got out of the car. "I'm a bit old for that, don't you think?"

"I got Sheryl's voicemails. Should have been waiting for them, honestly," he growled.

"She does this a lot?" Audrey asked.

"Every time," Mark grunted as he beat Audrey to the passenger door and wrenched it open. "Oh god, Sheryl!" he jumped back. She smiled weakly up at him, her eyes drooping. "You take her inside. I'll clean this up."

Audrey did as she was told without hesitation and carried her mother inside to drop her on the couch. She tossed a wet rag at her with instructions to clean herself off while she ran upstairs to get her a clean set of pajamas.

"Are you good now to wait for Mark?" she asked when Sheryl was cleaned and dressed with a glass of water. Sheryl nodded clumsily, muttering incoherently about getting in trouble, and Audrey pivoted towards the stairs, seething with anger. She was halfway there when she heard Sheryl's muffled voice.

"You're just like your father."

Audrey stopped dead just as the door shut loudly behind her. She jerked towards it to see Mark standing with a rag hanging from his hands, his jaw clenched. He'd heard it too.

"What'd you say?" she stammered.

"You heard me," Sheryl gibbered, sipping at her water. Audrey came back to herself and darted to the couch, sitting next to her, leaning forward in her exhilaration.

"What do you mean?" she coaxed gently, but the elation in her voice was clearly audible.

"Audrey –"

"Mark!" Audrey spun around to shoot him a warning glare. His mouth clamped shut but his wide eyes were worried and miserable. He shook his head quickly, urging her to stop. Audrey ignored him and turned back to Sheryl.

"Tell me!" she yelled. Sheryl's eyes moved sluggishly towards her daughter.

"He always wanted to be the hero," she growled, her slow, slurred tone lined with malice. "Always pointin' out what I was doin' wrong when he was just as bad off as I was. Worse, actually. He was a dead beat, Audrey, always was. Never goin' anywhere. Oh but he loved pointin' out everyone else's flaws."

"Is that how you see me?" Audrey hesitated, her voice cracked.

"Audrey – " Mark whimpered from behind. She threw her hand back to silence him, unwilling to turn and let him see the tears that formed in her eyes. Sheryl continued to glare at her, look her in the eye as she continued to spew incoherent malevolence towards her father.

"But I'm not a dead beat, Mom," she whispered. "I'm going to college in the fall. I'll make you and Dad and Mark and everyone proud." The old, dusty desperation to prove herself came scrambling back to the surface.

"You and I both know you're not really goin'," Sheryl scoffed.

"You don't think I'll leave," Audrey felt her voice coming back to her as fury replaced her gloom. "Is that such a bad thing? For me to stick around?"

But her mother didn't acknowledge that Audrey had even spoken. "You're goin' to end up just like him. Tryin' to be a hero and cleanin' up other people's messes when you're just as lousy and useless and make everyone depressed to look at."

"Shut up!" Audrey screeched, jumping from the couch. Tears gushed like rivers down her face. She wanted to scream at the wasted form in front of her but the words and emotions caught in her throat in their haste to get out, choking her. She turned and fled, running to the stairs.

"Audrey!" Mark caught her by the arm before she reached them and spun her around. "Audrey – "

"That's why you would never tell me about him, isn't it?" she yelled in his face. "Because he's something I should be ashamed of?"

"No, I did tell you – "

"Well I don't see how she's any different," Audrey spat through gritted teeth. "Talking about how useless he is and I am, when she sits there all day, wasting away."

"Audrey – "

"I don't care what you or Snow or anyone else says! I hate her! And I hate him! You'll be next on the list if you don't let me go!" she ripped her arm from his grasp and bolted up the stairs.

"Audrey, stop!" he shouted. "Get back down here! Don't run away from me when I'm talking to you!"

"You lost the right to lecture me when you told me you didn't even *want* to be my father!" She continued raging and swearing at him over her shoulder until she reached the top of the stairs. Mark called after her as she wiped away the tears before freezing midstride for the second time that night.

Ethan and Daniel stood in their doorways, staring up at her. Ethan's face was vacant while Daniel's was soaked with silent tears. Her eyes flicked from one to the other, still too stunned to move. Ethan scanned her entire body a few times, maintaining his stoic expression before meeting her eyes and shutting the door. Audrey choked on her sob as a fresh wave of guilt and despair flooded her.

He had checked her for signs of injury the way she used to check her mother.

"Audrey?" Daniel whined softly. Audrey couldn't take it. Without a glance at Daniel, she ran to her room and nearly slammed the door on Hermione. She locked it and threw herself on the floor by her bed, ripping the shoebox from beneath it. She tore it open, scattering old pictures of herself with Snow as kids, of Ethan and Daniel in their baseball uniforms, movie ticket stubs, and other such memorabilia until she found what she was looking for and frantically unfolded the picture Snow had drawn of her dad.

Audrey sobbed, her tears dropping onto her father's cheeks. Anger and abandonment she knew in her heart to be unjust filled her, fueled her rage. Her father trembled in her hands as she squeezed her fist around him, ripping the picture to shreds.

Hermione sat next to her, staring intently at her. Audrey slackened her tense muscles, reaching out to pet her. Hermione laid her head in her owner's lap as Audrey let out the rest of her grief in quiet tears.

Mark knocked sometime later, calling her name softly, but either he thought she was asleep or recognized the lost cause. He abandoned his attempt and left.

Audrey's phone buzzed on the bookshelf next to her. She ignored it, lying on her back and staring at the ceiling with Hermione's head on her stomach. Her eyes were sore and swollen.

Her phone buzzed.

If Sheryl was an irresponsible, irrational alcoholic and her father was a hypocritical miscreant, what did that make her? What would she inevitably become?

Her phone buzzed.

She felt guilty about the way she had acted the previous night, not for Sheryl's sake or even for Mark's. Even without fists thrown, hearing shouting like that, blatant screams of hatred within family members was not an easy thing to endure. And her brothers had witnessed it.

Her phone buzzed.

Daniel's memory of his parents screaming at each other was hazy and almost completely forgotten, but Ethan's was keener. Audrey had always sought to protect them from moments like the one she witnessed when she was Daniel's age, but she had failed. She was the one they would remember screaming at their mother.

Her phone buzzed.

Audrey grumbled loudly and yanked the phone from the

tall bookshelf. She flipped it open to a bombardment of text messages.

Satan: Come downstairs. I need a favor.

Satan: What happened last night?

Nerd: Please talk to me when I get home tonight. I'm sure we can get through this. I don't want you angry with me. I never held anything back from you.

Satan: Audrey Joanna Wyatt, get your ass down here. Mark's at work and I need you to do something.

Snow White: I'm on the plane. I think it's about to take off. Finally. I've been waiting for hours. I'll let you know when I arrive! XOXO

Satan: GET DOWN HERE NOW!!! I need you to take the boys to this play practice thing. I'm too hung over to do it.

"I'm going to kill her, Hermione," said Audrey. Hermione lifted her head at being addressed and wagged her tail. Audrey huffed and rolled off of the bed. Pulling on a pair of jeans and the NYU hoodie Snow had given her for Christmas the year prior, she went to round up the boys and head downstairs.

"Where am I supposed to be taking them?" Audrey asked, pulling on her bulky leather jacket. She couldn't look directly at Sheryl, so instead she shifted her gaze to the window. The two inches of icy snow they had received was already gone, trodden to mush by two overly excited boys.

"They're in this Christmas play at some kid's church," Sheryl grunted from somewhere in the living room.

"What church?"

"I don't know. It's that kid that always comes by to pick them up on Sundays."

"Chris?" Audrey asked.

"Yeah, sure." Audrey could tell she was just agreeing so she'd stop talking. Ethan and Daniel were already waiting in the car, which would seem unusual under any other circumstance.

"Do I need to stay there or is someone picking them up?" Audrey inquired.

"For god's sake, Audrey, I don't know! Stay there so I don't have to hear you! I'm way too hung over to deal with you right now." Sheryl flicked her wrist at Audrey, shooing her away. Audrey huffed and rolled her eyes, storming upstairs to retrieve *Crime and Punishment.*

"We're gonna be late," Ethan said flatly from the backseat as she got in Toretto.

"No we won't," Audrey tried to sound chipper.

"Practice starts at four," said Daniel, looking around awkwardly.

Audrey cursed loudly, but the boys didn't react. She had five minutes to get them on the other side of town.

She threw the gearshift in reverse and screeched out of the garage, yanked it in drive and floored it. The engine roared to life, and the tires squealed in protest as Audrey flung them onto the road. Once on the main highway, the traffic was unbearable, almost completely stopped with last-minute Christmas shoppers trying to scrape what was left from the stores three days before the biggest holiday of the year. Audrey cursed again.

"Please don't say that," Daniel whined, staring at the balled hands in his lap.

"Sorry, buddy," Audrey only half registered what she was saying as she weaved through traffic.

"It's Sycamore First Baptist, right?" she asked. Both boys nodded, and Audrey swerved left at the nearest traffic light.

"Where are we going?" Ethan asked.

"The long way, but it'll still be quicker than sitting in that traffic."

Audrey slammed her foot on the gas pedal, catapulting them forward. She didn't really care if they were late, but the deafening rumble of the engine, the vibrations it sent through her arms, the trees and mailboxes zooming past her at blurring speeds was almost therapeutic. It had the opposite effect, however on the boys.

"Slow down!" Daniel yelled. Ethan's eyes were golf balls as he clutched at the seat beside him. Audrey groaned dramatically, trying to make the atmosphere light hearted.

"Audrey, you're scaring me!" he cried.

"Fine, you fun suckers!" her feigned smile vanished when she heard the echo of her drunk mother from the night before.

She knew it was a mistake the moment her foot touched the brake.

The back tires skid over a patch of black ice and slung out from behind them, throwing them perpendicular to the road. Audrey tugged frantically at the steering wheel, trying desperately to straighten them out, but it only made it worse.

She lost control.

The last things Audrey heard were two screams and an ear-splitting crunch.

Then everything went black.

Chapter Fourteen

Seattle, Washington

The room was too bright. That was her first impression of the dressing room she had been escorted to. With its beige walls and carpet, a dramatic cream-colored sofa, and heavy white curtains that covered the large windows, everything appeared to glow in the morning sunlight that flitted into the room. A thick, plush rug adorned the center of the floor, and a white-framed full-length mirror sat propped against the wall next to the window. There were several vanity mirrors and tables along the wall, one for each of the six bridesmaids and the maid of honor. The only splash of color came from the mason jars strategically placed at the corner of every mirror on the tables, filled with strands of freshly cut lavender, and a clothing rack in the corner containing their dresses and robes.

Snow had offered to share her dressing room with Audrey, but Audrey had declined politely, rattling off some excuse she could no longer recall.

Audrey sighed heavily and pulled off her oxfords, using her toes to hold down the heel of the other shoe in order lift her foot free. She padded across the room, sinking into the thick rug, with Hermione following closely at her knee. She smiled to herself when she noted the robes: six silky lavender ones with the word Bridesmaid embroidered delicately into the fabric above each of their names. She didn't need to read her name to pick out the dark gray one as hers. She tugged her shirt over her head, ignoring the way her ribs were beginning to show when she stretched, and tied the robe around her, surprised at how smooth it felt against her skin.

Then she set to work. Taming her hair was always a chore

but one she endured more and more since her move to Seattle. Snow had hired a professional cosmetologist to get everyone ready, but Audrey refused. So she arrived three hours before the others to put her shoulder length hair in an acceptable position. Hermione stretched out on the fur rug and grunted with pleasure. Audrey grinned at her as she pinned back strands of hair until she was satisfied with the twists and curls and the strands that fell delicately from the bondage. She ran her fingers through the roots to loosen it the way Snow had shown her time and time again. Audrey did her hair and makeup methodically, mentally absent from the tedious work.

Her mind was on the last wedding she had been to. Barely over a decade ago. Sheryl had tugged a brush through her tangled hair, cursing with every moan of pain from her teenage daughter until she gave up completely. Audrey had stood on the altar with a mane of frizzy hair tied into a tight bun and watched her mother look lovingly up at the man who had invaded Audrey's life with intentions of playing daddy. She never saw the toast or the first dance or the cake being cut. As soon as the ceremony came to a close she'd run to the bathroom, crying, hiding from Snow so she wouldn't have to answer a bombardment of unwelcome questions.

Now it was Snow's turn. Audrey knew that the moment Snow made her vows and sealed them with a kiss, part of her would be taken from Audrey forever. Part of her heart would be closed off from her, given completely to someone else, held at a distance just out of her reach.

Marriage changed people. She'd read enough books to understand that. Their lives changed. Two would become one. There would be no more Snow Bailey and Audrey Wyatt. It would just be Amal and Elizabeth Ganesh and there was nothing Audrey could do to delay that moment any longer. In just a few short hours, Audrey would become an extra in the elegant theatrical production that was now Snow's life. She would be carelessly tacked on to the side as embellishment, a cushion for when the happy couple had a fight. Audrey was no longer Snow's world. But she hadn't been. Not for a long time. Part of her had known that.

Hair and makeup completed and, with an hour before the other bridesmaids arrived, Audrey sat in the floor, folding her legs in front of her, running a hand down Hermione's back.

"It'll be just us again, girl," she whispered. "Just like old times." A ghost of a smile teased at Audrey's mouth as Hermione stood up for a moment to adjust and collapsed onto Audrey's legs. Awkward and much too large, she curled into a ball in her master's lap. Audrey wrapped her arms around her and leaned over her, resting her head on Hermione's. She didn't know how long they stayed like that, but when she heard the door click and open behind her, she pulled herself into a sitting position with an protesting ache in her back. Hermione jumped out of the way as she stood up.

"Lizzie's asking for you," one of the nameless bridesmaids informed her.

Halfway down the hall, she met a face that she had prepared herself to confront, but it shook her nonetheless.

"Oh, Audrey," Mrs. Bailey exclaimed, stopping short at the sight of her before hastening forward to wrap her in a tight hug. Audrey let her hand pat lightly at the woman's back as a sort of return embrace. When Mrs. Bailey pulled back again, leaving her hands resting at Audrey's elbows, her pale green eyes were full of tears. She had grown plump in the years that had passed, her cropped hair more gray now than chestnut. "Look at you! All grown up and so beautiful! It's so good to see you, honey. How've you been?"

"Fine," Audrey answered. "I'm fine." Mrs. Bailey gave her a knowing look, her smile turning sad.

"Do you ever talk to your family?" her voice was the only thing that was tentative as she lunged for the big question.

"No," Audrey answered curtly. "Now if you'll excuse me, I've been summoned, and you can't keep a bride waiting, can you?" She hoped her parting smile was somewhat courteous as she walked past her toward the bridal dressing room. She closed the door behind her and leaned against it, looking at the floor and taking a deep breath to silence the voices before lifting her gaze.

Snow sat at her vanity table, her face downcast, but at the sound of Audrey's approach, she looked up with wide eyes brimmed with tears. Their gazes locked for a moment through the reflection of Snow's mirror, each vaguely aware of the other's thoughts. Oblivious to the thick emotion around her, Hermione bound over to Snow's chair, plopped down and stared up at her, begging for attention.

Audrey was the first to break the silence. She crossed the

room, placing her hands on Snow's shoulders, the blue silk robe thin and delicate beneath her fingers. Snow clamped her eyelids shut, a single tear falling down her cheek.

"If I tell you a secret, do you swear not to tell anyone?" Audrey's voice was surprisingly strong and unwavering. Snow smiled as the question that was so familiar to her own teenage lips fell from Audrey's mouth for the first time. She nodded vigorously. Audrey let herself smile. "Amal is the only one you've ever been with that I've deemed somewhat good enough for you." Snow looked up at her in the mirror with a shocked expression. Audrey shrugged. "That's why I don't like him."

"Why have you never said this before?" Snow asked, her voice thick with emotion.

"Because I don't go out of my way to say unnecessary nice things. You know this," Audrey joked scathingly. Snow giggled and wiped at her wet cheek. "You're making the right choice," Audrey smiled encouragingly.

"I know," said Snow in a reassuring tone that Audrey sensed was more for herself than her maid of honor. When Snow spoke again, the thickness of her previous tone returned. "I won't lose you, will I?"

"Never." Audrey smiled and gave her friend's shoulder a soft squeeze, pushing down her own corresponding fears.

At that moment, the door jerked open behind them as Mrs. Bailey bustled inside with the cosmetologist.

"Oh what's all this boo-hoo nonsense? It's your wedding day!" she exclaimed. Snow and Audrey exchanged glances and childish grins. Then the full day of preparation for the night's ceremony began.

The ceremony was gorgeous. Birdcages hung from the rafters containing strands of foliage, lavender, and purple roses. The chairs that lined the aisle were adorned with sheer ivory fabric tied in a decadent bow. An arch entwined with lavender sat elegantly on the altar behind the priest and Amal who waited impatiently for his bride.

Snow looked as though she'd stepped off of a magazine cover. Her ivory a-line gown with its high lace neckline that extended into mid-length sleeves caught every angle of her toned body. Her hair had been meticulously pulled into a bun atop her head, ornamented with jeweled pins.

Her maid of honor, however, was another matter. The pale skin of Audrey's face was tinted green with the nerve-induced nausea. Somewhere in the crowd he was waiting for her. She took several deep, jagged breaths to steady herself, unaware of her tightened grip on the best man's elbow.

"First wedding?" Thomas asked, leaning sideways at her.

"No, but hopefully the last," she breathed. He laughed with two short, deep chortles, and then the door opened ahead of them. Audrey cursed involuntarily. He laughed again and reached over to grasp her hand comfortingly before marching down the aisle.

All eyes were on the bride and groom's chosen favorites, as they made their way to the altar, Thomas with his hand still wrapped around the one at the crook of his arm to hide the way it trembled. Audrey hoped her smile was believable. She knew that somewhere on her left, a pair of blue eyes was fixated on her. With what emotion, she didn't venture to guess. She could only imagine his hatred. She kept her own eyes on Amal, who beamed excitedly at her, in order to keep from searching out the one who watched her.

Audrey blinked in confusion as Snow handed her the bouquet, grinning brightly. She cursed herself for missing her friend walk down the aisle, having been too concerned with her own anxiety. Still Audrey couldn't make herself search him out, not even chancing a glance in that direction in fear that her eyes would instantly land on him. The Ganeshes wouldn't want Audrey's tears in their wedding video. She felt faint and wished for nothing more than Thomas's arm to steady her again.

In what felt like a few short minutes, the bride and groom had exchanged vows, kissed to an eruption of applause, and returned down the aisle. Audrey took each step carefully, willing her legs to move.

"You can let go now, you know," Thomas said when they were halfway down the hall.

"Oh, right," she spluttered, pulling her hand free from his arm. He brushed away the creases she had left in the elbow of his tuxedo.

"Why are you still shaking? It's over now," he said, his deep blue eyes studying her.

Audrey clasped her hands behind her back. "Not for me, it isn't." Thomas gave her a questioning look, but she retreated before he could interrogate further.

Two hours into the reception, she still didn't think herself ready to see him, but she couldn't put it off any longer, afraid she would miss her only opportunity. She stood at the bar and scanned the crowd for his face, wondering how much it had changed through the years, if she would still recognize him. She knew that she would. But the pair of black eyes that met hers were not the ones she was looking for. He was staring at her with an intensity that would have made anyone else uncomfortable. His unkempt hair was shiny and windblown, reaching its full length at his shoulders. A corner of his lip formed a slight smile, but before she could respond, a different face obstructed her view. Her heart leapt to her throat when her eyes focused on him.

He looked just like his father. Not yet twenty, but dressed like a man in a charcoal gray three-piece suit, a black shirt, and a gray and red tie. His thick, bouffant hair had darkened through the years and was swept back to reveal a strong brow. His chin was broad like Richard's, jutting out slightly further than the rest of his face. He was taller than her now but thin, having lost his boyish roundness. But his eyes were the same clear blue that they had been as a child, and they were wet with tears.

In the long moments of tense silence that it took for Audrey to forget her memorized speech, he closed the gap between them and wrapped his arms tightly around her waist, bending down to rest his chin on her shoulder. She returned the embrace, closing her freckled arms around his neck as she choked on her tears.

"Has it really been six years?" she spluttered, trying and failing to be the strong one.

"More like a lifetime," he answered in a voice that was so unlike the one she remembered, deeper yet soft.

"I'm so sorry," she whispered, her voice strained. "I should never have left you. I should have – "

"Audrey," he interrupted her, pulling back to look her in the eye. The way he said her name was so foreign yet so familiar that it made her heart spasm violently. "Don't do that. I had my time to be angry with you, but I forgave you a long time ago."

Audrey nodded, unsure of what to say. He looked at her with a sad smile but with eyes that sung.

"You got old," she said, trying to lighten the atmosphere around them.

"So did you," he smiled a smile that time hadn't touched and laughed when she punched him in the arm.

"So, tell me how everything's going!" Audrey grinned.

"Can't complain too much," he shrugged. "I'm about to move out next month. Got a job over in Atlanta doing some work for the Braves."

"Oh, yeah?" Audrey's heart quickened at the mention of the Major League Baseball team, hoping she hadn't dashed his dreams of professional baseball after all. "Doing what?"

"Selling tickets," he answered. "Not exactly glamorous, but I've at least got my foot in the door. Besides, it was getting much too uncomfortable at the house."

"Uncomfortable?" Audrey tried to ignore the sinking sensation in her stomach when he explained his job.

"Yeah, Mark's remarried. I mean, Noel is great and all, but newlyweds," he feigned a repulsed shudder at the thought. "Plus the new house is smaller. They'll probably want the extra room."

"Ah," Audrey nodded. "So he and Sheryl then?"

"They divorced a few months after," his sentence completed itself in Audrey's mind, and she rushed to move the conversation forward, not wanting to dwell on the details.

"And you chose to live with Mark."

"I lived with my dad for a year or two, but let's face it. Mark was the best thing that ever happened to us," his mouth grinned, but his eyes were full of grief, a hidden sorrow temporarily unveiled. Audrey could only nod.

"So, he's happy now then? Mark?" she ventured on.

"Yeah, he's doing okay." This time his closed smile reached his eyes. Their conversation from there danced around marked landmines, neither willing to expose their scars and gaping wounds or address the vacant space to their side left open for someone who would never fill it, both reveling in the fleeting moment of camaraderie.

They were interrupted much too soon when the bride

shouted their names, awkwardly sprinting toward them with a young woman Audrey guessed to be her cousin. Audrey watched her brother extend his hand to the small, brown haired girl and entwine their fingers affectionately.

So much. I've missed so much. This time it was her own voice coming to persecute her.

"Audrey, help me, I'm trying to instigate something," Snow said in a loud, jubilant voice, putting her arm around Audrey's shoulder. "I think these two need to get married so that I can officially call you family!"

"Oh, for god's sake, Elizabeth!" Cecilia groaned dramatically, leaning heavily on her boyfriend. Only Audrey noticed the way his smile covered a wince as his full weight was pushed onto his right leg.

"Yes please don't encourage that. They're much too young," Audrey protested.

"I should have known you would suck the fun out of it," Snow grunted, pulling her arm down from Audrey's shoulders. "Oh, and by the way we're about to do the toasts, so I hope you have that speech ready." And with that, she went on her way to the next group of guests.

"You. Making a speech," her brother eyed her critically.

"I checked. There was no way of getting out of it," Audrey sighed. A repeated set of sharp pings of a serving spoon on glass silenced the crowd. Thomas announced for the toasts, and everyone took their seats. Per Audrey's request, Thomas made his speech first, taking on the pressure that went along with it, but it did nothing to alleviate her nerves. It wasn't the people that intimidated her. It was the quota of sentiment that was required from a maid of honor in her speech.

She was starting to regret her plea to go second. Thomas enraptured his audience and had them roaring with laughter at scandalous tales from Amal's college years. Audrey feared her own speech would pale and fall utterly bland after his neatly prepared anecdotes that turned heartfelt and sincere.

"Well I think I'll pass this on to the maid of honor now, shall I?" he beamed at Audrey from across the room. Snow gave her hand a squeeze before she stood hesitantly from her seat and made her way through the applauding crowd. Thomas handed her the microphone and winked encouragingly at her. Then she turned to face her audience. Snow's eyes were already glistening, her husband's smile shining brightly. Mr. and Mrs. Bailey exchanged glances with one another before looking up at Audrey with pitied expressions. Audrey found her brother easily. He nodded up with a grin. She still couldn't quite believe that she was with him again, something she had deemed impossible.

Her eyes grazed over the remaining plethora of faces but became ensnared when she saw the stranger from before. His gaze was penetrating, seeing through her. She felt exposed, vulnerable, and she straightened her shoulders in defiance. The corner of his mouth lifted in a crooked grin, sensing her discomfort.

Audrey cleared her throat as her second prepared speech of the day evaporated into thin air, and began, doing her best to avoid those onyx eyes.

"Hello," her voice was too high with the stress. She cleared her throat again. "I know most of you don't know me. I'm Audrey. I somehow have the privilege of being best friend to the bride. I don't deserve her, but then again no matter what you do you can never deserve someone like Snow – sorry Ganesh." Soft chuckles wafted across the crowd, helping her nerves settle slightly. Amal smiled and nodded in agreement. "I met Snow when I was twelve and immediately commented on how much she looked like Snow White. I don't think I've ever referred to her as anything else. I'm not even sure I know what her actual name if I can be honest." More hushed laughter. "What started as a reference to her complexion, soon turned into something more. She didn't just look like Snow White. She *was* Snow White. Pure of heart. Kind. Loving. Loyal to a fault. Oblivious to the evils of the world. But when she Skyped me from the other side of the world and showed me she'd found an Aladdin, I thought something was off." The laughter was a bit louder now. "And at first I didn't like him. I'm the best friend. It's my job. But Ganesh, you made me like you. Which of course made me hate you all the more, but you take care of her. You make her smile which is something I have trouble doing more often than not. I'm actually a lot of the reason she needs a smile put on her face in the first place." A hushed silence fell as she fought for the right words to say.

"Snow sees the world through a kaleidoscope. It's a distorted and deceiving view, of course, but one I was always jealous of. She sees color and light and love where no one else can see it. Which is how I am able to justify our friendship.

"Truth is, my life has been one big mess from the moment I was conceived. And I can honestly say that I wouldn't be here to give this awkwardly delivered speech if it wasn't for Snow," her voice cracked as she held back her tears. "So you take care of her Aladdin. And never let her go because you have found yourself a rare jewel."

The moment she relaxed her arm with the microphone at her side, Snow leapt from her chair and hurried toward her, pulling her into a characteristic bear hug. The audience clapped and cheered. Audrey hugged her back with her free arm, letting the other dangle at her side. Over Snow's shoulder, her brother clapped with wet eyes and the stranger gazed intently at her with an arm hanging over the back of his chair.

Chapter Fifteen

Madison, Alabama
December 2005

Mark sat in his spacious office and stared blankly at the linoleum floor, drumming his pen anxiously on the dark wood of his desk. His eyes flickered again to the clock on the wall. He muttered a curse and paused the drumming for a split second to check his watch, hopelessly willing the hands to speed up. It had only been six minutes since he last checked. There was still an hour to go.

He hated the way everything had happened the night before. He was always so careful to hide his wife from Audrey when she was in that state. From what he gathered, Audrey had spent fifteen years listening to Sheryl's drunken mutterings about how insignificant she was, how she was a mistake. He knew despite how hard he tried to make things okay between them, part of Sheryl would always blame Audrey for not only his own abandonment of her all those years ago, but for every one of her own failures and missed opportunities as well. And Audrey would never be able to forgive Sheryl for the things she'd been throwing at her for her entire life, especially after she blatantly destroyed the image she held of her father.

To compensate for the lack of parental love in her life, Mark watched as Audrey busied herself, constantly trying to prove herself worthy of the affection she was denied. Or was it to keep her own haunting thoughts at bay? He could only guess. What he did know was that her fading beacon of hope was the idea of her father. If she could only meet him, only notify him that she existed, he would fill the gaps in her heart. But Sheryl had obliterated that hope right in front of her. Mark had watched as Audrey's eyes darkened, had seen their luster dim.

He only hoped he could make her understand where he stood. He'd always seen her as a younger sister and loved her as much as he loved his own baby sister until he watched her recoil at her own mother's words, watched her crumble, the pieces catching fire, blazing and lashing at everyone around her. A protective instinct rose up in him, but Audrey wouldn't listen to anything he had to say.

"That was all she had," he'd seethed at his wife, biting back the lump tearing at his throat as Audrey retreated to her room. "Jesse was the only thing she had to hope for, and you just demolished it!"

"There's no use in false hope," Sheryl had mumbled.

His odd connection with Audrey was nothing compared to the emptiness he could almost visibly see in her. It had always been his desire to fill that emptiness, but she refused to accept him. He tried to buy her a dog, and when that didn't work, a car. She'd softened, and then he'd worked his way in, developed a bond he thought to be secure. He offered her what little he knew about the kid he only saw in the hallways of his high school, the scalawag he avoided at all cost. He wished it had been enough. He racked his brain for anything to help her now, but his mind was too busy counting the seconds.

"I can't do this," he said aloud, standing hurriedly to leave. Once out of his office, he navigated through the crowd of people and cubicles until he reached the door, ignoring the receptionist calling his name. He half ran to the parking garage, threw himself in his truck, and raced towards home.

The streets were packed with last-minute Christmas shoppers. He swore and slammed a fist on the horn, releasing some of the tension in his arms and chest with the obnoxious blast. He reached the house in triple the usual time and threw his keys on the counter.

"God, Audrey!" Sheryl yelped from the couch. She pulled the damp towel from her eyes and turned to him, her face contorted malevolently. When she saw him, her expression changed dramatically, a huge grin stretched her mouth and creased her droopy eyes.

"Oh, hey, honey. You're home early."

"Where is she?" he was about to burst with the need to apologize, to make things right, to make sure she was okay.

"Who? Audrey?" Sheryl scowled.

"Yes, Sheryl!" his voice boomed louder than he intended. "Where is she?"

"Alright calm down! She took Ethan and Dan to some church for play practice. Left about an hour ago." Sheryl settled back down on the couch and recovered her eyes with the towel. He nodded, unsure of what to do.

The kitchen phone rang shrilly. Sheryl clapped her hands over her ears and moaned. Shaking his head, Mark let it ring a few more times to antagonize her before he picked up the phone.

"Hello?"

"Is this a Mr. Mark Fields?" came an irritatingly calm voice.

"Yeah," he answered abruptly.

"I'm sorry, sir. There's been an accident..."

Mark barely registered anything she said after that. He clutched at his chest and hung up the phone when she had finished talking. His breath caught in his lungs as though someone had cracked every rib in his chest with a baseball bat. He didn't know his knees had buckled until they hit the tile floor.

"Mark?" Sheryl's worried voice sounded distant. "Mark, are you okay?"

Swallowing down his shock and grief with the bile that had risen in his throat, he shakily stood up. He had to be strong for her. She would need him more than ever.

"Sheryl, something's happened."

Philadelphia, Pennsylvania

Elizabeth leaned her head against the plane window, staring out as the city below grew larger with their descent. The Killers' latest hit, "Mr. Brightside," blared through her ear buds, but she couldn't hear it. A flight attendant tapped her shoulder and took her empty water cup.

Philadelphia. She'd always wanted to see it. It was technically driving distance from NYU's campus, but she'd never gotten around to going. Now that she was here, though, she wanted to be nowhere else but Alabama. The homesickness grew with every semester. She missed jogging through the neighborhood, waving at kids playing in the sprinklers. She missed her mom's fried chicken and green bean casserole and her dad's sweaty morning hugs that smelled like grass and lawnmower gasoline. She missed cheering on her favorite boys as they ran laps around a baseball diamond. She missed Audrey.

She massaged her temples as the rest of the passengers fumbled with their carry-on baggage. It had been a rough flight and her head was pounding. She turned on her phone to check for the usual bombardment of messages from Audrey while everyone scrambled off the plane. Her brow furrowed. Instead of mountains of bored texts, she only had a voicemail from her mom. She guessed it was a declaration of how much she missed her only child already.

"Excuse me, ma'am," the flight attendant interrupted her with a coo. "Everyone's gone."

"I'm sorry," Elizabeth muttered, flipping her phone shut. She readjusted her purse on her shoulder and sprinted off of the plane. Weaving through tourists and reuniting families, she made her way to baggage claim. She pulled her phone back out and went through the tedious process of calling voicemail and pressing the various numbers to get to her mom's message. Just outside of baggage claim, she was greeted warmly by her dark haired boyfriend. She smiled brightly at him, his soft eyes easing her nostalgic reflection.

"Hey baby," he said, bending down to kiss her. Elizabeth stopped abruptly, pushing him away a bit too forcefully when the voice on the other end of the phone gave a shaking gasp.

"Lizzie – " her mom paused to control her voice. "There's been an accident. Audrey's been hurt. Her brothers... Oh my god... you need to be here. It's bad. Call me when you land. I love you, Lizzie." She gave a shuddering sob before hanging up the phone.

The world seemed to spin off its axis. Elizabeth felt as though her feet had been lifted in the air, that she was floating. Her green eyes widened and her eyebrows hid behind her bangs as she stared up at Colin.

"What's wrong?" he beseeched. Elizabeth pushed passed him, hopelessly dialing Audrey's number. No answer. She collapsed against a nearby wall, and fought the building frenzy of her nerves.

She dialed her mother. She answered on the second ring.

"Lizzie?"

"Mom! What happened?" Elizabeth felt like she was screaming, but her voice was strangled.

"Audrey's car slipped on a patch of ice. They spun off the road and flipped a few times, I think. They hit a tree. It's bad, Liz," she explained. Her voice sounded raw.

"Is she okay?"

"She's in critical condition. They won't tell us anything right now."

"What about the boys?"

"It's the same with Ethan. He seems worse off than Audrey, though. His leg was so bloody," her mom slowly explained, shock still evident in her voice. Elizabeth fought her building, suffocating fear, wanting all of the information before she allowed herself to break. Colin stood next to her, rubbing her arm and searching her face for an explanation. She couldn't look at him.

"And Daniel?" she held her breath when her mom hesitated.

"He's gone."

Elizabeth froze, her gaze fixed ahead, staring unseeingly at a holiday reunion taking place in front of her. She grasped at her skirt, squeezing the fabric in her fist, not attempting to swallow down the lump in her throat.

"I'm so sorry, Lizzie," her mom croaked. Elizabeth flipped her phone shut and blinked, two massive tears leaking from her eyes as she pictured that darling boy with his shaggy hair and sparkling blue eyes.

"Liz!" Colin sounded so far away.

Daniel was dead. Audrey and Ethan could follow closely behind.

She turned to face Colin who looked miserable and anxious. All she wanted to do was to bury her face in his shoulder and cry, but she couldn't. Every second counted.

"I have to go," she said, wiping away her tears and pushing off the wall.

"But you only just got here," he protested. "Liz, what's happened?" He kept repeating her name in the hopes of calming her down, but it only made her more irritable.

"Audrey's in the hospital," she rushed through an

explanation as she sped off to the counter, "and her brother's dead. I need to be there." He stood back, looking stunned.

"I need the next flight to Huntsville, Alabama," she demanded at the desk. She hastily kissed Colin on the cheek and ran to her terminal and the gate that would take her back home.

She sat in a daze, barely taking in anything that was going on around her, whispering frantically, praying they would be okay. In seven hours she would be by her best friend's side. Audrey would wake up and smile at her. Everything would be okay.

But it wouldn't be. Audrey would wake to find her baby brother dead. Part of her would never truly wake up. Elizabeth pulled her legs in the chair, buried her eyes in her knees and cried.

Chapter Sixteen

Seattle, Washington

Audrey sat sideways on her gaudy sofa, cross-legged with coffee in hand, and stared down at Hermione, who lay stretched out in front of her with her head in Audrey's lap, taking up most of the room. She petted her absentmindedly.

"You should have seen him yesterday, Hermione," she said. "He's grown so much. He's a man now if you can believe it. Off to make his own way in the world. And with a girlfriend!" she blanched. "I don't like her much. She kept hanging all over him and whining. You wouldn't have liked her either. If Snow would have let you out of the dressing room, you'd know what I'm talking about." Hermione shifted her head slightly to get a view of her owner, but otherwise enjoyed her ritualistic morning massage.

The smile that was stretched across Audrey's face when she brought her coffee to her lips vanished by the time she brought it down again, leaving no evidence that it had ever existed in the first place. She gazed with unseeing eyes through the window as the sun brightened the bricks of the neighboring building.

The reunion with her brother had been nothing like what she had anticipated. The joy of having Ethan in front of her again, in her arms again, spread with a surprising warmth through her entire being but was soon shrouded by regret and agony and loss. Nearly every obstacle he had faced in the past six years could have been avoided if she had only kept her head about her that day. The missing piece in their hearts, in their lives could be traced back to one careless error, a thoughtless mistake that replayed itself every night when she closed her eyes. Their faces were painted on the back of her eyelids, and there was nothing she could do to bring them back, those boys with big hearts, big dreams, and bright futures.

Audrey tipped back the remaining drops of coffee, stubbed out her cigarette in the ashtray on the floor, and heaved herself from the sofa. She stretched until what was left of the stiffness in her back that came on in her sleep dissipated before padding to the bathroom to get ready. An hour later, she was leaning against the side of a restaurant with Hermione sitting at her heels and a cigarette propped between her fingers, her free hand resting in the pocket of her old leather jacket. She put the cigarette in her mouth and watched as she puffed out a slow, steady stream of smoke.

"Those things will kill you, you know," came a voice from a short distance away.

"Hadn't heard," Audrey quipped, smiling broadly, and dropped the cigarette butt, kneading it out with the toe of her oxford.

"Oh my god, is that Hermy?" his pitch got higher and higher as he got down on a knee to greet the dog. Hermione hesitated, sniffing him out, before wagging her tail exuberantly and accepting his scratches with a lolling tongue. Audrey laughed as he pet her and spoke in an excited baby voice.

"Is that how you get the ladies?" Audrey gibed.

"Works every time," he said, winking as he stood. Hermione pawed impatiently at his knee. "See? She's begging for more."

Audrey laughed. "Are you ready for the best sandwiches in Seattle?"

"Sandwiches," he repeated, looking disgusted.

"Yes, sandwiches. What's wrong with that?"

"Everything!" he waved his arms over his head. "You may have forgotten what it's like in the South, but I'm a Bama boy! I need meat!"

"They have cold cuts," Audrey insisted. He gagged dramatically. "Okay, there's a pub in the Marriott that's got steak and seafood if that's better suited for you." Rolling her eyes, she took him two blocks down to Hook & Plow where he feasted on a plate of lamb chop, chicken sausage, bacon, and steak with potatoes, mushrooms, and blistered tomato.

"I don't even," he started, befuddled by Audrey's plate. "What is that even supposed to be?"

"It's a kale salad."

"Seriously?" he asked with bulging eyes. "Yeah, I'm going to go throw up now."

They left the hotel and crossed the street to the waterfront. Audrey tried not to stare when his gait became uneven, favoring his left leg. She pushed back the acid that rose in her throat, promising herself to save her regrets for later, when he was on a plane Bama bound.

They strolled in silence down Alaskan Way towards a Ferris wheel that spun lazily in the distance until they reached a large pier. He leaned heavily against the railing and crossed his arms tightly against his chest, leaning over to gaze at the dark water that lapped against the poles.

"It's almost June right? I'm not going crazy?" he asked over his shoulder.

"Yeah, summers here are really short."

"How can you stand it?" he rubbed his arms to heat them with the created friction.

"London was colder."

"Seriously?"

"No," she laughed. "But I've always liked cold the best."

"So what are your plans?" he asked after a moment's pause. "Back to London now that Lizzie's been married off?"

"I've been here for so long now, it's kind of grown on me. I'll probably hang around for a bit longer."

"No chance I can talk you into Atlanta?" he beseeched.

She shook her head. "Too hot."

He smiled and turned to look out at the water. The wind tugged at their clothes and swiped at her hair. She struggled to keep the strands out of her mouth. The water slapped against the pier beneath them, reaching with each wake for the poles in a mad scramble to hold onto the wooden surface as the water rode by. The horn of a ferryboat could be heard bellowing in the distance, punctuating the monotonous hum of the traffic behind them and the splashing below them with its guttural groaning.

"I saw a whale out here once," said Audrey. "They don't come over here often, but we got lucky that day, I guess."

"I bet that was beautiful," he said, turning to look at her. She continued to stare out at the water.

"I saw a killer whale last year," she continued. "Ganesh drove us out to the state park last summer to whale watch. There was a pod of them swimming well away from the shore, but we saw them. That's something you don't forget." He didn't answer. They sat in silence, staring out at the gray water. The minutes went uncounted, but the clock proceeded to tick.

"What would he have been like, do you think?" Audrey's question was barely audible when she finally broke the silence. A moment's hesitation passed before she saw his head drop, heard his deep sigh before he turned around to face her, leaning his back against the railing, his arms still crossed tightly against his chest. She knew he was looking at her, but she stared unblinkingly ahead.

"He would be hilarious," he began. His was tone lighthearted as he recalled his little brother. "And a troublemaker. He would have graduated high school, but just barely, using mostly his charm to pass his classes." He chuckled breathily. "But without a doubt, he would have been extraordinary."

Audrey's chin quivered, and she shifted her watery eyes to meet his. What she didn't expect to find was the pity that swarmed there. She quickly looked away but could no longer keep hold of her fleeting resolve. She let out a choked sob and brought her hands to her face. He sighed again and reached across the distance that separated them, grabbing her wrist and pulling her into a wrapping embrace. After a minute or two of silent crying onto his windbreaker and simply enjoying his presence, his phone buzzed, signaling his expected departure to the airport. They pulled away for him to silence his phone. Audrey wiped at her eyes, but tears still trekked warm paths silently down her chapped cheeks. When he looked back at her, his face was stern and determined. His blue eyes flitted back and forth between her brown ones.

"I need you to promise me something," he said in a voice that matched his unwavering expression.

"Sure," the word sounded strangled in her throat. "Anything."

"Try to find happiness," he said causing a fresh wave of hot tears to rush to her eyes. "Please, Audrey. For me. Do whatever it takes. If you fail, you fail. But I want you to give it your all."

"Go big or go home right?" Audrey attempted to joke, but the smile never touched her lips.

"Something like that," he said and pulled her into another hug. "Promise me you'll keep in touch this time?" She nodded and walked him to the road where she hailed a cab and watched it drive away with her little brother inside.

Chapter Seventeen

Huntsville, Alabama
December 2005

The hospital was more crowded than usual. The halls and waiting rooms were subtly decorated with wreaths and mini Christmas trees. Families stopped by to spend Christmas morning with their ill family members before their traditional festivities. The nurses and doctors tried to filter in a sense of Christmas spirit, but whatever jolly atmosphere they managed to create evaporated around the edges of the fourth floor waiting room where one family awaited the news on whether or not two of their young members would be still be drawing breath by the end of the holiday.

Mark stood at the edge of the waiting room with a full cup of cold coffee. Sheryl sat in the chair beside him, staring at the wall. Dark tear tracks streaked down her face. A large, calloused hand held hers tightly. Richard's dark blonde hair was oily and stuck out in places where his hands constantly raked through it. His eyes were closed in a permanent grimace. A few empty chairs separated him from Mark's parents and the Baileys. Mrs. Bailey was flipping through a magazine, trying to keep herself occupied.

Elizabeth was slumped in her chair next to her mother. Dark circles shaded beneath her usually vibrant eyes. Her dirty brown hair had hung in shambles before her mother braided it for something to do. She still wore the black dress from the day before. Mark let his gaze rest on her for a moment longer. He could barely recognize her. He'd tried fruitlessly to get her to eat something, but in the three days since her plane brought her back, she'd only nibbled at a banana before tossing it into the garbage when she thought no one was looking.

Flashes of the day before danced in Mark's head despite his attempts to block them out for the time being. There was something unnatural in seeing a small casket lowered into the ground, knowing it contained a young boy who had barely lived.

Daniel's funeral was a closed casket one with only Sheryl and Richard having seen his body. At their request, Mark hadn't been allowed to see him. He told himself that seeing Daniel lying lifeless on a table was not something he had needed. He wanted to remember his stepson for who he was: an energetic little boy with a contagious grin and an unwavering joy. But Mark couldn't help but feel that not seeing Daniel's body had left him without closure. He'd sat at the funeral and seen a box buried six feet in the ground. He knew the box contained the little boy he'd helped to raise for over five years, but his heart wouldn't accept the reality. Daniel wasn't really gone. He couldn't be. The world wasn't that cruel.

Mark was pulled from his reverie at Dr. Jones' approach.

"I have some good news," she announced, trying to shed light on the dismal atmosphere. Elizabeth looked up for the first time in hours.

"Audrey's shone signs of recovery. The swelling in her brain has gone down significantly through the night. She's moving out of intensive care as we speak." Dr. Jones gave a warm smile. There was a collective sigh of relief, and Mark allowed himself a ghostly smile.

"Is she awake?" Elizabeth asked weakly.

"No," answered Dr. Jones, "but we can expect her to do so any time now. She can have visitors now, but no more than two at a time."

Elizabeth jumped up at the invitation and crossed the waiting room at a surprising speed.

"Do you want to see her?" Mark asked Sheryl. She shook her head vehemently, and he noticed for the first time that she was seething with anger. Without asking for an explanation, Mark followed Dr. Jones and Elizabeth to Audrey's new room. Elizabeth tensed when they came to her window. He looked down at her reassuringly, took her hand in his – for her support or his own he wasn't sure – and led her into the room.

Audrey lay in the bed with the blanket pulled to her waist. Her pasty skin looked even more washed out against the pale blue hospital gown. Wires from her arms, hands, and fingers connected her to the IV and the numerous monitors displaying indecipherable data that proved to Mark and Elizabeth that she was alive. The only color in the pale room was Audrey's long red hair, bushy from gentle brushing. Eleven stitches closed a cut above her temple, reaching deep into her hair, and dark green and purple bruises were scattered across the sickening pallor of her skin.

Elizabeth let go of Mark's hand as a tear fell from her eye. She pulled a chair up to the foot of Audrey's bed and slumped down. Her gaze never left Audrey's face. Mark exchanged a few words with Dr. Jones before taking a seat at Audrey's side. The monitor beeped its steady rhythm, punctuating the deathly silence with tangible signs of a life struggling to keep hold of the frail body it belonged to.

The hours stretched on while Mark traded out with his parents one at a time. Elizabeth wouldn't leave Audrey's side and no one asked her to. After lunch everyone had gone home to salvage what was left of Christmas, leaving Sheryl and Richard in the waiting room and Mark once again with Audrey. Elizabeth nodded off soon after his arrival.

Some time later, a slight movement caught Mark's eye. He looked up from the brochure on spinal injuries in his lap right into a pair of weak brown eyes.

"Audrey," he whispered. He scooted forward to the edge of his chair and wrapped her hand in his. She looked around drearily, taking in her surroundings as she began to welcome full consciousness.

"What," she rasped, pausing to clear her throat, "what happened?"

"What do you remember?" he asked, stalling, dread creeping like ice into his heart. After a moment's contemplation, Audrey's jaw clenched.

"I remember picking Sheryl up at the restaurant. I remember the fight. And Ethan and Daniel's faces..." she trailed off, her brow creased with puzzlement. "But I don't remember what happened after that."

Mark swallowed the lump in his throat as he prepared for what came next. He knew from the beginning that it would be his job to inform her of what had happened. He'd just never thought far enough ahead to prepare himself for when the moment came.

"You were in an accident," he proceeded cautiously. "You and Ethan and Daniel." He tried not to visibly wince at his own voice forming the syllables of Danny's name. Audrey's eyes widened.

"Are they okay?" she jerked upright, was overcome with dizziness, and collapsed back onto the bed. Mark wanted to tell her to be easy, but he couldn't form the words.

"Mark," she spat through gritted teeth, clutching a hand to her forehead and wincing at the pain. "Where are they? And don't sugarcoat it!"

"Ethan is in ICU. He's in a coma. His leg is pretty badly broken, and his spine is injured, but they won't know how bad it is until he wakes up," Mark's voice wavered, betraying his suppressed emotion. Audrey's grimace deepened. She bit hard onto her lips, waiting for the rest.

When it didn't come, she whispered, "Danny?"

"He didn't make it," Mark rasped.

Audrey's reaction to the news was nothing like what he had expected. Her pained expression vanished. She breathed deeply and opened her eyes. Tears didn't fall. Chin didn't tremble. Eyelids didn't flutter. She just stared ahead at the eggshell wall with her arms limp at her side.

"Audrey?" Mark was suddenly worried. "Audrey, say something please." She didn't acknowledge that he had spoken anything to her. "Audrey," he said in a slightly louder voice, waking Elizabeth. Upon seeing her best friend awake and alert, she let out a cry and hastened to her bedside. Mark stared dumbfounded at Audrey as Elizabeth took her hand from his. Even at this touch, Audrey didn't move. Elizabeth managed little choked phrases of thankful prayers and apologies.

Audrey didn't look at her, didn't return the grip on her hand. Her eyes were glazed over. The life seemed to have evacuated her. The only way Mark knew that she was alive at all was by the pattern of beeps on the monitor that had never changed its pace.

"Audrey's awake again if you want to go see her," Mark coaxed his wife the following afternoon.

"No," was all she said. It was all she had said for two days now.

"She's your daughter, Sheryl!" he tried to control his volume. "She almost died! She probably feels guiltier than she should about her brothers! She could really use her mother right now!"

"No."

Mark huffed and threw his hands in the air, wondering not for the first time what he'd seen in her when he married her. This was not the Sheryl I fell in love with, he thought, but he knew in his heart that she was. As much as he wished it did, her actions didn't surprise him. What did surprise him, however, was Richard.

"I want to see her," he said. Mark turned back around to face him incredulously.

"You what?"

"I would like to see her," Richard's voice was calm as he stood, his eyes boring into Mark's face. Mark tried and failed to read him, to guess his intentions. "If that's okay with you, of course."

"Okay, but I'm coming with you," Mark said firmly.

"No, I have somethin' I need to say to her. I'll do it on my own," Richard demanded, stepping closer to Mark.

"Whatever you have to say you can say in front of me. I'm not leaving you alone with her." Two pairs of blue eyes glowered into each other, faces set and rigid.

"Alright, fine," Richard yielded and pushed past him, stalking off to Audrey's room with Mark following close behind him.

"Elizabeth, can we have the room for a minute?" Mark asked when they opened the door.

"No," she answered without looking up.

"Snow," Mark's voice was soft, doing his best to keep it comforting and under control. Elizabeth's face shot up at the sound of her nickname, and when she took in the two men in front of her, she understood.

"Make it fast," she said and reluctantly left Audrey's side. "I don't know if she'll hear what you have to say. She hasn't moved at all." Mark ignored the worried despair in her voice as she closed the door behind her. Richard cleared his throat and sat down in Mark's chair while Mark stood as sentinel by the door.

"Hey, Audrey Jo," he said awkwardly. She remained

expressionless, unblinking, gazing with unfocused eyes at the wall ahead. Richard continued, "Do you remember that day when you were seven and Ethan was barely a month old, I came and got you from school early? You didn't say anythin' to me in the car, wouldn't even look at me until I bought you an ice cream. We sat on the tailgate with our cones, and you just looked at me with those giant brown eyes that you hadn't grown into yet. You were so pissed, I could tell. You just looked at me and said so calmly, 'She's havin' another baby, isn't she?' You knew the only other time we'd got you early from school was to tell you Sheryl was pregnant with Ethan. I said she was, and you got so mad you threw your cone on the ground and started yellin' at me." Mark stared at Richard dubiously as he chuckled to himself.

"It was so humid that day, and your hair was so huge, it stood half a foot above your head! You kept slappin' it out of your face while you yelled at me. You had little red handprints all over your cheeks. I don't remember what you said exactly. I just remember tryin' hard not to laugh. You were so mad that we were havin' another baby. Said you didn't want it. You asked if we could get rid of it like I did that stray cat you'd claimed before Ethan was born. We went back home, and you didn't say a word for days. I was worried you'd end up one of those kids who suffocated your baby siblings out of jealousy.

"But you weren't, were you? It wasn't jealousy at all, was it? You didn't want them to have to grow up the way you were growin' up. With us as parents. I see that now. At Dan's funeral, all I could think about was how much I had failed my boy." Richard trailed off, staring down at his hands. Mark saw a tear fall from his face. He felt awkward witnessing what was going on in front of him.

"If it wasn't for you..." Richard trailed off, looking into Audrey's lifeless face for the first time. "I don't blame you, Audrey. I don't blame you for what happened to my boy. He's dead, but he only lived because of you." Richard dropped his head in his hands and sobbed while Audrey didn't so much as blink. If she had heard anything Richard had said, she didn't acknowledge it.

Mark stood by the door and kept quiet while Richard broke apart in front of him. He had no sympathy for him, and he wondered if he should feel guilty for his callousness.

Chapter Eighteen

Seattle, Washington

"Did you get the ice?" Snow's voice carried from her bedroom.

"Yes, love," Amal sighed. "I've now answered that question four times." He shot a look at Audrey who humored him with a breathy giggle. She was stretched out on their much too soft sofa in a quite unbecoming position with her head on a pillow and one foot hanging off of the armrest while the other leg dangled from the side of the sofa. She flipped a completed Rubix Cube in her hands while Hermione curled awkwardly on the sofa by her leg.

"If anyone asks, I'm the one that finished this," she said, eyeing Amal as she tossed the Rubix Cube in the air, catching it expertly as it fell back toward her face.

"No one will believe you," he smirked.

Something was wrong. She could practically smell it. To the untrained eye there wasn't much to see other than a couple's frenzy to prepare for one of their many extravagant dinner parties. Snow's stress level was through the roof, which naturally mellowed out her best friend even more to further solidify their strange way of balancing each other out. Amal was equally stressed but attempted to keep it under wraps so as not to add to the chaos exuding from his wife. Bottles of wine and champagne were counted, extra tables and chairs pulled out, an old jazz vinyl spun on the turntable. Audrey served in her usual manner: as more of a decoration piece than a participant in the preparations. Why they still invited her over earlier than anyone else was beyond her.

"Hey, Audrey, come here for a minute," Snow called, tension evident in her overly jubilant voice. Normally Audrey would have protested in laziness, but she hoped she was about to be given some sort of an explanation. The sight that met her eyes, however, was not what she had prepared for. The bulbs above Snow's vanity were shining on makeup strewn across the table. Snow grinned sheepishly at her and gestured to the dress on the bed.

Suddenly aware of what was happening, Audrey tried to run away, to escape Snow's obvious plans of torture. To where she would run, she had no idea, but she didn't get the chance to contemplate further. Snow's warm fingers wrapped around her arm with surprising strength and pulled her back.

"Please just do this for me," Snow begged. There was that look again. The one that had unnerved Audrey the moment Snow had opened the door to grant her entrance into the apartment. A sense of despondency tucked away behind the orange spark in her vivid green eyes.

A second dose of it chilled Audrey long enough for Snow to guide her to the vanity and force her to a sitting position. Audrey's shoulder length hair was then combed and pulled and heated into larger, loose waves. Every tug on her scalp took her further away from her worries about Snow and led her to more shouted curses that earned a sharp bat on the head with the brush.

"Oh shut up," Snow finally groaned. "You look gorgeous!" Audrey shut her mouth long enough to take in her reflection. Her hair looked longer, unbound by its naturally curling fury, clipped tightly behind her left ear, exposing a diamond-studded earring in gold casing. Her lips were a delicate shade of rose, accenting her red hair. She couldn't deny that Snow's work was impressive, but when she caught sight of the dress in the mirror, her defiance clambered to the surface again.

Standing up, she protested, "But what's wrong with what I'm wearing?" She gestured to her gray button down and black pants.

"It's much too business like," she gave her a quick look over, "and gross."

"I wear this kind of stuff to all of your dinner parties," Audrey gritted her teeth.

"Yeah," Snow cringed, "I know."

Huffing and mumbling to herself, Audrey yanked the dress from the bed and stalked off to the bathroom to change.

"Now explain to me why you get to wear black, and I look

like the bloody Wizard of Oz!" Audrey called through the door.

"You sound bloody ridiculous!" Amal yelled from the kitchen. He hadn't missed a single opportunity to point out just how American she was in the four years she'd known him.

"I rarely wear black," Snow answered, ignoring her husband, "so when I do, it's classy and sophisticated."

"Whereas I look like a gothic slut," she retorted.

"You don't have to be a slut to look like one, Audrey, virgin or no."

"Wait, you're a virgin?" Amal called, suddenly closer in proximity as his interest peaked.

"Oh, piss off!" Audrey yelled through the door, and he sniggered in response.

Audrey rolled her eyes and looked at her reflection in the mirror. It was a simple dark emerald cocktail dress that cut just above her knees in a relaxed fashion. The single strap split at the shoulder beneath a gold clasp that held the two pieces of fabric together. A sash crossed around her middle, tightly hugging the flowing fabric to her thin waist. The black heels that Snow lent her made her feel as though she would tower over everyone.

When she reemerged from the bathroom, Snow's hands clapped to her mouth. "You look so beautiful," her voice was quiet and whiny through her fingers. Audrey blushed her thanks, the color clearly visible on her pale cheeks.

"First one's arrived," Amal poked his head in to announce, looking very dapper in his suit and freshly trimmed beard. "I've got a mission, now," he winked, giving Audrey a quick one over before ducking back out of the room. "How do you like your blokes?" he called over his shoulder. "Nice and clean cut or rugged and wild?"

Audrey sighed, "Jesus."

"Don't worry, he's just hyper. I gave him coffee."

"That was a mistake."

"You're telling me."

In a matter of half an hour, the spacious Ganesh apartment was full of a low buzz of murmuring conversation and in regular intervals a laugh that Audrey could pick out as Snow's. Louis Armstrong and Ella Fitzgerald reverberated off the walls, aiding to calm Audrey's nerves. The repeat guests knew well by now that it was pointless to approach her, but the newbies always tried to make conversation. She was never reproachful or rude and always made an attempt at conversation, but her responses came up dry, and she usually made a remark out of place that sent the conversation spiraling into an awkward silence. They'd stand around and study the walls while Audrey counted down the seconds until the other person would saunter off, pretending to see someone they knew.

When she caught a pair of green eyes, Snow grinned broadly and motioned for her to come over. One look at the people that swarmed around the hostess was all Audrey needed to see. She took a step in the opposite direction and walked to the corner window by the Ganesh's closed bedroom door, absentmindedly wondering where Snow had hidden her cigarettes.

"Is it too early to make a quiet exit?" she muttered to Hermione through the door.

"No, but I would be very disappointed if you left before I could get your name." Audrey swung around to meet a pair of liquid black eyes, the kind that seared itself onto your brain, never allowing you to forget them. "Sorry," he said with a sheepish laugh, "didn't mean to scare you." When she continued to stare, unsure of what to say, he went on. "So've you got a name, or what?"

"Audrey," she managed after clearing her throat.

"El's Audrey?" his eyebrows rose in feigned surprise.

"The one and only," she tried to smile, but it felt wrong on her face.

"Nice to finally meet you, Miss Wyatt. I'm Liam. I'm a friend of Amal's," he held his hand out for her and smirked. She put her own hand out tentatively but shook it with her firm business grasp, silently cursing herself for being so abrupt.

"I saw you at the wedding, didn't I?" she asked, hoping to divert the attention elsewhere.

"I'm surprised you remember me," he teased. "You kept running off."

"You were avidly creeping me out," she said, remembering his penetrating gaze. His white teeth gleamed at her, displaying through the thin part of his lips. The way his skin creased in fine lines around his eyes and mouth led Audrey to believe he was at least four or five years her senior. He had a strong face with a broad forehead and dark stubble that decorated his jaw. His long black hair, slightly oily at the roots was casually swept back and speckled slightly with hints of gray along the sides of his face. The buttons of his shirt were unfastened one too low beneath an open grey vest, and he eyed her sideways through a bushy set of brows.

In another life she would have found him stunning.

"A friend of Amal's," she repeated. "So what does that make you, then? Another surgeon type? Or something cheaper?" He laughed at that, and she fought the way the breathy rasp of it made the corners of her mouth twitch.

"Quite cheaper, I'm afraid."

"Nurse, then," Audrey teased.

"I'm a tattoo artist," he answered, quickly scanning her face to judge her reaction.

"A tattoo artist with no visible tattoos," she mused, eyeing the rolled sleeves of his white shirt. "Shocking."

"And permanently mar this gorgeous skin?" He moved a leather-cuffed hand to his torso in simulated astonishment. Audrey raised her eyebrows and chuckled in amusement. "No, but really, I've seen enough bad tattoos to know that I have nothing of such value that I want to parade around all the time."

"Surprisingly deep."

"Surprisingly?" Liam challenged.

She smiled, but changed the subject. "So how do you know Ganesh, then? Does he have some secret tattoo I should know about?"

"Not to my knowledge," he laughed again. "My brother, Thomas, was his college roommate. I met him when I was visiting campus for a concert. We've all kept in touch since then."

"This wouldn't be the same Thomas Farren that escorted me at the wedding, would it?" she asked.

"The very same," he said. Audrey smiled softly. They had the same nose now that she looked.

"Those two don't know how to lose touch with anyone," Audrey turned around to lean against the sliding door, watching Snow smile up at her husband as he told some exciting story that was lost in the distance that separated them.

"Yeah, they're gross like that," he quipped. Audrey snorted and nodded in agreement. Liam turned to her, but before he could say anything, Amal's voice rose above the noise, quieting the chatter.

"If everyone will take a seat, we'll start the toast and eat!" his emphasis on the last word brought cheers from his guests.

"Sit with me," the words were escaping Audrey's mouth before she could think the request through. The corner of his lip drug slowly upward in an almost mischievous crooked grin. She didn't need any more of an answer. She pushed herself off the door and navigated through the guests to the head of the first table. When Snow caught sight of Audrey, she grabbed her hand before she could disappear again.

"There you are! I was looking everywhere for you! There's someone I want you to meet! And not for Al's reasons. No. I actually think you'll like this one." Her eyes scanned a dozen faces before she noticed Liam behind Audrey. "Oh, never mind then," she grinned.

"Sorry, El, you were taking too long," he said over Audrey's shoulder. Audrey turned back to look at him and back to Snow, the realization of a what had taken place behind her back setting in. She took her seat, flashing a look at Liam whose eyes crinkled under his thick eyebrows. Thomas grinned sheepishly at her from his lounging posture across the table and winked at his brother. She was preparing to confront them all on their plot when Amal called for a toast, suddenly the posh and proper man everyone believed him to be. She glared up at him, willing him to crack up, to say something inappropriate or simply to let out something cockney.

"Elizabeth and I wanted to gather all of our closest friends and family here this evening to celebrate our first wedding anniversary and to make a special announcement." He wrapped his arm tightly around Snow's waist, pulling her closer to him, a blush rising to her cheeks. All of the signs Audrey had read that day came flashing back before her eyes, the revelation of what was taking place occurring to her moments before Amal made the official announcement.

"Unfortunately this will be our last dinner party for quite a while because," he looked down at his wife with his wine glass still raised in the air, "well because – "

"I'm pregnant!" Snow exclaimed. Shouts and cheers erupted from their guests. Liam stood and leaned across the table to shake Amal's hand in congratulation while Thomas laughed rambunctiously and wrapped his best friend in a hug, slapping him on the back.

Audrey stared blankly at her wine glass with her hands folded in her lap. Once again, Snow was taking the next step in her life, leaving Audrey behind as a pathetic stray that followed them around, pretended to enjoy the extravagance of her borrowed lifestyle. When she came to her senses and realized how selfish she was being, she looked up at Snow who was staring down at her with that same look of elation and anguish and understanding. Audrey smiled broadly at her and hastily stood from her chair to hug her and congratulate her.

"It's going to be okay," Snow whispered in her ear. Audrey pulled away and gaped at the worry stamped across Snow's face.

"Well of course it is!" Audrey nearly shouted. "You're having a baby! This is incredible!" They hugged again, and Audrey sat back down so everyone else could have their turn, delaying the toast even more, a drink that Audrey was anticipating with an increasing intensity.

The dinner clashed in the usual Ganesh fashion with Amal's upscale atmosphere and Snow's more Southern sense of game day, buffet style service. Audrey sat quietly through the entire dinner listening to Snow prattle on to friends about plans for the new baby. Liam made several attempts at conversation, but she shrugged them away with shortened answers, each attempt trying her already frayed nerves. His charming smile got under her skin, his laugh now made her cringe. Her mind revolved around the one question no one seemed to ask Snow, and she couldn't hold it in any longer.

"So, where will you put it?" she asked abruptly. Snow stopped midsentence about possible names and turned wide-eyed to Audrey's flared nostrils and tightened face. "Where will you put the baby?" she repeated dryly when Snow didn't answer.

"Audrey, can we not talk about this now?" Snow smiled uncomfortably but avoided her friend's fierce gaze.

"No I need to know," Audrey said firmly. Snow tried to keep calm as everyone around them became quiet. Audrey continued, "You've got no room for another one here. Neither of you have family in Washington." Snow looked more and more uncomfortable with every word while her husband stared at Audrey with an unreadable expression. She felt her voice drop to an icy volume, "I know you better than any one, Elizabeth Bailey. I know what you're planning, so you may as well tell me."

"Audrey," Liam's voice was low and soothing. She rounded on him, disgusted.

"Don't touch me," she hissed almost silently through gritted teeth and yanked her arm from his grasp. "Don't think I don't see through you too. You and this whole pretense you four have got going on." She wheeled around back to Snow, who stared down at her hands, blinking rapidly. Amal was seething, ready to interject in an instant if Audrey lay too hard into Snow.

"Just tell me," Audrey's voice was barely above a whisper. "I need you to say it."

"I need my mother, Audrey," she whispered. "I'll need her help with the baby." The confirmation of her fears must have been evident on Audrey's face because Snow reached for Audrey's hand, apologizing profusely, but Audrey pulled away from her reach.

"Now it all makes sense," she breathed. The patch of skin between Snow's eyebrows creased with her own confusion. A malevolent smile tugged at the corner of Audrey's mouth, and her eyes seemed to burn, a rare expression both Snow and Amal knew well. Amal leaned forward to say something before Audrey exploded, but he was too late.

"That's why he's here!" Audrey turned to Liam whose face displayed more pity than anger or trepidation like the Ganeshes. It fed her fires, but her voice remained tranquil. "I've been here almost three years, and not once have they ever mentioned you. Yet here you are, playing some charade, my knight in shining armor to make everything okay when the ones who drug me here up and leave." She swiveled back to Snow, ignoring the hair that swung free of the pin. "You don't think I can handle myself. Well I can handle my own much better than any of you. I don't need you or Seth Williams or Mark Fields or Mr. Tall Dark Mysterious here to sugarcoat my life because I can see it clearly. I don't have the privilege of seeing it any other way."

Before anyone could say anything, before she could see Snow burst into tears, Audrey threw the napkin in her lap onto the table, slamming the legs of her chair against the floor, silencing the remaining chatter, and stalked to the door. Liam must have followed her because halfway down the corridor, she heard him call her name. She tried to ignore him, but he caught up to her quickly.

"Hey," he said gruffly, catching her arm. She felt her anger melting away with every step, and she didn't want anyone around, him especially, when it left raw the emotions behind.

"Just get away from me," she grunted, yanking her arm free again.

"I just thought you might need these," he said, holding up her leather jacket and a leash. Hermione sat jovially at the other end. She hesitated before taking it and turned to leave. "You could have waited," he said, the bitterness evident in his tone.

"Waited for what?" she snapped, turning back around.

"For a better time!" he shouted, his manner hurting her more than she cared to admit.

"Then enlighten me. When would have been the perfect time, the most comfortable time for everyone else?"

"Oh, there's plenty of other opportunities!" his jaw tightened threateningly. "When there aren't two dozen people around for starters!" Audrey waved him off and turned again to leave, this time not pausing to listen to what he had to say. But he continued on anyway. "Oh and here's a thought, you could have let her have her day! Let them make their announcement and talk about what threatens your own security later!" She kept walking. He groaned emphatically behind her, the volume of it growing slightly fainter as she put the distance between them.

"Are you always this heartless?" he shouted after her.

"No, sweetie, you just caught me on a good day!" she called behind her, careful not to turn, to let him see her break.

Out on the street, her fires quenched and her resolve evaporated. She walked the few blocks to her apartment at a speed that drug Hermione behind, the weight of the night's occurrences pushing down on her shoulders and Liam's words resounding through her mind.

Chapter Nineteen

Seattle, Washington

"No, I'm right. You're wrong. That's just how things are. You're going to have to deal with it," Audrey said nonchalantly. Hermione eyed her from where her head hung off the edge of the sofa.

"Oh, don't give me that look. I know I'm right." Audrey slammed the pot of tea on the counter forcefully. "None of those big, judgey eyes. If she wants to talk to me, she'll call. Yes, I know it's been two weeks. You don't have to keep reminding me. She'll call." Hermione stared at her owner who groaned dramatically and grabbed a leash. Hermione stayed where she was.

"What are you waiting for?" Audrey called. "Come on, let's go." Not until Audrey motioned for her to come did Hermione drudgingly leap from the sofa, landing heavily, and padding slowly across the room. With a pang of sadness, Audrey knelt at eye level with her dog. She cupped her gray head in her hands and massaged behind her ears. "You're getting old," she said. "Old and sluggish. What am I going to do with you?"

Hermione stared up at her with her large brown orbs. After a few minutes, Audrey got to her feet and placed the leash on the counter, making the short trek to The Cobb apartment building alone. Amal opened the door when she knocked. He stared at her silently, waiting.

"Is Snow here or at the school?" she asked, fumbling for her words.

"She's out for the summer," he said dryly, avoiding an answer to her question. "Where's Hermione?"

"At the apartment. I don't think she was up for the walk today."

"I'm sorry," his voice seemed detached.

"Don't be. Things happen. Dogs get old. People are tactless and insensitive," she stared at the ground.

"Certain people? Or just people in general."

"You know what I mean," said Audrey, looking up at him. "I was tactless and insensitive. I was hoping to see Snow so I could apologize."

"Elizabeth's at the market," he said after a pause. "Gone to get ice cream or pickles or whatever she thinks she could possibly crave." He rolled his eyes, and Audrey giggled humorlessly. Amal sighed and moved out of the way to let her pass through into the apartment. He gestured towards the kitchen table. "Have a seat, Audrey."

She did as she was told. He returned shortly with cups of steaming tea.

"Sorry, Elizabeth got rid of all of our wine last week," he said, sliding a cup to her across the table.

"I'd prefer tea anyway," Audrey chortled. Amal smiled and shook his head.

"She wanted to tell you before the dinner," he said after a short silence. "She said she owed it to you, but she was terrified. She knew how you'd take it. But you surpassed all of our expectations." Audrey studied the wood grain in the tabletop and picked at a loose thread in the seam of her jeans.

"I'm sorry," her voice was weak and distant.

"Why don't you come with us?" he asked soothingly. Audrey shook her head minutely but fervently.

"I can't," she answered feebly.

"Why not?" he implored. "We found a house on the mountain more than half an hour away from where the two of you grew up. It should be fine. Trust me when I say Alabama is the last place I want to end up – "

"I can't!" her voice regained its power. Amal leaned back in his chair to study her, a stern look etched across his dark features. "I'm sorry. I just can't. Snow and I will stay in touch. I know we will. We've been further apart before. We'll be okay."

"That's not the impression we got at the dinner," he said calmly.

"Chalk it up to the heat of the moment," she tried to smile, using the joke to lighten the mood. Amal continued to stare at her.

"Again, I'm really sorry."

Before Amal could answer, the door burst open. The sound of rustling paper bags and Snow's panting filled the room. Amal stood from his chair to help her with the groceries.

"I couldn't decide on a flavor, so I just bought cookies n' cream, Neapolitan, and that brownie stuff that you like," she explained energetically.

"What, no cookie dough?" Audrey chimed in. The loud rustling stopped as Snow froze and turned toward Audrey's voice. She looked up at her husband, who nodded his reassurance. In a rush of energy, Snow crossed the room and clubbed her on the arm.

"I really can't stand you sometimes!" she exclaimed.

"I know," Audrey bit back a smile at her friend's passion. Snow began to laugh and forced Audrey into a hug, squeezing her tightly. "I'm sorry," Audrey whispered.

"Just never do that again, okay?"

"Yes ma'am."

"Hey, Al, did you pack the ice cream scooper already?" Snow called.

"Yes, love," Amal answered grumpily.

"Oh, attitude!" Audrey called. Snow giggled happily beside her.

"You know," Amal sounded exasperated, pinching the bridge of his nose when he came into view, "this would go a lot more quickly if you two would help."

"Sorry, can't," Audrey said with a shrug. "Mia wants ice cream." She turned her attention back to Snow, ignoring Amal's ensuing protest. "Looks like we'll have to do this high school style." She grabbed two spoons from a nearby box and took the carton of ice cream to the only piece of furniture left in the vast one bedroom apartment. They lay back on the couch, eating the frozen treat directly from the carton. Snow rested her hand on her growing stomach.

"God, I'm huge," she said with a mouthful of ice cream.

"Yeah, you are, but you're not even close to being done yet. Do you remember the whale we saw the summer after I moved here?" Audrey said with widened eyes, earning a cold smack from

Snow's spoon. A loud bang and a curse came from the next room, silencing their laughter.

"I should go help him," Snow said, handing the carton to Audrey and grunting to her feet.

"Nope." Audrey jumped up, grabbed Snow's wrist, and drug her to the door. "I called for backup." When she yanked the door open, she came face to face with a fist and jolted back.

"Oh, sorry Audrey, I was about to knock," said Thomas, offering an apologetic smile.

"No worries. Thanks for saving us," she smiled broadly, still clutching Snow's wrist. Thomas stepped into the apartment, kissing Snow's cheek in greeting and revealing the man behind him.

"You brought your brother," Audrey called over her shoulder. It was more of an accusation than a question. Liam's dark eyes burned into hers, but the smile that usually followed never came.

"Thought we could do with the help," came Thomas's explanation.

"Miss Wyatt," Liam nodded his head in acknowledgement.

"Farren," she addressed him, pulling Snow past him.

"You can let go of my arm now," said Snow when they were closed in the elevator. Audrey let out the breath she didn't know she was holding in a forced giggle and released her grip.

"I take it you haven't seen him since the dinner party," Snow observed.

"What gave it away?" Audrey asked. She didn't give Snow time to respond. The elevator door opened, and she climbed the remaining steps to the rooftop. Snow followed sluggishly behind. They made their way to the railing where Audrey had set up two chairs earlier in the day. Snow lowered herself into one, but Audrey leaned against the short concrete wall. The city expanded before her in what appeared to be organized disarray. Mount Rainier stood majestically behind it all, keeping watch over the city. The sun had begun to set, transforming the sky into a beautiful wash of pinks and purples. But Audrey saw none of it. Leaning over the wall, she gazed down at the ground, the building beneath her growing smaller and thinner before reaching its foundation in slabs of concrete.

"I have seen many sunsets in my day," Snow began, "but

none have ever compared to Alabama's."

"Yeah that's a pretty one," Audrey replied absently, her eyes fixated on the ground.

"But do you know what I miss the most?" Snow asked. When she didn't receive an answer, she continued. "I miss the fields. The crickets at night and the frogs. The neighbor's cows bellowing. The smell of the crop dusters and pesticides in the fall when we'd go out to pick a pumpkin for Halloween. Oh god how the summers were so hot! I'd be a sweaty mess before we made it anywhere. And so humid that your hair would basically be a frizzy Afro by the time you got to school. Oh and the winters! Remember the muddy snowman we made that January? It was so tiny. Bama snow is really just a bunch of ice." Snow stopped to laugh to herself.

"Well you'll get all of that soon enough." Audrey almost winced at her own icy tone.

"Will you stay here when we're gone?" Snow asked after a few minutes of strained silence.

"Yeah," Audrey nodded and sat down next to her friend. Snow reached over and took Audrey's hand. Normally she would protest, but this was their last night, and Snow was hormonal. So she didn't argue with her. "I have my job here. And I can't move Hermione. She's too old now to endure the change."

"Good old Hermoninny," Snow smiled sweetly in remembrance. "I need to go see her before we fly out tomorrow. I don't know when I'll be seeing her again." The silent understanding passed between them. Snow wouldn't be back in Seattle in time to see Hermione again. Realizing her mistake, she fought to change the subject. "Have you talked to your brother lately?"

"He's called a time or two," Audrey squirmed in her seat. "He seems pretty busy."

"Is he still liking Atlanta?" Snow asked.

"I should think so," Audrey stared blindly at the darkening Seattle skyline.

Snow sighed heavily next to her. "You've never answered his calls. Have you?" Audrey couldn't find the words. She shook her head. "God, Audrey!" Snow's evident frustration made Audrey turn her gaze to her oxfords. "When will you ever learn? I don't see what your problem is."

"He's different Snow," Audrey started. "He's Ethan, but he's not. He's not the little boy I remember."

"Well of course not, he's twenty-one years old!" Snow threw her arms up in exasperation.

"Exactly!" Audrey defended herself. "Look at how much I've missed! He counted on me to help him through the mess that *I* made, and I just left him."

"And you're just going to keep missing out on his life if you don't *talk* to him!"

"He'll be better off without me."

Snow stared at her in a loss for words. "You're so ignorant," she finally said. "I can't leave you here alone."

"I'll be fine," Audrey groaned.

"No you won't be! You reject the people I try to get you to meet, you ignore your brother, and your only other friend isn't going to be writing you any more."

"Seth Williams lived alone in London for decades, and he did just fine," Audrey protested, trying to ignore the pang in her chest at the mention of her friend who had died in his sleep two months earlier.

"Audrey – "

"And I won't be alone. I'll have Hermione, and we'll keep in touch, right?" She met her best friend's glistening green eyes.

"Of course we will," her voice was thick, and she gave Audrey's hand a gentle squeeze.

"It will all be okay," Audrey grinned reassuringly.

They turned back, Audrey Wyatt and Elizabeth Ganesh, back to the last fighting words of the fleeting sunset before the city was shrouded in darkness, shining its own light like a beacon through the windows of the towering buildings.

Chapter Twenty

Madison, Alabama
January 2006

More than two weeks had passed since Audrey had woken up, and although 2005 was dead and gone, not much had changed. Elizabeth only left the hospital at night to sleep in a proper bed. Mrs. Bailey stopped by every day when she got off of work. Ethan had stabilized a few days after Audrey just enough to be moved out of intensive care. He was still deep in a coma, and everyone's question was whether or not he would ever wake up. Sheryl rarely left his side, and Richard only stepped out to let Mark visit with his stepson when the obligation arose. Ethan was allowed two visitors at a time but only from his parents. Audrey's physical condition had improved enough for her to be discharged, but she was still detained due to her unstable psychological condition. She hadn't uttered a word, but she no longer stared blankly at the wall in front of her. She remained expressionless, but her eyes would jut around at everything and everyone that came near her. She would listen intently at updates on her brother's condition, but ignore anything else anyone said. Elizabeth continued to talk to her, hoping something would catch her interest and she would interject her own opinion into the conversation.

Everyone felt run down and at times overwhelmed. They were flooded with worry for Ethan and Audrey and grief for Daniel. With Ethan's life on the balance and Audrey's sanity, no one could properly mourn Daniel. The piercing pain at the thought of him had begun to chafe at their hearts, leaving them raw.

Mark stood up from his chair, kissed the top of his wife's head, and stole one last long look at Ethan. Like his sister, his dark bruises were a sickening yellowish green but visibly healing. A bulky cast wrapped around the length of his leg. How will he run? The thought raced through Mark's head for the fifteenth time. He pushed it away, saying all that mattered was Ethan's life. They could deal with his inability to play baseball later.

Mark nodded at Richard as he walked toward Audrey's room. Just outside the open door, he could hear Elizabeth's overly chipper voice.

"I go by and feed them when I leave here. You know how much Hermione misses you? She drives me crazy looking for you every time she sees me. I guess she just expects you to be with me. You know, if you start talking, they'll let you go home. You'll be able to see her."

Mark smiled at Elizabeth as he sat down in his chair.

"Hey, Audrey," Mark raised the tone of his voice in an attempt to sound cheerful. She moved her eyes to his face and gazed at him. It was still unnerving, the amount of uncharacteristic eye contact she made these days. "Having a good day today?"

Audrey blinked a few times without averting her eyes. The cut on her temple had healed into an ugly, ragged scar reaching up into her hair, and he tried not to look at it while Elizabeth bit her lip. Mark cleared his throat and turned to Elizabeth.

"Did you get that thing from the house that I asked you to grab?"

"Oh, yeah!" she jumped, digging through her large purse, and handed him a package.

"We got all of your stuff back," Mark said, carefully avoiding any specific mention of the accident. He smiled at Audrey who still stared at him. "Thought you might want this. Give your overactive brain something to do again."

He grinned broadly, hoping it wasn't too cheesy as he pulled the dilapidated novel out of the package and handed it to her. With a moment's hesitation, Audrey's eyes finally released him and fell down to his hands. She flinched so slightly when she beheld *Crime and Punishment*, that neither Mark nor Elizabeth could be sure it had actually happened. Within seconds her piercing stare was back on his face.

"I want to leave," she said. Her voice cracked with disuse but still had such a firm quality that it surprised both of her listeners. Mark and Elizabeth exchanged glances before Elizabeth rushed off to get a nurse.

"Of course," the first genuine smile of the new year stretched across Mark's face. "We'll leave as soon as possible."

Mark breathed a sigh of relief the moment the clock declared it was quitting time. Being back at work was both a blessing and a curse. It gave him the necessary distraction, but it never seemed to end. He grabbed his briefcase and car keys and rushed out of his office. Just outside, the receptionist cut him off. He tried not to groan too loudly as she smiled supportively up at him.

"Hi, Mr. Fields," she greeted him, "how are you holding up?"

"As well as can be expected I guess," he sighed, annoyed at the obstruction.

"I know I don't know you very well, and I can't imagine what you're going through, but I just wanted to let you know that your family has been in my prayers, and if there's anything you need, anything at all, I'm here." Her full lips stretched into a soft smile.

Mark stopped short and stared down at the slight woman in front of him. A head shorter than his five feet ten inches, her black hair fell in neat waves just above her shoulders. She had a very angular face with sharp cheekbones and smooth, dark skin. Her dark eyes glittered with compassion.

"Thanks, Noel," he muttered. He had been raised in the "Bible Belt", but never once had someone told him they were praying for him. He was astonished and taken aback at how comforting it was to hear. "I really appreciate it."

She nodded once with a shy grin and moved out of his way.

Once out on the highway, he dialed Sheryl's number. He didn't know if he needed to pick her up before heading to the hospital or if she'd gotten a ride with Richard. It was still weird to him how fully Richard was in the picture these days, even under such unnatural circumstances. He knew the man's pain, but he still couldn't help the bile that rose in his throat every time he saw him, especially when he came home from work to find him in his house.

Sheryl didn't answer the phone. Typical. Mark decided to stop by the house anyway to check on Audrey. If Sheryl was there, he'd go ahead and pick her up.

Elizabeth had made arrangements with NYU to skip over

the semester to help out with Audrey and Ethan if – *when* – he woke up and moved home. Audrey hadn't said a word since her declaration at the hospital, but Elizabeth did her best each and every day to lift her spirits. She'd even convinced Audrey to eat a few times, but she still refused her medication.

Mark sighed as he drove to a house that felt bigger and emptier than ever these days. Daniel had died, sucking the innocence and joy from the foundation of the house. Ethan was in a coma still, and despite his recent signs of near consciousness, anxiety of his condition when he awoke filled in the gaps left by the absence of Danny's cheerfulness. Audrey stayed locked in her room, lying on her side facing the wall with Hermione faithfully at her side. No one knew what went on in her head, but it didn't seem hard to guess. Elizabeth did everything in her power to divert her attention with a vigor that renewed every morning, but Audrey never budged.

He was a little over half a mile away from the house when Mark suddenly slammed on his brakes and skid to a stop, staring dumbfounded at the road. Walking in the middle of the opposite lane was a tall, gray and white dog.

"Dazzle?" Mark threw his truck in park and jumped out. "Dazzle! Here girl!" he called. Dazzle stopped walking and looked up at him. Her tail was tucked tightly between her legs, her eyes were glazed over, and she trembled violently. Mark's stomach dropped as he approached her. She flinched at his touch as if the thought of him terrified her.

"It's okay," he soothed, "come here." He scooped her up in his arms and laid her in the back seat of his truck. Different scenarios shot through his brain as he sped home, trying to come up with a possible explanation for Dazzle's behavior.

When he slung the truck into the driveway, he noticed the front door was opened wide. Yanking the keys from the ignition and flinging himself free, he bolted to the door to find Elizabeth sitting on the bottom step of the porch, hugging her legs, and sobbing powerfully into her knees.

"What happened?" he demanded. She lifted her head but didn't meet his eyes. Her sides heaved and she choked on her gasp like a child unable to control her crying. She gestured with her thumb inside the house, mouth open in a silent attempt to speak.

Mark leapt up the brick steps and through the door,

ignoring his urge to comfort her. Once inside, he began calling out for Audrey and Sheryl. Through the windows that lined the living room wall, he saw Sheryl sitting up, leaning on one hand while the other pressed onto the side of her head. Blood soaked her blonde hair and trickled through the creases of her fingers. Mark bolted through the open door and was at her side in a second.

"Sheryl! What happened? Are you okay? Can you see clearly? When did this happen?" The questions poured out of his mouth as he ripped off his shirt and pressed it against the side of his wife's head. He pulled out his phone to dial an ambulance. Sheryl muttered incoherently, but Mark was able to discern one word: *Audrey.*

Adrenaline pumped through him, surging him into action. With an ambulance on the way, he threw his phone aside and began to assess the damage. Sheryl's eyes were unfocused, but she was conscious. He fought to keep her that way, saying out loud everything that raced through his head.

"It's going to be okay, Sheryl. It's going to be fine. An ambulance is on the way. You'll be okay in no time. Don't go to sleep, Sheryl. Don't close your eyes. You've lost quite a bit of blood, and I'm positive you have a concussion."

"Audrey... I... she..."

His eyes raked over her again, and he noticed that splotched across her white t-shirt were drops of blood inconsistent with her injuries. Mark froze.

"Sheryl, whose blood is that?"

"Had to..."

Mark looked up to scan the yard for the first time, and what met his eyes turned his heart to a block of ice. He felt the weight of it sink down from his chest at the sight of the shotgun three feet away from them and the lump that lay on the ground ahead of it.

"Press this tightly here, okay, Sheryl?" he instructed. Jumping to his feet, he walked the few yards to the body on the ground. Its neck, leg, and side were soaked in blood from its flayed shoulder.

"No," he choked out, kneeling beside it. He reached a shaking hand out, hesitating, holding it in the air, before resting it on Flash's head, but there were too many unanswered questions to allow himself to grieve.

The police and an ambulance arrived and laid Sheryl on a stretcher. Upon seeing the murdered dog, they questioned Mark on what had occurred with both Sheryl and the lifeless animal, but he shook his head numbly, stating he wanted to know that himself.

Once the ambulance had taken his wife away, he poured a glass of water to take out to Elizabeth, who still sat wrapped in a blanket surrounded by three policemen, hugging her knees on the steps in her subsiding trauma.

"Thanks," she murmured. She held the water in her hand but didn't raise it to her mouth. They sat in silence for a moment, the frigid breeze whipping at their hair.

"Ma'am, can you tell us anything about what happened here?" an officer asked her tentatively. She opened her mouth to speak, but her teeth clamped shut as a fresh wave of tears began to fall.

"Elizabeth, I know this isn't fair, but we need you to tell us what happened," Mark encouraged her.

"I've never seen anything like it," Elizabeth said after a few minutes of silence. "The rage in their eyes." She wiped her cheeks with the meat of her palms and pushed her tangled hair out of her face. Mark wanted to comfort her, but answers mattered more to him in that moment than Elizabeth's feelings.

"Please, just start from the beginning," he coaxed.

"We were just sitting there," Elizabeth began. "Audrey was curled on her bed as usual. We had the door closed. We could hear Sheryl crying and yelling that Audrey had killed her baby. I put on a movie to block out the noise, but after a while, Hermione started growling. Audrey didn't move, but I knew it was weird for Hermione to growl. When she started barking hysterically, I got scared. She jumped off of the bed and started clawing at the door. I didn't know what to do, so I got up and opened the door to let her out. Then we heard more barking and that sharp cry that dogs do when they get hurt. Sheryl was shouting and cussing. I just stood there. I didn't know what to do."

An officer scratched away at his notepad, taking down everything she said.

"Then I could hear glass shattering, and that was when Audrey came up from behind me and shoved me out of the way and ran out. I followed her. We got downstairs just in time to see Sheryl kick Dazzle. Dazzle and Hermione hunkered back, but Flash was outside, looking all scared like I've never seen him. Audrey ran after Sheryl. I could see them outside, but I just stood there. I didn't know what to do. I didn't know what to do!" Elizabeth started to sob again, and Mark grabbed her shoulder firmly.

"Stay with me Snow! Tell me what happened!"

"Audrey tried to stop her! But she wasn't fast enough. Sheryl shot Flash, and Audrey screamed. She grabbed the gun from Sheryl and hit her really hard upside the head with the butt of it. I just stood there. I didn't know what to do! I thought she was dead! Audrey threw the gun and ran back in. She ran right past me without even looking at me. She ran upstairs and came back down with her suitcase. She grabbed Hermione and then she went straight to the front door without even looking at me. Dazzle ran out too. I followed them. I tried to stop her. I grabbed her and told her to stay, but she turned around and yelled at me. She said if I kept annoying her like that she'd kill herself. She said the last thing she needed was me acting as if nothing had happened because as far as she was concerned she was already dead. I just stood there and cried. She looked at me for a second before taking her dog and her suitcase and walking down the road. She just walked away like it wasn't a big deal."

Elizabeth's words became indiscernible as she sobbed. Mark stood up and ran to his truck, pulling Dazzle out, ignoring the officers' ensuing questions.

"I need you to calm down," he said to Elizabeth. "I need you to make sure Dazzle gets to the vet and make them hold her for a couple of days. Make sure she's okay. But I need you to calm down so you don't wreck and we have two more deaths on our hands." He flinched at his own harsh words, regretting them as they flowed from his mouth, but he didn't have time to apologize. He lowered Dazzle into Elizabeth's car and turned back to her. "Do you understand?"

She nodded frantically, wiping at her face.

"Now which way did Audrey go?"

Elizabeth pointed down the road. An officer grabbed his radio and began speaking into it when Mark interrupted him.

"We aren't pressing charges," he growled. "Do what you've got to do. I've got to find my girl." Without another word, he ran to his truck and sped out of the driveway.

It was well past two in the morning when Mark gave up his search for Audrey and stumbled through his front door. He tossed his keys on the counter and rubbed his eyes. The house was dark and empty. Daniel was dead. Ethan was still in a coma. Sheryl was in the hospital. And Audrey had vanished. Even the dogs had met the same fate as their owners.

The dogs.

Mark grabbed the wireless landline and shoved it in his pocket with his cell phone, just in case, and walked to the back door, crunching on glass along the way. He crossed the yard to the shed, avoiding the patches of blood stained grass and the limp and mangled dog. He grabbed a shovel, picked out a spot by the edge of the fence, and began to dig in the frozen ground.

Over an hour later he had a suitable hole. Zipping up his jacket against the icy wind, he trekked back to the house, again avoiding the signs of everything that had occurred that day. Pulling the pillowcase from Sheryl's body pillow in their bedroom closet, he made his way back outside. Finally gazing down at the corpse for a moment, he picked up the sticky, frozen body and carefully pulled the pillowcase around it. Mark tied off the opening, carried the body to the back of the yard, lowered it into the hole, and began to cover it with dirt.

He thought back to the countless pet funerals he'd had as a child with his sister, Clara. The family dog. Clara's cat. Clara's hamster. Clara's snake. Clara's turtle. Clara's fish – she insisted that flushing fish down the toilet was too inhumane. They'd once played with a frog for two hours before Clara had squeezed it too tightly. Their small back yard had been littered with makeshift gravestones until his dad had insisted that it looked like a cemetery and that they were to pull all of the plastic grave markers up. Clara had pitched such a fit about it until Dad said rather coarsely that she should feel bad about killing them instead. When she realized it was her own lack of care for them that had caused their inevitable demise, she'd sworn off of pets for the rest of her life. She made that vow at six years old. Now, two decades later, she stuck to that promise, never so much as buying a potted plant. She hadn't even carried a real bouquet at her wedding. Mark secretly hoped she and Simon never had kids.

She couldn't possibly do worse than me, though, Mark

thought to himself. Having Clara at the funeral had been like holding an umbrella in a hurricane. It kept him dry from above but the floods still swept him off of his feet. He'd driven her to the airport in silence. Neither said a word, but the silence held all of the love and memories he cherished.

Mark ladled another scoop of dirt onto the body. He tried to think of it as that. Just a body. Not Flash. Not the first thing he'd ever bought for his stepson that had slipped from his grasp.

Mark's pace began to quicken. Dirt flung in all directions, missing the hole more often than not. He piled the earth back in the hole so hastily that he barely heard his phone ring. Throwing down the spade and ripping both phones from his pocket, he pulled his cell to his ear.

"Hello?"

"Is she dead?"

Mark let out a deep sigh at the sound of her voice, the hardened tone of it washing through him, relieving the tension in his muscles. "Audrey."

"Is she dead? Did I kill her?" Her voice was firmer as she repeated herself.

"No she's fine. She's in the hospital. She's got a concussion and they had to give her some blood. She's staying the night so they can be sure though."

"Good."

"Where's your phone?" Mark asked after a long enough silence that he thought she'd hung up. "I didn't recognize the number."

"I left it with the manager at Waffle House. I'm using a pay phone."

"Oh. Where are you?"

"Nashville."

"What?" Mark's voice climbed an octave. "How'd you get there?"

"Had a cab pick me up at Waffle House."

"Oh."

"Yeah."

There was a silence in which Mark fought down the lump in his throat, knowing how this conversation would end.

"You're going somewhere." It wasn't a question. He knew the only reason she'd be in Nashville was for the airport.

"Yeah."

"Where?"

"Mark, I can't tell you that."

"Why not?"

"You'll follow me."

He had to admit the truth in her statement. "There's no talking you out of this, is there?"

"No."

Mark felt his very core begin to shake.

"Do you have any money?" he asked, trying to stall the inevitable end of their probable last phone call.

"Yeah, I packed a bag a few days ago when Elizabeth went to visit the hospital. I took the cash you keep in your study. And I had the cab stop at the bank so I could empty my savings account." He had never heard her call Elizabeth anything but Snow before, and it unnerved him.

"You know she was just trying to help," he said. "If you just talk to her, I'm sure it'll all be okay."

"Unless she has some kind of magic to turn back the clock..."

"I understand."

"Can you do me a favor?"

"Anything."

"If my brother wakes up – "

"When," Mark corrected. "The doctors say Ethan will wake up in a few days."

"If my brother wakes up," she repeated firmly, "tell him that I love him. I love him so much. Tell him that. And tell him I'm sorry." He could tell that she was crying even though her voice never wavered. Audrey always cried silently.

"Of course I will." Mark fought back his own tears.

"Thank you," she whispered. "I have to go."

"Audrey!" In that moment, Mark decided to break their unspoken rule. "I love you, Audrey."

He waited for her response, but all he got was a click and the buzz of a dead line. And just like that, she was gone. What felt like a club crashed through his only unbroken bone, and he crumbled onto the frozen ground.

Daniel was gone. Audrey was gone. Ethan could be permanently altered. He doubted he had much time at all left with

Sheryl. Even the dogs were gone. He was alone with a huge empty house and a half finished grave.

In less than a month, Mark Fields had lost everything.

Chapter Twenty-One

Seattle, Washington

Rain spattered against the windows, beckoning Audrey out into the present, a summons she easily ignored. Barely over a year had passed since Snow moved back to Alabama, and already their correspondence had become less frequent. Excuses poured from her friend's mouth for the first five minutes of every Skype conversation. First Snow and Amal had been busy with moving. Then the baby occupied all of their time. Snow's exhaustion kept her from picking up the phone more often than not. All veritable excuses, but it didn't leave Audrey any more thrilled to be left alone in a city she was only in because of Snow.

Her dog sat dozing with her head on Audrey's feet. At first Hermione hadn't been allowed inside the café, but after Audrey had words with the owner, he had finally conceded. Audrey tipped back the rest of her tea, dropped her barely eaten panini down to Hermione, and quietly made for the door.

Seattle had taken a rough hit that year with its floods, thunderstorms, tornados, frigid temperatures, and rainfall that broke records back in May. Summer had come and gone in a flash, but even then the temperature never reached higher than eighty-seven degrees. September, it seemed, would follow suit with the rest of the year's bizarre weather. Audrey pulled the collar of her new leather jacket tight on her neck to block out the wind, which these days could reach ungodly speeds. Lighting a cigarette, she puffed a pillar of smoke that was blown behind her, lost in the violent wind.

She often found herself eating less and smoking more. A bad habit, she knew. One that everyone had warned would kill her. But that wasn't what bothered her when she caught a glimpse of her reflections in windows on the street. She was starting to look more like her mother as she aged. Or maybe it was just the white stick in her fingertips.

Her hair, which now reached just below her shoulders, whipped her face mercilessly, but she kept her hands planted in her jacket pockets. Pockets that felt too high to her. The jacket was stylish, sure. Much better than the bulky one she'd worn since she was thirteen, but who put pockets at the midsection like that? She could only imagine how idiotic she looked with her elbows sticking out like the wings of some flightless bird.

It was only a short walk from the café to her apartment, but by the time they reached the elevator, Hermione was short of breath. The doors closed and the elevator pinged with each floor as it climbed nine levels. Hermione struggled to lie down on the cold floor.

"I don't know why you always do that," Audrey scoffed. "You know you'll just have to get back up." Hermione looked up at her with weak eyes, her tongue lolling out of her mouth as she panted. When the doors opened, she made no intentional move to get up. Rolling her eyes, Audrey bent down and scooped up the sixty-pound dog. She carried her into the apartment, set her on the gaudy sofa, and stroked the top of her head before lumbering heavily to the bathroom to shower.

It had been yet another stressful week at work, so she showered leisurely, letting the scalding water run from the top of her head and drip off different points of her face. When she finally got out, she squeezed the water out of her hair with a towel.

Wrapping her robe tightly around her figure, she ignored the evidence of how much weight she'd lost over the past few months and stepped out into her apartment. Upon seeing her, Hermione jumped down from the sofa. She landed at an awkward angle, and her leg slid out from under her. She let out a yelp but recovered quickly. It was then that Audrey noticed the limp. It was subtle, but Hermione seemed to put less weight on her hind leg than all the others. Audrey's heart sank, and her eyes sagged as she watched her jubilant puppy hobble towards her.

* * * * *

"It's called osteosarcoma."

The words hit her like a steam engine, blasting through her core. She knew before going in what the verdict would be, but something about the veterinarian in front of her, waving a pen around x-ray images of her dog's legs made it all so final.

"Bone cancer. It's very common in greyhounds unfortunately. They're more likely to get it than any other dog."

"What do I do?" she asked, knowing the answer already. Hermione lay on the table in front of them, and Audrey scratched her whitened head.

"Well, you have a few options," said Dr. Ross. He shoved his hands in the pockets of his scrubs with a grim expression on his face. "There are treatments available that could reduce the cancer cells, but they're all a bit on the expensive side. We could amputate the leg and put her through radiation and chemotherapy, but even then her life expectancy would be another year at best. And the cancer has already begun to spread to her lungs."

Audrey gazed down at Hermione. "Just tell me what I need to do," she whispered.

He paused for a moment, but his words were smooth. "The kindest thing for her would be to put her to sleep."

Audrey closed her eyes against the emotion that flared within her at the statement. Dr. Ross continued. "Every day, she would be in worse pain than the day before. She has maybe two months left in her, best case scenario."

Audrey sniffed and collected herself. Standing, she shook his hand and thanked him. He looked apologetically at her but said nothing. She wondered if so many years of giving the same news to different patients ever got easier or if he'd been hardened and his sympathy was feigned.

"Come on, Hermione," she tried to sound cheerful as she lifted her dog from the table. Hermione had started to feel old to her, but now that she was at death's door, she seemed much too young. She limped happily at her feet as they walked slowly to the lobby. Audrey felt like she was betraying her best friend as she made the appointment with Hermione right next to her. The receptionist told her she could wait and call to make the appointment when she'd let it all sink in, but Audrey needed it done.

Three weeks. Nineteen painful days were all Hermione had left on her quickly ticking clock. And those days passed like blinks of an eye. Each one came and went like waves beating mercilessly against the cliffs.

On Day Three, Audrey thought about calling Snow. She'd picked up the phone countless times, even logged onto Skype, but she never hit the green button that would bring her best friend across the country instantly into her apartment.

On Day Nine, she wrote a letter to Mr. Williams that he would never read, but still mailed it to his address like all the others. He'd loved Hermione as much as she did.

Day Fifteen was the worst. Just as every day, Audrey took Hermione to the park. They didn't run or play. They just sat under the same tree with blankets and jackets to guard against the building cold. Audrey smoked and read aloud, ignoring the stares from those around her. Each day brought her a fresh wave of pain, matching that of Hermione's, but she kept it together. She wouldn't allow herself to spend Hermione's last days crying. They watched the sun set behind the Seattle skyline then walked and limped slowly to the road where Audrey hailed a cab. As they stepped off the curb onto the road, Hermione yelped shrilly. Audrey's heart panged with the same sharpness as she scooped up her bundle and put her in the cab.

The driver made it to the apartment building more quickly than usual, uncomfortable with the constant wheezing and whining emitting from the greyhound. Audrey carried Hermione all the way from the cab to the sofa, struggling with the weight. She laid her down tenderly on the red, cream, and blue fabric. Audrey bit her cheek to hold back the tears when she looked Hermione over and discovered that her leg had been broken.

On Day Eighteen, Audrey tried to stay as cheerful as possible, only leaving the sofa to run to all of Hermione's favorite fast food restaurants and cafés. Hermione's last day was full of cheeseburgers and bagels, wagging tails and stifled tears.

The sun rose on Day Nineteen with Audrey still wide-awake. The day had come sooner than anticipated. Hermione had one last bagel before Audrey scooped her up and carried her to the door.

"You're either really strong, or she isn't as heavy as she looks," came a familiar uninvited voice as they waited for the elevator. Audrey ignored Ruby, who called after her in an attempt to continue the conversation, but the elevator doors muted the sound of her voice. Audrey sighed heavily.

She talked to Hermione as if nothing wrong was happening as they rode to the veterinary clinic. They came to a stop in front of the colorful sign, and Audrey froze. Hermione had minutes left and there was still so much to be said. The cabbie urged her out of his car. She handed him a fistful of crumpled bills and heaved her dog through the cab door and across the parking lot.

"I'm Audrey Wyatt," she managed to say when she reached the receptionist. Hermione pulled against Audrey's grasp in order to get a better look at the puppies in the waiting room. The receptionist offered a sad smile and ushered her to the operating room. Hermione grunted heavily when Audrey laid her on the table a little more clumsily than she should have. Her arms trembled when they were finally released from the dog's weight.

"We had a good run, didn't we girl?" she beseeched, searching her companion's face for an answer. She'd dragged her from one corner of the planet to the next, never staying in one place long enough for it to become a home. That kind of stuff mattered to children. Was it the same way for dogs? Did their locations matter to them at all? Or did they only care for the people in their lives?

Audrey was pulled from her contemplation when the door suddenly opened behind her. She didn't have to turn around to know that it was Dr. Ross coming to count down the seconds until Hermione lay dead before her.

She barely heard what he said. All she could hear was the ticking of the clock clanging in her ears. She only nodded when he asked her a question. She didn't know what she was agreeing to.

Audrey stood with Dr. Ross and an assistant over Hermione, who looked up at them curiously with pain evident in her dark orbs.

"Once this needle is in her vein, I'll inject the euthanasia serum. It should take only a few seconds for it to take its effect," Dr. Ross explained methodically. Audrey took a deep, ragged breath but didn't otherwise acknowledge that she'd heard him. She squatted down so that she was level with Hermione's head on the table. Black eyes met brown as Hermione held her gaze.

Audrey wondered if she was scared. If she questioned at all the events going on around her. She couldn't see past the pain and tightness in the weak orbs to see if any uncertainty lay there.

"You have been," Audrey's voice was thick as she choked out her words, "the best. I don't know where I would be right now without you." She reached up with a shaking hand and scratched Hermione behind the ear. She was only vaguely aware that the vet was injecting the serum into Hermione's front leg.

"I love you so much," Audrey whispered when the dog's eyes started to flutter and close. "Say hello to our brothers for me, will you?" she croaked. Hermione took a deep breath that was followed by several shallow ones. Audrey held her own breath, counting each small rise and fall of Hermione's side until she lay completely stilled. Audrey watched as the life left her best friend. With her hand on her fur, she could almost imagine she felt her heart cease to beat.

"I'll give you some time," said Dr. Ross. He left with his assistant at his heels. A deep, sharp gasp erupted in Audrey at the click of the closing door.

Audrey walked, alone and numb, in the frigid afternoon for miles until she reached her apartment. She climbed the stairs, each one a mountain, each flight a higher mountain range. The muscles in her legs ached by the time she reached the ninth floor. She unlocked the door and went inside, leaning heavily against the wood when it clicked to a close.

The studio apartment now felt cavernous and empty. The sofa too big for one person. The bowl on the floor too clean.

With trembling fingers, Audrey pulled out her phone and opened Snow's contact information. Big green eyes smiled up at her from the screen. Her thumb hovered over the Call icon, unable to find the strength to let it fall. Sixty-three days had come and gone since she last spoke to her. How would she even begin to explain to her how much had changed since then?

The raging sea seemed too tumultuous now for even her life raft to do much good in keeping her afloat.

Audrey sighed and pushed herself off the door. She lit a cigarette and uncorked the bottle of red wine that Snow had given her as a maid of honor gift and pressed her thumb on the cold glass over the icon labeled Delete Contact.

Part Two.
Five Years Later

"I know that you don't believe it, but
indeed, life will bring you through.
You will live it down in time. What
you need now is fresh air, fresh air,
fresh air!"

-Fyodor Doestevsky
Crime and Punishment

Chapter One

Gatlinburg, Tennessee

Owen Sharpe was a man of ambition and perseverance. Or so one would guess upon Googling him, which was what he was doing now. Over thirty years of a music career that had never shown much promise, he had hopped from band to band, but the other members had always found a reason to kick out their lead guitarist, never letting him stay for more than a four year stretch. They blamed things like drug abuse and exploits with the townies that he would consider to be his groupies. But once he'd gotten clean in his late thirties, he'd found a band that let him stick around. Eleven years clean but not sober. He still didn't feel right unless a bottle of George Dickel was trapped in his grasp.

Many different genres of music had strummed across the strings of his guitar in the past three decades, but his heart bled country. Not the crap he played now with the blues and alternative rock flare mixed in, but true country music. He and the rest of The Roadside Babel strayed away from the Merle Haggard, Willie Nelson sound that he pined for and more towards what he ignorantly described as hillbilly rock, but it was what their audience wanted. An audience that had grown steadily larger since Owen joined eight years ago. Tonight was their first night in the latest string of shows at a bar that held, at maximum capacity, three hundred people.

He wondered absently if she would be there. His mystery woman. The others teased him brutally about her. Next to him, the oldest in the group was forty-three, so the fact that a young woman would follow them to each show religiously with eyes intently gazed upon the aging guitarist was humorous to them. He always waved them off with disregard or made some crude joke, but his thoughts would often turn to her with haunting questions when he stumbled to the van the next morning.

He'd had many groupies follow them around for his sake, or so he told himself, but this one was different. Their tour the previous year had consisted of eight cities in the Southeast, starting in Nashville, and circling around the heart of the Deep South to make their way back to their home in Memphis, Tennessee. He first noticed her on the second stop of the tour on their third night in Chattanooga. Her long, stringy hair was casually thrown back behind shoulders that were clad in a leather vest. It had been a sweltering ninety degrees that day, but she'd still dressed in jeans. It's what caught his eye through the smoky atmosphere. There had been just over a hundred people in the bar, but when he caught her staring, he'd given her one of his most charming smiles. She'd turned back to her beer, and when the show was over, she was gone.

She turned up at every show after that, skipping only Atlanta, and always vanished when he left the stage to approach her. Evaporated into vapors right in front of him like a dazzling specter, a figment of his imagination. He blamed these hallucinations on the damage to his brain left by years of cocaine addiction until the others proved her existence with their taunting. Now he wondered if she would make another appearance this high up in the Smokey Mountains of Gatlinburg, Tennessee. He found himself hoping and swallowed the uncomfortable feeling down with a swig of Dickel.

"Come on, man. It's show time," Chad beat on the van door.

"I'm comin'," Owen grunted, tipping back the rest of his whiskey and tossing the empty bottle on the dashboard that had recently been cleaned. He ran a hand through his thinning hair, grabbed his Telecaster and carried it by the neck across the parking lot to the back of the bar. The rest of the band was standing behind the stage waiting on him. Their audience could be heard outside the door, chatting and ordering drinks.

"What took so long, geezer?" Mike jeered. "We were supposed to be on already!"

"Just leave it. He's here now isn't he?" Chad grumbled, walking between them towards the door. Mike rolled his eyes with a sneering grin and followed closely behind the front man. Milo, leaning against the bar, nodded a greeting, stubbed out his cigarette in the ashtray, and made his way to the stage. Owen followed them out grudgingly.

There was scattered applause when the four men stepped out into view, a few hoops and hollers. Someone in the back whistled. Owen took his place to Chad's right, pulled the guitar strap over his shoulder, and adjusted his microphone.

"We're The Roadside Babel," Chad gave his characteristically short introduction to a decent applause. Behind them, Milo tapped out four beats with his drumsticks, signaling for Owen to begin. The first song was an upbeat one with a loud, distorted guitar intro full of double-stops and hybrid picking, played so quickly that Owen's fingers seemed to blur in their dance across the strings. It led into a verse during which Owen sang backup with a hand placed on the strings to silence his guitar.

The drunks in the front of the crowd danced and sang a jumbled version of their lyrics, but most of their audience clapped along to the beat or tapped their foot. Others were smiling and cheering, but the ones in the back continued with their conversations. And Owen searched every face for hers.

He found her at the start of the fourth song. She'd taken a table to herself towards the back corner. The months had done little to his memory of her. The long curls and angular face were identical to the ones seared onto his brain, but from this distance, he could tell nothing else. He smiled at her during one of his favorite riffs and bent a few notes to give it a bit more of his signature twang. She lifted her beer to her mouth in response, her gaze unwavering.

They played a selection of songs from their latest album, and when the allotted time was up, Owen smiled at the crowd and waved, taking one last glance in the direction of his mystery woman. She was gone again. Despite his lack of surprise, he couldn't help the deeply rooted feeling of disappointment.

"You were off tempo for the last few songs, Mike," Chad spared no time in handing out his assessments once they were all crowded in the backroom. "You'll need to slow it down. You were throwing us all off. Milo sets the beat. Not you."

"Oh, can it, Chad, we did good!" Mike clapped a hand on the front man's shoulder with a sideways grin, resulting in a speech from their boss on respect.

You can take the teacher out of the classroom... Owen

thought as he made an early departure, leaving his guitar with the rest of the equipment. He stepped out into the fresh night air and pulled on his denim jacket, raising the collar against the mountain breeze. The warmth he had enjoyed during the day was now gone. He dug in the pocket for his bottle of Dickel and tipped it back. A loud, drunken cheer built up from inside the building. Mike must have gone back in for a drink.

"Got a light?"

Owen jumped at the sound of her voice, but recovered quickly.

"Sorry, ma'am. Don't smoke anymore." He turned to see the figure of a woman leaned against the wall of the bar, shrouded in shadow.

"Too bad," she said, putting a cigarette in her mouth. "Now I need to think of a different conversation starter." A flicker of flame illuminated a portion of her face for a moment. She clicked the lighter closed and shoved it in the pocket of her leather jacket. The end of her cigarette glowed brightly before she yanked it out of her mouth. Smoke rose lazily around her head while he stood by in stunned recognition.

"I thought you'd left," he muttered in astonishment.

"I just came out for a smoke like I always do."

He smirked and looked over his shoulder at the sign on the door. "You know you can smoke inside at this one, right?"

"Old habits, I guess," she sighed and bit the inside of her jaw, turning her gaze to the dimly lit street. "That whiskey?" she asked, nodding to the bottle in his hand.

He raised it slightly before answering, "Water's for teardrops, Dickel's for drinkin'."

"I've found the two go hand in hand in most occasions," she said in a soft, velvety tone.

"It's just a sayin'," he smiled. "Merle Haggard."

"I don't know who that is."

"You should check him out. If you like old country anyway."

She smiled a long smile, her closed lips stretching into a straight line. "You know," she started after another drag on her cigarette, "if you get someone in on the harmonica, it could really add a nice flare to 'God Bless a Sniper'."

"You'll have to take that up with Mike. That one's

technically his song."

"Should have guessed," she let out a tense laugh and raised a trembling hand to her mouth.

He took a step towards her to get a better view of her in the shadows, a step she subtly reciprocated in the opposite direction. "What's your name?" he asked, undaunted by her reservations.

"Joanna," she lifted her sharp chin as she spoke.

"Nice to finally meet you, Joanna. I'm Owen," he introduced himself with a smile, extending his hand toward her. She leaned forward tentatively but gave a surprisingly firm handshake.

"Mind if I call you Jo?" he asked, mustering up some charm.

"Please don't."

"Okay then," he laughed it off. He stuck his hands in his pockets, hoping the awkward silence wouldn't last for long.

"Good show in there," she pointed her cigarette to the bar behind them.

"Thanks," he grunted. He needed a drink but didn't reach for his whiskey again. "Want to head back in? I can buy you a beer or somethin' stronger if that's what you like."

"Next stop, Augusta, yeah?" she blatantly ignored his question.

"Yeah," he furrowed his brow in confusion.

"Well, I guess I'll be seeing you in Georgia then." Dropping her cigarette to the pavement and stamping it out, she set off across the lot to a motorcycle parked against the curb near the van. He scrambled for something to say in an attempt to keep her around, but all coherent thought deserted him.

"What no helmet?" he called after her, immediately cursing himself for it. She stopped and turned to look at him. Even from the distance he could clearly see the sad and pensive expression that tightened her lips. Then she revved the engine and peeled out of the parking lot.

Well he'd gotten what he wanted. But it wasn't what he'd expected. What *had* he expected? Some sweet Southern belle who had the hots for an older man? A young woman who fawned over him like some Hollywood movie star? At the very least he'd hoped for a cute smile when he finally introduced himself. No. That illusion evaporated the moment she opened her mouth. Sure, she seemed sweet, but she was closed off, as if she had tangible walls built around her. He couldn't place her accent, but it definitely wasn't Southern. One short conversation with her had left him with more questions than the ones that had plagued him for months.

He kicked at the loose gravel on the pavement and went back to the bar in search of more whiskey. A full week spread out before him until their next meeting in Augusta. Seven days to figure out exactly what to say to her.

"There he is!" Mike yelled when he walked through the door. "The devil himself!" Owen raised an eyebrow at him and gave a sideways grin. He liked Mike better drunk. "I've got a friend here who needs some work on the guitar for a song she's writin'." He winked at Owen and introduced him to his "friend." She was a woman in her early forties with sun-damaged skin and a pretty smile.

"And you are?" he asked her with a pursed smile and a cocked eyebrow, a look that drove the ladies mad when he was younger. It still seemed to have a certain effect on this woman as she blushed, be it from the drinks or timidity he couldn't tell.

"I'm Gail," she grinned. She had heavily lined watery blue eyes, and most of her lipstick had rubbed off on the countless glasses and bottles that had come across her path.

"Nice to meet you, Gail. Tell me about this song of yours."

Mike smacked Owen on the back of the shoulder with a grin and sauntered off. This one would be an easy catch. Not even a catch really. She practically leapt from the water into his boat, entangled in a net he hadn't cast, gutted and ready for the fryer. Her alleged song was clearly a ruse to make conversation with the band. She slid a napkin across the bar to him with a few lines of badly written lyrics scrawled across the surface. She had no real knowledge in music or the structures and patterns needed in creating poetic lyric. But he smiled and laughed at the right cues in order to get her where she needed to be for the night.

Much to his vexation, however, as Gail rambled on about something he wasn't paying attention to, his thoughts kept wandering to Joanna. There was something off about her, yet something quite familiar. He knew her. He could feel it in his bones. He ran his eyes over her in his head, searching for something about her that would trigger a long-forgotten memory. But in all of his recollections, she was cloaked in darkness and smoke. He could only capture the curl of her hair as it blew across her neck like a scarf in the cold mountain breeze and the savage point of her cleft chin as she jut it out when he finally asked for her name. The way she held her cigarette, not delicately between the tips of her fingers like most women but like the trigger of a gun with her thumb on the butt of it, flicking the ashes off the tip as though pulling back the hammer. How her hand had trembled with an unknown anxiety and how she'd stilled on her bike, arms hanging loosely with her hands wrapped lightly around the handles. The way that she'd sped off without so much as a glance back in his direction.

Well that part was all too familiar.

"Come on, Gail," he smiled, pushing the redhead from his thoughts. "How about you and me go somewhere quiet? What do you say?"

Chapter Two

Brighton, Alabama

Owen pissed in the gravel by the tire with distaste. God, he hated Alabama. Especially in the autumn. Give their universities a few national championships for their football teams and they think they own the South. Before they know your name, Alabamians ask who your team is. God forbid someone answer with the Tennessee Volunteers. If anything could calm the infamous Alabama and Auburn rivalry for even a minute, it would be their mutual hatred for the Vols. Cocky bastards.

He spit with more distaste, zipping his pants as he meandered toward the local diner where the rest of the band waited for their breakfasts. At ten in the morning in a sleepy part of town, they were the only ones inside. Pans clanged against counters in the kitchen, punctuating the silence with its racket. Alan Jackson's "Where I Come From" rang softly from a radio on the counter. A now half emptied pot of coffee awaited him at the table. With an aching back, he slumped down into one of the vacant chairs and poured himself a mug of the steaming drink.

"Why are we even here?" he grumbled.

"Chad had to go see his mother this mornin'," Mike explained with a sardonic tone. "She's about to kick the bucket. Don't be insensitive, geezer." Chad rolled his eyes at his menu but didn't add to the conversation.

Owen tore open a packet of sugar with too much force. It ripped in half, spreading the innumerable white grains across the table. Mike grinned his amusement through the side of his mouth as he chewed pointlessly on a toothpick. Chad gave him a hard look and sighed in aggravation, flipping the meat of his palm across the red painted plywood to wipe off the sugar in front of him. Owen ignored them and grabbed another packet as a large woman in a tight t-shirt approached the table, pulling a pad of notebook paper from her apron to take their orders.

"I'll just get a number two with extra hash brown casserole," Chad ordered, handing her the menu with a polite grin. Milo lifted his coffee mug and waved her off. Mike crossed his arms on the table and leaned forward with intrigue.

"I'll have a plate of bacon and gravy biscuit with a side order of you," he winked. The waitress flushed and wrote down his order.

"Lord, Mike, would you give it a rest?" Chad grunted. "It's too early in the morning for that crap." Mike grinned impishly and winked at the waitress again.

"For you, sir?" she asked in Owen's direction, still a shade too pink.

"Eggs," he grunted. "With some kind of meat." Her mouth opened to say something, but she thought better of it and bustled away.

"Seriously, Michael, get some class," Chad grumbled under his breath.

"Somebody's peachy this mornin'," Mike dismissed him and leaned further onto the table to face Owen. "Did you have fun with Gail the other night or did she go home with a younger, more capable man?"

"Can we go one day without you picking at him?" Chad groaned. "I swear you're worse than any of Laurel's boyfriends."

"Laurel's never had any boyfriends," Mike corrected with a high voice and a scrunched face.

"How do you know that?"

"You brag about it all the dang time! How she's got god-like high standards or some crap. Yeah, let me tell you, your daughter ain't no saint. That girl just likes to play the field and not bring any of them home to meet the parents."

Owen ignored the ensuing argument and gulped down the bitter coffee. Milo silently observed, his eyes flicking between the two men as though he could predict what each would say in turn. Within minutes, their table was full of food, which silenced the argument for the time being. Chad seethed over his plate while Milo sipped at his coffee and tucked a strand of stray hair behind his ear. Owen was greeted by a plate of just about everything the diner had on the menu. Except grits. He forgot the grits.

"Mm, that looks good," said a voice beside him. His head jolted up more quickly than he would have liked. She was pulling up a chair to the end of their table by the time his eyes rose to take her in. A smile teased his lips without his permission, and he pushed it away in the hopes that she hadn't noticed it. He'd never seen her in daytime before, and in the white light of the fluorescents, she was difficult to recognize. Her hair, much more orange than he remembered, was pulled loosely back beneath a baseball cap, and her freckled skin had an almost sickly pallor to it. Her cheeks were sharp, and dark shadows ran under her eyes. She wore ripped jeans with hiking boots and a faded Temple of the Dog t-shirt that bagged as though meant for someone of much larger stature. When the waitress approached her, she smiled politely, flashing oddly white teeth, and asked for coffee.

"You must be Joanna," Mike addressed her with a mouth full of bacon, leaning forward on his elbows to get a better look at her.

"You've heard of me, huh?" she smiled gracefully, color rising slightly to the translucent skin of her cheeks.

"Yeah, you stalk Owen," he answered matter-of-factly with a grin and a piece of bacon lodged between his teeth. Joanna's eyes widened, and she laughed sheepishly. Chad shook his head and muttered an apology for the bass player's behavior.

"I guess it could seem like stalking, couldn't it? I'm just," she paused in contemplation, "an avid fan."

"Well it's nice to finally meet you, Joanna," Chad offered politely. "Officially. If you don't already know, I'm Chad Wilkes. This is Milo Schroeder, our drummer, and that's Michael Butner, the bane of my existence." Mike smiled impishly and winked across the table.

"So where you from, Jo?" he asked.

"Oh, you know, here and there. I don't really stay in one place for very long," she smiled nervously and averted the attention from herself. "What about you guys?"

"You know where Osceola is?" Mike asked, chewing loudly on a mound of hash browns soaked in ketchup.

"I don't think so."

"Arkansas. Small town about an hour from Memphis. That's home for me."

"Do you still live there now when you're not on the road?" she asked, pouring herself a cup of coffee.

"Yeah," Owen interrupted with a snort, "he still lives in his Mom's basement."

Milo smirked and eyed Joanna over the rim of his mug.

"Tell me, geezer," Mike started with a mischievous grin, licking his lips in preparation for the insult brewing in his head, pausing for effect. He pointed his fork at Owen as he theatrically swallowed his food, "does that ex-wife of yours still pay your bills?"

"What else good is marriage for?" he quipped. Mike laughed and shrugged in agreement.

"I was born and raised here in Brighton," Chad tried to steer the conversation back to Joanna's question. "I live in Memphis with my wife and daughter, but I've got family here still."

"Ex-wife," Owen corrected with his mug in his mouth, looking off as though he hadn't said anything. He could feel Chad's scowl as it burned into the side of his face.

"Memphis sounds nice," Joanna commented, eyeing Owen with playful reprimand.

"It's a great place if you love music," said Owen.

"Is that where you're from too?"

"No, I grew up in Fayetteville, Tennessee. Know where that is?" She bit her upper lip with a set of gleaming bottom teeth and shook her head. "I didn't think so. It's about fifteen minutes north of the Alabama state line. I moved to Nashville when I graduated high school. Then Memphis in my thirties."

"That sounds nice," she said, her smile unwavering. She was starting to remind Owen of the Joker from the nineteen sixties Batman movies. "What about you, Milo?" she asked, turning her head to the drummer.

"New York," Milo said out of the side of his twisted mouth.

"I loved New York when I went!" she beamed with the first hint of enthusiasm. "Did you live in the city?"

"The Bronx."

"Oh. We never left Manhattan, I don't think."

"Most tourists don't." Milo's replies were characteristically short, but this didn't deter the inquisitive redhead. She cocked her head questioningly at him and started to say something when Mike made a scene of clearing his throat.

"So, Jo, is that your bike out there?"

"Yeah," she answered, turning in her seat to look at her motorcycle through the window. Mike winked sideways at Milo, who sipped his coffee unresponsively.

"Harley?"

"Honda," she smirked at him. "But nice guess."

"Bet you feel stupid," Owen gibed.

"You better watch yourself, geezer," Mike warned, pointing his fork at Owen again. Owen lifted his hands in mock surrender while Joanna laughed. It was a soft, colorless laugh, yet it made him grin.

Joanna never ordered any food. She just sipped at her coffee and offered up pieces of conversation when necessary. Her smile seemed too careful to Owen, as though nothing about it was genuine. Her eyes were dull, and her lids drooped as though sleep was something elusive to her. He wanted to hold her and stroke her hair while she told him about her life, but he shook away the thought as quickly as it had come. Those kinds of thoughts led to love. Love led to marriage. And he wasn't any good at that.

She said her goodbyes and climbed onto the back of her motorcycle with promises to see them again in Augusta. Owen watched her drive off until she was a miniscule dot in the distance.

"I like her," Chad said when Owen lowered himself into the back seat of their decrepit skeleton of a GMC conversion van. "She seems like a very nice gal."

"Bet she'd be real nice in bed," Mike chimed in beside him, leaned back with his legs spread out, his head lolled back on the seat. He gave an open-mouthed grin at Owen when Chad groaned in overwhelming frustration.

"Christ, Michael, do you have to foul every conversation?" Chad shouted as he threw the van in drive and sped out of the parking lot. They were several miles down the interstate when his relentless berating finally ended. He put a Hank Williams disk in the CD player as they resumed their trek to Augusta. Milo sat in the passenger seat, routinely calling out each notable town that they passed in a low grunt, marking their distance traveled. Mike interrupted after every quarter hour with a complaint or inappropriate comment, while Owen let his thoughts wander to Joanna.

Something beyond her red curls reminded him of his mother. She couldn't be much older than thirty, yet she bore the same bent, worn out expression that the haggard woman used to wear when she thought her young son wasn't looking. The way she sat quietly back in her chair with sagging shoulders and her hands folded in her lap, listening to a bunch of men share stories about the road and argue about what was and wasn't socially acceptable for Mike to say in a public environment, only speaking up when the others' questions were directed at her. She even had the same bony elbows, which threatened to burst through the thin, sallow skin when she crossed her arms. When she smiled, her face was engraved with premature lines that dug into her face with a ruthless passion.

He found himself captivated by her with an insatiable desire to know more, but he simply shrugged her out of his head and adjusted his position in the seat to alleviate the stiffness in his back. Joanna was just a fan and nothing more. He couldn't let himself get wrapped up in another person's life again. He wasn't that man anymore.

Chapter Three

I-95

"What is this crap?" Mike grumbled from the back seat, banging his head on the headrest in exasperation.

"We agreed Milo could choose the music when he drives," Chad explained for what felt like the fifteenth time, pinching the bridge of his nose.

"That doesn't answer my question," came his aggravated response.

Owen grunted his displeasure and picked up Milo's phone from the cup holder. "Vanna," he tossed over his shoulder, hoping the answer would silence him.

"I don't like it," Mike growled, crossing his arms like a defiant toddler.

"We know," Chad sighed.

I-95 splayed before them in a sun-cracked stretch of monotonous asphalt and tree lining, putting everyone's nerves on the edge of a knife. Minutes of silence, filled with Milo's selection of screaming rock music, trudged on in the lapses in conversation, accented at every chorus by Mike's guttural groaning.

"Buy some headphones before the next leg, will you?" Chad ordered. "But in the meantime we should probably talk about 'Story of a Fool', we can't seem to get the bridge to – "

"For god's sake, Chad," Mike yelled, throwing his head back against the seat with an intensity that would have cracked his skull if not for the padded cushion, lolling it around to gawk at their front man. "We have three days until the next show, can we talk about something other than technique for once?"

"Because you're so full of appropriate conversation topics," Chad snapped. "Tell me, Michael, what would you rather talk about? I'm all ears."

"Just to save us all some time," three heads jerked in the direction of Milo's low, husky voice, "he's going to say women."

"Hey, now there's a good subject," Mike piped up, leaning forward to clap his approval on the driver's shoulder. "Did anyone notice that chick with the blue hair last night?" He continued on in his shallow conversation with only a few interjections from the others.

Owen ignored Mike's growing monologue and watched Milo, grinning slightly in contemplation. The youngest member's gangly, veined arms were stretched out in front of him, gripping the steering wheel with whitening knuckles. They were arms that were graced with sporadic ink in no particular order. Two thick, black bands encircled his arm beneath his elbow. Across his inner forearm, etched in black, was calligraphy illegible to Owen. The symbols and writing were made to look as though carved into his skin, with inked swelling and dripping blood surrounding the edges. Elaborate roman numerals were written on each of his fingers. On his wrist a human skull rested with deep, hollow, penetrating eyes. A dead tree branched from the top of the skull with its roots encircling down on the top of the head, wrapping its tendrils chokingly around it. More images and writing decorated his biceps but were concealed beneath the black long-sleeved t-shirt that was casually pushed up to his elbows.

In the years that had passed since he and Milo met, Owen had uncovered nothing whatsoever as to the meaning of any of his numerous tattoos, but beneath the wide bands on his forearm, the skin was mangled and scarred from wounds badly healed. Milo never spoke about his past. He rarely spoke at all. But no one questioned him. It was a balance that none argued with when Mike was around.

"I think I preferred the silence," Chad complained, interrupting a running narrative of Mike's latest scandalous adventures.

"Come on, man," Mike grunted, "not all of us have a wife waitin' for us at home."

"Ex-wife," Owen corrected casually, craning his neck to follow a deer that stood at the edge of the tree line.

"Thanks, Owen," Chad replied scathingly. Owen threw a half-hearted salute from the side of his head.

"Okay, explain this to me," Mike turned in his seat to face his boss full on. "You and Sarah got a divorce, right? But neither of you moved out. How does that work?"

"We still haven't told Laurel," Chad answered to his reflection in the window. "We're waiting until she graduates. Don't want to give her any unnecessary distractions. Besides, with us on the road as often as we are, what's really the point in adding another mortgage right now?"

"Whatever," Mike slumped back in his seat, unscrewing the top of his flask. "You're just a bunch of prudes. All of you. Except you, Owen. But do you actually score with these women, or do you lecture them on their poor life choices and get so drunk you pass out and dream of little Miss Elusive Ginge?"

"Jacksonville," Owen called out as they passed the road sign, thankful for the diversion. He couldn't count how many times he'd passed out immediately upon entering his motel room.

"We're only halfway there?" Mike cursed and drank from his flask. The four sat in the silence that ensued while heavy guitar and screaming blared through the speakers. Before the song reached the bridge, Mike groaned loudly and jerked forward, grabbing Milo's phone. "I can't handle it, I'm sorry. Passcode?"

"Two zero zero four," Milo answered blandly.

"Dang," Mike huffed flipping through Milo's music menu, "You're one dark son of a bitch, aren't you? Now ZZ Top is someone I can appreciate." Soon "La Grange" replaced the deep, aggressive tones of "Humaphobia."

"Come on, old farts," he laughed, leaning over Owen, who cursed loudly at Mike's sudden proximity, and rolled down the window. Milo's dimples hid beneath the dark, scraggly beard on his pale face as he rolled his own window down and rested his arm on the door.

The white conversion van throttled down the interstate towards Daytona Beach, Florida, well above the legal limit. The sun had just begun its descent across the afternoon sky when she caught sight of the familiar bumper stickers. She tightened her grip on the handlebars and sped forward, the engine rumbling between the legs of her jeans. She pulled up next to them and slowed to meet their speed.

Milo looked in her direction, greasy strands of his dark hair breaking free from its bondage at the nape of his neck and flying wildly across his forehead. He smirked at her and waved wordlessly to the others in the car to get their attention. Owen leaned forward into view. His translucent eyebrows were knotted together as he squinted at her. Her face was masked behind the shaded visor of her new helmet but the orange braid that fell down between her shoulder blades was unmistakable. He smiled in disbelief. Two gloved fingers tapped the side of her helmet in salutation before she gripped the handlebars and sped off.

"Milo, how fast are you going?" Owen asked, concern etched across his face as he leaned forward, gripping the dashboard with calloused fingers.

"Eighty-five," he answered without checking the speedometer.

"She needs to slow down!" Owen couldn't tell if he was nervous or angry at her recklessness as he watched her slender, leather-clad figure lean over the handlebars and grow increasingly smaller in the distance.

"Leave her alone. That's her father's problem," Mike said absentmindedly. "By the way, if she ever gets bored of you, send her my way."

"If I have any respect at all for that woman, you're the last person I'd send her to."

Mike would have protested had he not been studying Milo's unsuppressed grin with a raised lip and squinted eyes. "Hey Schroeder, answer me this, do you wear eyeliner?" A black eyebrow traveled halfway up Milo's forehead as he shot a glance out of the corner of his eye and shook his head. "You sure?"

"Pretty sure," Milo answered. "I'm Italian and German if that answers your intrusive curiosity."

"An Italian New Yorker," Mike mused. "Shouldn't you be more mouthy then?"

"Leave him alone, Michael," Chad sighed.

"I'm just curious," he defended himself. A boyish grin decorated his tanned face before he continued. "Your pops was in the mafia, wasn't he?"

"Yep. Was yours in the KKK?" Milo quipped. Owen exploded with laughter as even Mike laughed with surprise.

"Easy now," Chad chuckled. "You're in a van full of

Southern boys."

"Just returning the stereotypes, boss," he smirked at the road. Mike's voice soon overrode the laughter as Metallica started to play over the speakers.

"Sorry, I can't do this anymore." He leaned forward to change out Milo's phone for his own. Soon Florida Georgia Line filled the van. Milo didn't protest. Owen watched him for a moment, wondering what had led him to leave the energy of the big city and join of a country band from Memphis.

He smiled out at the dirty windshield and absently stroked his graying chin. His own life hadn't been perfect, but he didn't regret a moment of it. It had taken fifty years but he'd finally found something that worked. Sure the guys didn't get along often, but they worked well together on stage. And that's what really mattered.

Milo pulled the van into the hotel parking lot in Daytona Beach, and the four men climbed out of the van and started unloading their suitcases. Owen threw his arms out and stretched his aching back muscles. He was getting too old for these road trips. He walked towards the back of the van to get his luggage when he saw the motorcycle.

"Looks like Jo's upped her stalker game," he chuckled to Milo who smiled crookedly in response.

"I checked us all in," Chad said, handing each of them their door keys. "Get unpacked and settled. We can't practice at the Crab Shack until Friday morning, and the rooms around us are booked. Since we aren't in our usual motels, we can't practice until Friday. So just enjoy the beach, I guess."

Owen took his key card and headed for his room on the sixth floor of the hotel. The door slid open noisily. He lumbered in and let his suitcase drop to the floor, helping himself to a drink from the mini bar, and collapsed on the bed. Flipping on the television, he scanned through the channels. He settled on an old John Wayne film and ordered a pizza for dinner. He was asleep by ten.

* * * * *

Daytona Beach, Florida

Owen stumbled off the platform of the Crab Shack. Since their arrival to Daytona Beach, he'd had a constant flow of alcohol that didn't agree with public performance. He'd flubbed up the bridge of "Wandering Eyes", missed a cue in the chorus of "A Good Man's Heart", and entirely forgot how to play "Where She Ran Off To", but at the moment he didn't care. He waved off Chad's lecture and packed his Telecaster in its case before making his way back into the restaurant in search of Joanna.

He found her at a table in the corner, engaged in an enthusiastic conversation with Milo, who leaned his elbow on the table with his head in his hand, watching her with an amused grin that squinted his eyes. She turned her attention to Owen as he approached. "Oh, good! Settle our argument."

"You're having an argument," he repeated, stupidly, helping himself to the empty chair beside the drummer, "with Milo Schroeder."

"I got him drunk to see if I could get him to talk, but all he's done is piss me off," she explained hastily. "Who would win in a fight, Iron Man or Batman?"

"Can that even happen?" Owen furrowed his brow in confusion.

"Technically no. They're different comics, but they're the same characters!" Jo argued. She rolled her eyes at Owen's dumbfounded expression and leaned forward with her elbows on the table, using her hands to help explain her strange position. "Both are just your average rich guy with a cool suit and fancy gadgets. Both have butlers that take care of them. Stark's just happens to be artificial intelligence. But I'm telling you, they're parallels!"

Owen pondered for a minute, amused at the excitement in her drunken eyes. "I'd say Iron Man."

"Ha!" Jo pointed to Milo, who smiled his defeat at his beer. "I told you! Iron Man can fly. You can't beat someone who can fly away from you."

"But Batman looks cooler," he argued, his head sliding

closer to the table as his elbow skid further away from him.

"That wasn't the question, though, was it?" she raised an eyebrow at him.

"You two are strange," Owen remarked, momentarily captivated by the new authenticity in Joanna's smile. Behind the drooping eyes and sallow cheeks, she was possibly one of the most beautiful women he'd ever seen. "Are you comin' with us to Tallahassee, Jo?" he asked.

"Joanna," she corrected, waving a pointed finger at him, staring down her finger like the scope of a gun as she tried to aim it at him.

"Are you comin' to Tallahassee, *Joanna*?" he laughed.

"That's the plan."

"And then Jackson after that?"

She nodded.

"Well why don't you just ride with us?"

"That'd be nice," she answered, her words beginning to slur as she took another drink of her beer. "But I've got my motorcycle. I can't just leave it here."

"We'll make Mike drive it," he shrugged. "It'd give us a much needed break from the bastard."

"Are you sure?"

"Of course! We'd love to have you."

"Sounds good," she grinned childishly. "As long as I can make out with Milo in the backseat." Milo let out a wheezing laugh and fell to the table, making Jo guffaw so loudly that it silenced the table next to them. Owen kept his grin plastered to his face, a sudden anger flashing in his gut as he eyed the drummer.

Just then, Jo's phone vibrated against the table. Her laughter stopped abruptly, the smile evaporating from her face, becoming once again the frown that left deep lines like parentheses around her mouth. She stared down at the glowing screen with that sullen expression without silencing or answering the commanding peal.

"You not gonna answer that?" he asked curiously.

"No," she shook her head and blinked heavily. "Don't recognize the number." The way she stared at the screen suggested otherwise. Owen shot Milo a questioning glace, but the man simply shrugged and leaned back in his seat, taking another drink of his beer.

"Hey!" Mike appeared beside him, wrapping a heavy arm around his shoulder. The heavy stench of tequila came off of him in waves as he spoke in Owen's ear in a failed attempt to whisper with a beer bottle by his mouth, acting as a blind to keep what he had to say a secret. "There's a blonde over at the bar. And she's real damn sexy and super drunk. And she's got a friend, so you need to come with me."

"Not tonight, Mike," Owen grunted and pulled himself from his chair. Ignoring the ensuing protest, he left the bar, breathing in heavily, and took a hefty pull from his bottle of Dickel before setting off toward the hotel. It was one in the morning by the time he got to his room, but instead of sitting in front of the television for the fourth night in a row, he opted for the balcony. Outside, a sharp wind blew humidity and slimy sea salt into his face, plastering his thin curls to his forehead. The starless sky was a deep black, but he could see the moonlight reflect off of the waves ahead of him like shards of broken glass clanking together as they crashed against the shore. He collapsed into the lounge chair and took another pull from the bottle.

He'd lost track of how long he sat in the salty chair when the gate to the pool below creaked open and slammed shut. He stood to peer over the rails, and what he saw made his heart sink like a stone thrown in a pond. Milo had Joanna by the hand, leading her towards the shallow end of the pool. She tripped over her own feet and giggled loudly. Milo laughed too but shushed her with a finger to his lips. He stripped down to his boxer shorts and dove headlong into the pool. Joanna followed after him. They waded through the water, giggling drunkenly and splashing, unconsciously gravitating toward one another until her arms were clasped around his shoulders.

Realizing then that he was intruding on an intimate moment, Owen retreated to his room, slamming the balcony door shut behind him. He fell heavily onto the bed and tried not to think as he sank into a deep slumber.

Chapter Four

Cherokee Landing
Malakoff, Texas

Owen leaned against the side of the rented RV and bobbed a toothpick between his teeth, staring out at the lake before him. The falling sun cast elongated shadows of the trees across the edge of the water, which made the branches dance like ghostly marionettes with long, knotted arms along its sparkling surface. Beneath the pink and orange sky, the lake expanded like a blackening void, broken only by the plops of a jumping fish and the hum of a motorboat that cut through the glassy water. Frogs and crickets were beginning to wake and sing their nocturnal melodies, and the shouts and laughter of a group of children in a nearby camper overcame the natural lullabies.

Mike was off somewhere introducing himself to their temporary neighbors, his hearty laugh traveling from some unknown distance, and Chad paced nervously, muttering loud and incoherent fragments into his iPhone. Milo walked toward the boat pier a little ways off with his greasy hair tied back, barely enough to fit in the rubber band. He handed a beer to Jo, who stood staring out at the water with her arms crossed, smoke rising from a cigarette trapped in her fingers. She smiled softly at Milo's approach, took his hand, and pulled him back towards the campsite.

Owen moved to the designated fire pit, stoking the pitiful heap of twigs and smoking leaves until it became a suitable fire. He grabbed his acoustic Ibanez by the neck and slumped down into one of the dirty lawn chairs that circled the fire pit. Taking a swig of Dickel, he plucked a string. It rang out flat. He twisted the corresponding peg slightly and plucked the string again, repeating the process with every string until his guitar was in tune. He played absentmindedly, running his fingers lazily along the fret board, and watched Jo and Milo stroll along the embankment towards the RV.

"Know any Alice Cooper?" she asked him when they reached the campsite. She plopped down in the chair next to him with Milo at her side.

"Can't say that I do," Owen answered.

"Shame." She drummed her fingers against the armrests in the silence that followed, keeping with the beat of Owen's guitar.

A white Honda CR-V crunched along the gravel lane and came to a stop behind their van. A short, thin girl with long brown hair and bright eyes rolled the window down and waved before cutting the engine. Chad rushed from the RV to meet her with a wrapping embrace and a brilliant smile.

"Must be Laurel," Jo guessed. Owen nodded to his front man's daughter in greeting. Jo stood to introduce herself. Owen smirked when she stiffened at the girl's friendly hug.

"There she is!" Mike came from around the corner. "How's my favorite high school graduate?" He wrapped Laurel in a hug that the girl was all too eager to return.

"I'm awesome!" she beamed, holding on to Mike for a moment too long. "Finally free of the shackles and bonds of public education! How's my favorite guitarist?"

"Bass guitarist, Laurel," Owen corrected her. Laurel lifted her hand to flick him off without taking her eyes off of Mike. Jo's mouth formed a tight O as she turned her wide eyes to a smirking Owen.

"I like her," she laughed.

Chad fired up the grill and soon filled the picnic table with burgers and hotdogs. The band grew silent as they stuffed their faces with the first hint of real food after weeks of fast food drive-thru restaurants and cheap roadside cafés while Laurel chattered on, mostly to Mike, about her senior year of high school. Jo held her hand over her mouth to cut in while chewing.

"You saw Smashing Pumpkins in concert?"

"Yeah! They were awesome! Do you like them?" Laurel answered energetically.

"Like them? I lived in Seattle for six years. I mean the grunge scene isn't what it was before Kurt Cobain, but I knew a guy who basically lived and breathed grunge metal. I didn't know Smashing Pumpkins were still around though."

"They're not as popular as they used to be," Laurel shrugged, "but they had a killer sound! My ears were ringing for days! And I had to take the ACT exam the next morning."

"I bet that was rough," Jo laughed.

Mike brought out a few cases of beer, and they all headed for the fire pit. Owen went to the RV for a whiskey before tending to the fire. Jo pulled a pack of Pall Malls from her jacket pocket.

"Hey, can I get one of those?" Laurel asked. Jo looked disconcerted for a moment before shrugging and handing her the pack. She put one in her mouth and took a light from Milo while her father stared in disbelief.

"You smoke now?"

"I'm eighteen, Dad. It's legal."

"Yeah, but it's gross!" he protested.

"Come on. All of y'all do it. Except Owen because he's old and could die." Owen shot her a playful disgusted look but didn't respond to the insult.

"But it's gross when girls do it. No offense, Jo," Chad eyed her apologetically. Jo waved her hand as if shooing away the comment.

"And who gave you a beer?" Chad's voice rose an octave when he noticed the bottle in his daughter's hand.

"I did," Mike answered for her with a shrug. "She's almost in college, Chad. Better she drink with us than unsupervised. That's how she gets into trouble and ends up with a baby. Or do like me and climb a water tower in the middle of a thunderstorm for a dare."

"You did that?" Laurel eyed him with awe.

"But she's underage, Michael!" Chad yelled before Mike could respond.

"Daddy, it's no big deal. It's just this one, I promise."

The argument sputtered on for a few minutes until all three parties decided to give up. Owen kept playing his guitar. Struggling with the tense silence, Laurel spat out the first thing that popped into her head. "If you were a body part, what would you be?" Her theatrical smile faltered only momentarily at the realization of how absurd she sounded.

"What?" Mike laughed in astonishment.

"Come on," Laurel encouraged, leaning over to grab his arm. "Just answer the question."

"I'd be the hands," Chad interrupted with a grunt before Mike had the chance to speak, "so I could repeatedly punch whatever part Michael is."

Jo snorted. "We all know what part Mike would be. You might want to change your mind, Chad."

Laurel tried not to laugh, but it escaped through her throat anyway in short, choked bursts. Mike pointed at Jo with a good-humored warning while Chad groaned his disapproval. "Christ! Can we not keep it rated PG? My daughter is *right there*!"

Mike raised his hands in surrender and laughed. "Hey, I didn't do it this time!"

"*I* would be the feet," Jo announced before Chad could reprimand her. "So I could go anywhere I wanted."

"Even if you could go wherever you wanted, you'd still stalk Owen," Mike quipped. Jo rolled her eyes and threw a rock across the fire at him, which he dodged with ease.

"What would you be?" she asked, turning her attention to Owen, who had been sitting quietly strumming his guitar. She gazed at him expectantly, her brown eyes glimmering softly in the light of the fire like two oil lamps spitting tiny balls of flames as they ran out of fuel.

"I don't know," he shrugged.

"The mouth," Mike snapped his fingers with the epiphany. "He couldn't drink his George Dickel if he wasn't the mouth." He held out his arms and cocked his head as though waiting for them to all applaud their approval.

"Oh, that's true," Jo nodded her agreement.

"I can be the brain," Laurel piped in. "Since I'm going to college, and none of you except Dad could finish high school in a timely manner."

"That works," Mike agreed, casually holding out his arm, shooting her the bird with his hand in her face. She shoved his arm away, holding onto his wrist for longer than was necessary, running her fingertips into his palm. "Which would leave Milo with either the stomach or the heart," Mike stated, slightly distracted.

"I'll take the heart," Milo shrugged.

"There," Mike grinned and stood from his chair. "We are one big, ugly body now. I can rest easy." He emptied the rest of the contents of his bottle with a renewed thirst and tossed it in the direction of the trashcan. "Night y'all." They all muttered their goodnights as Mike ambled toward the RV, scratching the back of his neck with his head turned down to his feet. Laurel watched him over her shoulder.

"He's so hot," she purred to Jo.

"Oh, gross!" she guffawed.

"Hey!" Chad interjected, overhearing the comment. Milo smirked, leaning back against Jo as she shook with laughter, her arm thrown casually down his shoulder with her hand on his chest. He reached up to play with her fingers as he watched Chad turn a new shade of red, sputtering like the dying engine of an old pickup truck. "You've only been here a few hours, and you're already – no – he's forty-one, Laurel!" Chad struggled to form his sentences.

"But she's not too young for him, you know," Milo added. Jo pulled her hand away from his to pop the side of his head without much conviction.

"Stop it," she laughed, leaving her fingers there to entangle them in his hair.

"I think I liked you better when you didn't talk," Chad shook his head and took a swig of his beer. Laurel shrugged with a sheepish grin.

Owen remained silent throughout the exchange, staring over the flames at Jo. She was wearing that same Temple of the Dog t-shirt that she always wore, and her curly hair was tossed over her left shoulder in its usual manner, but all day she'd seemed somehow different. The glow of the fire glinted in her dark eyes and melded with the red of her hair, setting her complexion ablaze. Her smile contained an authenticity that he'd only seen once before: two months ago on the day he asked her to travel with them. And her hearty laughter pulled at the corners of his own lips with its almost bewitching music.

Milo would probably agree. Milo, who sat on the blanketed ground with his head leaned back on her shoulder as her thin fingers laced through his dirty hair. Milo, who kept turning to look at her as though he thought she only existed when his eyes held her to the Earth. But Jo's gaze was always fixed on Laurel and Chad, mesmerized by their interactions, staring intently as though taking mental notes. Owen watched her smile turn sad, and he could almost see a thousand thoughts race through her head. When she turned unexpectedly to him, he was surprised at the depth in her eyes, as if she'd unintentionally let down her walls so he could really look at her, into her very soul. She turned away hastily and whispered to Milo.

"So, Jo, are you from Seattle then? Or Memphis like the rest of them." Laurel's question interrupted his thoughts.

"Oh, no," Jo answered. "I moved to Seattle when I was twenty-four. And I've never even been to Memphis."

"You should definitely come then! It's a beautiful city," Laurel beamed.

"Okay," Jo smiled admiringly at the girl.

"So, where's home for you then?"

Jo's smile faltered momentarily, the authenticity evaporating as the Joker grin returned. "I haven't stayed anywhere longer than a month for almost two years now." She averted her eyes and hid her expression with a swig of beer and a kiss to Milo's hair.

"That sounds awesome!" Laurel exclaimed. "That's what some of my friends and I are doing from August to October. Only in Europe."

"Europe?" Chad interrupted.

"We've been planning it for months, Daddy," she shrugged. "And we've all got tons of graduation money that we don't know what to do with."

"What about college?"

"I'm still going. I'm just starting a semester later than we planned."

"But, Laurel – "

"I lived in London for four years," Jo chimed in before another argument could arouse. Chad glared at her for the interruption.

"No way! That's what I'm most excited for!" Laurel interrogated Jo emphatically on the dos and don'ts of life in London while Owen sat in a stunned silence, attempting to picture Jo in the English capital. It occurred to him just how little he really knew about this roadie of theirs.

"Are you gonna answer that?" Laurel stopped rambling about her outrageous expectations when Jo's phone started ringing.

Jo shook her head. "No, it's probably just a telemarketer or something." As always she made no move to silence the ringing or decline the call. She simply stared at the screen, the white glare shining on her face, giving Owen a clear view as her expression relaxed and her eyes closed as though a tension previously unnoticed was released by the incessant chiming. "I think you'd like Seattle," she said when the ringing stopped and she turned back to her avid audience. "It'd be a great place for you to get started in your photo journalism if you still want to pursue that after college."

Forgetting Joanna's strange reaction to the phone call, Laurel throttled back into the conversation, raving on about her extravagant plans.

"I'm going to bed," Chad announced, the conversation topics making him more nervous and agitated as they went along. "You should, too."

"Okay, I'm getting kind of tired anyway," Laurel smiled. "Night, guys."

Owen stared at Jo as she watched Chad and Laurel walk towards the RV. An unreadable expression flickered across her face.

"I'm calling it a night, too," Milo graced her cheek with a bearded kiss and pulled himself up off the blanket. "Coming?"

"No, I'll hang out here for a bit," Jo answered, absently gazing into the flames. Owen and Jo sat in silence for what seemed like hours to him while he played his guitar.

"Wanna move to a chair?" his cracked voice seemed to boom after the prolonged silence, and he cleared his throat.

"Sure." She moved to sit next to him.

"She's a sweet girl, Laurel," Owen offered casually.

"Yeah, she is," Jo grinned. "She reminds me of someone I knew in high school."

"Poor thing doesn't know what's comin'. Chad's an idiot for keepin' the divorce from her like that."

"I don't know," she mused. "I think it's nice. She got to enjoy her last year of high school before the real world attacks her like a pack of savage dogs." She chewed the inside of her cheek and watched Owen's fingers play deftly at the strings of his guitar. "Think I could play for a bit? It's been a while."

"You play?" he asked in surprise.

"I know a song or two. It's been years, though." He passed

glances between Jo and his Ibanez before handing it off to her. She shifted uncertainly, adjusting the position of the guitar in her lap as though it were a foreign object. Her fingers moved nervously along the fret board until she found the right strings to press. Owen watched her with fascination as she began to strum. Some of the notes rang flat at first. He sniggered to himself as she cursed and restarted. When the sound finally came clear, a proud smile teased the corners of her lips.

"Bad Moon Rising?" Owen guessed, taking another pull from his bottle. Her grin broadened, and she began to sing.

"I see a bad moon rising. I see trouble on the way," she sang with an added country twang to her voice. Owen threw his arms wide with a loud holler of surprise.

"You sing, too?" he couldn't stop the astonished laugh that escaped his mouth. She ignored him, strumming each chord smoothly. Owen tapped his foot along with her and watched her with unreserved captivation until she finished the song and laughed at herself. "Where'd you learn that?" he asked, momentarily spellbound.

"I knew a guy," she answered with a shrug. "He didn't play a lot, but he taught me a few easy songs on rainy days. That's one of the few that isn't grunge rock, though."

"Must've been a lot of rainy days. I'm guessin' Seattle?" Owen's smile was still plastered to his face. He tried not to grimace at the subject change that wasn't as subtle as he would have hoped.

"I love this guitar," she ignored his question with a sigh and handed the Ibanez back to its owner. "It has a beautiful sound."

"It's not so bad," Owen responded with false modesty.

"Liam had a Gretsch." Owen noticed how she seemed to recoil when she said it, as though the statement had rushed from her mouth without her permission, but she recovered quickly and continued. "Chet Atkins hollow body, actually."

"You're lyin'," Owen stared at her in disbelief.

"It was a dark olive green with a golden pick guard," she smiled vacantly at the flames.

"You learned on a Chet Atkins?" he asked, dumbfounded at her casual mention of such a rare guitar. She grinned again and nodded.

"He inherited it from his uncle," she explained. "We didn't know how valuable those are until we sold it."

Owen struggled to form his response. "You sold it?" he finally choked out.

"Had to," she shrugged.

"Why?"

"Call it an unexpected cost of living spike," she said, turning her gaze back to the fire.

"No cost of living spike would be worth sellin' a Chet Atkins."

"Do you have any idea how much it costs to live in Seattle?" she laughed humorlessly. "We'd already gotten rid of my apartment and half of his already scant furniture. Trust me, it was a last resort." A heavy silence followed her answer. Owen brought the bottle to his mouth and studied her face as she gritted her teeth, the muscles in her jaw clenching beneath her ashen skin as she lit another cigarette. From her words, he judged this Liam to have been more than just a guitar teacher.

"Is he the one that calls you every night?" he asked tentatively.

"Yeah," she surprised him with an answer, her voice thick with smoke and agitation.

"Have you ever answered?"

"No."

"Why not?"

"I have nothing that needs saying." She dug the toe of her hiking boot in the dirt.

"He might."

"He doesn't," she snapped. He knew he'd crossed the line, but he couldn't stop himself.

"Is he still in Seattle, then?" he backpedaled, awkwardly attempting to salvage their conversation.

"I don't know," she sighed, her voice growing rigid. "That's where he was when I left them."

"Them?"

She sucked heavily on her cigarette and didn't answer.

"Do you mean Daniel?" he asked. Her head shot in his direction, and she leapt from her chair.

"How do you know that name?" she growled, attempting in vain to keep the desperation out of her voice.

Owen leaned forward in his chair, arms raised in surrender. "You talk in your sleep, Jo. You get pretty loud, and motel walls are pretty thin." She fidgeted for a moment, raking a shaking hand through her hair. Snagging her fingers in a tangle on the top of her scalp, she jerked her hand free and cursed, facing him with glinting eyes that burned in the firelight.

"What other names have you heard?" her voice was unsteady, heavy with a wretchedness that clashed with her external rage.

"Jo – "

"Just tell me."

He paused, unsure of how to respond. "I've only heard four," he started slowly. "Liam, Rosie, Daniel, and Ethan. Usually in that order." She grimaced with each name he listed as though he'd accompanied each with an arrow to her gut.

"Right," she nodded and gritted her teeth again before tossing the cigarette butt into the fire. "*Only* four," she laughed dangerously as her eyes began to glisten and turned to walk toward the RV.

"Jo, wait," he ran after her as she climbed the steps, and he reached for her arm, but she swiveled back to face him before he could touch her. He jerked back in surprise. Her mouth twitched while she fought for words, but her steady brown eyes were fixed on him, looking down at his frantic expression from her new height.

"Don't call me Jo," she finally whispered. Her eyes jumped between each of his. She leaned forward as though about to embrace him but instead turned back to the RV.

"Joanna," he called weakly as she shut the door behind her.

Chapter Five

Little Rock, Arkansas
Day 960

Have you read Zeno's paradox of the Tortoise and Achilles?

A soft breeze blew her hair around her face as the gray, soggy beach met her eyes and momentarily blinded her. Black waves rolled lazily against the shore in a near deafening whisper, frothing with sizzling white bubbles. Sun bleached logs littered the beach, and the tree-covered hills lined the coast in the distance with a layer of fog and mildew. The sky was as gray and heavy as the sand beneath her bare feet as she sunk to her ankles with the receding tide.

Achilles and the tortoise engage in a footrace. Aware of the tortoise's sluggish reputation, the haughty Achilles allows the tortoise a head start of a hundred meters.

She could hear him. Telling one of his mindboggling stories of philosophers long dead. She shot her head in the direction of his voice. He was sitting with one leg stretched out in front of him and the other pulled in. His black hair flipped out from under the toboggan that covered his ears. Her heart jolted forward seconds before her legs did. She raced toward him, her feet digging into the sand, propelling her onward.

Each racer travels at a constant speed. Achilles feels confident that with his strong, swift legs he will beat the tortoise to the finish line.

She ran to him faster than she had run away. Her chest burned not from the exertion but from exhilaration. Joy flooded through her body at the chance to make things right. The chance to make amends.

But before Achilles can pass the tortoise, he must first catch up.

She was halfway there, and with every step the image of him became clearer and clearer. She could just see the way his eyes wrinkled with his smile as he looked down at the little girl in his lap. She kept running, tears stabbing at her eyes but not yet blurring the perfect picture before her.

By the time Achilles reaches the tortoise's starting point, the tortoise has moved, creating a new gap. This gap is smaller, but the tortoise is still in the lead.

She should have gotten there by now. They should have heard her coming. She pushed harder, ran faster, ignoring the burn in her lungs that began to spread into her limbs.

As Achilles races to close the second gap, the tortoise has moved, producing yet another gap that Achilles now has to close.

She stopped. They were mere steps before her. She could see them perfectly. The man with the shining black eyes and the same unshaven face and the little one who held his hands and leaned back against him. Her curls were black like his, and they brushed across her forehead in the breeze. Her eyes were huge and black. A tear fell down her soft, round cheek. He looked down at her and laughed without sound. His lips moved silently as he spoke to her. She smiled and wiped a chubby hand across her face. He shook with his soundless laughter and wrapped his arms around her while she giggled.

Wanting nothing more than to hold them both in her own arms, she tried to close the distance. Panic gnawed at her insides when she realized regardless of how many steps she took, they kept moving away from her.

Mathematically speaking, no matter how quickly Achilles can close these gaps, the tortoise will always be in the lead, just beyond his reach.

She fell to her knees, sinking into the damp sand. They were inches in front of her. She called out to them, but the wind blew her words back into her face. She yelled for them, screamed their names, but they didn't hear her. They just kept laughing, watching something out at sea. She reached out to touch them. If they could just feel her, maybe they'd know she was with them. But her hand never made contact.

She screamed and beat her fists into the sand not taking

her eyes off them. Tears began to fill her eyes, blinding her.

No. Her tears wouldn't fall. They rose in her eyes like a black sheet, blocking her view of them. *No. No. No! NO!* She yelled their names in the dark. Why couldn't they hear her? Why couldn't she get to them?

She reached her hand out into the darkness, searching for them, but something cold and hard met her fingers. She pressed her hand against it. The frozen metal warmed slightly as the ice crept up her arm. She jerked her hand back, and her vision began to return.

A white mustang. Torn and broken. Wrapped around the trunk of a tree. Bile burned in her throat as she struggled with the image. Climbing to her feet, she ran to the car and pushed it away from the tree. It gave with little resistance. The rumpled passenger door fell from its hinges, revealing the boy inside. She ran to him and fell to her knees. Her fingers brushed gently across his forehead, moving the blood-matted hair away from his face. His blue eyes were pale and unfocused, lifeless. A sob gagged her, stifling his name in her throat. She wrapped her arms around him and pulled him from the car. He lay motionless and cold in her lap as she cradled him, rocked him. She tried to apologize, tried to tell him how much she loved him, tried to call him back to her, but her voice was trapped inside of her. She only held him closer, feeling his cool blood seep into her shirt.

She squeezed him against her, hoping to stop her own internal bleeding with his body. She would never let him go. She could never leave him.

Suddenly his frigid body evaporated, leaving her cradling air. She gasped heavily as oxygen violently returned to her. She screamed at the top of her lungs, his name searing her throat like liquid fire as she searched for him, for any sign of where he'd gone. She stumbled through the icy forest calling out his name.

"Audrey!" shouted a stern voice that stopped her in her tracks. She panted and heaved with tearless sobs, trying to ignore the way her brother's blood froze on her skin. "Why did you leave us, Audrey?"

She pivoted on her unsteady legs to face him. He stood before her like she had last seen him. A man grown but with the eyes of a boy. He walked towards her, limping heavily, staggering with the pain in his mangled, twisted leg yet his face showed no sign of physical anguish. As he got closer, his expression distorted with a rage that burned behind his piercing eyes. He grabbed her by the arms and shook her.

"Where were you? Why did you abandon me? I was so lost, so alone, and you deserted me," he spat viciously while she blubbered incoherently and sobbed.

"I – I, Ethan – I'm sorry –" she choked.

"You killed him! You killed my brother! You *murdered him!*"

"I'm sorry, Ethan. I'm so, so sorry." Her legs began to give out. She sank to the ground, but he came with her, still clutching her arms, still shouting maliciously in her face.

"Joanna."

"Ethan. Please."

"Joanna, wake up."

Audrey shuddered to consciousness. Every muscle in her body was tensed and shaking. She held back the tears that weren't allowed to escape in the dream and sat up, throwing her legs over the side of the bed.

"I'm sorry," she whispered when she'd somewhat composed herself.

"Are you okay?"

She put on a smile before turning to face Milo. "Yeah, go back to sleep."

Owen sat up in his bed in the next room and rubbed his temples, burying his face in his hands. Those names again. He'd woken to them so often now that the surprise factor had diminished. On nights like tonight, she'd wake everyone up before Milo finally decided to end her suffering sleep. If you could call it sleep. Why the man didn't wake her up when her dreams started, Owen would never understand.

Cursing to himself, he jerked back the blankets and made his way to the window. Jamming his finger through the blinds and pulling them down, he could see her sitting on the curb in her comic book pajama pants and leather jacket, cigarette in hand. Before he could talk himself out of his decision, he jerked the door open and stepped out into the cool June air.

"Curiosity finally got the better of you, huh?" she asked

without looking back at him.

"What?" he asked slightly disconcerted.

"I know you watch me every time I come out for some air."

"Some air," he scoffed with an added grunt as he sat down next to her. "Yet you smoke."

"I'm full of contradictions," she gibed dully.

"You do smoke too much."

"I've done worse."

"Really?" he asked, slightly dumbfounded.

"Yup."

"Me too."

"I know."

He clapped his hands together loudly to puncture the awkward silence while he thought of something to say. "Been clean thirteen years now."

"Thirty-two months."

"You count the months?"

"I count the days."

"Ah. What made you quit?"

Joanna hesitated, searching for the right words. "Got a tattoo."

He eyed her curiously. "And?"

"Woke up with the tattoo artist."

A mischievous grin teased his mouth and deepened his wrinkles. Joanna rolled her eyes. "It wasn't like that."

"Okay then," Owen raised his hands, his grin widening. "Tell me. What was it like then?"

She gave only a sideways glance and a cloud of smoke in response. He tried not to let her see his growing impatience as he ran headlong into another of her walls. He picked up a fistful of gravel and bounced the pebbles in his hand, separating them like pills until they lay in one flat layer across his palm while he searched for a way around her defenses.

"What do you dream about, Jo?" he asked the question that had been burning within him for months now. She shook her head and looked back down at her feet. The orange glow of the street lamp illuminated her stoic expression like a mask of glowing amber, emphasizing her hollow cheeks and sunken eyes. He continued, "Those names you – "

"Owen."

"Who's Ethan?"

"Owen, stop!" she barked, rounding on him. Her jaw clenched as her eyes bore into him, but her voice was steady when she finally spoke. "Do you know what I like so much about Milo?" Owen didn't answer. "He doesn't ask any questions."

Owen nodded in defeat, exhaling his trapped breath when she released him from her burning gaze. "Can I just ask you one thing? Then I'll leave you alone."

"What," she sighed with annoyance.

"I just want to know where you got those pants," he said, fighting a smile. She stared at him in disbelief. "What? I like them!"

A breathy chuckle escaped her mouth as she shook her head, but it soon faded back to her default solemn expression. "They're from Liam," she sighed and turned to him. Sadness filled her eyes like a ghost. He stared at her unrestrained emotion, transfixed by the depth of her mesmerizing brown eyes.

"Chet Adkins guy?"

She nodded. "He's the one that got me clean," she tried to explained in a shaky voice. "More or less." He waited, watching the wheels turn in her head as she chewed on her lips. "I don't count the days since I got clean out of some weak sense of pride for not shooting up in nine hundred sixty days. My entire life changed that day. Getting clean was just a side effect." A tear escaped her eye, and she turned away, wiping it with her finger and muttered an apology.

"You're sorry for crying?" his heart broke as she buried her face in her hand.

"I haven't cried since," she paused and swallowed heavily, "It's been over two years now." She sniffed and wiped at her eyes. He wanted to comfort her, but he didn't know how. He reached out his hand and placed it on her shoulder. She flinched at his touch and moved away. Clearing her throat, she stood up and dropped the half-smoked cigarette to the ground. "Well, it's getting late," she said, stamping out the butt. "I should get some sleep. See you in the morning, Jesse."

Jesse?

Panic flashed across her face at the realization of what she'd said, and she sprinted to her motel room door before he could say anything. How did she know his name? He hadn't gone by his first name since high school. He was just beginning to get to know her, and with one little word came a dozen more questions. He put his head in his hands, raked his fingers through his thinning hair, and stood up. Going back to bed wasn't really an option at this point. He grabbed a bottle from his stash of Dickel in the van, and started walking.

Joanna didn't need his help. She needed therapy. The way she always stared out of the van window fiddling with that charm bracelet of hers, always deep in thought, never really speaking her mind. He thought being with someone every day for four months would constitute some form of knowing the person, but she was still a stranger to him. Always just out of reach. And then she called him by his first name.

She's keeping something from me, he thought. A lot of somethings was his guess.

Chapter Six

Memphis, Tennessee

Owen sat on his own sofa in his own house watching his own television, but his thoughts were still on the road. On the screen a woman cried with her children as her husband left for war. Which war, he didn't know. The volume was down. Could be one of the World Wars or even Vietnam. He didn't know the time periods that well. Did they even make movies about Vietnam?

He pulled himself off the couch and went to the bedroom to dig for a clean shirt in his still packed suitcase. He grabbed his Telecaster and amplifier and searched for his car keys. Within minutes he hit a small wave of traffic on the outskirts of Memphis. He cursed and turned up the radio. Dierks Bentley's "Am I the Only One" soon filled the cab of his truck, and he found himself singing along several times. The parking lot behind his regular bar was virtually empty except for two pick up trucks, a motorcycle, and several empty and broken beer bottles. Music from an afternoon house band poured into the street from a nearby restaurant as Owen lugged his guitar into the bar.

"Hey Jake, how's it going?" he greeted the bartender with a wave.

"Well look who it is! Our favorite guitar guy! Haven't seen you in a couple days," Jake laughed, slapping his rag on the counter. "You know we had Luke Bryan in here on Tuesday? I've never seen this place so packed!"

"Luke Bryan did a bar gig?"

"No. He had a show over there at the arena. He just came in for a burger and a drink. Some girl put it on Twitter, and ten minutes later it was so packed in here, I had to send Rachel out for more tequila. On a Tuesday if you can believe it!" His thick beard bobbed back and forth as he spoke.

"Sounds like celebrities are good for business."

"You ain't kiddin'! I should get a Twitter in case someone else comes in," he mused to himself.

"Hey I've got my guitar in the truck. I was thinkin' of playin' some tonight, what do you say?" Owen asked, putting on his most charming smile.

"Well now Owen, you don't do solo gigs anymore. And The Roadside Babel isn't booked here until New Year's Eve. You know that."

"Yeah, Jake, but listen," he bargained, leaning with his elbows against the bar, "I haven't done any of my old songs in years. It'd be a nice change up."

"No one would come."

"Of course people will come! I'm in The Roadside Babel, dammit! We packed out every bar we went to on this last tour. We're really makin' a name for ourselves!"

"I know you are man, I know you are, but look. Owen Sharpe by himself isn't enough to bring in the same kind of crowd."

"What are you tryin' to say, Jake?"

"I'm just sayin' your band is doing real well. Real well. But Chad's the real talent, and Mike and that quiet one on the drum set are the eye candy for the ladies. I even had a fella in here the other day askin' about that redhead chick that's with you now. He looked like money. Actually he looked like Richie Rich. Made me mad just lookin' at him. I should have given him her number. If I had her number. Hey you should give me her number."

"Jo?"

"That's the one."

"Ah hell, Jake, you've got me blushin' over here," he said, ignoring Jake's characteristic rambling. "You don't have to pay me or anythin'. I just want to play. Just put my first drink or two on the house. That's all I'm askin' of you."

"I'm sorry. It just won't work."

Owen started to raise his voice when he was interrupted.

"I thought I'd find you here." He turned to find Joanna leaning up against the bar next to him, coffee in hand. "Milo says you practically live here."

"He drinks enough on his own for me to pay the rent," Jake laughed. "You must be this Jo I've heard so much about."

"Joanna," she corrected politely, reaching out to shake his hand. She eyed Owen's irritated stance and asked, "I've interrupted something, haven't I?"

"Jake here was just bein' an ornery prick," Owen snapped. Jake shrugged and moved down the bar to a dark haired woman who had just taken a seat at the end. Owen sighed. "Anyway what are you doing here?"

"Looking for you. I thought that was clear. I'm your stalker, remember?" Her lips curved with a ghost of a smile as she lifted her coffee half an inch from the counter and dropped it back down repeatedly and annoyingly.

"Well, you found me. Now what?"

"Someone's bitter," she laughed. "I just came to see if you wanted to grab a bite to eat this Saturday, or will you still have your knickers in a twist?"

"My what?"

"Your panties in a knot! Jesus, it's like talking to a child."

Owen ignored the comment. "But Saturday's Christmas."

"So?"

"What, you and Milo don't have any plans for Christmas? Family to see?"

"Do either of us look like we've got family to see?" she asked, intending for it to sound sarcastic, but her eyes darted away from his inquisitive stare and her lips stretched into a taut line. "Besides I don't do Christmas."

"What do you mean you don't do Christmas?" he questioned, staring at her dubiously.

"I just don't celebrate it." She brought her coffee to her lips, shrugging as though not celebrating Christmas was a common thing.

"That's not very Christian of you," Owen joked.

She furrowed her brows at him. "Says the guy who drinks enough to pay a bar's rent." He laughed and raised his hands. "So will I see you Saturday or not?"

"Saturday's fine with me."

"Cool," she said, stepping back from the bar and pulling a pack of Pall Malls from her jacket pocket. She walked backwards towards the door as she instructed him. "You can pick me up around three. You know where Milo lives?" He nodded. "Cool. Take me somewhere I've never been, which is anywhere in this city. We don't get out much, if you catch my drift." She winked and waved at Jack and then she was gone.

"She seems nice enough," Jake commented, coming back from a needy day drinker.

"She's a thorn in my side," Owen grunted. "Make yourself useful and get me a Dickel, will you? Neat."

Owen pulled up in front of the dingy two-story apartment complex and threw the truck in park. A stray cat was rifling through an upturned garbage bin, and dogs barked to each other somewhere far off while a person unseen yelled for them to shut up. A door opened on the second floor a few houses down, and Joanna stepped through. Owen moved the truck to meet her. She greeted him with a smile.

"Where to?" she asked.

"That depends. Do you want barbecue or milkshakes?" he asked, waiting for an opening in the line of cars on the road.

"Milkshakes? Really? It's December."

"You don't understand, Jo. These are the best milkshakes in the country."

"Well in that case, lets get milkshakes. And Joanna, Owen. It's Joanna," she shook her head and turned her face to the window.

They rode in silence with Hank Williams on the radio. She leaned forward to turn up the volume.

"Can I be honest with you?" she asked, raising her voice over the music.

"Sure," he answered, trying to think of the best way to get to the restaurant from this edge of the city.

"I don't like country music, but – "

"You don't like country music?" he repeated, nearly running off the road in his shock. He gaped at her in astonishment and disbelief. "You wrote practically half our songs on this new album!"

"But I grew up in the South, and it always got on my nerves," she waved him off. Before he could ask any further questions, she continued, "I don't like country music but I have always loved Hank Williams."

"How is that even possible? Hank is just about as country as it gets! You don't get more country than yodeling," he argued.

"I know. My step dad used to listen to country all the time, and Hank Williams was the only one I could tolerate. I remember sitting in the back of his truck with my brothers, listening to his voice and his guitar. He wrote such sad music, but he was so real. Even at a young age I could identify with his songs. Sometimes his lyrics would be so melancholy, but the music was more light and upbeat. I only listened to him when Richard played it, but listening to him, I'd feel like I was being transported to a simpler time where nothing mattered but the people you loved with drinks on Saturday and church on Sunday."

"He drank more than just on Saturdays, you know," Owen added with a laugh.

"Well yeah," she grudgingly agreed. "But still." She paused and smiled at a memory. "My brothers used to sing 'Hey, Good Lookin'' all the time. Of course they only knew the first lines, and they'd sing it to me so I'd get them something to eat. They liked to yodel. They did it too much really, exaggerated every line of his songs."

Her voice trailed off into her memories. Owen turned the truck into the parking lot for the famous Arcade Restaurant. They would have been there earlier, but when he noticed she was telling him more than just a preference for a musician, he drove a couple times around the block.

"We're here," he said, pulling the keys from the ignition. Jo blinked and shook her head.

"Sorry, got off track there for a bit."

"It's fine," he tried to encourage her. "You've never talked about them before."

"I have my reasons."

They took seats at the bar of the brightly lit retro diner. Owen ordered two chocolate shakes and fried peanut butter banana sandwiches.

"That sounds atrocious," Jo blanched.

"You have to like it or you're not a true Memphis citizen," Owen grinned.

"Is that so?"

He nodded. "The King himself loved those sandwiches."

"Okay now I know you're lying," she laughed.

"No, really," he pointed to a framed autographed photo of Elvis on the adjacent wall.

"Oh!" Jo guffawed. He turned back to find her with her head on the bar, shaking with laughter. He stared down at her in confusion. When she rose back up, she pushed her hair out of her teary eyes. "I thought you meant the King of England!"

Owen laughed slowly in astonishment. "Why the hell would the King of England come to Memphis?"

"Well I don't know!" she shook her head, her shoulders shaking with now silent laughter. "I feel so stupid!"

"You should!" They laughed until the waitress brought their orders.

"Is there anything else I can get you?" she asked them.

"Yeah," Owen answered, still recovering from their outburst, "a new dinner date!" Jo punched him playfully in the arm and went for a sip of her milkshake.

"Ah come on now," the waitress giggled, turning to Jo, "don't be givin' Dad a hard time."

"Dad?" Owen repeated in confusion. Joanna choked on her milkshake.

"Are you not her dad?"

Owen raised an eyebrow at the waitress. "No, darlin', she's not my daughter."

"I'm sorry," the waitress smiled apologetically. "I just thought you two looked alike is all." She hurried away in embarrassment. Owen turned to Jo with his eyebrow still cocked.

"Must be the hair," Jo shrugged and dug into her sandwich. Holding a hand over her mouth, she said, "Not bad."

"Good enough for the King of England?" Owen taunted her. She flicked him off without taking her eyes off of her plate. They ate a few bites of their sandwiches before he turned back to their previous conversation. "So you grew up down here with the rest of us, huh?"

"Yep," she answered, wiping crumbs from her mouth.

"Tennessee?"

"Alabama."

He gagged dramatically onto his plate. "That's the worst of the bunch!"

"Are you serious, right now?" she asked, slightly taken aback.

"Alabama or Auburn?"

"What?"

"Alabama or Auburn? The college football teams?"

"Oh. We never really watched football until my mother remarried. But Mark was an Alabama alum. He never missed a game. Made us all into Bama fans, I guess."

"You're an Alabama girl," he scoffed and shook his head, feeling betrayed. "I can't believe it. All Alabamians care about is their college football."

"And Tennessee is so different," Audrey gibed.

"Well," he laughed, "we're not as bad."

"And how many national championships has that modesty won you?"

"That's not important," he argued.

Jo shook her head and paused as their laughter subsided. "I didn't necessarily hate the state, but I left as soon as an opportunity arose," she explained.

"Would you ever go back?"

"No," she said it with a force that ended the conversation. Owen bit into his sandwich and smiled as she pushed a wad of tangled curls behind her ear.

"So how's the boy toy doing?" he asked.

"He's fine," she answered with a shrug.

"Figure out what his tattoos mean yet?"

Jo snorted. "Half of them don't mean anything. I asked him why he has bolts in his neck, and all I got in response was 'I liked the movie, Frankenstein.' And then he came back to the apartment a couple of weeks ago and said, 'Hey Joanna I got a tattoo for you', lifted up his shirt, and showed it to me. I was expecting my name or some cheesy crap like that, but no. He got Hel."

"Hel?"

"She's a being in Norse mythology."

"What the hell?"

"Clever," she smirked at him.

"I'm here all week," he winked. She shook her head and continued on as if he hadn't said anything.

"The day before he got it, he'd found out that I've been to Iceland. I told him about this café that I went to, Café Loki. I explained how different the original mythology is compared to the comic books and how I've always loved how Loki just goes crazy and does whatever he feels like whenever he feels like it. Milo said he went in for a Loki tattoo but the pictures of Loki's daughter were apparently much cooler. So in short, Milo got a tattoo of a woman who is basically the Norse goddess of death and dedicated it to me."

"Charming," Owen laughed.

"I didn't tell him what she was," Jo added with a slight smile. "I just let him think he did something sweet."

"Well that as nice of you."

"I try," she grinned her Joker grin.

"You've got a tattoo, right?" he asked. She nodded with a mouth full of peanut butter and banana. "What's it of?"

She finished chewing before taking off her jacket and pulling at the back of her shirt. "It's on my shoulder if you pull the neckline down."

Owen stiffly reached for her shirt and pulled it down to get a look at the ink on her pasty, lightly freckled skin. An elaborate crescent moon covered a large portion of her shoulder blade with two stars at its center. Inside the stars were delicately curving lines that swirled into numbers. They were vague and he didn't notice them at first, but they were definitely there. On the top star was the number eight. The bottom one was ninety-nine.

"What are the numbers for?" he asked.

"They're my brothers' baseball numbers." She pulled her shirt back to its appropriate place and turned her face to the bar. Her jaw was clenched. "I was originally going to get their names in the moon. But Liam said I started crying. I wouldn't tell him their names, so I gave him their baseball numbers. He added the stars on his own intuition. I was pretty drunk and most likely high, so I don't really remember." She stirred her milkshake with her straw absentmindedly.

"You said you don't have family to spend Christmas with," Owen started.

"Yeah," she said, turning back to him with a smile and drooping eyes. "I don't. And I'd really rather not talk about it. I've said too much as it is. Christmas is just not a good time for me."

"I was married once," he said, hoping to gain her trust by telling her a bit about himself. "But I was always on the road, drinkin' and doin' drugs. I was unfaithful. I got back from tourin', and she handed me divorce papers. She helped me out with bills a few times while I was tryin' to get clean. But it was never the same with old Bridgette. Guess I still love her."

"I know what that's like," Jo said to the counter.

"I'm over it, though. She ain't comin' back. What's the use in cryin' over it?" A silence ensued while Jo played with her straw, both of them deep in their own memories.

"I never knew my dad," she said after a deep sigh. "Not growing up anyway. My mom had a string of lovers and two husbands – that I know of – and somehow I'm the only one of my siblings who ended up a bastard."

Owen didn't know what to say as she paused and picked up a fry to draw indistinct pictures in her ketchup.

"I used to fantasize about him," she added. "When I was really young, before my brothers came along, I imagined him buying a loaf of bread and taking me to the park to feed the ducks. He'd read to me at night before I went to bed and put me on his shoulders when we went to amusement parks." She trailed off, lost in thought.

"Did you ever meet him?" Owen found himself asking.

"Yeah."

"Was he what you expected?"

"Is anyone ever?" she retorted with a sad smile, turning to face him. "He would never have read to me, that's for sure. He isn't one for the books." Her smile turned genuine as she went on, "And he's more nosey than he is caring, but his heart's in the right place. He likes to find out everyone's baggage so he doesn't have to feel so bad about his own."

"Do you still talk to him?"

"I don't keep in touch with anyone once I leave them," she shrugged, but Owen sensed there was something she wasn't telling him. He decided not to dig further, afraid he'd push too far and close her walls back up for her.

"Can I ask you somethin'?" he asked, changing the subject.

"You can ask, but I may not answer," she quipped halfheartedly.

"How did you know my name?"

"Jesse Owen Sharpe," she sang his name with a smile and put her straw in her mouth. "I'm your stalker remember?"

The image of Joanna hiding out at the back of the bar, sipping quietly at her glass, flashed before his eyes. "You've never really struck me as a crazed fan," he admitted.

"You go by your middle name, so I started going by mine,"

she shrugged. "Does that qualify me as a crazed fan?"

"Not really, no," he shook his head. "A bit weird maybe, but not crazy."

She didn't meet his eyes as she said, "I'm a fan, and I'm crazy. Just because the crazed part isn't an adjective for the fan part doesn't make much difference."

"Crazy people don't know they're crazy," Owen argued with a cock of his head. She stared down at the bar and twisted a strand of hair in her fingertips. "So what's your first name then?" he asked.

"No," she said bluntly with widened eyes and a nervous smile, waving at the waitress, who bustled over to them at the summons.

"Can I get y'all anything?" she asked them.

"Check, please," Owen answered, and she waddled off. "Does Chet Adkins still call you?" he asked Joanna.

"Nope."

"Want to go to the bar?"

"Yep."

Chapter Seven

Seattle, Washington

The weak morning sun pushed its way through the blinds and dotted the blankets with patches of broken light. He'd watched the black room grow steadily brighter and the long beams shorten as the sun rose higher in the sky. He sat up slowly and stretched his stiff muscles. Throwing his legs over the side of the bed and reaching for his black, plastic rimmed glasses, he lumbered to the kitchen to pour himself a cup of coffee.

Steam rose from the mug as he set it next to his laptop and made himself comfortable at the small kitchen table. A picture of a little girl kissing a stuffed humpback whale on the nose popped up on the screen when he opened his laptop. He blew into his coffee, waiting for the Internet to connect, and ran a hand through his short, spiky hair. Minutes later, he was hunched over the keypad searching the Internet, picking up where he'd left off the last time. How long had it been since then? Four months? Must be a new record.

In the past year and a half, he'd managed to pick up traces, but when it was all accumulated, the clues didn't add up to much. He had very little to go on in the beginning. Nothing but her name, date of birth, and where she grew up. Nothing at all about the man he hoped she was looking for. It had taken him months of fruitless hunting, futile phone calls, and painful dead ends to finally get some traction, but the exhilaration he'd felt when he'd found Owen Sharpe was indescribable.

First came the relief. All of his foraging had finally paid off. It hadn't all been for naught. Then came the fist pumps. Silent fist pumps of course. Couldn't risk waking her up and have her asking questions. Then he'd clasped his hands in front of his face as the unexpected melancholy set in. He couldn't tell anyone of his discovery. If the others knew what he knew, they'd go rabid.

Then came the despair. He'd searched for this man on a hunch that she would too, but he had no real way of knowing what her intentions were when she left him almost three years ago. The image of the empty hospital room and crisp sheets flashed before his eyes. There wasn't so much as a letter on the pillow. He didn't care a thing about this man he'd spent so much time and energy tracking down. The year and a half it took to find him would mean nothing if Audrey didn't do the same. He didn't know what he would do if he found her. Probably nothing. He just wanted to know where she ended up is all. How she was doing. If she was happy.

Of course his efforts were not solely focused on finding the ginger haired hick whose face now filled his computer screen. He searched for her too, but she was a ghost. By now she was likely an expert at disappearing. She'd gone off the radar so many times, he wasn't surprised that finding her directly was so impossible.

"Do you know who I am?" she slurred.

"You act as if you're someone easily forgotten, Miss Wyatt," he said to her bleary eyes.

"I just need to know if you remember me. Because if you do, I need to go somewhere else. Tattoos are permanent after all." A pause followed before she snorted.

He released a breathy chuckle, leaned back in his chair and put a hand over his heart. "Just tell me what you want, and I won't stray from it. No matter how much you piss me off."

"Is that a promise, Mr. Farren?"

Liam started his search with a quick glance at The Roadside Babel's website. Nothing new but the approaching release date for their new album, "Like Wildfire". Then he searched for any news articles pertaining to the band and carefully read through all of them. Most were short accounts of the up-and-comers gracing a club or bar with their presence or interviews with their local Memphis paper. He took a gulp of coffee and leaned forward to put the mug back on the table when the next article pulled up. In his shock, the mug missed the edge of the table and clattered to the floor. The hem of his pants were splattered with hot coffee, but he spared it only a glance.

A news article from two months earlier in Jackson,

Mississippi, displayed on his screen, and with it came the first view in twenty-eight months of the woman he loved.

The four band members stood at the entrance to the bar. By now he knew all of their names. Chad and Mike stood at the right end of the group. Mike was throwing his signature rock and roll hand gesture while Chad stood smiling. Milo, with his mop of dark hair covering part of his left eye, smoldered at the camera with his arm thrown casually around her shoulders, keeping her tucked closely to his side. Owen was on the end with his hands in the pockets of shorts that were an inch or two too short, smiling midsentence down at her. Her arm was wrapped around Milo's waist, but her wide eyes were locked on Owen, laughing heartily at whatever he was saying.

Liam couldn't remember the last time he saw her smile like that. Actually he could. He liked to think he was the one who taught her how to laugh again. How to love, even though she never admitted it. Maybe it was just a trick of the camera or the strength of the Southern sun, but there was a glow to her skin, and *that* he had never seen before. She looked healthy. The bones in her face were still sharp, but she didn't look so emaciated. Her hair had gotten so long. The wiry strands tangled together in the same unkempt curls that he'd once spent hours running his fingers through. He let himself smile, warding off the jealousy invoked by Milo's proximity to her. After a lifetime of haunting questions, she'd finally found him. Before now, with Owen's picture pulled up on his laptop screen, Liam could never see the resemblance, but looking at them next to each other, it was almost obvious. Their shared red curls and almond brown eyes were unmistakable. She'd found her father. And he made her smile.

Tearing his eyes from her, he read the article.

RISING STARS HAVE JACKSON BABBLING FOR DAYS

Last Friday, Memphis-based country artists, The Roadside Babel, stunned audiences at Joe's Liquor Cabinet. Mixing traditional country blues with an alt-rock flare, they have brought something exotic to the music industry. When asked about their origins, front man Chad Wilkes answered, "Three of us love country. Milo prefers rock, so we compromised." Simple enough.

As the quartet took the stage to a deafening applause, no doubt was left as to the growing fame of the country stars. Joe's Liquor Cabinet was filled to its maximum capacity of five hundred people with countless others watching from the street windows.

Although country and rock hybrids are nothing new, The Roadside Babel will surely revolutionize the genre and inspire garage bands across the nation. With their hit song, "Love the Sinner", viral on YouTube and a new album in the works – with the added help of new writer, faithful roadie, and Milo Schroeder's rumored flame, Joanna Farren – great things can be expected to come their way.

Liam stared at the screen in disbelief with a lump building in his throat. She was using his name. What prompted her to take on an alias, he could only guess, but from her new name alone, he cared a little less about the "rumored flame". She hadn't forgotten them.

"Daddy." Her soft voice pulled him from his reveries. The coffee that soaked his pant leg was now cold. He closed his laptop and turned toward her. She walked sluggishly, wiping roughly at her eye with the palm of her hand. She wore thick high socks and a baggy Pearl Jam t-shirt, and her hair was tangled and stuck to the side of her face.

"Good morning!" he smiled at the sleepy toddler and scooped her up in his arms. "Sleep good?" She yawned and nodded, resting her forehead on his shoulder. His face twitched involuntarily at the itch of her bushy hair on his skin. He set her down on the counter and gathered as much of it as he could behind her head. "What do you want for breakfast?"

"Coffee," she muttered.

"Okay, and what else?"

"A donut."

"A donut?" he feigned disbelief as he pulled an elastic from his wrist, tied it around the ball of her hair, and rested his arms on either side of her. "We don't have donuts. We have cereal and cereal and, let me see, more cereal."

"Fine, I'll have cereal," she conceded, obviously disheartened. He set her down on the floor and heard her waddle off as he poured a bowl of cereal and chocolate milk in a coffee mug. He stared at the faded Union flag on the mug and the barely legible letters on the rim.

"You're up early," he said in the direction of the gaudy sofa, absently shoving his long hair back from his face.

"No, you're just up late," she quipped without taking her eyes off of the pages of her book.

"Is there any coffee ready?"

"Nope, we're out," she raised her mug in his direction. "You can have the rest of this, though."

"Thanks," he mumbled and took a sip, spluttering with surprise. "This is tea!"

"I said we're out of coffee," she said with a suppressed smirk. With a quick swipe, he snatched the book from her grasp.

"Liam!" she jolted forward to reclaim what was hers, but he hastily hid it behind his back. She glared at him with a hardened brow but with eyes that glittered with the feelings that she adamantly refused to give voice to.

"Who reads Paradise Lost first thing in the morning, anyway?" he teased.

"Give it back," she protested, sucking her lips in her mouth the way she always did when she didn't want him to see her smile. It was almost surprising that the action didn't cause her cheekbones to cut through her thin, ivory skin. Still, there was a noticeable improvement. There was a renewed spark of life in her eyes.

"Not until you tell me good morning," he beamed impishly at her.

"Seriously," she raised an eyebrow. His smile grew wider, and he pushed the tip of his tongue between his teeth to form her favorite smile. She closed her eyes and, shaking her head, leaned onto her toes to kiss him. Her lips were soft, but her fingers were cold against his cheeks. She slid her hands to his shoulders as she pulled back.

"You still didn't say good morning," he whispered.

"Morning," she rolled her eyes, tapping his cheek in a mock slap. "Now hand it over." He made a show of contemplation before shaking his head and pulled her down onto the sofa with him. She leaned back into him, and he wrapped his arm around her, squeezing her hands to warm them.

"Where were you?" he asked. She pointed to a stanza

towards the bottom of the page. " 'What though the field be lost? All is not Lost; the unconquerable will, and study of revenge, immortal hate, and the courage never to submit or yield...' "

"Daddy!" she called impatiently, elongating the word into way too many syllables.

"Coming, Rosie." He shook away the memory, poured himself another cup of coffee, and joined his daughter on the sofa. Setting up his laptop on the table in front of them, he put in a scratched DVD of Dexter's Laboratory. Soon she was wide-awake and sitting in his lap doing her best impersonation of the boy scientist as she drank her chocolate milk with her breakfast.

Minutes passed before he realized she'd gone quiet and was softly tracing her finger along his forearm for the thousandth time while he watched her little brow crease in contemplation.

"What are you thinking about?"

"Why does it have thorns on it?" she asked, not taking her eyes off of the tattoo that she continued to outline.

"Because it's a rose, and roses have thorns," he explained.

"Well I don't like thorns," she said after a short pause.

"You're not supposed to," he chuckled softly, "but they make you appreciate the roses so much more, don't they?" She shrugged and turned her attention back to the screen. He kissed her hair and laughed when she tried to wipe it away. She looked back up at him with a grin that crinkled her nose and pressed her dark eyes into slits.

He understood her questions. Why her daddy would get vines of thorns with only a single rose permanently engraved into his skin didn't appeal to her innocence. He hoped she would never understand first hand what it was like to build a life, to see your entire future laid out before you, only to be left in the cold with only one thing that kept you going. Even if it was such a beautiful little thing.

The familiar bitterness began to crawl its way back in as he looked at her. He knew Audrey well enough not to trust the smile in the picture. She hated posed photographs. "People cover so much of themselves when they know a camera is pointed at them," she would always say. Of course, he wanted her to be happy. Nothing she did could ever make him wish any harm on her. But then he'd look at his little Rosie.

Like her namesake, she bloomed in a world of thorns.

Thorns to harm her and thorns to protect her. His Rose smiled with disappearing eyes as though blinded by an untarnished joy to the injustice that surrounded her being. He had given his Rose as a gift, a gift that was forsaken and returned. His baby girl would grow up with endless questions about where her mother was and why she had left her. The same questions Audrey had asked herself time and time again. She knew the effects of living with that kind of abandonment, yet she willingly inflicted that same inner turmoil on her own daughter. And somewhere tucked deep inside of him, he knew that he wouldn't bat an eye if she were miserable.

Chapter Eight

Memphis, Tennessee
Day 1261

Audrey Wyatt was miserable. She pulled the comforter over her face to block out the late morning sun that stabbed like daggers behind her eyes. Her racing pulse resounded like medieval battle drums against her skull. She groaned and flinched at the noise of it. She leaned back in the pillow and ran her fingers through her hair, breathing steadily to calm the heart that was frantically pounding against her ribs.

She didn't scream this time, so that was good. Did that mean she was making progress? Doubtful.

She'd been back on that Washington beach again, and in the distance he sat with the girl on his lap, staring out at the sea. Audrey was running, always running, but this time there was a numbness where her joy usually festered. It expanded from her chest and through her limbs, causing her legs to falter. She stumbled and fell to the sand. Tears blurred her vision and fell down the tip of her nose. She wiped them away with sandy fingers and rose to her knees. They no longer sat in the sand, but stood, Liam with his back to her, his long black hair uncovered, the ends stuffed inside the collar of his coat. At his feet, Rosie tugged at his hand and pointed out at the water. Liam stood motionless, ignoring his daughter's pleas for attention.

Anger flared in her gut and refueled her resolve. She called Rosie's name and froze in shock when those black eyes turned to her.

"You can hear me?" Audrey whispered in disbelief. Rosie stood, still clutching her father's coat sleeve and pushed her frenzy of curls from her expressionless face to get a look at her mother. The months had begun to lean her, shedding a bit of the infant roundness from her cheeks. Audrey scrambled up only to fall back down at her daughter's feet. She stared at her little girl with teary longing, shoulders and chest heaving from the exertion. Rosie cocked her head and studied Audrey's face. She reached out a tiny hand to wipe away her mother's tears. Audrey gasped at the touch she couldn't feel and grabbed her hand, pressing it against her face, but she still couldn't feel it. She lunged forward, caressing Rosie's cheeks, her hair, her shoulders, until finally she wrapped her tightly in her arms. Rosie's mouth flew open with laughter, but only silence escaped from her throat. Nevertheless, joy flooded through Audrey as she stood and spun them around.

She pulled back to get a look at the little girl smiling back at her. In her overwhelming sense of bliss, Audrey threw the girl in the air. Her face scrunched with glee and a silent, jovial shriek as she experienced a brief moment of weightlessness before plummeting back down to her mother's grasp. Audrey tossed her again and again, laughing along with her before she caught his eye. He'd turned back to them. His nostrils flared and his eyes burned with malice and pain, his dark hair blowing across his twisted face.

"Why did you leave us, Audrey?" Liam growled with a voice that wasn't his own. Every nerve in her body seemed to explode within her. Rosie fell back down into her arms, but it felt wrong. She was much heavier, limp and ice cold. Audrey's eyes shot back to the child in her grasp, but it wasn't her little girl.

"No!" Audrey cried chokingly at Daniel's frigid body in her arms. She sank to the sand and cradled him, trying to wipe away the blood from his face.

"Why did you leave us, Audrey?" came Ethan's voice again.

"I'm sorry," Audrey sobbed, dropping her head to Daniel's chest, tears mixing with the thick, congealed blood.

"We needed you, and you left us!" he shouted. Daniel's body vanished, and she screamed, frantically searching for him in the sand around her, calling out his name. Ethan grabbed a handful of her hair and shoved her back into the sand, thrusting his knee in her gut to keep her from getting up. Her screams caught in her throat, choking her, suffocating her.

"Ethan, I – " she coughed out a mouthful of sand, but before she could finish her sentence, Ethan was in her face.

"I needed you!" he spat. He wrapped his fingers around her throat and shoved her deeper into the wet sand. His grip crushed her windpipe as her mouth flailed open unable to gasp for air. A cold wave crashed into her, filling her mouth and nose with stinging seawater. Ethan's eyes burned inches above her as he repeated his vile words over and over, spraying her face with his rage. Everything around her began to blur and darken as she felt the life leave her wretched body.

Audrey had woken in a layer of sweat, coughing up phlegm, desperately trying to catch her breath. She lay in bed trying to calm her breathing. Not a night went by that she wasn't haunted by the ghosts of her past, but some dreams were more pungent than others. They were getting worse if she was honest with herself, but her recovery time in the mornings had gotten shorter.

"Therapy would do you some good." Elizabeth's words echoed through her head. She couldn't discern if it came from a memory or her imagination. But it sounded like something Snow would say.

Finally she decided to brave the world outside of the bed, make some coffee, and maybe get something on her stomach. Something besides the weight that was thrown across it.

She pushed back the blankets to find Milo sprawled across the bed on his stomach, his decorated arm stretched across her abdomen, an empty bottle of moonshine in his hand. That explains the headache, she thought, taking the bottle from his flaccid grasp and tossing his arm aside. He moaned in response and rolled over to his side. The floor felt cold against her toes, but it wasn't an altogether unpleasant sensation. She poured water in the back of the coffee maker, massaging her aching temples. She stumbled around for the leather jacket and, pulling the half empty pack of Pall Malls from the pocket, lit a cigarette, took a long drag at it, and stared through the exhaled smoke at the man in the bed.

Milo slept with his back to her, his arms tucked in to his bare chest as though clutching something close, afraid to let it go. Like his arms, his back was ornamented with black ink in almost haphazard disarray. A wishbone adorned one shoulder blade while the other sported the elaborate head of a lioness. The neck of a guitar with drumsticks in place of the frets covered his spine and reached into his hair. On his left side, half hidden beneath the blankets was the Norse mythological being, Hel. Half woman, half skeleton. Goddess of death.

Death was something as familiar to him as it was to Audrey. Each night, a young Milo Schroeder would stiffen at the sound of the footsteps in the hall outside of his Bronx apartment. If his father was sober, he'd walk in, collapse on the sofa, switch on the television set, and order Milo to his room. If he wasn't, Milo would cower in a corner while his mother took a beating meant for someone else, hoping his father's rage wouldn't turn to him. More often than not, Milo sat alone on the bus to his elementary school rehearsing the story his mother had given him on where his new injuries came from.

At fifteen, he dropped out of high school and worked selling hot dogs on street corners in Manhattan, hoping to raise enough money to cart his fragile mother away from New York and out from under his father's despotic mauling. At seventeen, he found her curled in her bed, overdosed on a mixture of prescription painkillers two months before his planned escape. He'd skipped her funeral in order to pack his things without the watchful eye of his father.

At nineteen, Milo awoke in a Philadelphia hospital with his entire left forearm wrapped thickly in a bandage. His girlfriend, Tonya, had found him in a puddle of his own blood, a box cutter in hand. He used that blade again a year later after forcing her to get an abortion. This time no one sat next to his hospital bed when he woke confused and drugged with dulled pain in his right arm.

Audrey took another drag at her cigarette. When she looked at Milo, she saw Liam. The dark hair and dark eyes were almost the same. Milo differed only in his slighter stature and his tattoos. As much as she tried to force herself to love him, however, he could never fully take Liam's place. Over the past year, Audrey had unintentionally become for Milo much of what Liam had been for her. He confided in her and confessed to her things he'd never wished to utter aloud. He found in her a sense of freedom. He could trust her more than anyone. His Joanna.

Audrey scoffed at the irony and stubbed out the cigarette butt in the ashtray on the bedside table before climbing back beneath the comforter and sliding close behind Milo. He flinched awake at the icy touch of her fingers against his bare chest. Another difference from Liam. No chest hair. She felt the raised flesh of where the needle had been shoved too deeply into his skin during his first tattoo. Bruna. His mother's name.

"Morning," she muttered, kissing the wishbone.

"Hey," he grunted sleepily, coming to his senses. He squeezed her hand in his and kissed her knuckles. "I don't see how your hands are this cold in April."

"Jesus Christ, Aud, your fingers are like ice!"

"You said that last year," she said, ignoring Liam's voice in her head.

Milo rolled to face her and wrapped her in his sinewy arms, resting his chin on her head. Audrey breathed in his musky scent and leaned her forehead against him, interlocking her fingers behind his back. Her attraction to Milo was more than just his physical resemblance to the only man she ever loved. Being with someone with more inner darkness than herself was intoxicating. Thirty-four years of constant encouragement and "Keep your head up, you'll get through this," from people who knew nothing of her pain had exhausted her in more ways than she'd realized. Being with Milo was like sinking in a numbing yet serene pool of inky black nothingness. It enveloped her like a thick, cool fog every time he touched her. Without him the people, the sunlight, the cars, the blues music blaring through the open doorways of every downtown bar, everything seemed so harsh, so severe, so bright. She wished she could love him. But he was only her addiction. She'd traded her tubes and injection needles for something else entirely to cloud her mental functions and dull the ever-present gnawing pain and emptiness.

"Hey, Aud, are you home?" she heard her name. He sounded so far away. He cursed. "You relapsed again?" His thumb pulled back her eyelid. He's so beautiful. And tan. Where did he get a tan? His dark hair was wet from the rain. He looked like an angel. He must be Jesus.

"It's not a relapse when you're not addicted, Liam," she mumbled.

"Like hell you're not addicted," he growled. He was scrounging around for something. Her heroin stash, no doubt. He wouldn't find any. It was still with Ruby. She rolled onto her elbows to get a view of him on his hands and knees, searching under the bed and through their drawers. He swore again and pushed back on his knees, jerking his head to get his hair out of his face. His thick brows

knit together to form a straight, stern, intimidating line. She grinned awkwardly, her cheek pressed up against her eye where she rested her head in her hand.

"You're so handsome."

"And you're high," he seethed through clenched teeth.

"Just a little bit." She collapsed back on the bed. Did they have three ceiling fans?

"Okay," Liam grunted as he got to his feet. "You're going to sleep this off so I can yell at you." He lay down on the bed next to her and extended a thick arm as an invitation. She offered him a corner of the blanket she was wrapped in. He rolled his eyes and pulled her close, purposefully hiding his face from view. She could feel the tension in his arms and knew as she laid her head on his chest that his eyes were welling with tears. Too numb to let it bother her, she nestled closely to him and let the erratic rhythm of his heartbeat and the steady rise and fall of his torso lull her into a deep, dreamless sleep.

Milo broke the silence with a muttered curse. "I was saving that moonshine for our anniversary."

"You said yesterday was our anniversary."

"Was it?"

"I suppose so."

Milo paused and stroked her hair. "And we were supposed to save some for Mike."

"Mike can deal with it," Audrey chuckled and pulled out of his embrace. "I like to watch his hissy fits anyway." She crossed the dingy apartment to the coffee pot and poured two mugs, adding a sugar cube to Milo's.

"Get me an aspirin, will you?" he rasped from the bed.

"We're out." She tossed her cigarettes at him and brought him the coffee. They smoked in silence until the sun passed its midpoint and began its long descent towards night. It was another thing she liked about Milo. His silence.

But how long could it last? Surely it was only a matter of time before Milo wisened up to her pretense. Nothing he loved about her was real. Not even her name. The moment he saw her for who she really was would be the moment she would lose him. He'd be gone in the blink of an eye just like everyone else. Just like Liam. But Liam was different. She'd had nine months to say goodbye and two years to answer the phone when he called every night. There was even a return address on the letter he sent. But she hadn't been strong enough to stay. Another day in the hospital and she would have asked to see her baby, anchoring her with them for the rest of her life. Answering the phone even once would have put her on the first plane back to Seattle. They deserved better than that.

Rosie deserved better than her.

Chapter Nine

Phoenix, Arizona

Owen took several drinks from his bottle of Dickel and stashed it under the passenger seat. He pulled his guitar and amplifier from the back of the van and made his way across the parking lot. Once inside, he sidled past the bar, winked at the bartender who sat on a stool painting her nails, and joined the rest of the band on the platform set up at the back of the club.

Milo was meticulously setting up his drum set while Mike chatted with Joanna who raised her eyebrows and laughed in astonishment at whatever conversational limit he had breached. Chad sat cross-legged at the edge of the platform dressed in slacks and an old pair of vans. He was hunched over a binder of their new songs, scrutinizing every page. His hair was shaggy and he'd grown out the makings of a beard. He and Sarah must've officially divorced, Owen thought.

"Oh good. You're here," Chad said, pulling himself to his feet. "We have a few hours before the club opens. We need to rehearse until then. We haven't done any of these new songs live, and I really want to try these that Jo wrote." Mike smiled proudly at Jo. She only rolled her eyes in response.

They practiced songs from their new album, stopping after each one for Chad to lecture them like his old high school marching band students. For once, Owen was taking more heat than Mike. His fingers slid clumsily into their placements on the fret board, and on more than one occasion, he tensed in frustration, strumming too violently against the strings. The notes blared through the amplifier, ricocheting off of the walls and bouncing back to them to drown out Chad's voice. During their third run of Jo's song, "The Forsaken Rose", he missed his cue from Milo to begin his guitar solo.

"Alright, stop! Stop," Chad waved the microphone to silence them. "What's the matter with you, man? You act like you've never played before!"

"We haven't done this song since the studio, Chad," Owen grunted, massaging his face. "I'm not used to havin' a solo. You know that."

"You know the song, dammit! You helped her write it!"

"Heck, Chad, if you'd quit rough talkin' us all the time, maybe we'd get enough practice in!" Owen raised his voice, snapping back more than was necessary as his anger flared.

"If y'all'd do it right, I wouldn't have to keep stopping you!"

"I don't need this crap," Owen waved him off. He yanked the strap from around his shoulder and carried his guitar by the neck from the stage. Chad called after him, but he ignored him. The back door slammed against the outside wall when he kicked it open and stalked off to the van. He yanked the sliding door open, tossed his guitar across the seat, and reached for his whiskey.

"Hey!" Jo yelled from behind him. The door threatened to snap from its hinges as it cracked against the building a second time. Owen dropped his head with an exasperated groan, roughing up his hair in an attempt to alleviate some of the rage that coursed through his veins, tensing up in the joints in his fingers. He snapped back up at her voice, ready to counter whatever she had to say. He turned to see her storming across the parking lot, her face as red and wild as her hair. "What in god's name is wrong with you?" He rolled his eyes and tipped back the bottle. "No, give me that." She yanked the bottle from his mouth, and he swore.

"Oh, quit your hollerin'," he growled. "I won't miss my cues come show time."

"Yes you will! What's wrong with you? You wrote the bloody music!" She took a step closer and sniffed him. He cursed again and flinched back. "How much of this have you had?" she snarled, clenching her jaw with a force that could have broken her teeth.

"Not enough to listen to you run your mouth," he grunted, reaching for the bottle in her hand. She jerked it out of his reach.

"Yeah, fat chance Bad Blake."

"Bad Blake? Who the hell's Bad Blake? Just give me the dadgum whiskey."

Fire flashed in her eyes, and she smashed the bottle against the asphalt, spraying both of their pant legs with whiskey. Owen gave a start and jumped back away from her, looking down at the dark pieces of shattered glass.

"You need to get yourself together," she cautioned, her voice strained as she attempted to calm herself. "You're going to lose this." When he looked at her, her eyes were shut and her chest heaved as she struggled to calm herself.

"What the hell are you talkin' about?" he breathed, shaking his head in exasperation.

"They're going to kick you out of the band," she admitted, pursing her lips. Her brown eyes bore into him, round and full of pity.

"What?" he stammered when the news finally set in.

"They're only talking about it right now, but your drinking is getting out of control and inhibiting your performance on stage. They feel threatened. They don't want you dragging them down with you."

"Ah well they can all go to hell!" he roared, hoping the others could hear. He wheeled around and punched the side of the van. He cried out in agony, his knuckles throbbing.

"You need to go," Jo demanded, the wrath rising back in her voice, slithering through her teeth like a malignant snake coming out of hiding. "Get out of here. Get yourself sober. And for the love of God, get that bloody song down!" She spun around and marched back into the club.

Owen bellowed a storm of cursing nonsense with veins popping out of his neck and forehead and made the short walk to the motel. His thoughts raced through his head in a jumbled chaos as he threw open the door to Joanna's motel room. He wrenched open the drawers in her bedside table and immediately found what he was looking for. He kicked away a pair of discarded jeans, sat on the edge of the bed, and yanked open the packet, but there were no cigarettes inside. Swearing loudly at an absent Joanna, he looked back at the rather tattered pack and dug his fingers inside, pulling out a wad of papers. Holding the box up to his eye, he found no hidden cigarette. He cursed again.

Grumbling incoherently under his breath, he began flipping through the papers, stopping short after one glance at their contents. His rage evaporated with one quick lick of flame, gone in smoke. The ashes sank down in his chest.

They were a bunch of black and white photographs taken on an old, instant camera and a folded up sheet of paper. A voice somewhere inside him told him to put them back, a voice of which he ignored.

The first and most ragged looking picture was of two boys. Probably around ten or eleven years old if he could guess. The brothers she had mentioned last Christmas, maybe? They were goofing off in baseball uniforms. He flipped to the next one.

A young woman with long dark hair was sitting on a stack of cardboard boxes. She was laughing at something and not looking at the camera. Despite the hazy quality of the photograph and her baggy, unflattering sweatpants, she was beautiful.

The next one was an ugly dog with giant eyes sniffing the camera.

A familiar face greeted him next. He couldn't place it, but he knew that weird boyish grin from somewhere.

A young blonde man was leaning against the railing of a dock somewhere, looking out at the ocean. Maybe he was Chet Adkins?

Nope. This one's Chet Adkins. A man with long black hair sat eating cereal with his elbow propped up on the table, a cigarette in his fingers. It looked like Jo had tried to sneak a picture of him, and he'd caught her. His eyes peeked up at the camera through a set of bushy eyebrows.

Owen was captivated by the next photograph. Maybe it was simply because it was the only one that wasn't black and white. Or maybe she was just that beautiful. She was so little with black, curly hair and eyes the size of golf balls, a tear falling down her chubby cheek. She was quite possibly the most gorgeous little girl he had ever seen. He paused for a moment before flipping to the next one.

A chill sank like fangs into his spine as he stared into a pair of familiar, beady eyes. It was a cutout of a high school yearbook photo from the eighties. A man with short curls and a strong, square jaw. Jesse Owen Sharpe was typed out in bland font beneath the picture. Questions soared through his brain as to why Joanna had his senior portrait at all, much less stashed away with what he presumed to be her valuables. He never bought her brash explanation of being a crazed fan. Hastily, he reached for the folded paper, hoping to find the answers.

It was a letter, handwritten in small, relaxed letters, and addressed to a woman named Audrey.

Hey Aud.

The last time I called you, I left you a voicemail. I said it was the last you would hear from me.

Well it wasn't.

Obviously.

When you left, that was supposed to be it. I was angry with you. I didn't tell you that. But I was. The first week, I thought I could do it. But I couldn't. Well physically I could. I became the world's best diaper changer. Well maybe just in Seattle. Okay I was the best diaper changer in the apartment building. I won't tell you I was the only diaper changer in the apartment building because that would be stupid. I was though.

Anyway I did better than I thought I would. But once she was in bed at night, I couldn't help but think of how badly I wanted you to know her. I wanted to share the cute little moments with you. And of course I thought everything she did was cute.

Everything.

So I started calling you. I'd apologize if it made things harder on you, but I'm not actually sorry. You deserved it.

But I know you better than you think I do. I knew you'd try to find your father. So I tried to find him too. Every spare minute I had − which I didn't have many − I was searching for clues of where he ended up. I went full Sherlock Holmes on his ass. I knew that if I could find him, I could find you.

It worked.

Obviously.

I can't tell you how it felt to see you in that photograph. Not looking at the camera of course. Typical. You were smiling at him. I admit it was strange to see the two of you together at first. I can see the resemblance though. And of course the pretentious bastards have a fan mail address. I fought the urge to mail you a picture of her for months.

But I caved.

Obviously.

That's what's in the other envelope. A picture of our little girl. She's two now. She's grown up so fast. I wanted to send you a picture, but narrowing down the hundreds that I have was hard. So when I took this one, I knew it was the one, but you need to know the story behind it to really get it.

She has nightmares. A lot. One Saturday she woke up at four in the morning, and I could tell going back to sleep wasn't in the cards for either of us. So I grabbed our coats and toboggans, wrapped her up like an Eskimo, and took her to the beach. In November. Shut up. I know it was a bad idea, but I'm a guy. I think there's something in the Y chromosome that allows some leeway for me to make stupid decisions like that. According to the highly esteemed Philosopher Wyatt anyway.

That's you by the way.

In case you've forgotten who you really are, Miss Joanna Farren.

Anyway we sat in the sand and watched the sun come up over the ocean when a humpback whale jumped clean out of the water. I think she jumped as high as it did. She'd never seen one breach before. She was in awe. When I looked down at her, she was crying. So I took a picture. I figured you should see her first whale.

Then I laughed. I know. Terrible dad move, laughing at your daughter's tears, but it was just so cute. But she laughed too, so it was okay.

I guess since it's getting to the end of the letter, I should tell you one of the main reasons I'm writing this. I've started seeing someone. I guess after two years, I'm telling you this more for my sake than for yours. And I know you hated it when I said it, but I love you, Audrey. More than I ever thought I could love anyone. But I've given up hope that you'll come back. I preached to you for years about moving on, and here I am waiting on you to show up at our doorstep. At some point I've got to take my own advice and let you go.

Rosie and I will probably always be here. She has an obsession with whales now. If we left Seattle it would be with me dragging her kicking and screaming. If The Roadside Babel is ever in the neighborhood, look us up. She'd love to meet you.

If I can ask one thing of you — and I think we both know that you owe me that much — it would be that you never forget her. I know you won't. I just have to say it. Because you know better than anyone that you will never be far from her thoughts.

Or from mine.

Liam.

Owen sat in silence for a moment, contemplating what he had just read. The last year spun through his head like a tornado, unraveling everything he thought he knew. Every moment with Joanna shifted. Every conversation. Every look in her eyes. He noticed things he hadn't before. Every word she ever said took on new meaning as his answers began to click into place.

"No," he whispered. "She's not mine. She can't be mine." He tried to rationalize it all in his head, but all of the clues pointed to one inevitable outcome. The words in the letter repeated in his head.

your father... The Roadside Babel... I knew you'd find him... Joanna was his daughter.

It explained everything. Why she'd followed him for a year before approaching him. The unexplainable connection he'd always had with her. The look of adoration in her eyes when he did something impressive. Her strange behavior around Chad and Laurel. Their conversation at the diner. How she'd known his first name.

He reread the letter and went back through the photographs, stopping again at the little girl. Rosie. His granddaughter. He shoved the photos and the letter back in the empty cigarette packet and tossed it back in the drawer, slamming it shut. He stumbled out of Joanna's room and towards his own, his heart pounding violently against his ribcage.

Chapter Ten

Phoenix, Arizona
Day 1365

They said, "The truth will set you free." They put it on bumper stickers and church t-shirts, plastered it on banners, and recited it in group therapy sessions. But what they would never admit to you was that funny little line drawn lightly in the sand, that when crossed, your own personal freedom would endanger those around you. From what she'd seen that day, the truth was something no one really wanted to hear. It might give the confessor a sick sense of freedom, but was it really fair to gain such liberation when the truth bound others? When it weighed them down and set fire to their fragile sense of security that was held up by support beams of lies and fabricated personal histories. It wasn't right. But there was nothing she could do about it now. She leaned back against the headboard, biting down on her cigarette as she thought back to the events of the day, wondering if there was anything she could have done to change the outcome.

Audrey sat at the empty bar contemplating her next move as The Roadside Babel practiced without their guitarist. She hadn't planned far ahead when she'd fled Seattle. Finding Owen had been easier than she'd expected thanks to the Internet and her father's pathetic need for attention and subsequent quest for fame, but now once again she was faced with the demolition of her stable world. She was as happy as she allowed herself to be. She had her father. She had her distraction.

Milo caught her gaze and stretched his twisted mouth into

a grin without missing a beat as he pounded the drums. She smiled back but averted her eyes, flicking them to her fingers absently pulsating against the bar.

She would have to choose soon.

The music sounded strange without the lead guitarist. Chad attempted to fill in for him with his rudimentary guitar skills, reading the music from a stand in front of him. He flubbed again on the chorus and stopped singing, bursting into a cursing rage.

"I'm done y'all!" he exclaimed. "We'll just do the best with what we've got tonight." He laid the guitar on the platform and jumped down heavily. "Someone make sure that jackass shows up." He stormed toward the door. Mike and Milo exchanged perplexed glances. Mike shrugged and pulled his guitar strap over his head, sauntering off the stage to the bar.

"Well that was dramatic," he drawled, reaching over the counter for a drink.

"You sure you want to do that after all that happened earlier?" Audrey asked, giving him a sideways glance.

"Yeah. Owen'll show up completely faced and I'll look sober as a priest next to him."

"I wouldn't count on it. I told him it was in his best interest to sober up before the show tonight."

"You think he listened?"

Audrey didn't answer. She smiled at Milo's approach as he drew up behind her and wrapped his arms around her shoulders, burying his face in her hair. Mike smirked and raised his eyebrows knowingly at Audrey as her muscles involuntarily tensed at Milo's affection. She rolled her eyes.

"I reckon there's a burger joint down the road that's supposed to be pretty good," Mike said. "Think I'll get a bite to eat. Tell Chad if you see him. Don't need him pissin' his britches." Mike strolled out of the club, leaving Milo and Audrey alone. She groaned internally as Milo released her from his grasp and took the seat next to her.

"Have you thought anymore about it?" he asked.

"Nope." She lit a cigarette.

"Why not?"

"Because I don't see the point, Milo. How many times do I have to tell you that?"

He turned his head and gazed unseeingly at the bottles of

liquor arranged in neat rows on the back wall. Audrey sighed.

"We already live together. I just don't see why we need to get married."

"Because we love each other," he shrugged. "It's what people who love each other do."

"Wow you're such a romantic," she quipped humorlessly, ignoring the way that word made her gut roil. When he didn't respond, she continued, "I just like how things are right now, Mi. I don't want to think about something like that. I've seen too many marriages go nuclear, and the ashes never settle easily. So have you."

"At least think about it," he urged.

"Look, Milo. I really don't think – "

The door burst open. Both of them jerked their heads toward the clamor to find Owen staggering through like an injured animal. Audrey cursed and rushed to his side. He shoved her off with a grunt and lumbered to the bar.

"I told you to sober up!" she yelled in disbelief. "I broke your whiskey! How are you even drunker?"

"You think that was my only bottle?" he slurred. He set himself down in her seat and lolled his head to Milo. "I see it now," he said, pointing to Audrey, "with my eyes. She's not what you think. She has the same eyes, Audrey."

Audrey froze, afraid to process his words that echoed through her mind, resounding like air raid sirens that filled her stomach with a crippling dread. Milo blinked in confusion.

"Audrey?" her name sounded wrong in his deep rasp. Unnatural. "That's Joanna."

"Nope," he belched. Milo turned to Audrey with a furrowed brow.

She laughed nervously and ran to the bar. "I'm afraid you've had way too much to drink, sir. You're getting confused."

"I know who you are," he pointed to her. "You're a liar."

Milo glared at Owen with unabashed disgust and slid the tin of peanuts toward him. "We go on in two hours," he muttered and stood, pushing past Audrey to the door.

"Where are you going?" she asked, her desperation rising. Somehow Owen knew who she was. The way he glared at her, taking her in from his slouched position at the bar, twisted her gut in knots. And she didn't want to be alone with him.

"To get Chad," Milo growled.

Audrey collected what was left of her nerve and smiled pleasantly at her father. "Let's get you sobered up, shall we? I think Chad just might kill you if he sees you like this."

"Your hair is so curly," he mumbled.

"Yep," she smiled.

"And red."

"You're very observant."

"And your face is so – " he reached his calloused fingers to the side of her face. She shoved his arm away, her breath catching in her throat. His head lolled as she threw him off balance. "I know you, Audrey."

His bleary eyes bore into her. Her face burned with hot needles, and her stomach turned to lead. She laughed. "Jesus, you're drunker than I thought." She pushed the peanuts in his direction as his unrelenting gaze shattered through her remaining resolve. "For the love of god! Eat the bloody peanuts!" She picked up the tin and slammed it on the bar in front of him, sending peanuts flying in all directions.

"Hey!" she barked at the bartender. Her blonde hair swung around in a golden cascade as she spun around to Audrey's voice. Audrey shook the glass in her hand. The ice clinked against the sides, inaudible with The Roadside Babel's deafening sound from the platform. The club was packed with listeners and drinkers raising their glasses and singing along with the music. Few seemed to notice how terribly they were playing.

Milo unconsciously sped up the beat, Mike struggled to keep up, and the words sounded jumbled as they flew from Chad's mouth. The front man signaled Milo to slow down, but after a few measures, he'd speed it up again. Owen played clumsily, his chords littered with dead strings, and his notes rang out flat. He strummed too many strings with most of his chords, and his fingers seemed to tangle along the neck of the guitar. Audrey had managed to sober him up enough to stand and hold his Telecaster, but she grimaced with every misplayed chord.

She tossed back her vodka and slammed the glass against the bar, pushing herself from her seat. She weaved through the mass of sweating bodies and out into the stifling night air. She lit a cigarette and pulled the smoke deep into her lungs, holding it there until her head whirled with lack of oxygen before she released it. It was burned out in four puffs, and she lit another.

Owen knew who she was, but how? She was always so careful around him. Except the night she called him Jesse, but that was months ago. And it didn't explain how he knew her name. She ran her hand across her scalp, ignoring how her fingers snagged a tangle of hair.

It didn't matter how he figured it out. Not now anyway. What mattered was what to do next. She could leave. Right now she could walk to the motel and climb onto her Honda, leaving The Roadside Babel behind. But where would she go?

She lit a third cigarette and worked to calm her heart rate, which mimicked Milo's speeding rhythm on the drums.

A loud crash wrenched her from her thoughts. The music broke off, and the crowd gasped. A deafening silence followed as Audrey wheeled around and flung the door open. Inside she could hear the hushed whisper that spread through the crowd like a contagion. Three men stood on the platform, staring down at the floor in front of them, shaking their heads in revulsion. She pushed people aside until she got to the front and found her father sprawled out on the ground, unconscious.

"Looks like we'll have to end it here, folks," Chad's tense voice amplified above her as she crouched down to Owen's side. Unhooking his guitar strap, she rolled him onto his back and off of his Telecaster. Mike appeared with a glass of water, dumping it on Owen's face. The drunken guitarist spluttered back to consciousness.

"Get up," Mike growled. He and Audrey lifted him up by his elbows and toted him outside. They sat him down, leaning him back against the cool brick wall. Milo brought him a glass of water. None said a word until Chad burst through the door, cursing wildly.

"That's it, Owen. You're done."

"What?" Audrey screeched, swinging around to face him.

"Chad, you can't be serious," Mike demurred from behind her. "I know we talked about finding a new guitarist, but you can't just kick him out here and now."

"You're damn right I can! You can play guitar. We'll manage better without him than with him screwing up every song."

"Chad, please," Owen mumbled from his slump by the wall.

"He had a bit of a shock today," Audrey tried to reason with him. "Just give him another chance."

Chad shook his head and waved a shaking finger at Owen's crumpled form. "I will not play another song with that drunk." He turned, still shaking his hand, and stormed off toward the motel.

"Chad, give him another chance or I'm out, too!" she called after him. The words tumbled from her mouth without her permission, but she didn't regret them. Chad turned back to her with a bewildered and exasperated expression.

"Why do you care that much?"

"Because," she paused and swallowed, "because he's my father." Three pairs of eyes locked onto her in a stunned silence.

Mike sighed a curse behind her. "Now it all makes sense."

"You're kidding," Milo breathed. "Right?"

"Unfortunately not," Owen answered for her.

"I won't leave him," Audrey said in an unsteady voice, still staring at Chad. "Not like this."

Chad paused, staring at her with piteous eyes that made her cringe. "Then it looks like this is the end of the line for you, too." He shook his head as he turned back to the motel. Audrey was unable to move, unable to breathe as Mike yelled after Chad and ran to catch up with him. Finally, she turned to face the remaining two.

"Are you serious, Joanna?" Milo's voice was thick, rising in pitch with every painful word that he visibly forced from his throat. He approached her, and she crossed her arms to ward off his touch.

"My name isn't Joanna," she swallowed back the lump in her throat, silently preparing for what the rest of the night had in store. "Well it is, but – "

Milo blinked rapidly as the reality of it all clicked in his head. "Audrey?"

She breathed, staring into his pained eyes, biting down on her lips. "My name is Audrey Joanna Wyatt. Farren is Liam's name." She looked at the asphalt beneath her feet. "And my daughter's." The breath that left Milo's lungs brought tears to her eyes, pushing the oxygen from her chest. He brushed past her in his move toward the motel. She pressed her hand to her mouth to silence her building cry and lifted her stinging eyes to Owen, who met them with a burning malice.

"I don't need you to stay with me," he jeered.

"Tough," she spat, swallowing her tears as her throat constricted and expanded in its effort to expel the lump that settled itself there. She left him crouched in the parking lot and chased after Milo. She found him in the bathroom of their motel room, violently shoving his few belongings into his bag, deliberately avoiding his own reflection in the mirror.

"Milo," she choked out and cleared her throat. "Please talk to me." He ignored her, checking beneath the sink for the third time in his attempt to evade her for as long as possible. "Please – "

"What do you want me to say, Audrey?" he spun around, his hair falling into his contorted face. Tears filled his eyes as if the taste of her real name had stabbed daggers in his tongue on its way out, and he turned away from her.

"Just come sit down," she pleaded, keeping her voice calm. She reached out to touch his arm, but he jerked it away. She recoiled slowly as if waiting for him to strike. "Please."

Milo paused, tension rolling through his taut arms, and he relaxed his fingers. He nodded dolefully and walked past her to sit on the bed. She turned slowly to face him as his legs sprawled out in front of him, and he lit a cigarette. He nodded his head to the spot next to him, the light of the flame burning against his face. She crossed the room and hesitantly sat down next to him, her muscles rigid as she prepared herself for the conversation ahead. He handed her a cigarette, and they smoked in silence for what felt like hours before his gravelly voice broke in.

"Do you love me?"

Audrey blew out a cloud of smoke and winced at the sound of her own hoarse voice as she whispered, "No."

"Did you ever?"

"No," she shook her head and stared down at her lap.

He bit down on the inside of his cheek. "Did you love this Liam guy?"

"Yes," she admitted aloud for the first time. It was an oddly freeing exclamation despite the gnawing sensation in her chest.

"Do you still?"

She didn't answer as silent tears began to fall from her eyes in steady rivulets.

"Of course you do. You had his kid," he said, his voice rigid with pain.

"Milo – "

"I told you about Tonya's abortion," he whispered. He crossed his arms to keep his hands from shaking and turned his head away from her. She awkwardly reached a hand out to comfort him but thought better of it and retreated.

"You did, and I should have told you about Rosie. I know that, but – "

"Yeah you should have!" he spat, rounding on her.

She shoved the cigarette in her mouth and singed her lips as it burned to the butt.

"I should have asked you about those names," he scolded himself.

"I wouldn't have told you."

"No I suppose not."

"So this is it then, huh?" Mike smiled gingerly at her. The van door slammed as Milo and Chad loaded their suitcases in the back.

"Looks like it," she smiled back. He held his arms out in invitation. She hugged him tightly.

"I'll miss you, little Miss Elusive Ginge," he breathed into her hair.

"Just do something for me, okay?" she swallowed the burning lump in her throat, staring over his shoulder at Milo leaning against the van. Mike released her, sliding his hand along her arms to hold her wrists.

"Sure, anything."

"Get rid of the blonde tips."

He snorted and shook his head, running a hand through his dyed hair with a sheepish grin. "Ah, but I thought they were workin' for me."

"They're not," she grinned. His lips formed a sad smile as his glittering eyes stared down at her. "And take care of him," she said through the knot in her throat. "Make sure he's okay."

"I will. I promise," he raised her hand to his face and kissed her knuckles before walking off to the van.

"You sure you don't want to come with us?" Chad asked, approaching her with his hands in his pockets. "He may be your dad, but he's a jackass."

"Yeah he is," she chortled. "I won't stay with him for long.

I'll make sure he gets back to Memphis okay, and then I'll be on my way."

"He sold his place in Memphis," Chad informed her with another irritatingly piteous expression. "It was in his ex wife's name. He wanted a fresh start or whatever."

"I'll figure something out," she assured him, silently cursing her father.

"Well if you're sure, then." He hugged her stiffly. "And thanks for the songs, Jo."

She held onto him for a moment too long to blink away her tears before he could see them. "If you could make sure 'The Forsaken Rose' gets at least one good run I'd really appreciate it."

"Sure thing," he smiled. "And let me know where you end up. You'll be getting royalties on those songs." She nodded, and he turned to climb in the driver's seat.

She finally tore her eyes from the van to meet Milo's. He glared at her with such abhorrence that she felt as though she would combust and he would watch her burn. She stepped toward him, but he kicked off the bumper and disappeared behind the sliding door of the van's backseat. The break lights flashed momentarily as Chad changed gears, and the remaining members of the Roadside Babel pulled out of the empty parking lot. She followed them into the road and watched as the dust clouds dissipated until the old white van receded on the horizon. Only then did her breath return to her.

She kicked the tire of her motorcycle, dropped onto the curb in front of Owen's motel room, pulled out a cigarette, and stared out at the expanse of desert wasteland before her, wiping the dusty tears from her face.

Having to think of what to say to those men reminded her of why she always left before anyone had the chance to say goodbye. Nothing that formed in her head seemed appropriate. There weren't words to befit a suitable farewell to those few that she held close to her heart. And it took everything in her not to run after them as they drove away.

Chapter Eleven

Buckeye, Arizona
Day 1378

"Get up," Audrey yelled and kicked the door closed behind her, ignoring his startled cursing. She tossed the shopping bag on his bed. "Up, up, up. It's almost noon." She pulled the crisp button down and dark wash jeans from their plastic wrappings and flung them on top of his groaning form.

"Get out, Audrey!" he grunted, rolling away from the sunlight that poured through the window.

"I've got you another interview. You said you used to bartend, right?"

"Yeah, but – "

"Good. You should get the job then," she interrupted his protest, standing at the foot of the bed with her hands on her hips. "Get up. And get showered because I can smell you from here. I got you these because you'll have to look sharp, Mr. Sharpe." She winked and snorted humorously at herself.

When he finally rolled out of bed and muttered under his breath as he lumbered to the bathroom, she flipped on the television. A local channel was showing an all-day Harry Potter marathon. It was midway through The Chamber of Secrets when she tuned in.

"Hey, Audrey! Guess what Mark just bought us on DVD!" he bubbled with excitement. His cheeks were red, and he shoved his sweaty hair away from his face.

"What?" she feigned curiosity.

"The new Harry Potter movie!" He pulled a Wal-Mart bag from behind his back and waved it in her face. "Can we watch it

now?"

    "Right now?"
    He nodded exuberantly.
    "Sure. Go get your brother."
    She could almost feel Daniel curled up against her side, cheering on the wizard boy on screen.
    "How's this?" Owen asked groggily, stepping out of the bathroom.
    "You look great," she lied. He still had indentions on his cheeks from his pillow. She lugged him out the door and led him down the gravel sidewalk to Serge's Bar. It was only half a mile trek, but by the time they reached the front door, they were both drenched in sweat.
    "Tuck your shirt in," Audrey instructed.
    "I'm not tuckin' my shirt in," he grumbled.
    "Do it."
    Owen rolled his eyes and did as he was told, ignoring her triumphant smirk.
    "Remember, just smile and be your charming self," she encouraged. "You'll do great. Hi, Serge."
    At one in the afternoon, the bar was deserted. The wooden floors were freshly swept, but the air around them smelled of stale cigarettes. A wiry, old man with a scraggly beard and sun spotted skin stepped out from a back room.
    "Ms. Williams," the bar's owner nodded towards her. Owen shot her a questioning glance, which she ignored. She smiled pleasantly at Serge as he greeted Owen with a stern expression plastered to his leathery face and led him to the bar. Audrey took a seat in the corner and stared out at the street through the dust caked windowpane.
    When The Roadside Babel left them two weeks ago on a Phoenix roadside with nothing but her Honda, Owen's guitars, and a couple of wadded bills tucked into Audrey's pocket, she'd watched them drive off with a pang of regret. With those four men, her efforts to forget where she came from had become almost easy. The moment Chad pushed the gas pedal, she wished she'd chosen them instead, but the only reason she'd been with them in the first place was Owen. She couldn't leave him alone and helpless in the desert in a near permanent drunken stupor. She had an obligation to him as his daughter to make sure he was taken care of. Or so she

told herself. She didn't want to think about how much she'd hurt Milo. He would never forgive her for lying and keeping so many secrets, and without Owen, she had no one. So she decided to stay.

Unable to find him work in Phoenix, she'd dragged him from town to town, hitchhiking his rides while she drove behind them on her Honda, until they reached the sweltering town of Buckeye, Arizona.

The thermostat on the motel wall earlier that morning read 102°F. She'd stared at it for a long moment, puffing on a cigarette and contemplating her own immediate future. Once Owen was settled in with a job and a place to sleep, she'd kick this town's dust from her boots, climb on her motorcycle, and be on her way. To where, she had no idea.

She pushed Seattle's ever-present summons from her mind and thought of all of the places she'd been. Oddly enough, she found herself thinking of Denver. In the months she spent searching for her estranged father, she'd followed a false lead to the Mile-High City and spent a couple of weeks there. Over eight hundred miles separated her from Colorado now, but she enjoyed the monotony of the interstate. The predictability. She had enough gas money, and she didn't need much food. The prospect of a fresh start should have excited her, but nothing really did that these days. And she'd had enough of fresh starts.

Audrey leaned back in the booth and pat her jean pockets until she found the one that held her lighter.

"Tell me why I should hire you," Serge growled.

"I've been a bartender before," Owen muttered. "I know how it works."

"Right," his interviewer responded, clearly unimpressed. Owen blinked heavily, trying to expel the remaining sleep from his eyes and the ache from his temples. Serge nodded past Owen to the corner where Audrey sat. "I'll be honest with you Mr. Sharpe, I only agreed to this interview because of your daughter's enthusiasm. I've tended to my own bar for twenty years, Mr. Sharpe. I don't need you doing it for me."

"I understand," Owen sighed, already slightly irritated by the man's continual usage of his name. He had to stop himself from laughing. What façade had Audrey used to trick this poor man into thinking her enthusiastic? "And now I'll be honest with you, Sergeant, I couldn't tell you for certain where I am right now or even what this bar's name is."

"Serge's Bar," he commented blandly.

Owen eyed him blandly. "Thing is, that woman's dragged me from bars to restaurants to god knows what else trying to get me a job. It's been exhausting, but no matter what I say, she won't give it a rest."

"Well, Mr. Sharpe, I'm not going to hire you," Serge asserted, "but I'd be lying if I said business was doing good. I get the same customers in here every night that I've gotten for the last fifteen years. This bar will die with them, and with the state of their livers, that's not far off," he laughed grimly and continued. "Maybe a woman like Ms. Williams is just what this bar needs to get back on its feet. Maybe bring in a younger clientele. Could be nice having a woman around here, too."

"What are you gettin' at exactly?" Owen asked.

"I'll hire your daughter if she wants the job," he explained impatiently. Owen leaned back in understanding and looked over his shoulder at Audrey already dragging at a cigarette. She gazed blindly through the windows with solemn contemplation etched around her drooping eyes. That look had adorned her expression several times in the past two weeks, and if he'd learned anything in his fifty-three years, it's that a woman with that look on her face was woman about to run off. He found himself blowing job interview after job interview, unable to confront her about her intentions. He couldn't let her leave.

"I'll talk to her about it," Owen blurted out. "I'm sure she'll take it though. She's probably tired of luggin' me around just as much as I'm tired of being lugged around." He laughed hoarsely. Serge hinted at a grin, slightly bearing slimy teeth.

"I look forward to hearing from her." The two men stood and shook hands. Before turning to leave, Serge nodded in response to Audrey's wave and mumbled under his breath at Owen. "I hope you don't mind me asking, but what the hell kind of a name is Percy for a little girl anyway?"

"Her mother was crazy," Owen quipped. Percy Williams? What the hell kind of an alias was Percy Williams?

"How'd it go?" Percy Williams asked expectantly when she caught up with him on the sidewalk outside the bar.

"He said he'd call," Owen lied. "Percy Williams?" he repeated aloud.

"Joanna Farren has been compromised," she joked.

"But Percy?"

"Yeah," she shrugged. "Like Persephone. The Greek goddess?" she rolled her eyes when he still didn't understand. "They called her the bringer of death."

"Well that's morbid," he grunted. "You're terrible at makin' aliases. I thought you liked the Iceland mythology anyway."

"I like the Thor comic books. They're different. But you never questioned me for a second when I was Joanna Farren until you snooped through my things," she sneered. "Anyway what's for lunch?"

"Get whatever you want. I need a break from you. You're overbearin' and annoying." He stalked off before she could respond.

Audrey walked into their motel room and pulled her hiking boots off with her toes before grabbing a pillow and curling up on the foot of her bed with her knees pulled in and her hands clasped beneath her chin. The television was still on, showing another of the Harry Potter movies.

" 'Sorry, Professor, but I must not tell lies,' " she quoted mutely along with Harry.

"Would you stop?" he laughed. "You basically just killed one of the best moments in the history of television! I thought you said you haven't seen this movie."

"I haven't," she shrugged. "But I read the books countless times. You don't forget a line like that."

"Oh, you're one of those!" Liam groaned loudly, covering his face with a thick hand.

"What's that supposed to mean?

"It just means you're annoying." He looked at her from across the sofa with eyes like black holes, inadvertently drawing her in. For a moment, she forgot who she was. Her smile faded.

"Will you read them to the baby?"

His lips tightened. "Stay and read them yourself."

Her voice caught in her throat and wheezed its way out in a whimper. "I can't."

He reached across the couch to take her hand. She flinched at the touch, so familiar, like the ghost of a distant memory. He brought her knuckles to his lips for a scratchy kiss, and she swallowed the lump forming in her throat. It had been months since she'd allowed him to touch her. She turned her head back to the television so he wouldn't see the tears building in her eyes and moved her hand to her round stomach.

Audrey wondered if he ever read *Harry Potter* to his little Rosie. She pictured Liam lying in Rosie's small bed with his legs crossed at the ankles, holding the heavy book with two hands, the curly headed little girl snuggled close against him. Her heart stuttered and she pushed the image away.

The door creaked open, and Owen stumbled in. She didn't spare him a glance.

"That was quite a long lunch."

"Went house huntin'," he slurred.

"And bottle chasing?"

He didn't answer. She guessed he was nodding.

"I take it you got the job then?"

"Nope."

"Then why go house hunting when you don't have a way to pay for it?"

"You got the job."

Audrey sat up to face him. "Excuse me?"

"Serge didn't want me. He wanted you. Said somethin' about your enthusiasm."

"Well I'm not taking it, so we'll just have to find you another place to work."

"I like it here."

"In Buckeye? It's hot as hell here."

"I bought a house," he grunted, throwing himself across his bed.

"Right," she scoffed. "With what money?"

He belched. "I sold your motorcycle."

She gaped at him in disbelief. "That's hilarious, Owen. Where'd you really get the money?" He lay back with his hands behind his head and didn't respond. Lurching off the bed, she threw open the door and darted outside. Her Honda was nowhere to be seen.

Collapsing onto the curb, she dropped her head in her

hands. She was stranded here in this desolate hell with her drunkard father and no tears left to cry. Her heart throbbed, heavy and worn, in her ears as she stared at the empty parking spot. Sparing only a short moment for despair, she ran her fingers along her scalp and trudged inside, closing the door behind her and glaring down at her father's dozing form.

"I hate you," she muttered dryly. He saluted her lazily and fell asleep. She lay back down on her bed and turned up the volume to drown out his snores.

Chapter Twelve

Huntsville, Alabama

"Did you get the ice?" Elizabeth called to her husband from the bathroom, adding a layer of mascara to her lashes with practiced ease.

"Was I supposed to?" he asked after a suspiciously long pause.

"Yes," she couldn't keep the malice from her tone.

"But the freezer has an ice maker."

"That won't make enough ice for forty people!" She slammed the wand back inside the tube of mascara.

"Okay I'll get some on the way back from the airport, then," he huffed.

"Seriously, how many years of medical school and you can't figure this stuff out?" she mumbled under her breath as she heard him leave. She wondered again why they were having this party. Why couldn't they just throw a normal birthday party for a ten-year-old girl instead of making it some huge reunion fiasco?

A high-pitched squeal carried from the floor above her. Elizabeth closed her eyes and breathed, hoping to calm herself before dealing with the day ahead.

"MOOOOOM!"

"Yes Mia," Elizabeth answered a little too sternly to the beckoning call. When she came to the bottom of the stairs and beheld her son leaning over the balcony in a tiara, she couldn't help the smile that stretched her dark-coated lips.

"He took my tiara and he won't let me use his phone charger!" her eldest shrieked.

"Why can't you just use your own?" Elizabeth asked absentmindedly as she walked to the kitchen to search for the paper plates, her kids following closely behind her.

"I left it at Lacey's house, and now my phone's dead and I can't tell her how big of an idiot my brother is!" she rounded on Ezra.

"Don't call him an idiot, please."

"But it's my *birthday*!" she stamped her foot.

"No it's not," Ezra corrected his sister, adjusting the tiara that was beginning to slide down his silky hair. "Your birthday's on Tuesday." Mia screamed and made a move for the tiara, accidentally shoving it further on his head in her effort.

"Ow!" he yelled as the combed ends scratched his scalp.

"Give it a rest, will you?" Elizabeth snapped at Mia, pulling the combs from her son's hair, and handed the tiara to the spoiled princess. Mia placed it gently on the top of her long, meticulously curled locks, then spun around and trotted off without another word.

"She needs a spanking," Ezra stared after her, rubbing the side of his head.

"Agreed," Elizabeth grinned down at him. "Why are you still in your pajamas? Go get dressed. Uncle Ethan will be here soon."

"Oh!" he sped off to his room to change.

Clapping her hands together, Elizabeth turned back to make an inventory of the party supplies. Plates, cups, napkins, forks, spoons, knives, cake, pasta, garlic bread, and a hoard of soft drinks and kool-aid. She racked her brain for anything that was missing. She texted Amal to pick up some sweet tea. Ethan loved sweet tea. She received a short 10-4 in response. She tried not to think of the stunned announcement he'd made the night before. That man and his timing.

The doorbell interrupted her thoughts. She checked her reflection in the door of the microwave before running to get the front door. From the sound of her daughter's voice, Mia had beaten her to it.

"Hey Zoe! Come on, I have tiaras for everyone in my room! Mine's the biggest one of course, but still." Her voice carried as she ran upstairs and Zoe struggled to keep up.

By the time Elizabeth made it to the foyer, they had disappeared.

"Hey, guys," she smiled apologetically at the couple

standing in the gaping doorway. She hugged Mark and Noel in turn and led them through to the kitchen, pouring them a drink. "There's two of them, right? Or am I going crazy?"

"Ethan took Ronan for a joyride in that new Camero of his," Mark answered with a chuckle.

"He says joyride, but I don't think the kid ever goes over sixty," Noel added. "I'm pretty sure I drive my minivan faster."

Elizabeth laughed. Twins. It could be worse, right? At least theirs were both well behaved. How do you unspoil a spoiled brat?

The next half hour passed with the uneventful arrival of Mia's friends and their parents. The spacious Ganesh home was soon teeming with activity.

The rev of an engine sounded from outside. An excited smile wrinkled Elizabeth's eyes as she sprinted to the door. In the driveway, Ronan Fields was hanging out of the passenger side window of a sleek black Camero, waving his fists in the air. Ethan's grin was just visible as he revved the engine again. Elizabeth gave Ronan a fist bump before shoving the top of his head back down into the seat.

"Nice car. Can I get a ride?" she said, leaning down to peer through the window.

Ethan bit his smile and winked. "Give me a kiss and I just might," he flirted, cutting the engine and climbing out of the car. She met him at the front and wrapped him in a tight hug.

"How've you been?" she asked.

"Good, obviously," he gestured to the car. "You?"

"Ah, can't complain."

Another engine roared, interrupting their conversation as Amal's Jaguar pulled up next to them. He revved the engine again. Ethan's grin didn't waver as he casually flipped Amal the bird, disregarding the passengers in the car. Elizabeth rolled her eyes.

"Sorry, but I have to say it. Jaguars are still better," Amal bragged, coming around the hood.

"Jag-you-uh?" Ethan feigned confusion at Amal's accent. "What's a jag-you-uh?"

"You know, that's still funny seven times running," Amal quipped with heavily layered sarcasm.

"Still though, can't beat the American muscle."

"Ah but it lacks that British charm, don't you think?" With their testosterone battle at its conclusion, they hugged in greeting.

"Also I believe Southern hospitality has won out over your English sense of manners. You haven't introduced me to this beautiful woman." Ethan smiled politely at the woman, whose cheekbones told of one too many rounds of Botox injections, and kissed her hand as she approached.

"Sorry," Amal hastily apologized. "This is Thomas, his *wife* Nancy, and his brother, William."

"Ah, yeah Thomas! I met you at the wedding!" Ethan shook his hand. "It's good to meet you, William."

"Liam," he corrected gruffly and shook the offered hand.

"And who's this?" Ethan knelt down to get on eye level with the young girl keeping close to Liam's side.

"Dania," she answered and politely extended her hand to Ethan.

"It's wonderful to meet you, Dania," he laughed and kissed the back of her hand. "My name's Ethan."

"It's nice to meet you, too," she muttered shyly.

Liam's eyes jolted to Elizabeth in recognition. She nodded softly and turned her attention to her husband with a pointed glance, all too aware of the hoards of young girls running rampant through her house.

"Why don't we move this inside?" Amal suggested, taking the hint from his already frazzled wife.

"Sounds like a plan," Ethan jumped up. "Hey Dani, can I call you Dani? What's your favorite color?"

"Blue," she answered quietly.

"Blue? That's so cool! I like pink. Pink is cool. What's so funny?"

"So that's Ethan, huh?" Liam asked Elizabeth, watching his daughter laugh.

"The one and only."

"He seems happy."

"He's certainly the life of the party," Elizabeth smiled.

"I wish Aud could have seen him like this."

"She could have," she responded dryly before changing the subject. "So that's Miss Dania Rose, is it?"

"The one and only," Liam beamed.

"She's a cutie."

"Thanks, she gets it from her dad," he winked.

"Right," Elizabeth scoffed. "Where's Beverly?" she asked,

craning her neck to look for the platinum blonde ticking away at her cell phone.

"She couldn't come," he shrugged. "Couldn't get away from work or something like that. I think she just didn't want to endure a plane ride with Rose."

"That's still a thing?" she asked, knowing the girl's aversion to any of her father's friends outside of her family.

"She hates literally everyone," Liam added with a laugh that sounded a little too emphatic to be believable.

"Wonder where she gets that from," Elizabeth mumbled sullenly under her breath. Liam's smile faded as he turned his eyes to study the bitterness in her expression.

Liam watched from his seat on a barstool that he was sure cost more than his house as Elizabeth busied herself with hosting a party that progressed without a seam. He saw it all as a bit too structured. But with a kid like Mia, structure was probably important. God, he hoped Rosie wouldn't turn out like that.

Unfortunately the poor girl had inherited the loner tendencies of her parents, and being the youngest of the group didn't help things. She got on okay with Ronan when at the kids table, but when she wasn't glued to her daddy's side, Ethan was making her laugh. Even now, she was sitting next to him in the living room talking more than he'd ever seen her talk without breaking, but Ethan listened with constant rapture, his attention never wavering. He took in every word she said, interjecting only to make some comment that would send her into a fit of giggles.

The corner of Liam's mouth teased at a smile. Even if they were both unaware of their connection, it was the first time Rosie had been in contact with her mother's family. And he was glad to see Ethan so happy. All Liam knew about him was what Aud had told him through the years. But with her dark and morose perspectives, he had always seen Ethan as a sad and broken child. He had never been so glad to be wrong.

"Wow, she can talk." Ethan laughed when Rosie ran off with Ronan to watch Mia open her hoard of presents. He stole a beer from the fridge and popped the cap off on the countertop.

"She's usually pretty shy," Liam said. "I think she just likes you."

"Really? I can't picture it." After a short silence, Ethan looked around as though to make sure they were the only ones in the kitchen and leaned back against the counter. "Y'all are from Seattle, right?"

"Yeah."

"That's a real nice place. My sister lived there for a few years."

"Six and a half years," Liam interrupted. He knew what Ethan was getting at and didn't want to waste any time.

"So you knew her then." It wasn't a question.

"Yeah."

"Were y'all close?"

"Pretty close, yeah." He kept his answers short and hoped the questions about what she had been like in those days would follow and end there, but he was wrong. Ethan looked at the ground and gritted his teeth.

"Please tell me Dania isn't my niece," he demanded, shooting Liam a furious look. He didn't answer. "Jesus," Ethan ran his fingers through his hair and turned to punch the countertop. Liam let him seethe for a moment.

"It's not what you think," he began.

"Oh it's not, is it?" Ethan fumed. "Well, please, enlighten me because it sure as hell looks like she ran off and left y'all behind. She's good at that by the way." He took a hefty swig of his beer and slammed the bottle down on the counter with a loud clink.

"When Rosie was born, Aud wasn't in a very good state," Liam started to explain.

"My sister hasn't been in a 'good state' for almost twenty years," Ethan spat, "but it doesn't give her the right to continually abandon the people who love her."

"She thought she was doing the right thing," Liam recited.

"Oh yeah?" he laughed maliciously. "And how did she justify it this time? What, she thought you and Dani would be better off coping without her? That her interference – no – her mere presence would only make things worse?"

"She said she wished her mother would have done the same for her," Liam's volume rose with his temper.

"What?" Ethan's face contorted in bewilderment, but the statement silenced him for long enough to finally listen. Liam took a deep breath to calm himself before divulging pieces of Audrey he'd never wanted to share, much less with her brother, but Ethan deserved an explanation more than anyone.

"Your sister wished she'd been put up for adoption. If she wasn't a part of your family, she wouldn't have been driving the car that morning." Liam waited as his words sunk in. Ethan seemed to understand, but his anger didn't dissipate. The muscles in his jaws clenched before he spoke again.

"She said that?"

"I loved Audrey," Liam admitted, the words sliding off his tongue with a familiar ease as they had countless times through the years. "She's the strongest, bravest woman I've ever known. But when she found me again after Amal and El left, she was almost constantly strung out on heroin." He waited as the news settled with Ethan, who leaned back heavily against the counter.

"No," he whispered, his brow furrowed in denial, but he didn't look surprised, only disappointed.

"She'd been getting it from her neighbor. So I moved her into my place and got her clean, but without the drugs, her nightmares came back."

"Nightmares?"

"I don't think she ever would have told me about you and your brother if she didn't call out your names every night."

Ethan looked down, crossing his arms and kneading his toe into the floor. "She never moved on, did she?"

"Why do you think she asked me to name our girl Dania?" Ethan shook his head. "When she got pregnant, she was in a sort of hysterics. Her first reaction was to abort the pregnancy. I talked her out of it with some rather harsh methods if I'm being honest."

Do you really want another child's death on your hands? He flinched as his own words bellowed back at him. The hurt and betrayal in her eyes stabbed like a blade of ice in the back of his skull. He'd never forgive himself for that.

"Then she told me she was leaving," he continued. The memory played before him like a scene from a movie: Aud with her sunken face and frizzy hair looking him in the eyes. *"When it's born, that's it. I'm gone. I can't stay here anymore."*

"I tried everything to get her to stay. But she'd made up her mind."

"Man, I'm sorry," Ethan broke the subsequent silence. "It couldn't have been easy on you."

"Look, guy," Liam asserted firmly, "I wasn't planning on telling anyone about Rosie, especially you. So if you could just keep it to yourself – "

"Yeah, no problem."

As if on cue, Rosie came barreling into the kitchen with Ronan bouncing ecstatically at her heels. "Daddy, Daddy, look! Ronan lost a tooth!" She raised an outstretched hand as close to Liam's face as she could reach.

"That's – " Liam blanched at the bloody tooth in his daughter's palm, "freaking gross! Why do *you* have it?"

"She's the one that pulled it!" Ronan yelled exuberantly and ran off to find his parents. Ethan threw back his head in a loud, guttural roar of laughter while Liam grimaced at his daughter in disbelief.

"That's just disturbing, Rose. Here," he handed her a napkin, "go give it back to Ronan." She smiled proudly and trotted off to find her friend. "And keep your hands out of other people's mouths!" he called after her.

"Ronan Shane!" Noel's disgusted yet unsurprised shriek could be heard from the neighboring room. Liam and Ethan laughed to themselves at the absurdity when Elizabeth marched into the kitchen with an armful of trash bags.

"Here, El, I'll take that out for you," Liam offered.

"You're an angel!" she gasped.

"I know," he winked and threw the bags over his shoulder, heading for the garage.

Elizabeth looked to Ethan and painted on a smile. "Having a good time?"

"I know Dani is Audrey's daughter," he stated plainly, his elation evaporating.

"Okay," she replied with her hands on her hips. "And how'd you take it?"

"I could really learn to hate her," he frowned in disapproval.

"Get in line," Elizabeth muttered and sprinted out of the kitchen to clean off the dining room table.

The rest of the party went by in a blur of shrieks from young girls and gossip from their parents. Maybe she was just getting old, but Elizabeth was really beginning to hate parties. Finally it was time for everyone to go. Amal showed the Farrens upstairs to the guest rooms while Elizabeth said goodbye to Mark and his family.

"Some party," he smiled.

"I think we're done with birthday parties until the sweet sixteen," Elizabeth sighed heavily.

"Oh that'll be fun," he shook his head. Both of them tried not to think of their daughters as teenagers. "I remember taking girls up to the Monte Sano Park over here in high school," he reminisced.

"Wait you had more than one high school girlfriend?" she teased.

"Yeah!" he defended himself. "I had two, thank you very much." When they laughed, their laughter was tense.

"Do they have any news?" he asked finally.

"News?"

"The Seattle friends. Do they know anything about Audrey?"

"I doubt it," Elizabeth spat. "She left Seattle years ago to whore around the country with a bunch of gross rednecks. And for the record, I stopped caring about her whereabouts when she decided to end our friendship over her freaking dog. All she has ever done is run from her problems. So just give it some time, and she'll leave Father Dearest in the dust, too. Then I'm sure you'll be able to sleep at night. But don't bother me about it."

"Hey, I'm sorry, I didn't mean – "

"It's fine, I'm sorry," she winced when she realized what she'd said, rubbing her temples with a thumb and forefinger. "I shouldn't have gone off like that. It's just been a long couple of days."

"I understand. We've been praying for your family," he smiled reassuringly at her, reaching out to squeeze her arm comfortingly.

"Thanks." She waved them off and collapsed on the bottom of the stairs, leaning her head against the wall as she listened to the conversations floating down from the top floor.

"Woooooow," came Rosie's high voice. "That's a lot of Legos!"

"You can put them right on the wall, see?" Ezra explained.

"Dad glued the Lego plates on the wall so I can build extra cool things. I built the rocket once from the Space and Rocket Center if you want to see it!"

"Can I make a whale?" she asked.

"Yeah!" his response was followed by the sound of hundreds of Legos being dumped into the floor. "I'll make a dragon and they can fight each other!"

Elizabeth smiled to herself, recalling all the times as a teenager when she imagined herself as a mom, drinking cocktails on the back patio with Audrey while their kids played in the backyard. This wasn't at all how she'd imagined it, but she would take it.

A quick glance around the house at the mess that awaited her was all she could handle, and she made her way down to the bottom floor, stepping out onto the dark planks of the patio. The sweet scent of the woods soothed her frayed nerves as the late autumn breeze rustled the drying leaves in the darkness that enveloped her. Bryant bounded up the steps, panting excitedly, and wagged his tail happily at her feet as she tangled her fingers in his thick fur.

The events of the day had wreaked havoc on her already fragile emotions. With the Farrens there, it reminded everyone of Audrey. Everyone who knew her had hounded Elizabeth with questions. Luckily only one of them was smart enough to put it together that Dania Rose was Audrey's daughter. Unluckily, that one person was Ethan. Add that to a bunch of screaming preteen girls, her mother's incessant questioning, and her fight with Amal the night before. Maybe it would have all been less strenuous if he had been by her side, but he felt so far away, almost completely out of reach. Yes, things had changed in their fourteen years together, but had they really reached this point?

The screen door creaked behind her and clicked shut, interrupting her thoughts. Unsure of where the night would lead, she didn't turn around, but he surprised her by wrapping his arms around her shoulders and resting his chin on her head.

"I won't go if you don't want me to."

"If you really meant that, you would have talked to me about it from the beginning instead of planning it for months behind my back," she stated dryly.

"I tried to tell you a few times," he said. "I just never found the right moment."

"Oh, and throwing it out casually after I tell you I'm pregnant is absolute perfect timing. Way to go." She pulled herself from his grip and trudged across the patio, collapsing heavily into a chair. He sat down next to her, pushing the giant Newfoundland down from his lap.

"I'm terribly sorry, Elizabeth."

"You talked about saving the planet when we first got married, but I thought once we had Mia, it wasn't in the picture anymore because you said you didn't want to miss anything. But what if you're gone when this one's born? Did you think of that?" Her voice rose in pitch with every syllable.

"Of course I did, but I didn't exactly expect you to get pregnant again when I signed up," he responded defensively.

"Oh, and you think I did?" she countered. "You think I really expected this? For god's sake, Al, I'll be forty when I have this baby! Which means I'll be paying for college and your nursing home bills at the same time!"

"You'll toss me in a home?" She tried to ignore the playful hurt in his eyes.

"At this rate? For sure putting you in a home," she answered.

"Fair enough." He laughed softly for a moment. The anger gone, Elizabeth's fears began to set in.

"But Somalia," she voiced her disbelief. "What if something happens to you? I can't raise three kids without you." Before she'd finished he was already knelt in front of her. He took her hands in his and stared intently up at her.

"Nothing is going to happen," he assured her, enunciating his words with a squeeze on her fingers. "It's just a four month mission. It'll be simple examinations and surgeries. Routine stuff. I'll be back before the baby's born. I promise. And I'll change every diaper for the first two months."

She leaned forward, her face inches from his. "*Every* diaper?"

"Every single one," he grinned.

"Double it to four months, and I'll consider it."

He smiled sweetly and kissed her. She wrapped her arms around his shoulders and buried her face in his neck.

"Just be safe, okay?"

"Yes ma'am."

Chapter Thirteen

Buckeye, Arizona

The air was stale, but he breathed heavily anyway. The heat was stifling, but he pulled the thin quilt above his head to block out the sunlight that poured through the window. He cursed that nagging chain-smoker of a daughter of his for taking down his aluminum foil shades. His head felt like it was splitting in two. He was too old to be getting that drunk. He promised himself he wouldn't do it again. A promise he planned on breaking that coming Friday. He had another gig at some bar in Goodyear. At least she'd be rid of him for a night. That's what she wanted, he assumed.

Grunting heavily, he swung his legs over the side of the bed and stared down at his sagging, inflated stomach. It's a beer gut, he thought. No other word for it. He scratched it absently as he tried to stand, but a searing pain stabbed his lower back and forced him back down on the bed. The second try wasn't so bad. He found the three-day-old shirt in the floor and pulled it on. It was still damp with sweat from the day before. He hobbled down the hall and through the living room, pushed open the screen door, and let it slam shut behind him. The afternoon sun momentarily blinded him as he lumbered groggily across the porch and collapsed into the faded lawn chair next to his daughter.

"You're up early," Audrey mumbled, finally acknowledging his entrance with one of those extra long cigarettes bobbing between her pale lips. She removed it to blow into her tea.

"Am I?" he grunted.

"The sun's up, isn't it?"

"Is that what the sun looks like?" He quipped, laughing at his own joke. She showed no sign of amusement but took a sip of her tea. It must have burned her mouth because she made a sharp hissing noise as she rubbed her tongue against the roof of her mouth and reinserted the cigarette. He sighed and cleared his throat. Audrey was so difficult to talk to these days. It was hard to overlook the fact that it was his fault. He was the reason she was stuck here after all.

"You workin' today?" he asked stupidly, knowing the answer.

"I work every day." The ice in her tone did nothing to cool the surrounding temperature.

"Right," he drew back, his pulse pounded violently against his skull. Fatigue stretched out and made itself comfortable in his aging limbs. "Do we have any aspirin?"

"Nope," she answered. "Ran out last week. If you need aspirin, you buy it. That was the deal."

Owen rested his elbows on his knees and massaged his temples. He assumed she'd been bluffing when she'd made that rule. He mustered up the energy he needed to storm off angrily and rose to go back inside.

"Get some water and a rag to cover your eyes," she called over her shoulder when he got to the door. "But come back out here. Our air conditioning unit's broken again."

"Yeah, I noticed," he bit back. It was a dang sauna in there.

"You'll at least get a breeze out here," she continued as if he hadn't interrupted her. He ignored her and flipped on the fan on the coffee table. Ripping off his shirt and collapsing onto the cracked leather of the sofa, Owen stared blankly at the ceiling, watching as the ceiling fan made its lazy rotations only to stir the musty air. The couch felt cool against the bare skin of his back, and it made him drowsy. The numerous fans strewn around their tiny house did little to lower the temperature.

The house was a furnished lease, adorned with colorful pastel walls and wood paneled ceilings. Each room was a different color, from blues to yellows to oranges. The sofa was a deep purple, and each piece of furniture was handmade from wood. Freakin' hippie tenants before them really screwed them over.

Since moving in, neither Owen nor Audrey had put forth much effort into making the place their own. Other than a trail of liquor bottles and off brand Doritos bags, Owen's guitar cases sat in the corner of the living room along with an old carpet bag he took with him to his gigs in neighboring towns. Audrey kept her things in her room, which contained a bed with a denim comforter, a flimsily built bookshelf, and a small dresser with burn marks from her routine smokes in bed. A single book lay on the dusty shelves. It was one he'd seen her thumb through a few times through the years. The spine of it had been ripped and reinforced with masking tape so many times that it was hard to tell what exactly it was that she was reading. The cover had been torn off somewhere down the line, leaving the dilapidated pages exposed.

Owen had just begun to doze off when he heard Audrey's footsteps on the porch and the second screen door slam shut. He waited a few minutes, letting her get an acceptable distance from the house before pulling himself to his feet. He lumbered to the kitchen, pulled a bottle of George Dickel from the top of the cabinets and tipped it back, but nothing came out. He held it out and found it empty. Cursing to himself, he put it back and wrenched open the refrigerator, taking a case of Audrey's beers to the screened-in porch. He would never admit it, but she was right. It felt better outside than it did in that oven of a house.

He stared out at the desert wasteland in front of him and popped the top off of one of the beers, taking a hefty swig. It washed down his throat, and he sighed heavily.

Of all of the women to come across his path in his lifetime, Audrey Wyatt was the last person he expected to get stranded in a godforsaken desert with. Not a day passed that he didn't regret selling her motorcycle. If he hadn't, she would have left ages ago, and he wouldn't have to deal with her. One would think that after all this time she would have gotten over it, especially after she took out her revenge by selling his Telecaster to buy a bicycle. No, Owen had endured almost three years of her cold shoulder, her unremitting silence.

Her hair was cropped to her chin now to ward off some of the excessive heat, and her clothing was thin with cut off sleeves. He rarely saw her eat, and her bones seemed to protrude from the skin. It didn't take a genius to see that she was unhappy, but she had a job – a job that he'd procured for her, in case anyone forgot. She could leave any time she wanted. Yet every morning at two thirty, he'd wake to the sound of her leaning her bike against the porch, trudging into the house, and collapsing onto her bed. Most of the time that followed with the pungent stench of her menthol cigarettes. She seldom slept, and when she did, he'd wake again to the same list of names she'd been calling out since the day he met her. Her voice was softer now, no more screaming, but the wall that separated their rooms was thin.

His thoughts wandered absently to his granddaughter. He guessed she was six or seven now, probably attending some fancy elementary school in that big city. Her round, dark eyes so full of wonder, and those unruly curls that she obviously inherited from her mother. From him. He hoped to meet her some day, but he knew it was highly unlikely. He asked about Rosie on occasion, but Audrey never acknowledged the questions. She'd just stare ahead with vacant eyes and a tight jaw, puffing away at her cigarette.

Owen slammed the door of his rusty, unfaithful pickup truck and walked around to the passenger seat to grab his guitar case and amplifier. It had rained on the way to Goodyear, enough to clean the windshield but not enough to wash away the thick layer of dust that covered the truck. He walked into the bar with a few hours to kill and took in the empty, dark atmosphere.

"I'm Owen Sharpe," he addressed the bartender.

"Chrissy Monaghan," she said sardonically, unimpressed, not looking up from the counter that she was scrubbing clean. Her hair was curled, dark on top and bleached at the ends. She looked about forty and frustrated with her life. "What can I get you?" she grunted. He let out a sharp laugh.

"I'm playin' tonight."

She finally looked up with piercing blue eyes, and he lifted his guitar for her to see.

"Oh," was all she said as she turned to put up the freshly cleaned glasses.

"Got somewhere for me to set up?" he asked, slightly disconcerted by her offhand nature.

"Over there," she nodded her head toward a small platform in the corner with a microphone stand. Owen shuffled over to it and plugged in his amplifier. Grabbing a chair from a nearby table, he snapped open his guitar case and pulled his acoustic Ibanez out to tune it, running in his head through a list of songs to play for the evening. He plucked the strings and turned the pegs until the notes rang out in tune. Sparing only a glance at the clock by the door, he made his way to the bar. He took a seat on a stool in the middle and pulled out his wallet, counting the bills and change left over from his last gig outside of Phoenix barely a month prior.

Sliding it forward, he said, "Get me however much Dickel this will buy." Chrissy eyed him and then the bills. He watched her reach up to the glasses that hung above the liquor bottles, pulling up the hem of her shirt, revealing a turtle tattoo between the dimples of her lower back. The bottom half of it was hidden beneath her high-waist jeans, and he wondered what the rest of it looked like. "Leave the bottle, will you?" he said with his most charming smile when she set the glass in front of him and filled it halfway with whiskey. She shrugged and went back to her inventory.

" 'Keep a shot of Dickel within heart attack range at all times,' " he smirked, raising the glass to his lips. "Know who said that?"

"Nope," she said to the back wall.

"Merle Haggard," he stated proudly. "Know who that is?"

"Nope."

"Oh he was only a creative genius when it came to country music!" he grinned, waiting for her to turn around with an impressed smile and lean over the counter, eager to hear more. When she continued counting bottles of liquor, he cleared his throat and asked, "Live here long?"

"My whole life," she answered.

"Like it?" He took a drink and sighed as it swept down his throat, beginning to feel the relaxing effect of the alcohol as it entered his system.

"Have to," she shrugged. "Can't leave, so I may as well enjoy it."

"I know how that is." He waited for her to respond, but when she didn't, he scrambled for something else to say. "I got stranded in Buckeye a couple years ago."

"Hm."

"It's not terrible," he said. "Can't complain. I do miss Memphis sometimes, though. There's nothin' quite like it." He eyed her thin form again, tanned and smooth with just a hint of cleavage visible from the V of her button down shirt. "Ever been there?"

"Nope."

"You should go sometime." She never answered, and he spent the next hour drinking and chattering on about life before Buckeye, trying in vain to impress her.

"Shouldn't you go on now?" she snapped, gesturing toward the platform. He glanced back and noticed the bar beginning to fill with people.

"Probably should," he said. "Save this for me, will you?" He handed her the bottle and carried his glass to the platform and sat in the chair, absently strumming his guitar, running through the warm-up scales with deft ease. A thin man in his twenties approached the platform with his girlfriend. His dark hair was slicked back and his meager mustache was curled at the ends. She was short and plump and wore a purple dress that buttoned to her neck.

"Hi," he said and turned red. "You're from The Roadside Babel, aren't you?" Owen nodded. There was always one at every gig that still wanted to see him for The Roadside Babel, usually the ones that couldn't afford the real Babel shows, with their flashy new blues guitarist and arena concerts that sold out within weeks.

"I'm Justin, and this is Margo," he seemed flustered, reaching out a hand for him to shake. "We've been big fans for years."

"Owen Sharpe," he grunted, shaking both of their hands.

"Mr. Sharpe," Margo started, blushing a brighter shade of red than her boyfriend, "do you think you could play 'Story of a Fool'? It's my favorite song." She smiled pleasantly, dimpling her fat cheeks in a way that would have made him smile had she not asked the question.

"Can't," he responded. "It's not my song." She nodded in understanding, and the couple left. Owen shook his head, ashamed of his abruptness. He needed all the fans he could get. It didn't do him any good to keep scaring them off.

"Alright y'all," he said into the microphone, addressing his meager audience for the night. No more than fifty people sat at tables or stood at the bar, ordering drinks. Only a few acknowledged him. "I'm Owen Sharpe. I'm gonna play a few songs for y'all tonight. This first one's called 'My What a Gal'." He smiled broadly and winked at Margo, who sat at the table nearest to the platform. Even in the dim lighting he could see her blush.

He ran through his songs methodically, choosing from the

plethora of songs from previous bands as well as covers of his favorite country songs. As the night progressed, his audience grew just short of one hundred guests, and he gained the attention of some that ignored him in the beginning. His skill on the guitar always surprised even those that were difficult to please. He tipped back his whiskey and leaned back into the mic.

"I'm gonna slow it down some," he said. "Now, I don't have the rights by law to this song, seein' as it belongs to those no-good Roadside Babel bastards, but seein' as it was written by my daughter about my granddaughter, I have rights by blood."

But that's about all I have rights to, he thought bitterly as an awkward cheer rose from the audience, their excitement tampered by his unexpected description of his former band. He adjusted his position in the seat and took another swig of whiskey.

"This one's called 'The Forsaken Rose'." Justin and Margo could be heard over the quiet cheer as they whooped obnoxiously, flushed not from nerves but from the empty beer bottles that now littered their table.

He picked the intro softly for a few measures and then strummed the simple chords that led into the first verse. He'd written the guitar for the song with easy chords and strumming patterns in the hopes that he would have someday been able to teach it to Joanna. But Audrey never showed any interest in learning.

"My dearest Rose," he began the song with a tight throat, picturing the little girl with curly black hair and a tear on her chubby cheek. The picture he'd sneak out of Audrey's cigarette box when she wasn't at the house.

> My dearest Rose
> With the soft black petals and the beautiful eyes
> You could have made me whole
> You could have made me rise
> From the darkest hole, made smiles from the lows
> I never should have left you
>
> My dearest Rose
> Give a petal to the ones you don't want to die
> Take the time to feel the breeze
> Ignore the thorns and learn how to fly

Baby girl I'm beggin' you please
Leave a petal for me

My dearest Rose
I'm not much of the prayin' kind
But if I could ask God for just one thing
It would be that my Rose could find
The things that'll make your heart sing
Oh Rose if I could turn back time
I'd be there to count your fingers and your toes
I wouldn't make you the forsaken Rose
Baby girl I'm beggin' you please
Leave a petal for me

He sang the chorus an extra time and ended the song to a quiet applause. He smiled and thanked the audience, bidding them goodnight. He packed up his guitar and loaded everything back in the truck before returning for his bottle of George Dickel, ignoring the emotions invoked by the song. He wondered – not for the first time – how different his life would have turned out if whichever of his high school flings birthed Audrey had told him she was having his baby. Maybe he would have been a part of Audrey's life. Maybe he'd be a part of Rosie's.

"That was pretty good," Chrissy said with the hint of a smile. She slid a shot glass across the bar. "On the house." She winked. Owen raised his eyebrows in surprise and smiled.

"Only if you do one with me," he grinned, raising his shot glass.

"Just one," she said without contemplation.

Owen parked the truck in their invisible dirt driveway just as the sun began to set behind the distant mountains. He pulled the keys from the ignition and laid his head back against the seat. There was no sign of Audrey's bicycle. She was still working, no doubt.

He trudged into the house, tossed his keys blindly onto the counter, and collapsed into bed, exhausted from his short trip. He'd stayed the night with Chrissy, who he was slightly pleased to learn had never heard of The Roadside Babel.

"Cocky bastards," he muttered as he drifted off to sleep. He woke with a start a few hours later in a fresh layer of sweat and kicked off the blanket. Not bothering with dressing, he made his way to the kitchen.

"Hey, Audrey?" he called. "We got any coffee?" He stood waiting for a reply that never came. Frustrated, he called her name again with no response. Grumbling to himself, he beat on her bedroom door, which surprisingly gave without resistance. Her room was as she left it. Her bed was unmade, and cigarette butts littered her bedside table. But something wasn't right. He foolishly searched the rest of their small house, but she was nowhere to be found.

The clock above the stove read 10:43. Audrey was never this late getting back. He shrugged it off as best as he could but by three that afternoon, his stomach was in his throat. He picked up the phone and dialed one of the only numbers he knew by heart. Serge answered after four rings.

"This is Serge."

"Howdy, Serge. This is Owen, Percy's dad," he said, almost forgetting Audrey's alias.

"She said you'd call," he muttered blandly.

"She did?" Owen asked in confusion.

"She called me from the airport this morning. Quit her job. No, I don't know where she's going." Serge seemed exhausted from the effort of holding a conversation.

Owen sat in stunned silence for a moment. "Well thanks, Serge. I won't keep you." He hung up the phone and leaned with his hands on the counter.

Audrey quit her job? Where was she going? The creases in his forehead deepened into canyons as he contemplated his daughter's exodus. He went for his keys, unsure exactly where he was going, but he had to find her. Beneath his nearly empty keychain sat a note and a handful of wrinkled dollar bills. He picked up the note and scanned it. In Audrey's hurried scrawl, he read:

Owen –

I'm leaving. I won't be coming back. I've left you some money for rent. Spend it on rent.

Audrey

Owen slammed the note back on the counter and squeezed his fist around it. In the blink of an eye, she'd vanished without so much as a goodbye. Anger and betrayal welled within him but neither could outweigh the heavy sorrow that sunk in his heart. Blinking away the burning tears, he grabbed the money and his keys and drove to the liquor store.

Chapter Fourteen

Huntsville, Alabama
Day 2385

"Payment's been taken care of, Miss," the driver nodded with a grin. "Your luggage will be waiting at the house when you arrive." Audrey pursed her lips and got out of the car. She stood on the curb at the entrance into Bridge Street Town Centre as the black Bentley drove away. She pulled a cigarette from her pocket and took in the scene before her. Boutique shops and restaurants lined a cobblestone pathway with dark canvas awnings over every door and neatly trimmed hedges and trees dotting the lane. A security guard was reprimanding two unattended children that had decided to take a dip in the large fountain that stretched along the length of the main entrance. Shoppers and lunch goers were scattered about, mostly consisting of small groups of teenagers enjoying the warming rays of the sun that signaled the beginning of their summer vacation. A middle-aged woman sat on the far edge of the fountain fanning herself with a brochure to ward off the early May heat.

Audrey smirked and dropped the cigarette to the ground before stepping into the nearest café. It took a moment for her eyes to adjust to the dim lighting of the rustic coffee shop. A bouncing blonde smiled in greeting.

"What can I get you?" she asked.

"Just a black coffee," Audrey answered. The place reminded her of the joint she and Elizabeth frequented in Seattle.

"What kind?" the barista inquired further, catching Audrey off guard.

"Just black," she asserted, jutting out her chin in irritation.

"Yeah, but all of our coffee beans are imported. We also have organic coffee and – "

"Just get me a cup of coffee," Audrey interjected, raising her voice. "I really don't care where the bloody beans were grown."

"What's the name?" the barista asked as she turned and bustled off to the various machines behind her.

"Wyatt," Audrey answered honestly for the first time in years.

"Audrey?" came a familiar voice. She turned to find a short, round woman with a pleasant smile.

"Mrs. Bailey," she greeted the woman callously.

"I didn't recognize you with your hair so short," Elizabeth's mother beamed.

"Yeah and I'm sure aging twenty years didn't help."

"Oh, we've all aged twenty years," she added, her smile unwavering.

"Mm," Audrey grunted, running an eye over the woman. Her shoulder-length, stylishly layered hair had long gone gray, and her soft eyes were heavily wrinkled. Audrey guessed she was pushing seventy.

"Wyatt," the barista pulled her away from her observation. She didn't meet Audrey's eyes as she handed her the coffee. Audrey took it and left without paying, forcing Mrs. Bailey to hurry forward and cover to ticket. The aging woman led her up a planked staircase to a second floor with brick walls and wooden tables with miscellaneous seating. They took a seat at a table in the corner where Mrs. Bailey's sandwich awaited them.

"Are you sure you don't want anything to eat?" she questioned her, eyeing her skeletal figure. "The tomato pesto paninis are to die for."

"I'll stick with coffee, thanks," Audrey snapped. Mrs. Bailey grinned down at the table.

"This place was just a lake last time you were here, wasn't it?" she asked in another attempt at small talk.

"Yeah," Audrey huffed, lifting her coffee an inch from the table and letting it fall back down several times with her building irritation. "So, Elizabeth gets a taste of discomfort and can't cope with it, huh?"

"I wouldn't call the death of her husband something like discomfort," the woman snapped with her first hint of impatience.

Audrey cleared her throat, pushing out the pang in her chest at the woman's words.

"You didn't say in your letter what happened to him," she said to her coffee.

"Amal was doing four months of humanitarian work in Somalia," Mrs. Bailey explained. "Two weeks before he was scheduled to come home, some local men raided the hospital and open fired. He and three other doctors were killed." Her voice grew heavy as spoke. Elizabeth smirked despite the gnawing sensation in her gut.

"He always was the hero type," she sighed. "Mr. Altruism, himself."

"You should have seen him with those kids," Mrs. Bailey smiled sadly. "He was the only one who could calm Mia during a tantrum. And oh how Ezra adored him! He followed him around so closely Amal would trip over him. Which of course would always lead to a wrestling match." She chuckled softly.

"I'm guessing Ezra is their son?" Audrey presumed. Mrs. Bailey nodded. "How old are they now?"

"Mia is ten. Ezra's eight," she stared down at her untouched sandwich. "Much too young to lose their father.

"So what of Elizabeth?" Audrey changed the subject, steeling over her expression to hide the building turmoil in the emotions that had remained stagnant for years. "She isn't coping well, I imagine. I don't see why I'd be needed here if she was winning Mom of the Year."

"I don't think I've ever heard you use her name," Elizabeth's mother mused. Audrey gritted her teeth.

"How is she?"

"She's broken," Mrs. Bailey explained with a heavy sigh. "She doesn't eat. She rarely even sees the children anymore. She just shuts herself in her room and cries."

"How long has she been like that?" Audrey asked without much sympathy.

"It's been almost a month. I'm worried about her. And my grandchildren. Ezra seems to be coping okay, but he's so young, he doesn't entirely understand. Mia has barely spoken a word, which if you knew her you'd know how uncharacteristic that is. They need their mother."

"So naturally, you bring me out of hiding to swoop in and

save the day," Audrey sneered. "I don't see what good I can do. You're from Hazel Green, I'm sure you've heard that I'm not exactly great in a crisis."

Mrs. Bailey nodded slowly. "I'm desperate. My daughter needs help, and I don't know how to help her. She never had a friend quite as close as you, and with your experience – "

"My experience," Audrey repeated disdainfully. "What, because I handle death so well? I am probably the last person Elizabeth wants to see right now!"

"You're probably right," she agreed. "But you may be what she needs." Audrey sat back in her chair and stared down at her coffee while the woman continued. "She was so devastated when she found out you'd deserted her."

"Me?" Audrey shrieked. "*I* deserted her? I was alone in a huge city! I had my neighbor, sure, but I'm sure you heard what Ruby and I got up to!" Mrs. Bailey averted her eyes. A dulled rage built up in Audrey's gut at the memory of Ruby knocking on her door after Audrey had thrown picture frames, glass dishes, and Hermione's dog bowls against their shared wall, screaming in agony.

"Want to come over? I think I know something that can help you."

Audrey shook away the voice and went on. "I was lost without her! I didn't know how to cope! And I'm sure she didn't even notice until a good six months after I blocked her that I'd removed her completely from my life! And even still, I heard Liam on the phone with her giving her updates on my condition like I was some sort of terminal invalid! He asked her every single time if she wanted him to give me the phone, but he never did. I was crushed every time."

"You're the one that shut her out!" Mrs. Bailey defended her daughter. "You can't always blame her for your drug addiction.

Audrey shot up from her chair, appalled by the woman's accusation. "I'd like to leave now." Mrs. Bailey glared up at her before gathering her things and leaving her sandwich untouched.

"You'll be staying in one of Elizabeth's guest rooms," she stated methodically. "It's a bit of a drive from here. I'll take you up there."

"I'd rather not," Audrey protested. "Give me the number of that driver or any taxi service and I'll call." Mrs. Bailey sighed and dug through her purse, producing a small key.

"Here's a key to the house. Your room is on the top floor. Once you go up the stairs, take a left. It'll be the door on the right, next to the library. I'll give Kevin a call. He knows the address." With that, Mrs. Bailey made her way down the stairs. Audrey scraped her fingers along her scalp in exasperation and sped out of the café. Four cigarette butts lay at her feet before the Bentley pulled back up in front of her. She dropped the fifth one and climbed in the back seat.

"Good to see you again, Miss Wyatt," the driver smiled at her in the rear view mirror.

"Don't call me that," she spat.

"Well what should I call you then, Miss?"

"Don't call me anything. Especially not 'Miss'. I've got a good ten years on you," she snapped. "Just stop talking and drive me to the bloody house." Without a word, he pulled out of the parking lot. She stared through the window as he merged onto the interstate. She gazed up at the towering Saturn V rocket that was visible from many points of the town and marked one's entrance into Rocket City.

"Tall isn't it?" Mark noted beside her.

"How observant of you," Audrey stated flatly.

"You know there's another model of it inside. It's suspended horizontally, and all of the parts are separated and labeled so you know what it all does."

"Fascinating."

"Can we go inside?" Danny groaned. "It's hot!"

"Yeah," Mark called after him. Ethan and Daniel ran inside the neighboring building. "You coming, Audrey?"

"No, I'll just sit out here," she replied dully to her new step dad and sat on one of the round blocks of concrete. She crossed her legs in defiance and stared up at the point of the rocket.

"Okay," Mark conceded. "Just don't wander off." Audrey gazed up at the towering spacecraft, dreaming of taking her brothers inside and launching them to another planet where things weren't quite so austere.

"Audrey! Come look!" Ethan yelled from the door a few minutes later. "There's a giant rocket in there, and you can touch it and get inside of it!" She groaned and pulled herself to her feet. "Hurry up!"

"I'm coming. I'm coming."

Audrey swallowed back the memory as the car trekked up Monte Sano Mountain. Near the top, the driver pulled the Bentley into a long driveway that curved in front of an elaborate red brick house.

"The cleaning lady said she put your bag in your room, ma'am," he drawled.

"Thanks," Audrey muttered, suddenly ashamed of her earlier treatment to the driver. She stood on the pavement and waited until the car was out of sight before climbing the brick steps to the front door. Two dark, heavy wooden doors with golden handles wore a half moon window like a crown and loomed ominously before her. She rang the doorbell, but didn't receive a response. She waited and rang the bell again before pulling the key from her pocket.

"Figures," she said as she stepped into the house, leaning her weight onto one leg.

The foyer expanded into a vast living room with a high, pointed arched ceiling. The right wall reached only halfway to the ceiling and opened into the top floor with balconies overlooking the opulent fireplace with an intricately carved, white mantle on the opposite wall. On the wall across from her, three tiers of artistically designed windows reached to the ceiling and overlooked the rolling downward slope of the mountain. A large, russet colored, L-shaped sofa sat at the heart of the room with a glass coffee table at its center atop a long, Aztec rug. Abstract paintings adorned the beige walls and a photograph of Elizabeth's family covered the wall above the fireplace.

Audrey stepped up to the portrait and bit her lips to keep back the gnawing sense of loss that she didn't have the right to feel. The four were standing on a deserted road through a forest. Amal faced Elizabeth with his arms around her while she threw her head back with laughter. Clutching her hand was a four-year-old Mia, smiling sweetly at the camera with her head cocked and her long, curled, brown hair cascading down her shoulder. At their feet sat a toddler with jet-black hair and Elizabeth's pale skin. His almond-shaped eyes gazed ahead, his mouth gaping open. Audrey's eyes lingered on her friend who had aged so beautifully before she tore herself away to meander through the rest of the house.

A staircase by the front door lead both upstairs and down.

The bottom floor was clearly Amal's hiding place – or a man cave, as Thomas used to call it. A pool table sat in the center of the room and the walls were decorated with framed World War II propaganda posters. A large sofa faced a flat screen television that was mounted above another immaculate fireplace. Like the floor above, windows stretched from the floor to the ceiling and opened up to a dark planked porch that overlooked the mountainside.

She pushed open the glass door and stepped out onto the patio, leaning against the rail and gazing down the side of the mountain. In the distance, the city splayed out like a board game, its players shuffling about methodically with no clear winner.

A shuffle below her drew her attention away from the busy town. She jumped back with a shriek when she beheld the large black bear staring up at her. Their eyes were locked as her heart thudded against her chest. It cocked its head and lolled its tongue out.

"Oh," Audrey sighed aloud. "You're a dog." At the sound of her voice, it bounded up the stairs to the porch and sat panting at her feet. She stared motionlessly as it sniffed her pant leg and pawed at her for attention.

"He doesn't bite," came a voice from behind her, and she whipped around to face him. She recognized Ezra from the portrait on the mantle. He was older now, leaner with shaggy hair and sad eyes. "His name's Bryant. He's my dad's dog." Audrey glanced back down at the bear at her feet. "My dad's dead," he said it so casually that she almost missed it. She eyed him curiously. "What's your name?" he asked.

"Audrey. Are you Ezra?" He nodded.

"I'm supposed to bring Bryant inside when we get off the bus from day care," he explained, wiping his nose on his sleeve.

"Well let's go inside then," Audrey smiled at the boy and ushered him inside. Her heart faltered as he took her hand and led her up the stairs. He brought her through the living room and into the lavish kitchen.

"You can leave food here if you brought any," he dropped her hand and went for the double refrigerator with Bryant following at his waist. Audrey took in the mahogany cabinets and dark granite countertops. A double paned window adorned the wall above the sink beside a stainless steel dishwasher. There was a matching stove and oven on the adjacent wall, and above the cabinets along the wall were colored drawings, each one signed by one of Elizabeth's children. The refrigerator shut noiselessly and Ezra crunched loudly into an apple. "So did you?"

"I'm sorry?" Audrey asked.

"Bring food?"

"Oh. No, I didn't."

"Oh," Ezra walked towards the archway into the living room. "A lot of people bring us food now. Since Dad died." He stopped and turned back to her, eyeing her suspiciously. "So why are you here then?"

"I'm a friend of your mom's. I thought I'd come and help out around the house if I'm needed," she tried to explain in terms that wouldn't make her sound horrible. Ezra turned his frown to his feet, spinning the apple in his hand like a baseball.

"Mom doesn't talk much," he stated blankly. "She used to read to me. She doesn't anymore." Audrey took a seat on the sofa. Ezra sat next to her.

"What does she read to you?" she implored.

"*Percy Jackson and the Olympians.*"

"I've not heard of that one. What's it about?"

"A boy who's a demigod. His dad is Poseidon," he explained.

"Sounds interesting," Audrey smiled at him. He grinned at his feet. She was beginning to feel oddly more comfortable the more time she spent with this boy, as though she was slipping back into the role she was always meant to play. "Where is your mom right now?" she asked.

"Probably at the grocery store. Nana makes her do stuff like that so she doesn't stay in her room all the time." He turned back to her. "Are you the one Nana said was going to stay with us?"

"I believe so."

"Oh!" he jumped down excitely. "You're next to my room! Want to see it?" Before Audrey could mutter a 'sure', Ezra grabbed her hand and lugged her up the stairs. "That's Mia's room," he pointed to the first door. "I'm not allowed to go in there. This is my room. You can come in here all you want. It's the best room in the house." He pushed open the door into the most fascinating room Audrey had ever seen.

Three of the walls were light blue. Across the length of one wall were glued sheets of Lego boards. Ezra pulled a large box from under his bed and ripped the top off of it.

"It's really cool," he started with a building enthusiasm. "You can stick Legos all over the wall if you want. You can spell words or draw pictures! I made a light saber once. It stuck out so far that it couldn't stay straight and it bent and touched the ground."

"That sounds awesome," Audrey couldn't help the grin that stretched her lips.

"Who are you?" snapped a voice behind her. Audrey turned to see Mia in the doorway with her arms crossed. Audrey stood in shock at the sudden appearance of the girl, remembering how she had watched Elizabeth grow, teasing her relentlessly about her weight gain. Now here she was, ten years old and absolutely stunning, even as she turned her nose to the ceiling and scowled at the stranger in her brother's room. "Are you the woman Nana was talking about?"

"I assume," Audrey muttered, slightly daunted by the girl's narrowed eyes.

"Mom doesn't know you're coming," she simpered. "Nana told us not to tell her because she's going to be mad."

"Is she?" Audrey's heart sank in her chest at the confrontation in her future. Mia shrugged and walked off. The slam of a door followed soon after the girl's departure. Moments later, the sound of the front door opening interrupted Ezra's description of the latest episode of his favorite television show.

"Mom's home," he said almost ominously. Audrey got to her feet, walked through the door, and leaned over the balcony rails. She watched from above as her old friend shuffled through the door with an armload of grocery bags. Flipping her long bangs from her face, her eyes caught Audrey. Surprise flickered across them for a moment. Then they burned like an emerald furnace as they fixed on the gaunt woman leaning against her balcony rail.

Chapter Fifteen

Huntsville, Alabama
Day 2385

"Well if it isn't Audrey Wyatt," Elizabeth huffed, letting her bag laden arms fall to her side loudly as she scowled up at her. She stalked off to the kitchen and called over her shoulder, "This is my mother's doing, no doubt." Pushing herself heavily off the rail, Audrey followed after her, fighting the way her heart jittered in her chest at having her best friend in her sights again.

"She contacted me, yes," Audrey stuttered, unsure of what to say.

"I should have known that's what she was up to when I caught her on the phone with Liam Farren," she spat his name as though the taste of it on her tongue was repulsive. She shook her head and unloaded the groceries. "Should have freaking known."

"She's worried about you," Audrey oddly found herself defending Mrs. Bailey, pushing aside the knot in her gut that accompanied Liam's name.

"She needs to mind her own business is what she needs to do," she grumbled.

"I'm only here to help you, Elizabeth."

"I don't need anyone's help!" she snapped with an added, "Especially yours," under her breath. She slung open the refrigerator door and began tossing the groceries inside.

"But you don't have to go through this alone," Audrey struggled to keep her own emotions in check as her best friend mumbled to herself.

"Oh that's rich coming from you," Elizabeth laughed horribly. "You, who always run away when things go south. What are you going to do? Teach me how to shut everyone out? I was crushed when I realized you'd cut me out. And I never understood why. It plagued me for over a year until Liam called Al – " she broke off, her eyes filling with tears at the mention of her husband's name. She screamed a curse and slammed the refrigerator door.

Audrey heard a shuffle of feet and turned to see Ezra retreat from his post at the balcony into his room. He shut the door softly so his mother wouldn't hear. She turned back to find Elizabeth bent with her elbows on the counter and her head in her hands. Audrey walked around the side of the counter to comfort her, but she froze in her tracks before she could get to her.

"Elizabeth," Audrey swallowed hard to steady her voice, "are you pregnant?" Elizabeth nodded with her head still in her hands. "Did he know before he left for Somalia?" She nodded again. Anger boiled in Audrey's gut and writhed in her veins. She wished Amal was alive so she could murder him herself.

"Saving lives here was never enough for him," she said bitterly, raising up and stuffing her hands in the pocket of her hoodie. "He always wanted to do humanitarian work. It never crossed our minds that I would get pregnant at this age. But he still wanted to do it before there were three of them to take care of." She stared blankly at the wall ahead of her.

"I know you don't want me here," Audrey said after a moment's pause, "but I'm here. I'm still not sure what good I'll be, but now that I'm here I don't want to be anywhere else. I'll do whatever you need me to do."

"Right," she jeered, "because you're so selfless! You haven't thought of anyone but yourself since Daniel died. Not even for your own flesh and blood! Why should this be any different?"

Audrey swallowed hard and cleared her throat before answering. "I would move heaven and earth for you, Elizabeth. You know that."

"You are such a liar!" she screamed. "You pushed me out! And you've done it every time hell decided to upturn your life, but I have always wanted nothing more than to hold your hand through it. I gave you slack when you took off the first time. Maybe I was just young and naïve for it, but I always knew you'd get in touch with me when you were ready. But then you do it again because your freaking dog died, Audrey, your dog that was old and dying anyway! And then you threw your own life down to crap, and made poor Liam fix you back up again!"

"I never asked him to do that," Audrey whispered, not trusting her voice.

"Oh, whatever, Audrey!" Elizabeth sighed, throwing her arms up in defeat.

"I cut you out because I knew where my life was headed," she admitted. "I could see it, and I could also see how perfect yours was. Nothing bad ever happened to you, while I got a double portion. I was just tired of being the one to drag you down."

"You never dragged me down, Audrey!" she said, her eyes filling with tears. "You can't keep doing this to yourself. Think about it. Everything you've ever been through, other than the accident, has been completely self-inflicted. You always, *always* chose the path that led you to more pain."

"Look at you," Audrey wheezed through the lump in her throat. "Still trying to help me out when you've fallen to pieces." Elizabeth averted her eyes and crossed her arms. "I'm not here for your counsel. I'm here for you. For you and your children. Nothing more."

Her friend sniffed and turned her head to Audrey, leaning with her hands on the counter. "Do you know how to make hamburger helper?" she asked, not meeting her eyes. Audrey shrugged. "The kids are tired of these big meals from all the neighbors and church friends. They'd probably love some hamburger helper. Or McDonald's if you don't know how to make it." Elizabeth edged past her and walked to her bedroom on the other side of the living room.

Audrey stared after her with her clenched fists in her pockets. In the years that passed since she deleted Elizabeth's number from her phone's address book, she'd often wondered how her life had turned out. Now she was standing in the embers of where her friend's dreams had burned. She sighed and shook her head.

Running a hand through her short hair, she pushed off of the counter and trudged upstairs to the room Ezra had pointed out as hers. The guestroom was very simply decorated with dark wooden furniture, a bed with an olive green duvet and burnt orange pillows, and a large pale shaded lamp. Burgundy curtains draped across a window with a forest view. A tapestry hung on the wall above the bed, and a single framed photograph sat on the bedside table. Audrey picked it up and smiled.

In the small wooden frame that Mrs. Bailey had most likely set out for her as a reminder of why she was there was a picture from Elizabeth's wedding. Elizabeth had her arms thrown around her maid of honor's shoulders, squeezing her in a tight hug. She smiled with a gaping mouth at the camera, her eyes creased into slits while Audrey looked away with a raised eyebrow and a crooked, closed grin.

"My lord, Audrey!" Snow grumbled. "Why can't you ever look at the camera? At least smile, for God's sake!"

"You know how much I hate getting my bloody picture taken!" Audrey protested with a laugh.

"But you couldn't just take one decent picture could you?" she huffed. *"Not one! Not even on my wedding day!"*

"Hey Audrey?" Amal called lazily from the sofa behind them, exhausted from an extra shift at the hospital.

"I know, I know," Audrey waved him off, turning on the bar stool to face him. "I sound bloody ridiculous," she mimicked his cockney accent. He smiled at her with his eyes closed and shot her with a finger gun.

"Could you not have at least faked one?" Snow continued with her complaint, ignoring their interruption. "Just one! That's all I ask!"

"Like this, then?" Audrey stretched her mouth into an unflattering grin and pushed her head back, squishing the skin of her neck into a double chin.

"Stop that," her friend snorted. "That's hideous."

"Better her be her brooding self than fake a smile and pretend to be a pleasantly happy human being," Amal hummed.

"See?" Audrey laughed. "He gets it!"

"Can't you just take my side on this?" Snow whined, getting up from her seat to stand in front of her husband. He shushed her and reached for her hand, pulling her down onto the couch next to him. He lay down on the sofa, forcing her down as he went, and rested his head on her chest, still shushing her.

"Just be my pillow," he droned. Snow smiled and shook her head, pulling off his Seahawks hat to run her fingers through his hair.

"You're going to be a great mom," Audrey whispered, intending it to sound sarcastic.

"I know," Snow tossed one of her loosely braided pigtails

over her shoulder with a dramatic flick of the wrist. Annoyed that there was no room left on the couch for her, Hermione snorted and leapt onto Amal's back, plopping down and laying her long muzzle on his head, staring up at Snow, begging for attention.

"Oi!" Amal jolted awake. Hermione struggled to keep her balance on his back. "Sod off, will you!" he yelled, waving a hand behind him to swat at her. Audrey and Snow burst with laughter as he shot various curses at the dog until she retreated back to Audrey's side.

Audrey sank onto the bed as she stared at the picture. Amal's life had been tragically cut short, ripped away from his family and all of those that loved him. Her friend was dead and gone, and she wondered just how much of Snow was left in Elizabeth, if any at all.

Day 2399

"Audrey?"

"We needed you, Audrey! And you left us!"

"Ethan, please –"

"Audrey, wake up."

"You murdered him!"

"Hellooooo!" Ezra shook her arm vigorously until she jolted awake with a gasp that sent her into a coughing fit. He stared patiently at her until she finally stopped hacking. "You were having a nightmare so I woke you up," he informed her with his hands clasped behind his back.

"Thanks, kid," Audrey managed to wheeze when she caught her breath.

"Are you going to be okay, or do I need to stay with you?" he asked with an impartial intonation. Audrey stared at the boy incredulously. "I'll stay with you," he announced and climbed into the bed next to her. She backed away to give him room, still frozen with astonishment. He adjusted the comforter around him and clasped his hands on his chest before turning back to her. "So what was your dream about?"

"Um," Audrey stammered, still unsure why he'd welcomed himself into her bed.

"Dad always told me that talking about your nightmares helps you to see how unreal they are, and you can go back to sleep easier. He always got in bed with me until I told him about my dream."

"Did he, now?" she asked, attempting to calm her still racing heart rate. In the week that she'd been with the Ganeshes, she'd learned a lot about Ezra and his relationship with the other members of his family, but Elizabeth and Mia barely acknowledged her presence.

"Yeah," he nodded, his untrimmed, black hair splayed out on the pillow beneath him. "So if you tell me about your dream, you can see that it wasn't real, and you can go back to sleep."

"I can't do that," she tried to smile for him.

"Sure you can," he encouraged her with a nudge, batting his dark green eyes and abnormally long lashes at her.

"See, my nightmares aren't just dreams. They are actually real to me."

"Tell me about them," he coaxed. He pursed his lips expectantly.

She sighed heavily and gave in. "Did your mom ever tell you I had brothers?"

"Yeah," he nodded. "Uncle Ethan."

"Uncle Ethan?" she repeated, knitting her brows together.

"Well he's not really our uncle, but we call him that because he's so much fun."

"I bet," Audrey laughed nervously. "Do you see him often?"

"Not really. He lives in Atlanta so he doesn't come over much," he explained. "I saw him at Dad's funeral, but he wasn't as fun as he usually is. Before that, though, he came over for Mia's birthday party, but he didn't play with me much then either. He played with Dania most of the time."

Audrey's pounding heart froze in her chest. "Who's Dania?"

"She's a girl from Seattle," he said with a shrug. "Our parents are friends." Audrey gazed at the ceiling as the tears welled in her eyes. Ethan met Rosie. And he played with her.

"What's she like?" she whispered.

"She's nice, I guess," Ezra shrugged again. "She's really quiet though. And she got really mad when my Lego dragon destroyed her Lego whale. She ran and tattled, and then her dad said she was being a baby. She got all offended and rebuilt her whale and then took it home with her. But then Uncle Thomas sent me a new box of Legos, so it was okay. He's not my actual uncle either. He's Dad's best friend. Or he was anyway." He shook his head, perplexed. Audrey didn't answer. Her throat constricted, blocking her airway as she blinked away her tears.

"Did you dream about Uncle Ethan?" he asked her when the silence went on too long for him. Audrey nodded and swallowed back the lump in her throat. "Do you ever see him?"

"No," she said, her voice was thick but steady.

"Is that why you're so sad?"

Audrey rolled onto her side to face him. Ezra did the same.

"What makes you think I'm sad?" she asked.

"Sometimes you look like Mom does when she thinks about Dad," he stated.

"Well aren't you observant, Sherlock Holmes," Audrey laughed humorlessly.

"Dad said I asked too many questions," he giggled back.

"Do you miss your dad?" she found herself asking.

He nodded. "I miss wrestling with him and watching Doctor Who with him. He said that when I'm out of school for the summer, we would build a real Tardis and travel all of time and space together."

"I'm sorry, kid," she said, absently reaching out to move a strand of silky hair out of his face.

"Mom used to do that when we watched a movie," he said. "She always played with my hair because she said it was the softest hair in the world."

"I'd have to agree with her," Audrey smiled. "Is she the one that cuts it?"

"Yeah, but she hasn't cut it since Dad died. That's why I look homeless." Ezra pursed his lips and looked thoughtful for a moment. "I miss her too," he said nonchalantly.

"Why do you say that?" Audrey asked, propping herself up on her elbow.

"Because she never talks to me anymore," he said. "She always wrote notes on my napkins in my lunchbox, and she'd take us to the park and eat peanut butter sandwiches on the edge of the mountain. But she doesn't do that anymore. And she doesn't let me feel the baby kick anymore, either."

"I had another brother besides Uncle Ethan. Did you know that?" she changed the subject, unsure of how to respond. Ezra eyed her with a furrowed brow. "He was our baby brother. His name was Daniel."

"What happened to him?" he asked.

"He died when he was very young," Audrey confessed aloud to the boy what she'd only ever told to Liam. "But instead of helping Ethan when he was sad, I ran away."

"Why?"

"Everyone reacts differently when they lose someone. I ran away because I blamed myself for what happened to Daniel. I still loved Ethan more than anything in the world, but I couldn't stay. Just like your mother still loves you. She's just going through a really tough time right now."

Ezra nodded. "I just miss her."

Audrey sighed heavily. "I do too, kid. I do too."

Chapter Sixteen

Huntsville, Alabama
Day 2409

Audrey spent most of the days alone in the sprawling Ganesh home while Elizabeth was out on errands for her vexed mother and the kids were at daycare, enduring hours of interaction with other kids their age, something Mrs. Bailey said was needed in their situation. In the beginning she would roam from room to room, piecing together the parts of their lives that she'd missed. Photographs hung on the walls and decorated shelves, displaying birthdays, vacations, kindergarten graduations, karate belt tests, theater performances, and milestone photography sessions depicting the family at each new stage of life.

The library was her favorite. The room was relatively small when compared to the kids' bedrooms, but two of the walls were lined with floor to ceiling bookshelves filled with old paperbacks, elegant leather bound volumes, and colorful hard copies of books that graced the New York Times Bestseller list. At first, Audrey would flip through various books that littered the wooden shelves, but she soon found that many were medical journals and scientific essays that made her dizzy to read. Elizabeth's shelves were crammed with romance novels. Audrey picked one up once, flipped it open, and put it back seconds later feeling intensely violated. A long, ornate wooden desk sat against the wall beneath a long window. She would sit in the black, leather chair, spinning idly, smoking a cigarette – having never seen anyone venture to that corner of the house, it was the only room she smoked in – and gaze through the window that didn't have much of a view. The tree line was so thick on that side of the house that one could only just see hints of a fading sunbeam through the leaves for a few minutes each day.

Wherever she went, she was shadowed closely by Bryant. With his drooling tongue and shaggy coat, he lumbered behind her and lay down on the long, decorative rug to stare at her with an unyielding perseverance. But even with the pervasive canine at her hip, she was dreadfully aware of how utterly and bitterly alone she was. The deafening echo of her footsteps resounded like the horrible, cackling laughter of a playground bully, taunting her mercilessly with every step.

When she was around Elizabeth and her children, she buried her own emotions deep inside of herself in order to lend a smiling hand wherever she was needed. It fooled the children but not Elizabeth, who watched her sometimes with grim, narrow eyes, but she never said anything.

The loneliness and guilt that gnawed slowly and steadily on her heart piled up on top of one another and suffocated her, intensified by the silence that bore down on her from all sides. She tried to stifle the blaring quiet by blasting earsplitting classic rock music through the ceiling speakers, but then the brilliant sunbeams that glared through the window wall of the living room blinded her, burning holes in the dams of her soul, bringing back all that she'd worked through the morning to push out.

On this particular morning, she decided not to fight it, to let it all in with the hope that, with all emotion spent, the numbness would set in, giving her reprieve for a few days. She ran her finger along the spines of books on the staggered shelves, pulling one out every now and again to open it and smell the pages.

"What are you doing?" she asked icily. Liam was laid back on the sofa with Crime and Punishment *opened and lying across his face.*

"I found this in your stuff," he answered simply, sitting up and studying the pages of her book.

"You went through my stuff?" she shrilled. He eyed her through his bushy eyebrows.

"It's a small apartment, Aud," he sighed. "I didn't go through your stuff, it was under the mattress when I took off the sheets to clean off your vomit." He emphasized the last word as though her

sick was excuse enough to rummage through her things. Audrey crossed her arms and moved her weight to her other leg, jutting out her chin to seem unaffected by the embarrassment. "Clever hiding place really," *he continued.* "Very original."

She stomped over to him and snatched the book from his grasp before heading for the door. He sighed heavily and pulled himself off the couch to follow her.

"Where are you going?"

"To see Ruby," *she answered curtly. She yanked the chain from the door and jerked it open a crack only to have it slammed shut again, a large hand barring her exit. She huffed, clenched her teeth, and swung around to face him.* "Get out of the way."

"No," *he said casually, replacing the chain lock on the door.* "You aren't going to Ruby's."

"You think you can stop me?" *she hissed.* "Just because you charmed my landlord into breaking my lease early doesn't mean that I'm forever yours to command."

"You signed the papers, Aud."

"I was high," *she seethed through gritted teeth, embarrassed of the admission.*

"Exactly," *his lips formed a tight, grim line.* "Which is why you aren't going to Ruby's. You are so strong, Aud. You don't have to keep doing this." *His tone was almost pleading.*

She laughed viciously. "Strong. Right." *She tried the door again but he pushed it shut, much to her irritation.*

"You really are," *his voice was soft, contrasting heavily with his grip on the door.* "You are without a doubt the strongest person I know. You've been through hell. I know that. But you're still here. That should count for something shouldn't it? I can see it in your eyes, Audrey. You're a warrior." *His words stirred inside of her an almost humorous guilt at how easily she seemed to have deceived him.*

"I'm not strong, Liam," *she said, dropping her hand from the doorknob.* "In fact, I'm the opposite of strong. I cower, and I run. I take the easy way out," *she spoke it over herself as though condemning every decision she'd ever made. His answering groan surprised her and he threw his hands in the air.*

"Why do you always have to be so unhappy?"

"If you'd done what I've done, you'd be the same way," *she spat, reaching again for the door. He caught her wrist and pulled it* to his chest, tugging her off balance in an effort to keep the doorknob out of her reach. She staggered toward him but backed up as soon as she saw how close his face was to hers.

"Maybe I would be," he agreed, his eyes locked onto hers. "But luckily you've got someone like me to help you."

She turned her head and scoffed. "You think you're so special."

"You've been doing so well! Don't do this," he pleaded, ignoring her snide comment..

"Oh, I've been doing well," she repeated sardonically, "says the vomit stain on your sheets."

"Audrey," he sighed, rubbing his face with two thick hands and running them along his scalp. He threw down his arms in defeat, gazing at her with liquid black eyes. She felt vulnerable, like she needed to zip up her leather jacket and run before he could penetrate her defenses.

"Fine. Do what you want," he breathed, turning back and collapsing heavily on the sofa with a foot extended on the coffee table. He was still dressed from work in his usual attire. A grey shirt unbuttoned nearly to his navel, displaying a broad chest that was specked with dark hair. His sleeves were rolled up to flaunt the thick leather cuff on his wrist that had gone out of style a decade earlier. A small pendant fell against his chest, suspended by a leather chord, and two small diamonds studded his ears.

"You dress like an idiot," she grumbled and dropped onto the couch next to him, crossing her arms and resting her bare feet on the table beside his. He smiled broadly with a breathy laugh and draped his arm around her shoulders. Her heart fluttered in her stomach at his touch, and she reacted by tossing the book in his lap abruptly and asking with a voice that came out louder than she intended, "Why were you smelling my book anyway?"

"You can read a lot about a person by a careful examination of their books," he shrugged, using the voice she'd begun to associate with his odd philosophical conversations. "Without realizing it, you leave traces of yourself in the pages. Look," he used his free arm to point to a small blotch on the corner of a page. "You drink coffee while you read."

"That was tea actually," she corrected in a soft, fascinated voice. His eyes were on her and when she met them, her chin bobbed soundlessly before she continued. "I was in London at a little teashop on Dering Street."

He smirked down at her. "Tea then."

"What else can you discern about me, Philosopher Farren?" she cleared her throat and asked with a pristine voice. He turned back to the book in his hand.

"Well there's the obvious," he flipped to the white backside of the cover. "You love this book. I could tell that from the spine alone, but you love it so much that you keep a record of how often you read it." He trailed his finger down each column of handwritten dates as if with the touch, he was transported to each moment that she turned the pages. He watched her curled up in bed with her dog, on planes and in London teashops, on the stone ledges of Reykjavik and atop bleachers in baseball parks before numbers eight and ninety-nine took to the field. "You read it two to three times a year for three years, then ritually every December starting in 2005. But you didn't this past December. Why is that?"

He looked at her, studied her expressions, waiting patiently for her answer, but she couldn't put to words how vile and menacing the book had become as it glared at her from across rooms, judging her ruthlessly as she held the lighter under the spoon. She didn't hide it under the mattress to keep Liam from finding it. She hid it so she didn't have to look at it. She turned her gaze from him to the book in his lap. Reaching over to thumb the pages, she said, "You still haven't told me why you were smelling it," and nearly flinched as the thumb of his right hand caressed her arm comfortingly, as if he were aware that she didn't quite trust him enough to divulge with him the ghosts that haunted her.

"Most books smell the same," he said. "But sometimes when a person really pours their heart into what they're reading, it takes on a different aroma. One more fitting to the reader. It kind of becomes an extension of that person and starts to smell differently."

"What does mine smell like?" she asked his hand on her book.

He laughed a throaty laugh that caught her attention. "Cigarettes."

He continued to laugh as the image of her mother with a cigarette in her mouth jerked the book out of her young daughter's hands and flung it across the room, screaming at her with a long forgotten motive, flashed before Audrey's eyes, pushing the air from her lungs in a sharp huff.

"Audrey?" he murmured when he caught her dazed expression, but all she heard was her mother's screams. Two fingers gently pulled her chin in his direction. Two dark eyes bored into her beneath knitted brows. Her heart beat violently against her chest, and she closed the gap between them and kissed him softly. Stunned by how quickly it happened, it took a moment for Liam to register that she was kissing him, but he returned the embrace with a tenderness that matched her own. His face was scratchy and he tasted like coffee and cigarettes, but she reveled in it, in him. It was her first kiss in over ten years and she felt clumsy, but she didn't care.

Silent tears cascaded down Audrey's cheeks as she sat on the library rug with Bryant lying against her thigh. Tattered black and white photographs from the cigarette packet that she never opened were scattered around the floor in front of her. Liam was in her hand, and she ran her finger across his face and down his hair, recalling how later that night, she'd stared at his sleeping features and become so overwhelmed by happiness and guilt and fear that she'd snuck out of bed to find Ruby.

Her drug habit had begun less than a week after Hermione's death when her neighbor knocked on her door and offered her a way to dull her pain. Audrey had shut the door in her face with a grunted 'no', sure that Ruby was only offering because she had grown tired of hearing Audrey's cries through the thin wall. But then she'd turned back to her apartment. The bar stools were lying on their sides where she'd thrown them in a drunken rage, and her flashy sofa spread jackknifed across the floor. Broken glass from drained liquor bottles turned her floor into a minefield.

But her apartment was empty. For the first time in her life, she was completely alone. Alone with her shame.

Liam brought her back to that same empty apartment after she'd gotten her tattoo, but when he turned to leave, she could hear the whispers of familiar, haunting voices in the dark corners of the room.

"Don't go," she'd slurred, and he'd stayed. He slept on her sofa, and she stared at him until she fell asleep, making sure he wouldn't disappear. The next morning he got up to make breakfast and found her pantry bare except for a few packs of crackers and a box containing heroin, injection needles, tubes, a roll of tin foil, and lighters, and he took it upon himself to clean her up. But as he did so, she was falling for him. It was a strange feeling, one she'd never experienced before, and she denied it every time it rose within her. In the small moments when he would catch her staring and smirk or when he got lost in his own retellings of Socrates, Zeno, and Anaximander, droning on and on with pure excitement gleaming in his eyes, in those moments she would feel a new happiness well within her. She would smile and he would stop midsentence to point it out.

"Is that an actual smile I see, Miss Wyatt?"

Her slivers of joy would immediately be poisoned with guilt. Why should she get to be happy? Why should she have that privilege when she'd ripped it away from her own baby brother? Daniel would never have the chance to immerse himself in someone else's smile, to laugh with his friends, to fall in love. So why should she get that chance?

Those were the days that she would relapse, the days when Liam would clench his jaw and make her sleep it off, shouting and cursing and pleading with her the moment she woke up.

The day she stared with her heart in her mouth at two thin lines on a white stick was the day she threw out her supplies. She never touched heroin again. But now, 2,414 days later, she longed for a fix that would take away the regret that she cradled in her arms when all she wanted was to hold her daughter.

Without warning, two arms wound their way around her, and Snow rested her chin on her best friend's shoulder.

"It's going to be okay," she assured her. Her voice was thick as she began to cry. "You'll get through this." Audrey's sobs coughed out audibly as she moved to return the comforting embrace, and for the first time since she was a teenager crying onto Mark's shoulder over a father she was better off not knowing, she allowed someone to see her fall apart.

Chapter Seventeen

Huntsville, Alabama
Day 2413

"Hey, kid!" Audrey said, popping her head in the boy's room. He was busy creating a new lego spaceship next to the elaborate one he'd built the day before. He spun around, sending his dark hair flying. "Want to help me paint your baby sister's room?" she grinned and held up the buckets of paint.

"Oh, yeah!" he exclaimed and jumped up from his post on the floor. Audrey held his door open wide enough for him to bolt through. He led her to the room on the other side of the library on the far side of the hall. The furniture had already been hauled out, leaving the white walls and carpet bland and blinding. Audrey crossed the room to open the window. An early summer breeze fluttered in with the sound of leaves rustling on their branches. The birds sent up their twittering music, welcoming in the summer months on the last day of May.

"Are those clothes okay to paint in?" she asked, eyeing his blue button down pajama shirt and matching pants. He looked down at them too and shrugged. "I don't want you getting in trouble," she added.

"Mom won't care," he shrugged again and grabbed a paintbrush. Audrey plugged a portable stereo into the wall outlet and loaded a CD she'd found in the family's collection. "What's that?" he asked with a cock of his head as a bass guitar enunciated the beat through the speaker at the song's introduction.

"Queen," Audrey answered with slight revulsion at the question.

"No, I know that," he rolled his eyes at her. "What's that

thing you put in there?"

"A CD?" she questioned, slightly confused.

"So it's what's playing the music?" he asked. She nodded slowly. "How many songs does it hold?" Audrey blinked before looking down at the case.

"This one's got ten tracks on it," she answered dumbly. Ezra rolled his eyes again.

"My phone holds like a million songs," he declared, puffing out his chest with pride.

"Why would you need a million songs?" she laughed in disbelief.

"I don't know," he shrugged. "But it can have that many if I want it to." Audrey shook her head and worked the lid off of the can of paint.

"We're doing those three walls pink, and the one with the window grey so we can hang some pink curtains on it," she explained.

"Have you ever painted a wall before?" he asked with his hands on his hips, looking down at her with a haughty expression plastered to his thin face.

"Nope. Have you?"

"I helped Dad once when Mia wanted polka dots on her wall. I can teach you," he held out a hand in reassurance.

"Hey, do you think Mia would want to help?" Audrey suggested.

Ezra shrugged. "You can ask her, but I don't think she will."

"Don't touch the paint until I get back," she instructed as she left the room. Standing outside Mia's door, she found herself suddenly nervous. Taking a slow, steadying breath, she rapped gently against the wood.

"Who is it?" came the soft reply.

"It's Audrey," she answered and cleared her throat. A moment later the door opened, and Mia stepped through, staring up at her with arched eyebrows as though the effort to get out of bed for something so pointless was irritating.

"What do you want?" she snapped.

"Ezra and I are painting the baby's room if you want to join us," Audrey offered with an unsteady smile.

"Yeah, no. I'd rather not," she started to close the door, but Audrey found herself pushing it back open.

"Why don't you just come and watch then," she suggested. "Ezra misses you."

"No he doesn't," Mia seemed appalled at the prospect.

"Well we'll be in there if you change your mind." The door was closed before Audrey could form a smile.

"No luck?" Ezra called from the nursery doorway.

"Looks like it's just us," Audrey said as she made her way back to the pale room.

"Told you," he shrugged again and handed her a paint roller. They worked silently on the first wall for a long while with Ezra occasionally offering up little words of encouragement and advice on how to correctly paint the wall without any streaks.

"This is such an ugly pink, isn't it?" she broke the silence when they finished the first wall.

"Oh, I hate it," Ezra blanched. "But Mom thinks its 'Princess Perfect'," he made quotation marks with his fingers as he quoted his mother, using a much higher tone to imitate her feminine inflection. Audrey giggled at him and started to ask him what his favorite color was when she heard a loud crash from downstairs. Ezra looked up at Audrey with round, frightened eyes, both of them frozen in their places. Then came the scream. Audrey lurched into action, racing down the stairs at full speed with Ezra trailing behind him. Mia opened her door curiously to watch the scene unfold.

"Elizabeth?" Audrey called anxiously. She got a cry in response and turned the sharp corner to the master bedroom. She found her crumpled on the floor with her arm around her round stomach. Audrey ran to her side and maneuvered her into a sitting position, moving her hair out of her sopping face. She panted and heaved, trying to catch her breath.

"Mom!" Ezra screamed. "Are you okay?"

"The baby. She's coming," she managed to wheeze.

"What?" Audrey stammered. "Are you sure?"

"I've done this twice, Audrey! Of course I'm freaking sure!" she screeched, squeezing the blood from Audrey's hand. She winced at her grip and frantically searched for her phone to call an ambulance.

"But you're not due for – "

"Don't you think I know that!" she shrieked. "Just drive me. The keys to the van are on the hook by the door." Audrey stared into her friend's panicked eyes and felt her heart throb against her ribs as she raised the phone to her ear.

"I can't," she breathed.

"Yes you can," Elizabeth worked to control her breathing. "I can tell you how to get there. An ambulance will take too long."

"I haven't driven a car in eighteen years!" Audrey yelled. Elizabeth glowered at her with pained eyes. "Hello! I need an ambulance. My friend is in labor."

Audrey sat in the waiting room of the hospital with Mia and Ezra on either side of her, waiting for news of her friend's progress. Elizabeth's parents had arrived shortly after they did, and Mrs. Bailey rushed in the delivery room to be with her daughter. Mia slept against her grandfather's shoulder while Audrey avoided Mr. Bailey eyes as best as she could. Ezra reached over the armrest to clutch Audrey's hand. She stared down at his little hand and fought the tears that formed in her eyes. How many times had her two little brothers held her hand like that?

Finally the doctor walked into the waiting room. Audrey jumped from her seat aside Mr. Bailey as they searched the doctor's face eagerly for news, but Audrey heard nothing after, "She's fine. They're both fine."

She slumped back in her seat with her spinning head in her hands. The image of Elizabeth crumpled on the floor in agony plagued her mind. She would have gotten to the hospital much more quickly had Audrey driven her instead of waiting for the ambulance to make the trek up the mountainside, but the image from her dreams of Daniel's torn body crippled her.

"Ms. Wyatt," the doctor pulled her away from her guilt. "Ms. Ganesh is asking for you." He smiled politely and exchanged a few words with Mr. Bailey. Audrey found herself looking down at the boy still grasping her hand. He let go and swayed back and forth on his heels.

"You should go," he said. "Mom gets mad if we make her wait when she calls us." Audrey swallowed heavily and trudged down the hall to Elizabeth's room. The door creaked softly as she opened it. Elizabeth was ghostly pale with dark bags under her eyes. Her sweaty hair was tied back, and her weak eyes smiled up at her when she entered.

"Hey," she croaked.

"Hi," Audrey whispered, afraid to break the tranquil silence.

"How are my kids?"

"They're fine," she answered. "They're great."

"Good," Elizabeth nodded slowly.

"Look, Elizabeth, I'm really sorry about what happened. I should have driven you –"

"No, you shouldn't have," she interrupted Audrey's apology. "I shouldn't have asked that of you. Even if you did drive, your head would have been in the wrong place, and it could have been disastrous."

"Yeah, you're right," Audrey said to her boots.

"They moved Lilian to the NICU," Elizabeth said after a moment's pause. "They've got her in an incubator."

Audrey struggled with her answer before settling on, "Lilian's a beautiful name." Elizabeth laughed hoarsely and turned her head to the ceiling.

"She doesn't have a middle name," her voice was heavy, and when Audrey looked up, her green eyes were full of tears. "Al and I could never agree on names, so I always chose the first name. He got the middle name."

"What are you going to do?" Audrey asked, sitting down on the edge of the bed, and reached for her friend's hands. Elizabeth stared at their clasped hands for a long while before answering with a shaky voice.

"She doesn't have to have a middle name. Lilian Ganesh is recognizable enough," she tried to laugh, but tears rolled down her cheek and stifled it in her throat.

"How about Amalie?" Audrey offered, leaning forward in an effort to distract Elizabeth from her sorrow. "Since Amal never chose a name, name her after him."

"Lilian Amalie," she tasted the name and smiled. "That's a lot of L's." Audrey smiled back and released a choked laugh. "But it's beautiful." Elizabeth gazed at the wall ahead, lost in her own mind. Audrey sat quietly so as not to disturb her.

Moments later there was a soft knock at the door and Mr. Bailey popped his head in. "How's my little girl?"

Audrey ducked out of the room once Elizabeth's dad brought in the kids. She broke out of the hospital at a light run and lit a cigarette before she left the revolving door, the smell of the hospital triggering a plethora of unwelcomed memories.

"You were in an accident. You and Ethan and Daniel. Ethan is in ICU. He's in a coma."

"And Danny?" she forced herself to ask, afraid the answer would only confirm her dread.

"He didn't make it."

Audrey pushed out Mark's voice with a puff of smoke, but it only left room for Liam's modulated pleading.

"Jesus, Aud," he breathed. *His voice was light, and she could hear his smile. She pressed her eyelids together, gritting her teeth against the temptation. Her heart stopped with every soft grunt and short cry that came from his arms.* *"You've got to see her."*

Then he started to cry. Her eyes fluttered as she almost forgot why they were closed in the first place. In their four years together, she had never once seen Liam cry. *"Hello, beautiful."*

He exchanged short words with a nurse, and she waited until she heard the door shut again.

"You're safe," he sighed bitterly. *She let out a long breath and drug her eyes open. He sat leaning on her bed with blissful, dark eyes but a set jaw.* *"So what's your plan, Aud?"*

She gazed at him until her vision blurred with tears. She reached out a shaking hand to touch his scratchy face. He placed a thick hand over hers, moving it to kiss her palm and press it against his cheek, and closed his eyes.

"Just look at her," he pleaded. *"Just once. That's all I'm asking. She's beautiful, Aud. She's the most beautiful thing I've ever seen."*

She. Audrey felt her heart sink into the mattress behind her. She had a little girl.

Swallowing the lump in her throat, she moved her hand to his hair that fell just past his shoulders. *"I can't,"* she whispered, *twisting the end around her finger for the last time. She ran her hand along his shoulder and squeezed a handful of the soft, black fabric of his shirt to choke back her emotions. Gasping with a tearless sob, she pulled him down with all of her remaining strength and wrapped her arms around him. He held her tightly and dug his face into her neck.*

She opened her mouth to speak, but choked on the words. I love you. *She wanted to scream it, wanted to let him know just once before she left, but her tongue turned to lead in her mouth.*

Audrey coughed violently and held onto a ledge for support, her chest heaving with the memory, the soft cries of her baby girl and the desperate entreaties from the man she loved.

"Honey, are you okay?" Mrs. Bailey called behind her, laying a hand on her back as she coughed. Tears from strain and grief filled her eyes as she nodded and caught her breath.

"This hospital," she started, gasping for air. "It's where my brothers were born. It's where he –"

"Oh, honey," Mrs. Bailey wrapped Audrey in a warm hug that she found uncomfortable at first, but soon she melted into the motherly embrace. But she didn't let the tears fall. After a moment, Mrs. Bailey pulled back. "Do you want to see Lilian? I can get you a car back to the house if you'd rather."

Everything in her screamed no, but she nodded and followed the woman back into the hospital. She led her through the halls and to the NICU where Audrey was escorted alone by a nurse to the incubator that held Elizabeth's last child. The nurse scuttled away, leaving Audrey standing in front of the clear box. She sat down tentatively and stared at the tiny baby inside.

The first thing she noticed was how small she was, with bony arms and legs and miniscule fingers and toes. Her skin was wrinkled and dark, almost as dark as her fathers, with wisps of black hair on her tiny head. Her large eyes were closed, but her mouth was slightly ajar, revealing the toothless gums inside.

Audrey's eyes filled with tears as she reached a finger through the hole in the incubator and lightly stroked her little arm. Her skin felt feathery light and delicate to the touch.

"Hello, beautiful," she croaked. "You are going to have such a wonderful life. You don't know it yet, but you have such an amazing mother who will always love you and take care of you. And you have a brother and a sister who will always have your back, and grandparents who will spoil you. And I am so sorry your daddy never got to meet you." She paused to wipe away a tear as she began to smile. "But I'm so very glad I got to."

Chapter Eighteen

Huntsville, Alabama
Day 2518

"Dinner's ready!" Audrey called over her shoulder, ladling heaps of steaming hamburger helper into three bowls. The weakening autumn sun drifted lazily through the window and fell across the tiled floor, covering the kitchen with its pale light. Ezra trotted in, grabbed a bowl, and left without a word. "Where are you going, kid?" she asked, glancing at the table she'd begun to set with cups and forks.

"We're eating downstairs so we can watch a movie," he stated matter-of-factly.

"Oh we're watching a movie are we?" she laughed.

"Yep!" he yelled, already halfway down the stairs. Mia trudged in, her long hair tangled and plastered to the side of her head. She'd been lying in bed with her door closed since she got back from school the day before.

"What about you, Mia?" Audrey asked, using a hopeful tone that still sounded foreign in her throat. "Want to watch a movie?"

The girl shook her head, grabbed her bowl, and stalked back to her room, closing the door behind her softly so as not to call any attention to her from her mother, who sat on the window seat in the dining room's bay windows, rocking Lilian and staring blankly out at the leaf covered lawn. Audrey exchanged the remaining bowl for the tiny baby and sat at Elizabeth's feet. Lilian barely registered the change of arms, her eyes clamped shut and her fists resting against her stomach. Her thin black hair stood up in awkward angles, and Audrey smoothed it down, pushing back the way her smooth skin made her stomach churn.

"I wish she'd sleep like this at night," Audrey commented with strained effort, her voice pushing past the tightness of her throat. She stared down at the baby, not trusting her stinging eyes to hide the emotion from Elizabeth.

"You and me both. I think she's slowing down though on the whole Operation: Keep Mommy Awake For As Long As Possible," she chortled through a mouthful of hamburger helper. Her dirty hair was tied on top of her head, her bangs clipped back. She hadn't changed her sweatpants in three days. "Did you save yourself any of this?"

"No," Audrey shook her head. Her friend responded by shoving her toes into Audrey's side. "You need to eat something."

"I'm fine, really," she tried to sound believable. Bryant sat at her feet, whining and staring longingly up at Elizabeth's food. "Come on, boy," Audrey got his attention. "Let's go outside." She left her friend in the dining room before she could say anything else and made her way downstairs where Ezra waited patiently, scrutinizing the movies he'd strewn across the floor in front of him.

"We have a whole bunch of movies," he declared, his eyes still scanning the cover art on the cases. "You can choose what we watch if you want."

"Thanks kid," she replied absently. "Here, take your sister." She handed the baby off to Ezra and slid open the door to the patio to light a cigarette. Bryant bounded through the door in an excited rush that almost knocked Audrey off her feet, and ran down the steps into the fenced yard. She blew out a stream of smoke that carried out into the air and through the bare branches of the trees.

Ezra coughed dramatically from the doorway behind her. "Those things are nasty!" he exclaimed.

"What, you don't want a puff?" she joked, holding the cigarette out in his direction. He blanched and struggled to close the door without dropping his baby sister while Audrey snickered to herself. She turned back to the yard and leaned against the patio railing. The trees that lined the fence in rows reached their scraggly, nearly empty branches upward and outward like arms simultaneously entangling their knobby fingers with those of their neighbor while reaching up into the heavens as though trying to capture God in their twisted grasp. She half expected them to move like in the cartoons her brothers used to watch, bending down in one swift motion, trapping the jubilant dog it their witch's finger cages, but they simply swayed in the wind in a subtle, tranquil dance.

Audrey stared down the side of the mountain, through the gap in the trees' fingers and down into the bustling city at its feet, her thoughts lingering on the only safe topic these days: Owen.

She'd left her father in a mad rush to be at her best friend's side, but now two months later, she wondered how he was fairing without her. She wondered if he was still in that house, surrounded by the remnants of the free spirited tenants before them, or if he'd been evicted in his pursuit of alcohol. Part of her thought she should regret not saying goodbye, but it wasn't a very strong feeling. She'd never forgiven him for selling her motorcycle, not because it was all she really had, but because in realizing just how much he'd screwed up his own life, he'd made sure to drag her down with him. She might have forgiven him and moved on if he did it out of some desperate notion to keep his daughter around, but he only did it so he wouldn't have to be alone.

Of course, she'd thought of taking a bus to the airport every day when she left Serge's Bar smelling of smoke, sweat, and alcohol, but somehow she'd always found herself peddling on her rusty bicycle back to that grungy old house in the middle of the desert. She didn't really have anywhere else to go, and leaving him to fend for himself had never sounded very appealing, no matter what he'd done to her.

She lit another cigarette and watched the bear-dog make laps around the box yard, sniffing out foreign smells. She imagined him shaved and eighty pounds lighter with short grey fur and bulging brown orbs for eyes, sniffing puddles in the streets of London or Reykjavik or Seattle.

Lilian's sharp, piercing cry stabbed through Audrey's chest, and she pushed out Hermione's weary face from her mind as she called for Bryant and went back into Amal's man cave that smelled of shampooed carpet and disuse.

"You stink now," Ezra grumbled, handing off his shrieking sister as if her cries were some unidentified poison.

"Thanks kid," Audrey laughed, bouncing Lilian in her arms. The baby stopped crying almost instantaneously and gazed up at her with almond, black eyes. Eyes similar to what Audrey imagined Rosie's were like. Clearing her throat and shaking the painful image from her mind, she turned her attention back to Ezra. "What movies have you got?"

"A whole bunch," he repeated. "Batman v. Superman with Ben Affleck and Henry Cavill. The Jungle Book – both of them. One with Idris Elba as Shere Khan, and the other one with Benedict Cumberbatch, which is funny because he played Sherlock in Sherlock and Khan in Star Trek, and when you put it together, you get Shere Khan. But we've also got all of the Hobbit movies and all of the new and old Star Trek movies – but not the one with Benedict Cumberbatch. Dad didn't like the way mom looked at him. Oh and there's Fantastic Mr. Fox, too. It's got George Clooney in it. It's funny because they don't cuss. They say the word cuss. I tried that once. I said, 'Hey, Dad! Where's my cussin' Legos?' "

"How'd that go?" Audrey laughed.

"He took my Legos away for a week."

"I would too."

"Do you like Benedict Cumberbatch?" he asked.

"I don't know who that is."

"He's awesome. Mia likes him, too. We have a lot of his movies, except Star Trek. We've got all of the Hobbit movies – I already said that – and all of the Sherlocks. And then there's The Imitation Game, but I don't understand that one much. And there's Doctor Strange and Zoolander 2 and Magik and Penguins of Madagascar – "

"Penguins of what?" Audrey interrupted him, suddenly interested in the long list of movies that streamed from the young boy's mouth in what sounded like English mixed with some foreign language that she didn't understand.

"Madagascar!" he repeated, holding up the case. "It's about the four penguins in the Madagascar movies. Benedict Cumberbatch isn't a penguin, though. He's a wolf. His name is classified. Not like, 'Hi my name's Classified. What's yours?' but like 'My name is top secret. You can't know what it is.' " He deepened his voice to imitate the British actor.

"Let's watch that," she smiled nervously, hoping her dangerous choice in movie wouldn't cause a breakdown in front of Ezra. He put in the movie and curled up next to her, reaching his hand across her to touch the tip of his finger to Lilian's palm. Audrey smiled as the movie started, remembering Ethan and Daniel sitting on either side of her, quoting the four escaped zoo animals, and imagined watching a movie with her own baby in her lap and Liam at her side. She sighed and kissed the top of Ezra's shaggy head.

"What was that for?" he asked in confusion.

"You're all right, kid," she said and he smiled, a stretched grin with gaps and missing teeth, and she let herself be content.

Audrey woke suddenly with the screams of someone else for once. Ever since Lilian was brought to her new home, she woke the whole house with her ear splitting shrieks. Audrey groaned and rolled over with the pillow over her ear, drowning not only the child's cries, but also the images of an exhausted Liam rolling out of bed to calm his little girl's wailing. She was pushing the pillow tighter against her ear when she heard the steady beat of music in a neighboring room.

Giving up on ever getting any sleep, she threw back the comforter and swung her legs over the side of the bed. She opened the door and winced at the new volume of the baby's cries from the sofa downstairs, and she almost wished her lungs were still slightly undeveloped. She leaned over the rail to find Elizabeth rocking her on the couch with Bryant staring curiously up at her as if wishing to silence it.

Doing okay?" Audrey called down to her friend. Elizabeth waved a hand in her direction without a word and returned her attention to the baby. Grinning, Audrey went back to search out the music's origin. She cracked open Ezra's door to find him snoring softly with his arm over the edge of the bed and the comforter around his ankles. He moved with little resistance as she pushed him back onto the mattress and pulled the blankets around his shoulders. Running a hand on his hair, she snuck back out of the room. She paused outside of Mia's locked door, soft music pouring out from under the door. She knocked loudly enough to be heard.

"Who is it?" the girl called.

"It's Audrey," she answered, no longer nervous but slightly frustrated with lack of sleep. The lock turned and the door opened slightly. Mia eyed her from within.

"What do you want?" she snapped again. Audrey crossed her arms.

"Can I come in?" she asked with more of a commanding tone than a questioning one. The girl paused before walking back to her bed. Audrey pushed the door wide enough for her to step through.

"Close it," Mia ordered. Audrey obeyed and took in the room around her that showed the remnants of a childhood that she was slowly outgrowing. American Girl dolls and large stuffed animals sat unused on a shelf with an autographed poster of all five members of some boy band. Makeup and hair products adorned a small vanity desk with a mirror surrounded by unlit bulbs, and a full length mirror hung on the door to what Audrey guessed was her closet. She ignored her frail and dangerously skinny reflection in the mirror and turned back to the girl lounging back on her bed with her arms crossed.

"I like your room," Audrey muttered in her direction and took a seat on the edge of the bed. Then she noticed the music flowing from the stereo. "Is this Of Monsters and Men?" she asked in astonishment. The girl nodded softly, pulling the blankets back around her and picking up her phone from the bedside table. "I didn't realize they actually got famous. I haven't heard this song." She waited for the girl to respond, but when she didn't Audrey continued. "Did you know I saw them in concert when I was in Iceland before they actually got famous?"

"That's cool," Mia commented blandly, staring at her phone.

"What are you doing?" Audrey eyed the pink cased smartphone in her hand.

"Playing a game."

"What game?"

"It's just a game!" Mia shot, glaring up at Audrey with an intense fury in her eyes. Audrey scowled down at her.

"Please don't speak to me like that," she found herself reprimanding the girl. Mia rolled her eyes and tossed her phone on the bed next to her.

"I don't even know you!" she screeched. "You just showed up at my house! You're not my mother!"

"You're right. I'm not," Audrey broke in. "But I'm here to help you guys."

"I don't need your help," she protested.

"Your mom said the same thing, but I'm here anyway."

"Well I don't want you here," she glowered at Audrey.

"Did you know I was your mom's best friend before you were born?" Audrey tried to calm her.

"I don't care!" Mia yelled. "You're not *my* best friend, so why don't you just get out of my room?" Audrey stared at her, caught unaware by the unfamiliar feeling that enveloped her: pity. Is this what people feel when they look at me? she thought. Tears stung at her eyes when she responded with a smile.

"You look just like your dad."

Mia stilled and averted her eyes to her knees. "People always say I look like my mom."

"I can see that," Audrey continued. "But you've got his eyes and his smile."

"I haven't smiled at you," she snapped, suddenly defensive again.

"But I can tell you've got his smile," she chuckled. "Your dad had the most contagious smile. Even me, who rarely ever smiled at anyone. He could make me grin and laugh at just about anything. I can tell that when you're not being such a brat, you are the same way."

Mia's eyes welled with tears and her lip quivered. Audrey was suddenly nervous and uncomfortable again at the girl's change in stance. She reached tentatively across the bed and placed a hand on her knee.

"It's okay to miss him," she whispered. At that, Mia broke. Tears flooded from her eyes as she wept into her knees, squeezing them tightly against her chest. Unsure of how to react, Audrey sidled up next to her and drew her close. She didn't resist her touch, but leaned into her, clutching at the worn fabric of her old Temple of the Dog shirt, and sobbed into her shoulder. Audrey pulled the girl into her lap and wrapped her arms around her, shushing her comfortingly and stroking her hair as her own tears bit at her eyes.

She held her like she'd held her brothers, like she should have held her own daughter. She nuzzled her face into the girl's hair.

"I'm so sorry," she whispered.

"It was my fault," the girl whimpered. "It's all my fault." Audrey jerked back and pulled her out so she could face her. She wiped Mia's hair out of her wet face and turned her chin up to face her.

"How could you think something like that?" Audrey asked almost harshly in her bewilderment. "He was overseas. It wasn't your fault."

"But maybe if I wasn't such a brat like you said, he would have wanted to stay," she confessed, staring into Audrey with bleary brown eyes. Audrey's heart shattered in her chest, and she wrapped the girl in a tight embrace again.

"Don't you ever, ever blame yourself," she shushed her. "Never ever blame yourself for what happened. He loved you so much. He went there to help people, not to get away from you."

"Do you promise?" she coughed.

"I promise," Audrey assured her through the lump in her throat and rocked her gently side to side until her sighing ceased and was replaced with the deep, slow breaths of sleep. Audrey leaned her head back against the headboard, closing her eyes against the protective nature she'd developed for Mia. She saw so much of herself in her oval, heavy eyes, and she willed away the burden of guilt that seemed to suffocate the girl, wishing somehow to take it onto herself.

The door creaked open and Elizabeth's worn face peeked in. "Is she okay?" she asked. "I heard her yelling."

"Yeah," Audrey whispered, sliding her arm from behind Mia's head and tucking her into bed. She crossed the room silently and closed the door. "She'll be okay."

Chapter Nineteen

Huntsville, Alabama
Day 2618

Audrey leaned against the patio railing with a cigarette and a glass of wine. The collar of her leather jacket was pulled up around her bare neck to fight off the bitterly cold breeze that seemed to carry ice with it, plunging the microscopic crystals into her skin. She gazed unseeingly down the mountainside while Bryant ran haphazard laps around the yard.

"Skipping coffee this morning, are we?" Elizabeth's voice sounded behind her. Audrey turned to see her and curved the corner of her mouth into what she hoped looked like a smile. She trapped a strand of hair behind her ear so it wouldn't blow across her face. Elizabeth sidled up next to her, reaching for the pack of cigarettes that was balanced on the rail. She lit it and blew out a stream of smoke.

"What kind of name is Bryant for a dog?" Audrey asked when she heard Elizabeth's intake of breath that signaled the beginning of a question that she probably didn't want to answer.

"Dad named him," she answered with a shrug, pulling her sweater more tightly around her. "Al could never decide on a name, and Dad said he looked like a bear. So being the Alabama fan that he is, he started calling him Bryant after Bear Bryant. He started responding to the name before Al could think of something else, so it just stuck."

Audrey continued to watch the Newfoundland bound across the yard jubilantly, unmoved by the crisp morning air that rustled his thick, shaggy coat. She couldn't think of anything else to say. Her mind was dominated by the date on the calendar.

"I went to the library this morning," Elizabeth stated. "I noticed a Harry Potter book is missing." Audrey lifted *Harry Potter and the Prisoner of Azkaban* languidly and set it back down on the rail, sipping at her glass of wine. She'd ventured into the Ganesh library with the hopes of finding Danny's favorite book. Even with two walls covered with filled bookshelves, it wasn't hard to find on the second shelf from the bottom within Ezra's reach.

"I'm going to see him," Audrey said. "As soon as it's light out."

"How are you getting there?" Elizabeth asked.

"You've got a bicycle," she noted.

"You'll get lost," her friend protested. "Or wreck trying to get down the mountain. And it's miles away. I already called a taxi for you. They'll be here in half an hour tops."

"Thanks," Audrey murmured.

"Just don't torture yourself, okay?" When she didn't receive an answer, Elizabeth sighed and tossed the half smoked cigarette in the ashtray, turning back to the house. Audrey downed the last of her wine and lit another cigarette, ignoring every voice but his.

"Will you come throw baseball with me? I have to practice so me and Ethan can play for the real life Red Sox. Wherever they are."

She heard the cab pull into the driveway and made her way through the house to the front door where Elizabeth stood waiting her. She didn't say anything, but her green eyes implored her. She reached out and pulled her into a tight embrace. Audrey stood frozen for a moment before awkwardly resting a hand on her friend's back.

The drive to the cemetery was a long one, but when she stood under the metal arched entrance, she still wasn't ready to face him. The field before her was white with a thick layer of frost, and the grass screamed in agony as it crunched beneath her boots. A thin mist hung like a ghost over the ground, waiting patiently for the first beams of the sun to evaporate it before its next shift began at sundown. Her legs moved without permission as she ambled through the neatly organized rows of headstones, stopping at each one to read the name. After twenty minutes, she found the one she was looking for and choked on her own breath.

In loving memory of
Daniel Brennan Mills
Beloved son and brother
February 9, 1994 – December 22, 2005

Audrey sank to her knees in front of her baby brother's headstone as the sun began to rise over the horizon.

"Hey buddy," she croaked, the sound of those unused words brought forth a fresh wave of anguish. "I brought you something." She held up the hardback copy of *Harry Potter* as if he could see it. "I know I'm not Mark, but I hope I'll do." She leaned back against a headstone and ripped her eyes from her brother's name.

She cleared her throat and began.

Audrey shouted loudly as she read, the excitement building during an intense chapter. She was deep into the story, almost forgetting where she sat. She didn't hear the footsteps as he approached her.

"Audrey?" he called to her with an unsteady voice. Audrey jumped, startled at the sudden break of silence. Her hair swished in her face as she jerked towards him.

"Mark?" she gawked, hoisting herself up from the frozen ground. He breathed a grin and stepped closer to her with glowing eyes.

"I never thought I'd see you again," he beamed, deep wrinkles crowding his eyes.

"You got old," she jested despite the rock lodged in a valve in her heart and nudged his arm. His smile widened.

"Am I a more appropriate age for you now?" he quipped.

"Getting there."

"So how've you been?" he asked. "Last I heard you were riding around the country on tour with a band!"

"Everyone knows then, do they?" she huffed, making sure her smile stayed plastered to her face.

"It's a small town," he waved off the comment.

"No it *was* a small town," she corrected him. "I seriously think this place exploded since I was last here."

"That it has," he agreed. "So what happened to the country

band?"

"They kicked out their guitarist. Last I heard they were on their way to Europe for a big tour."

"Oh yeah?" he grinned. "Then why'd you leave?"

"You know why," she eyed him. "That last charm the boys got me? The guitar? That was a hint wasn't it?"

"Yeah, it was," he nodded sheepishly. They stood in silence for a long while before he finally thought of something to say. "*Prisoner of Azkaban*, huh?"

"Yeah, it was his favorite," she turned back to look at Daniel's gravestone.

"He did love those books."

Audrey sat back down in the dead grass, and Mark followed, sliding down next to her with a groan.

"What about you?" she asked. "I heard you remarried. Is that still a thing?"

"Yeah that's still a thing," he said, leaning to the side to pull his phone from his back pocket. "We've got twins now." He scrolled through his photo album full of photographs until he came to a little girl with winking round eyes and an arm around a boy with short, fuzzy hair and a toothless grin.

"That's Zoe, and that's Ronan," he pointed out.

"They're beautiful," she commented, taking the phone from him.

"They're a handful," he laughed, reaching over to scroll to another photograph. "Oh this one's a funny story actually. We were at the Ganesh's for Mia's birthday party, and Ronan ran in with this little girl that had apparently pulled out his tooth for him."

Audrey felt ice shoot through her veins, freezing her where she sat. Her eyes locked on the young girl grinning proudly behind Ronan. Her eyes were squinted shut with the smile and her long hair twisted with unruly curls. Audrey's chest burned, and her throat clamped shut. She couldn't breathe.

"I guessed as much," Mark broke her from her reverie and took his phone from her, tearing her daughter from her grasp. "She's yours, isn't she?"

"I don't know what you're talking about," she gulped, longing to take his phone again.

"Come on, Audrey. I'd know those curls anywhere." He swiped through his phone. "I snapped some more of her if you want to see them." She didn't answer, gazing at the phone that he held out to her. Against her better judgment, she took it from him and looked down at the screen.

Her head buzzed at the photo in her hand. Ethan smiled broadly at the camera with his niece in his lap, his chin on her shoulder as his arms wrapped around her in a tight squeeze, and she smiled with a wrinkled nose and disappearing eyes.

Regret sawed into her bones with the next one. Liam sat at Elizabeth's kitchen table with his arms crossed leaning against the table while his daughter squeezed onto his arm, hiding half of her face from view. His black stubble and short hair were flecked with grey, and the rolled sleeves of his shirt revealed an elaborate rose tattoo on his forearm surrounded by vines of thorns. He smirked down at his daughter almost as if he knew Audrey was gazing at them and the thought made him uncomfortable. Her heart sang as she saw the two of them together, wishing more than anything to watch them talk, to watch him push her on the swings or take her to the beach to see the whales.

"Dania's really a sweet girl," Mark assured her. "You'd be proud of her."

"You take a lot of pictures," Audrey said blandly, handing the phone back to him.

"Yeah, well, I didn't take enough of Danny, so," he trailed off, pulling up a handful of dead grass.

"There wasn't time to take enough pictures of Danny," she murmured.

"No, there wasn't," he cleared his throat before he continued. "I have a confession to make." He held up a worn copy of *Harry Potter and the Order of the Phoenix*.

"You too, huh?" Audrey snickered.

"I come here every year on the day he passed and read to him. Just to let him know I haven't forgotten him."

"Thank you," she whispered. They sat in silence for a while, staring at the small headstone in front of them while an old anger built up within her again as she read his name. "She made sure to bury him before I woke up, didn't she?" Audrey seethed.

"What are you talking about?"

"Sheryl. She had his funeral while I was in a coma so I couldn't be here. So she wouldn't have to look at me, her son's killer, while they lowered him into the ground," her throat tightened as she spoke and she lit a cigarette.

"Oh don't start that," Mark groaned. "Of course she didn't do it on purpose. She just wanted to bury her son sooner rather than later so she could have a bit of closure. She wanted to get it over with"

"You're still defending her," Audrey spat in wide-eyed disbelief. "You aren't married to her anymore, Mark. You can speak your mind."

"I will absolutely still defend her when she's being wrongfully accused!" he argued. "Your mother was in more pain than anyone should have to bear. Yes, of course, she handled it wrong when it came to you, but purposefully burying him without you present was not one of those instances."

"But why?" she heaved, tears stinging her eyes. "Why did it have to happen to him? Why does someone so young and innocent have to go like that?" The way Mark stared at her with unabashed pity fueled her flames, and her fury writhed in her veins.

"The way I see it, maybe his life would have been too full of turmoil, riddled with disappointments and heartache. Maybe God just chose to spare him from all of that."

Audrey scoffed. "Is that supposed to make me feel better?"

"No," he smiled sadly at her, "I guess not. It just depends on how you look at it." Audrey stared at Daniel's name as her anger evaporated.

"Say I believe you," she started, fiddling with the hem of her t-shirt. "Why couldn't God have done the same for me? Why couldn't He have taken me too?"

"Don't say that," Mark protested. "You survived for a reason. You made it out with just one scar. Just one. Right there," he smiled and ran his finger along the faded line above her temple. "He does everything for a reason."

She snickered bitterly. "Care to tell me what that reason is?"

"I don't know," he smiled kindly. "But I'll bet she's got your chin and Liam's eyes." Her chin trembled and she dropped her head onto his shoulder in exhaustion.

"I'm so tired," she wheezed. "I'm so tired of hurting. I'm tired of running. I just want it all to be over."

"Then stop running."

Audrey let out a shaky breath, and he squeezed her knee.

Without another word, he picked up Elizabeth's copy of Harry Potter and opened it to where she left off. Audrey left her head on Mark's shoulder as he read. She lost herself in the sound of his voice, laughing softly when he used another dreadful English accent. He read until the sun sank below the horizon, until Audrey's body went limp as she slipped off into a dreamless sleep. He closed the book and stared up at the empty expanse of sky, watching it fill with stars as the light of the sun faded steadily.

"You'll be okay," he whispered in her hair, and for the first time in eighteen years, he actually believed it. He turned and pressed his lips to the top of her head before waking her and driving her up the mountain where Snow waited with a comforting smile and two pints of cookie dough ice cream.

Chapter Twenty

Huntsville, Alabama
Day 2702

Audrey sat on her bed and weighed her old book in her hand. The spine had ripped in half twice, reinforced with Scotch tape, but the cover had long since disappeared. She ran her finger over the blotch of tea and lifted the open pages to her nose, inhaling deeply the vanilla scent tinged with cigarette smoke. She smiled sadly at the memories that accompanied it and set *Crime and Punishment* on the nightstand next to the framed photograph of Snow and her maid of honor.

Throwing her legs over the edge of the bed, she went to the window and forced it open. The warm March breeze blew pollen across her face as she climbed out onto the roof. She lay back and gazed up at the stars that filled the night sky, willing the cloud of smoke that billowed from her mouth to travel its way to the parental gas giants burning away in the black velvet above her.

Her muscles were pleasantly sore from a long week of backbreaking woodwork. She and Mr. Bailey had spent three days sawing and cutting boards down to a proper size and nailing them together in a painstaking process of following a vague set of instructions. Ezra sat on the steps of the back porch with Bryant, shouting out how incorrectly they were doing everything.

"I'm going to hit him with this plank," Audrey grunted under her breath. Mr. Bailey laughed and nodded his agreement but didn't say anything. By the end of the third day, her arms and hands were cut, bruised, and splintered so badly that she couldn't tell where most of the blood was coming from. Elizabeth sat her down and tended to her with the first aid kit. Audrey shouted curses and threats with every pinch of the tweezers and drop of hydrogen peroxide.

"Oh, please. You're worse than Mia," Elizabeth snickered. Audrey turned to give Ezra an offended look when she noticed how he stiffly he stood as though he were waiting patiently for someone to allow him to speak.

"What's up, kid?" she asked.

"Dad said not to use hydrogen peroxide on cuts because it can just irritate the wounded tissue even more," he recited and pranced back up the stairs to the kitchen. Audrey glared down at Elizabeth whose lips were pursed in half-hearted shame.

"I'm going to punch you in the face," Audrey said calmly and Elizabeth snorted. "And then I'm going to pour peroxide on it." Elizabeth laughed unabashedly, leaning back with the effort, and Audrey smiled, grateful to witness the deepening creases in her friend's snowy white skin.

The next two days were filled with paintbrushes and squeals as they coated the new, freshly built Tardis with a blue paint that Ezra assured them was called Tardis blue.

"It's the bluest blue of all blues," he stated.

"That's a very specific way to describe it," Audrey said. More of the paint ended up on their clothes and skin than it did on the makeshift time machine. Mia stormed off more than once to seethe in anger and gripe about the unfairness of the world when her brother painted her on purpose, but she always came back when the laughter that filled the yard lured her out again.

As they painted, they fantasized about what they would do when they finished the ship that could travel through all of time and space. No one gave serious answers, afraid to tamper with the delicate, tranquil atmosphere. Elizabeth dreamed of Paris and Italy while her eldest daughter pined for Broadway. Ezra wanted to see dragons and samurais and ancient alien invaders that he adamantly refused to disbelieve in.

"Where would you go, Audrey?" Mia asked her after a dramatic rendition of "The Wizard and I" from the Broadway musical, *Wicked*.

"Ah," Audrey thought for a moment. "I'd go to a baseball game."

Elizabeth passed her a knowing smile, and Ezra shouted, "In space! Can you imagine a baseball game in space?"

When they finally finished painting, Mr. Bailey brought out the tin Police Public Call Box sign that adorned the top panel of the box, and Ezra bolted inside, dragging his sister with him.

"Right, then!" he shouted with a perfect English accent. "We can go anywhere you want! Any time you want! One condition – it has to be amazing!"

Audrey turned to see Elizabeth with Lilian on her hip, gazing at the closed doors of the Tardis with glistening eyes.

"I wish Al could see this," she whispered. Audrey took Lilian from her arms and nodded toward the Tardis.

"Go," she ordered. "If you hurry, you can reach them before they get to Mordor." Elizabeth blinked away her tears and ran into the space ship.

"Oh no!" her voice called from within. "They've taken the hobbits to Isengard!"

"NO!" Ezra screamed. "Not the cute little hobbits! We have to save them!"

"But what about the Ring of Power?" Mia challenged. "It has to be destroyed!"

"It's a *time machine*," her brother groaned with impatience. "We can save the hobbits, destroy the Ring of Power, kill all of the orcs, and bring balance to the Force, and still be home in time for tea!"

Audrey laughed and looked down at the baby in her arms. "You'll be a nerd, too, someday. And you can travel the stars just like them." She kissed her fat cheek and smiled at the velvety touch of her skin. She let herself linger, taking in Lilian's sweet sent.

Out on the roof, Audrey gazed up at the night sky, picking away the blue paint that was dried onto her skin and into the fabric of her Temple of the Dog t-shirt. The Ganesh family was still healing, each in their own way, from the six foot three inch hole in their heart, but they were making the best of it. It was obvious to Audrey that they no longer needed her.

So here she was on another rooftop, staring down a mountainside that sloped down into another blooming city. Huntsville had sprouted and grown in the eighteen years she'd spent running, and it was nowhere close to being finished. A town with a name like Rocket City, full of engineers and fresh-faced businessmen, was destined to spread its arms and reach for the stars. But she wouldn't be around to see it happen.

"I come bearing gifts," came a voice from behind her. Elizabeth's bright green eyes came into view from the window as she stepped out onto the roof and sat next to her best friend, handing her a glass of wine. They gazed out at the moving lights of the town at the foot of the mountain that almost reciprocated the stars above it. "How's your arms?"

"I can't feel my fingers," Audrey laughed.

"That's probably not a good thing."

"No, probably not," Audrey's smile faded as she listened to the chatter down below her. "Are they still traveling through space?"

"They refuse to leave that darned box. They played the time machine card, saying they'll finish traveling and come back at bed time."

"They're clever," Audrey laughed. "I don't think there's a smarter kid on the planet than that Ezra."

"Oh I know! He stunned even Amal sometimes. That kid knows everything there is to know about the film industry, but you can't let on if you're completely lost and don't know what he's talking about because he'll get really impatient and irritated. When he was in kindergarten, he told us we had the brains of an infant."

"I can see that," Audrey laughed. "He quoted some movie the other day, and I didn't catch it. He put his hand on my shoulder and said, 'You're an imbecile. But that's okay because you're a redhead.' "

"What?" Elizabeth guffawed. "That doesn't even make any sense!"

"I know! I just stared at him, and he just sauntered off, shaking his head with such disappointment!"

Their laughter died down, and they sipped awkwardly at their wine as neither of them wanted to confront the situation growing around them.

"How are you doing?" Audrey finally asked.

"I'm getting there," her friend sighed with a soft smile.

"I feel like I wasn't much help at all," she said to her cigarette.

"You were. I was happy to see you despite how I reacted."

"I deserved it, though."

"It took a lot for you to come back here. I don't think I'll ever be able to thank you enough for what you've done for my kids." Elizabeth sighed and gestured to the roof beneath her. "But judging by your choice of scenery, you're leaving soon."

"I fly out tomorrow," Audrey answered.

"Were you going to say goodbye?"

"That's what I'm trying to decide," she stared at the wine glass, swirling the contents into a miniature whirlpool. Saying goodbye to Elizabeth and the kids was inevitable, but it terrified her almost as much as the flight that would follow.

"You have to," Elizabeth ordered. "They'll be crushed if you don't. Even Mia's grown pretty fond of you. She refuses to say it, of course, but she loves you."

"Okay," Audrey yielded.

"I hate we missed the sunset," her friend mused, turning her head to the stars. "You should've watched it one last time."

"Sunsets are sunsets," Audrey spat dryly.

"None quite like Alabama though," she sang, her voice full of awe. They sat in silence, listening to the crickets and frogs weave an intricate web of melodies and harmonies around the boisterous fantasies of the children below. "Are you going to miss it?"

"What?"

"Alabama."

Audrey snorted. "Not at all. I'll miss you guys, sure, but this place to me is haunted."

"A place is only what you make it, Audrey – "

"And you call this a mountain?" Audrey interrupted, her tone raising an octave. "It doesn't hold a candle to Mount Rainier!"

"I never said it did," Elizabeth found herself laughing. She reached over and took her friend's trembling hand. "You're doing the right thing."

"How do you know?" Audrey asked sourly. "You don't even know where I'm going."

"Come on, I can read your mind Joanna Farren."

Audrey grimaced and laughed despite of herself. "Really, what was the point in using an alias?"

"Disappearing is next to impossible to do in today's world. Not nearly as easy as it was in those macho movies you loved," Elizabeth chuckled softly and then turned serious, gazing out at the glowing city. "When I finally drug it out of him that he'd found you and that you took his name, I knew it was only a matter of time before you went back for him."

"I'm not going back for him," she snapped. "I'm going back for my daughter. I've screwed things up too much to salvage anything with Liam."

"I wouldn't be so sure," Elizabeth said. "He's got Beverly now, but I know he still cares for you. My money's on him dropping her as soon as you show up."

"Don't even try, Snow Bailey. I'm not one to believe in false hope."

"I'm just saying," her friend raised her hands in surrender. "Take my advice. As a widow." Audrey flinched at the words on her friend's tongue. "Don't let your reservations and guilt stop you from going after the ones you love. Because they can be gone in the blink of an eye, and you'll just be left with regret."

"I know. I killed my brother, remember?"

"Stop saying that!" Elizabeth shouted. "It was an accident! You didn't kill him!" She sighed to collect herself. "Excuse me for a moment." She disappeared through the open window and returned minutes later with a box wrapped

in blue paper. "He told me not to give you this until you deserved it."

Audrey eyed her friend suspiciously and took the box from her pale hands. Elizabeth gestured to the note folded on top of it and drained her wine. Confusion wrapping itself around her head, Audrey unfolded the note. Her eyes stung at the familiar handwriting.

Give her all my love, sis.
− E.

"When did he give you this?" Audrey whispered, not trusting her voice as she traced a finger over her brother's handwriting, handwriting that hadn't changed since he was twelve years old.

"He mailed it to me at Christmas," Elizabeth answered.

Audrey's fingers trembled as she tore off the paper and opened the box. Inside was a new, hardcover copy of *Crime and Punishment*. A bookmark was already in place, and when she opened it to the page, a passage was highlighted.

Don't be overwise; fling yourself straight into life,
without deliberation; don't be afraid – the flood will
bear you to the bank and set you safe on your feet
again.

She smiled and wiped a tear from her cheek.

"There's more," Elizabeth said. Audrey looked back in the
box and clasped a hand around her mouth. Inside was a small
velvet bag. Her heart thundered against her chest as she lifted it
and pulled open the drawstring, emptying the contents into her
palm.

It was a rose charm.

Chapter Twenty-One

Seattle, Washington
Day 2703

Audrey shook with more than just turbulence as her plane drew nearer and nearer to its destination. Various scenarios ran through her head of how the evening would go, and none seemed to play out in her favor. The pilot announced their imminent descent, and she felt sick, her nerves clenching up in fiery balls in her hands, elbows, and shoulders. The familiar skyline stretched beneath her and seemed to laugh contemptuously at her. Even the mountains stared at her with disdain. The plane touched ground with a clamor that sent her heart racing, pumping acid through her veins. She ambled through the airport in a daze until she came out onto the street and got a cab. Mumbling the address, she stared through the window at the familiar streets and buildings that began to tower above her, staring down at her accusingly as she let her thoughts wander back to the morning.

Elizabeth was loading Audrey's suitcase in the back of her car while Mia clung onto Audrey's waist.

"I wish you didn't have to go," she whined. Audrey rubbed her back, unsure of how to respond.

"I'm sure I'll see you again," she found herself saying. "You'll have to come see me sometime."

"Okay," the girl cried and backed away, wiping at her eyes with the meat of her palm. Ezra sat on the steps, playing with a Star Wars action figure.

"Hey kid," Audrey called. "Come tell me bye."

"Bye," he said to BB8.

"Really? Is that all I get?" Heaving himself to his feet he

trudged toward her and gave her a half-hearted hug. She held him close and whispered into his freshly cut hair, "Before I go, I want you to know: you were fantastic. Absolutely fantastic. And you know what?" She pulled him back to stare into his dark green eyes. "So was I."

A grin stretched his mouth, and he said, "The Doctor said that."

"Yes he did," Audrey smiled. "So am I still an imbecile?"

He paused thoughtfully for a moment and then nodded. "Just a little one though. Because you looked it up on the Internet and didn't actually watch Doctor Who."

"I can't win," she threw her arms out in half-hearted exasperation. Ezra laughed, beaming up at her with a toothless grin.

"We should get going, Audrey," Elizabeth called behind her. With a heavy heart that beat steadily faster and faster, they drove down the mountain towards the airport. "Have you got everything?" her friend asked when they stood outside the door.

"I can't do this, Snow," Audrey panicked.

"Okay, none of that," she pulled her into a hug. "I have never been more proud of you."

"But I'll die. I'll get on the plane and die. I think I'm having a bloody heart attack."

Elizabeth pulled back, leaving her hand on Audrey's shoulder and gazed scornfully at her. "You sound bloody ridiculous." Audrey smiled and let her friend's tranquil eyes momentarily calm her. "Does he know you're coming?" she asked.

"No, I never could call him," Audrey admitted.

"Do you want me to?"

"No, it's fine," she tried to smile. If Liam didn't know she was coming, it would be easier to live with herself if her legs faltered and refused to carry her to his street.

"Call me tonight?"

"Yeah, of course."

"Promise me."

"Okay, I promise," Audrey assured her.

"Okay, that's it. I'm leaving. You've got a plane to catch!" Elizabeth pulled her into another hug and watched her as she made her way through security.

Audrey sat in the back of the cab and mentally rehearsed

what she would say when she saw him. "Hi Liam, I know you hate me, and I have no right to ask this of you, but I would really love to meet my Rosie." She picked it apart and edited it, refining it until it sounded more like, "Hello William. It's Audrey. If it wouldn't be an inconvenience to you, do you think you could possibly allow me to meet your daughter? It would bring me great pleasure."

"Stop the car!" she screamed. She jumped out to catch her breath, throwing money at the driver when he yelled for her payment. He sped off with her luggage in the trunk, but she didn't notice. She ran her hand through her hair and squeezed until the pressure on her scalp made her eyes sting. Nothing seemed right to say to the father of her child to make up for seven years of neglect and abandonment.

She paused to get a sense of her bearings. Maybe if she walked the rest of the way, she'd have thought of something by the time she reached him. She ran to the end of the block where the sign read Lenora Street. She was only half a mile away. Without thinking, she catapulted forward, racing down the street, passing apartment buildings, restaurants, and garages without seeing them. She burst out onto Bell Street like a bolt of lightning and skid to a stop two buildings down from The Tattooed Lady. Bile rose in her throat at the thought of seeing him again, and her hands trembled violently.

The glass door of the shop beside her gave her a view of her sweaty figure. She was much too thin and her hair curled awkwardly despite the shape Elizabeth had tried to give it before she left. Her face was wet and her eyes bulged with anxiety. But she still had nothing to say.

Pushing back her fear and nausea, she took a tentative step forward and let her thoughts venture to Daniel with his mop of blonde hair and eyes that glimmered with an innocent joy. She could feel him reach out and hold her hand, leading her forward, assuring her that everything would be okay.

She was so lost in the feel of her brother's hand in hers that she almost walked past the little tattoo shop at the end of the block. Frozen in place, she turned to the window, and her racing heart leapt into her throat.

Liam sat at his station, with his tongue between his teeth as he focused on a woman's arm, running the machine along her skin as she talked. His dark hair was longer than in the picture on

Mark's phone but buzzed close to his scalp underneath. It brushed into his eyes as he bent to get a closer look at his work. He stopped to wipe her arm with a folded paper towel, looking up at her to smile and interject in the silent conversation. He laughed, and Audrey could almost hear its music through the glass and brick that separated them.

She stared at him through the window for what felt to her like a few moments, but it must have been longer because he finished and bandaged the tattoo, smiling again as the woman spoke to him. He stood and talked to her for a minute longer before she turned to leave the shop. Audrey felt her heart kick start back into action when the woman opened the door and the draft from the air conditioning blew chills across her skin. Liam was looking down as he pulled off his gloves and strolled to the front desk. As he typed in the computer, pushing his graying hair out of his eyes, Audrey fought with her legs that screamed in protest, refusing to move.

Liam ran a hand through the top of his hair again, and as he turned his head with the motion, he caught sight of the woman staring at him on the sidewalk. Audrey felt her nerves catch fire when his liquid black eyes turned to her. He took her in motionlessly before shaking his head in disbelief. Then he was walking to the door. Without taking his eyes from her, he came out onto the street and stood close enough to touch.

Her entire body shook violently, and she stuffed her fists into her jacket pockets, barely able to breathe as she met the penetrating eyes that gazed down at her with an unreadable expression, wiping her mind of all prepared speeches. Her chin danced soundlessly as she struggled to form a sentence.

But then his mouth curled slightly upward into a breathtaking smile that immediately calmed the raging chaos of her brain.

With a sharp intake of the cool Seattle air, she said, "I made a mistake."

"Was it all put into words, or did both understand that they had the same thing at heart and in their minds, so that there was no need to speak of it aloud, and better not to speak of it?"
-Fyodor Doestevsky
Crime and Punishment

Epilogue

Seattle, Washington

Dania Rose grew up without a mother. She had an amazing father and an aunt and uncle who spoiled her, but not a mother. When she was very young and would watch other moms pick up her friends from preschool, the abandonment would resonate with her like the aftershock of an earthquake. Why did her mother leave her? Was she unlovable? Was there something wrong with her?

But then she'd realized one day as she sat at a restaurant with her father, Uncle Thomas, and Aunt Nancy that she didn't really need her. She had all she could ever want. Sure, she was still curious about who her mother was, but she didn't want her. Dania Rose thought of herself just as her father described her: as a pretty little Rose. She'd finally understood why his tattoo had thorns. Her mother must have been the thorns. No woman who would leave her pretty little Rose could be a flower.

Her father had shown her a picture once of a skinny woman with wild red hair and a pink tongue sticking out of her thin lips. She held her hands up to block her eyes with a cigarette jutting out from between her bony fingers. Dania Rose had stared at the picture for a long time, contemplating this woman with no eyes.

"That's my mom?" she'd asked.

"Yeah, that's her," her father had nodded, rubbing her hand from across the table and studying her face.

"Cool," she'd shrugged. She never asked about her mother again. She had other things to do. The survival of an entire species rested on her shoulders.

By five years old, she'd founded a Save the Whales campaign at her elementary school. There were only three other members (and that included the supervising teacher), but they had a mission: to raise money to save their gentle giant neighbors. She went door to door every other weekend, selling candy and raffle tickets for the sake of the whales. She'd smile extra brightly when a woman answered the door. They always bought more and laughed at everything her father said. On Saturdays she watched Whale Wars and seethed with anger every time her father covered her eyes.

"I know they're killing the whales, Daddy," she'd shout.

"I just don't think you're old enough to watch this, Rosie," he'd say.

She'd huff and turn to glare at him. "There's blood all in the water because the whalers shot a peaceful creature with a harpoon. And now it's dying." He'd sigh in defeat and lower his hand. "I'm going to join Sea Shepherd when I grow up and stop all the whalers," she'd declare, much to her father's chagrin.

"I believe you," he'd laugh nervously.

Dania Rose loved her life in her little house in Des Moines, Washington. She had her father all to herself, except for the handful of times he tried to get a girlfriend, but she always took care of that. Except this blonde one was proving to be a much more difficult task than what she was used to. But in time, Beverley would get what was coming to her. Dania Rose would see to that.

Then one day the unthinkable happened. Her father drove them out to the city to her favorite restaurant and bought her a milkshake. She eyed him suspiciously when he wasn't looking because she only got milkshakes on special occasions, and as far as she knew it wasn't her birthday. She hadn't just finished a speech on cleaning the environment or done something nice without being told to do it. That's when she noticed he was trembling. She'd never seen her father nervous. He wasn't scared of anything. But now he sat next to her at the table (which didn't make sense because there was a perfectly decent empty seat across from her where she could see him better), and he was shaking.

Dania Rose watched her father quake like the San Andreas Fault and reached out to hold his big hand in her little fingers. He smiled down at her and leaned over to kiss the top of her head. Usually she'd wipe it off to annoy him, but his dark eyes seemed anxious, and she didn't understand why. He ran his free hand through his hair and let out a breath to calm his nerves.

"What's wrong?" she asked.

"There's someone I want you to meet, Rosie," he said. Then his eyes focused on something in the distance, and she saw her father smile. Confused, she followed his gaze, and her young heart sped like a giant horse in her chest and her long eyelashes fluttered in disbelief. Her father stood and hugged the woman when she approached. Then he turned to Dania Rose with his hand on the skinny woman's back.

"Rosie, this is your mother," he said.

That was the day Dania Rose met the woman who didn't want her. That was the day her life changed forever.

Playlist

1. Dearest Forsaken – Iron & Wine
2. Bloom – The Paper Kites
3. Middle Of My Mind – Tom Rosenthal
4. Peaceful Easy Feeling – Eagles
5. The Love We Stole – Bear's Den
6. Pumpin Blood - Acoustic – NONONO
7. Hold On – Wildwood Kin
8. Strange Dreams – Whiskey Myers
9. Where I Come From – Alan Jackson
10. Your Way – Michael Padgett
11. Too Dry to Cry – Willis Earl Beal
12. Flight – Lifehouse
13. Hello My Old Heart – The Oh Hellos
14. Landslide – Smashing Pumpkins

About the Author

Meagan Walker is a student at the University of Montevallo where she studies English. She enjoys traveling and photography. When not on campus at Montevallo, she lives with her family and her dog, Tobias, in Huntsville, Alabama, which inspired the setting for *The Forsaken Rose*.

Learn more at
Facebook.com/MeaganWalkerAuthor

Made in the USA
Lexington, KY
19 June 2016